Hot Breath

Also by Sarah Harrison

THE FLOWERS OF THE FIELD
A FLOWER THAT'S FREE

SARAH HARRISON

Hot Breath

Macdonald

A Macdonald Book

First published in Great Britain in 1985
by Macdonald & Co (Publishers) Ltd
London & Sydney

British Library Cataloguing in Publication Data

Harrison, Sarah, 1946-
Hot breath.
I. Title
823'.914[F]   PR6058.A6942/

ISBN 0-356-10992-5

Typeset by Fleet Graphics, Enfield, Middlesex

Reproduced, printed and bound in Great Britain by
Hazell Watson & Viney Limited,
Member of the BPCC Group,
Aylesbury, Bucks

Macdonald & Co (Publishers) Ltd
Maxwell House
74 Worship Street
London EC2A 2EN
A BPCC plc Company

FOR
Sue and Tim

Chapter One

It has always been my contention that it's a crime to waste good, fresh morning brainpower on domestic chores. I have therefore trained myself, with almost complete success, to resist the silent siren call of unmade beds, and bowls on the inside of which the Brekki-Nuts are forming a pimply collage, and to spend five minutes getting my mind into another, higher gear, suitable for what is known as 'creative writing'. The morning in question was no exception. In fact, with a new book to start I actually allowed the period of mental preparation to extend from five to twenty minutes, and employed all the recognised aids for release of the imaginative powers. That is to say a nice cup of coffee, a perusal of the popular press and the amiable background prattle of a well-known Irish disc-jockey.

It worked a treat. With the children at school and the sun streaming benignly through my kitchen windows, everything seemed possible. And it continued to seem so, for a minute or two after I left the table and began to trudge up the stairs. My mood of quite unfounded optimism even saw me through my study door and over to my desk.

I addressed my tripewriter and stuck a piece of A4 into its

grinning maw. But the sight of that pristine acreage as white, empty and inhospitable as the Russian steppe, did for me.

I picked up a biro and my notebook and wrote, feverishly: 'Mince Spag Whiskas Post Veg'. And then, as an afterthought: 'Bread'. This last sparked off a rapid association of ideas and, for reasons more mercenery than literary, I began to type.

Maria Trevelyan, I wrote, *gazed out of the window in the great library of Kersey House. She was utterly alone* – Were there degrees of aloneness? I allowed this knotty problem to occupy me for a full three minutes, and had still not resolved it when I continued. – *in this new and strange place. Beyond the window the gardens of Kersey stretched away in awesome grandeur. A formal terrace ran the length of the house above smooth emerald lawn, which was in turn bordered on the far side by a sweeping gravel walk. Beyond this, as far as the eye could see, there extended rolling parkland where herds of fallow deer grazed between the mighty trees.*

I paused, drained, and looked out of the window at my own garden. Here, cracked concrete lapped weed-strewn turf, and in the herbaceous border my cat, Fluffy, was sedulously covering the still-steaming evidence. It was the day for Declan, my gardener, to do his weekly stint, and animal-lover though I was I almost wished he would sweep down on the slant-eyed bastard with a bottle of rat bane and a dustbin liner. I watched Fluffy saunter off, stretching each leg fastidiously behind him with a teeny shake of the paw, and thought that next time my publisher's PR department asked for a list of my hobbies I could not in all conscience include gardening.

I looked back at the tripewriter. Seeing that I had actually made a few black marks on the virgin white I experienced a small surge of inspiration and wrote: *Maria caught sight* –

At precisely this moment I myself caught sight of my neighbour, Brenda Tunnel, returning I presumed from seeing her youngest child on to the school bus. She stopped on the corner by my front gate to conduct her usual shouted exchange of scurrilous small talk with Baba Moorcroft over the road. Brenda spoke, laughed, listened with eyebrows raised, and laughed again, this time almost uncontrollably.

I returned to the page: – *of her reflection in the glass. She saw a pale, heart-shaped face framed by* – ' I glanced again at Brenda

Tunnel – *abundant brown hair, caught back in a velvet snood. Her figure was trim and neat; she was not displeased with it.* Maybe not, but how much of her figure would have been reflected in the glass? Not a lot, presumably, unless she was standing on the window seat. But then which mattered more, stringent realism, or the speedy establishment of Maria Trevelyan as a raver? I continued: *Her breasts were high and firm, waist narrow, legs straight and strong as a boy's.*

Brenda flapped her hands at Baba in an agony of mirth. In the breast and waist department my neighbour afforded little inspiration, being built like an Aga. But on the other hand if I was cracking Maria up to be a feisty sort of lass, I could have worse models. Kersey House and its aristocratic inhabitants could scarcely offer more opportunities for licentious behaviour than the public bar at the Wagon and Horses where Brenda pulled pints of an evening.

I turned my mind to matters of seventeenth-century dress, so promisingly begun with the velvet snood, but images of Brenda in a farthingale kept rising to stick in my creative craw.

Fortunately the phone rang and I went downstairs with my usual sense of relief to answer it.

'Hallo! Harriet?'

'Hallo, Vanessa.' It was my editor from Era Books

'I'm sorry to disturb you when I know you're *bound* to be writing – '

'That's okay.' All this time and she hadn't learnt that writers only write in the hope of being disturbed.

' – but I wanted to know how you were. And of course to find out how *The Remembrance Tree* is coming along . . . ?' She named the historical romance the first few lines of which protruded from the tripewriter upstairs.

'It's beginning to take shape,' I said weightily. Brenda Tunnel passed the window, had a damn good look in, caught my eye, and having the decency to look embarrassed, waved her carrier bag in a salute to which I did not respond.

' – so much interest already,' Vanessa was saying, 'it's quite fantastic, I can't wait to read some of it.'

This was an unhealthy development. 'I feel a bit secretive

9

about it at present,' I confessed with engaging diffidence. 'It's a big project and I'm feeling my way rather, I'm sure you understand . . . '

'Of course, Harriet, say no more! It will be all the more thrilling when it arrives,' trilled Vanessa. I could picture her in her elegant office off Southampton Row, surrounded by huge plants amongst which her plain, docile, but efficient teenage secretary lurked like a ruminating tapir.

'But you will ring if there's the least thing I can do?' she asked. 'I mean I'm always here, even if you just feel like a good *talk . . .* '

Yeah, yeah, yeah. 'Yes,' I said. At lunchtime Vanessa would, no doubt, be off to some recherché watering-hole to promote more interest in my book, tripping through Covent Garden in her hand-tooled cowboy boots. What a load of Chelsea Cobblers.

'The great thing is,' she enquired earnestly, 'are you *enjoying* it?' I could not imagine where Vanessa, with six years in publishing under her belt (and I use the phrase advisedly), picked up the idea that authors enjoy writing.

'It's coming,' I said cryptically. 'It's coming. You know how it is.'

'Absolutely. That's the main thing,' effused Vanessa, hearing what she wanted to hear. 'I'll keep in touch, anyway. All the best with the writing.'

As I left the sitting room I could hear my daughter's guinea pigs making noises like tugboats greeting the QE2 out in the yard. I opened the back door and glanced out. There was the cat, not content with defecating on the bedding plants, sitting on the roof of the hutch as if trying to hatch it out.

'Gertcha!' I cried amid a chorus of agitated tootings from the caveys. Fluffy poured himself down the side of the hutch like furry custard, and prowled away.

I returned to nubile Maria in her mullioned window. Time, I considered, for the first, premonitory flicker of lust in her hitherto latently sensual loins.

As Maria gazed out, a figure entered the empty landscape. It was – I paused – *one of the –* I paused again – *young under-gardeners* (this title had a peculiar aptness for what I had in mind). *As she looked he stopped, and seemed to return her stare. He was no more than twenty yards away.* Were yards anachronistic? I pencilled a question mark and went on: *Maria was unsettled by those burning dark eyes, the tangled gypsy-black hair, the body full of animal strength and grace. Broad shoulders, long, thick-thewed legs* – I called another halt. What exactly were these 'thews' to which I so carelessly referred? I scanned the shelf for my dictionary, but it wasn't there. It would be in Gareth's room, appropriated for home-work.

Temporarily stumped, I looked out of the window. There was my own gardener, Declan O'Connell, clipping the hedge with an electric strimmer. He wielded this tool slung round his barrel-shaped body in a leather harness where it reared and shuddered like a gigantic motorised prick. Declan was a gardener of the rip-strip-and-clip variety, never so happy as when he was bludgeoning vegetation into submission with one of his arsenal of electrical gadgets.

Idly I wondered if Declan had thews, and if so, where they were. If he did, they were certainly all he had in common with the sultry horticulturalist of *The Remembrance Tree*. Declan was fiftyish, plug-ugly, and of a disposition so choleric that a girl would have had to be a full-blown masochist to court his attentions.

But like Maria's under-gardener he too seemed to sense my appraising eye on him through the window and returned my stare. Not knowing what else to do I waved, and immediately wished I hadn't, for Declan switched off the strimmer, lowered it to the ground and mouthed something at me with ferocious emphasis.

I turned off the tripewriter and opened the window: 'Is anything the matter?'

'It's this focking strimmer,' explained Declan. His speech struggled, hissing and sputtering, from a glutinous bog of an Irish accent. 'It keeps going off.'

'Why, do you think?' I asked politely.

'If I knew why, I'd have fixed it, so I would!' He nudged the offending implement with his foot. 'It could be the box in the yard. Where does he keep the fuse wire?'

The name of my absentee husband was never uttered by

11

Declan. George was either just 'he', or 'that bloddy fule' as in 'what bloddy fule put the garage so close to this hedge?'

'Perhaps,' I said, 'you could look for it, Declan. I am trying to work.' I knew this would cut no ice, since only manual labour of the most taxing nature constituted work in Declan's book. Nonetheless, I closed the window and switched the tripewriter back on, so that its hypnotic hum drowned his mumbled imprecations. Via my peripheral vision I saw him go round the back of the house to the yard. The strimmer lay on the grass like a beached marine monster, trailing tentacles of wire and leather strap.

I got back to Maria's libidinous musings. Those thews sprang off the page at me again, but I decided not to let them detain me any longer at this juncture.

. . . *thick-thewed legs, added to her first impression of a zestful animal nature kept but scantly in check.* From 'but scantly' my reader would at once infer that Maria inhabited an historical context.

As those dark eyes found, and then held, her own, she felt a flush spreading on her cheek. Cheek? Why cheek in the singular? I considered this and concluded that it was because 'cheeks' made it sound as though her bottom were blushing. As indeed it very probably was if she were the sort of girl who pulled under-gardeners at twenty paces. That was it, paces, not yards.

She experienced a strange and frightening quickening of the pulse, a pounding of the heart and racing of the blood which caused her in a moment to rise from the window seat and –

At this point I experienced some quickening, pounding and racing of my own as the back door opened and my dog, who had till now been lying like an overstuffed pyjama case on the stairs, burst into life with a volley of maniacal barking, fit to wake the dead.

'Bad dog, Spot!' I screamed cheerily as I trotted down the stairs in his wake.

I found Declan standing just inside the kitchen door like the Stag at Bay while Spot slavered and bristled most gratifyingly at a distance of some four feet. At this moment I remarked a striking similarity between the two of them. The dog with his upraised hackles, glaring eyes and bared fangs;

Declan with his pateful of vertical wire wool, gleaming horn-rims and ranks of yellow dentures exposed in a horrible grimace.

'What is it now, Declan?'

'I can't find the fuse wire, so I can't,' he snarled. 'You could do yourselves a favour by tidying up that bloddy yard.'

I ignored this gratuitous sally and swept past him, cutting through the aura of bone meal, Ambre Solaire and sweaty chilprufe which hung round Declan through the long hot summer.

As I led the way to the yard he followed, grumbling and grunting like some pungent and refractory farm animal.

The yard was certainly a mess, but my instinct as to the fuse wire's whereabouts proved correct. I handed it to him without a word and he did not thank me, while the guinea pigs poop-pooped winsomely in the background.

Back upstairs with Maria I wondered gloomily why it had fallen to my lot to have Declan's malodorous, recalcitrant bulk heaving about my back garden when I might have been thrilling to thick-thewed legs and burning black eyes.

I recapped and continued: – *and move back into the dim seclusion of the library. It seemed odd that she should now feel safe in that great, forbidding, book-lined chamber where only this morning* – I was about to introduce, smoothly, an action replay of the indignities visited upon Maria to date in the library. But my attention was caught by the study door, which moved slightly ajar. Declan's face, or part of it, became visible in the aperture, suffused and accusatory. He was one of those creatures who seem comparatively normal out of doors, but who appear less and less so as they approach the civilised confines of the house. Now, on my carpeted landing with its Laura Ashley wallpaper, Declan's presence was rebarbative to a degree. It was like discovering a plucked turkey in one's underwear drawer.

'Well, Declan?' I asked, with what I hoped was the hauteur of the authoritarian employer.

'Where's the fuse box?'

'Why?'

'You're in all sorts of trouble, so you are.' There was a

fleeting flash of the NHS choppers, a predatory glitter behind the hornrims.

I progressed to Olympian detachment. 'Well, Declan, I look to you to get me out of it. The fuse box is in the main bedroom.'

'What?' He pushed the door wide and stood arms akimbo. 'It can't be.'

'It is.'

'Mother of God, what kind of pantomime is that, to go putting the bloddy fuse box in a bedroom?'

With murderous rage held, like my hero's animalism, but scantly in check, I rose, went past Declan, crossed the landing and entered the bedroom. My satisfaction over being right about the fuse box was tempered with chagrin over the state of the room, which embodied just the kind of middle-class squalor most abhorred by Declan. How bitterly I now regretted the rigorous self-discipline which had prompted me to free my mind with caffeine, horoscopes and Radio Two when I might have indulged myself (and saved face) by making the beds.

I pointed. 'Declan, fuse box. Fuse box, Declan.'

My literary allusion was wasted on him I could tell. He approached the fuse box like an animal negotiating treacherous ground – nostrils flaring, eyes rolling, respiration sterterous.

Reaching it, he crouched down, glared at it, then at me.

'Are you for telling me the chap has to come up here every time just to read the meter?' he growled rhetorically. It was obvious that his astonished disbelief was not for the original fault in planning, but for the fortitude of the official from the electricity board.

'We manage,' I assured him. 'Now if you'll excuse me I must get back to work.'

I shut the door of the study firmly behind me, and sat down at the desk. Turning on the tripewriter I began to expound on the formative experiences of Maria in the library. But after only a few minutes the hum of the tripewriter ceased. The keys froze beneath my fingers. Indeed the silence was so complete that for a moment I wondered if I had achieved complete suspension of disbelief, and had been transported back three centuries to join my heroine in her tribulations. But there, by the hedge, lay the strimmer. And here, before me, my sophisticated and presently useless tripewriter.

I strained my ears. No fridge humming, no trundle and whirr of the washing machine. Nothing.

The door opened a chink. 'Did you not know one of your trip switches is up the spout?' asked Declan.

'No, I didn't know that. Declan, why is nothing working?'

'I turned everything off, so I did!' He was triumphant.

'May I ask why?'

'If your trip switch isn't working and something plays up you're going to get a bloddy great bang.'

I rose and went over to him. I could give Declan about four inches. 'But Declan, my typewriter's not working. I can't get on.'

He bridled. 'No more can I, the focking strimmer's dead.'

'There are shears and a stepladder in the yard.'

Declan's eyes narrowed. 'What's the ladder like?'

'Long, with rungs.'

'If the ladder's not high enough, it's a death-trap, so it is. If I fall and break me back, and me with no insurance, who'll care for the wife and kiddies?'

This did not seem the right moment to remind Declan that he was fiddling the DHSS hand over fist. I could think of no possible answer to his question which did not sound either defensive or callous.

'I'll show you the ladder. In the meantime, would you please turn the electricity back on?'

He did so. I then escorted him to the shed and furnished him with shears and ladder. Bearing in mind his gloomy prognosis I phoned the electricity board and arranged for an engineer to come out at vast expense after five the same evening.

Considerably energised by this confrontation, I pounded on: *Maria had been keenly aware, since arriving at Kersey, of her lowly status as a dependent relative. Her Hawkhurst cousins were infinitely wealthier, more cultured and better looking (she thought) than she. In*

particular she felt that her eldest cousin, Richard Hawkhurst, des-
pised her. Those ice-blue eyes assessed her with a surgeon's delicate
accuracy.

I halted. Another anachronism? I doubted that surgeons of the period were noted for either delicacy or accuracy. For some reason I pictured a flagon of small beer and a gore-bedewed meat cleaver.

At this moment there was a bellow from the garden. I looked out of the window to see Declan, at the foot of the ladder, turning round and round on the spot with his right hand clamped beneath his left armpit, trumpeting and bowing like a wounded elephant engaged in some obscure rite of court-ship, or the marking out of territory.

I flung up the window. 'Declan! Are you all right?'

'Mother of God, I cot meself! I'm bleeding!'

On the way downstairs, I glanced at my watch: ten forty-five. If I put my foot down I could get Declan to the surgery at Basset Parva. But by the time I'd done so the morning would be gone, and with it my chance of advancing Maria's story.

So it was with extreme briskness that I bathed Declan's wound at the kitchen sink – he had sliced the flap of skin between the thumb and forefinger – bound it up with cotton wool and elastic bandage, and drove him at speed the two and a half miles to Basset Parva.

At the surgery, the receptionist said: 'You're late, really. Surgery's over.'

'I'm bleeding, woman!' said Declan.

'He should see a doctor,' I affirmed. The receptionist peered over the counter at the blood-soaked cotton wool.

'It looks like an Outpatients job to me,' she commented.

'But the hospital's miles, and I'm supposed to be working. I'd like to save myself the trip if possible.'

She looked pained. 'There's only Dr Ghikas here now,' she said. 'But I'll ring through and find out if he'll see you. If you'll just take a seat.' Dr Ghikas was of Greek extraction, and new to the practice. I had not met him, but as Declan and I sat down, with a flatulent sound, on the red vinyl banquette, it appeared his reputation had gone before him.

'Da Greek doctor!' exploded Declan in a squeaky stage whisper. He might have been referring to Charles Manson. 'I'm boggered if I'll be patched up by any focking Greek!'

'Declan,' I said. 'Shut up.'

The receptionist put down the internal phone and addressed us.

'Dr Ghikas will see you. Patient's name?'

'Mr O'Connell,' I supplied, nanny-like.

'Initial?'

'D.'

'C.D.,' corrected Declan. So he had secrets.

'Address?'

'20 Bog's Gap, Basset Magna,' he growled.

'Are you registered with this practice, Mr O'Connell?'

'I'm a patient of Dr Salmon.' Declan named the senior partner. 'And the wife and kiddies too.'

'Thank you!' the receptionist chimed like a doorbell.

Declan folded his arms. The under-arm area of his shirt was stained crimson where he'd sandwiched his injured hand, and this had the effect of making him appear to sweat blood. I experienced the sweet sensation of having Declan on toast.

I jiggled the knife a bit. 'I'm sure Dr Ghikas is first-rate,' I opined. 'After all, the Hippocratic oath derives from – '

'You're responsible, so you are!' snarled Declan, poking my bicep with a corny finger. 'If the Greek's an incompetent!'

'Mr O'Connell, would you step this way please?'

I accompanied Declan, less from solicitude than a desire to watch him squirm. We crossed the narrow passage to Dr Ghikas's consulting room. There were three doctors in the Basset Parva practice, and their respective rooms accurately reflected the pecking order. Dr Salmon (respected elder states-man) occupied a spacious apartment at the rear, complete with tropical fish and access to parking; Dr Donleavy (a whizz with women's plumbing) had the room next door to the waiting room; and Dr Ghikas (the lowest form of medical life) presided over a crepuscular cell between the pharmacy and the loo.

I chivvied Declan before me like a sheepdog driving a cantankerous ram to market. Dr Ghikas was washing his hands

17

at a basin in a corner. I saw a tall fair-haired, rangy figure, dressed in an English tweed suit of the type only to be found in Paris. The metal earpieces of his stethoscope rested on the back of his neck like the hands of a clinging woman.

Drying his hands, he turned to face us. And sentenced me, with a single polite smile, to the lubricious purgatory from which I was not, for the foreseeable future, to emerge.

Chapter Two

Of course, I was ripe for it. Thirty-five, fit and solvent, with children at school and the sweet scent of freedom in my nostrils: more or less a textbook case.

When George had said that he was off to build a leisure centre for the oil sheikhs for a year, my first reaction was that the children and I would go too. My second was that we wouldn't. First of all, and quite idly, the prospect of twelve months off the marital leash was not abhorrent to me. I pictured myself like some hard-working dray horse from the streets of London, taken to the country for a brief spell and rolling on the greensward with its legs in the air. But I had no idea then what an accurate picture this would turn out to be. Secondly, a bored, introspective community of venal expatriots banged up in some concrete oasis in the desert struck me as the milieu least likely to be attended by the literary muse. It was hard enough conjuring up the quickening manhoods and heaving bosoms of Merrie Englande in the rural peace of Basset Magna, let alone in a country where women had no freedom, drink was outlawed and the outlook was uniformly arid. Thirdly (and I finally managed an altruistic impulse) it would be an upheaval for the children. Gareth was thirteen and Clara nearly twelve, crucial ages educationally speaking, when it would be much better not to disturb them.

The three of us would enjoy a kind of sabbatical from George's improving influence. I would work, and have frequent recourse to convenience food, and allow the children to watch too much television. But my husband's vanity has always been a healthy plant. He was convinced that I would pine without the physical and emotional nourishment which only he, his erotic skills and his BMW could provide. And the children, he foresaw, would run riot without his naturally authoritative supervision. He overlooked the fact that in his absence I would be able to rant at them like a fishwife with the additional advantage of looking the part. Practically speaking I had Declan to keep Mother Nature in check, and an address book stuffed with the names of Little Men, that ghostly army of jobbing plumbers, electricians, glaziers, joiners and sweeps, who ensure that life continues, even in the absence of the pater-familias.

I also had a charperson, in the form of Damon. As an amanuensis, Damon was a curate's egg, and the parts that were good were not immediately apparent since he was an outstandingly unprepossessing youth.

Damon had been sent to me through the good offices of a new job creation scheme for unemployed teenagers in the Basset area. The scheme was officially entitled Jobs Incorporated, but had been dubbed JINX by its dissatisfied patrons, who were legion. From the local market town of Basset Regis the Mohicans, glam rockers, punks and New Wave mods spread in all directions like an unhealthy rash, body-popping their way into the homes of an unsuspecting citizenry, pulling up rose bushes, rotivating croquet lawns, painting over keyholes and allowing pedigree bitches to be screwed by passing mongrels. Against the hail of complaints which rattled down on the JINX office, its well-intentioned supremos could only offer assurances of youthful fulfilment, which was small consolation to a householder standing amid the smoking ruins of his largest single investment.

Damon had come into my employ after five years at the

local comprehensive (that now attended by Gareth) where he had gained CSEs in Home Economics and, mysteriously, German. While these may have qualified him to be manager of the Munich Hilton, they in no way fitted him for private domestic service. His first job for me – intended at the time, to use his own phrase, to be just 'a one-off gig' – had been the laying of some vinyl flooring in the utility room. He had taken a very long time, but the flooring had been laid, with just one small tumulus near the freezer where Damon had sealed a Scotch egg for ever to the floor. This episode neatly typified Damon's qualities as a worker: he was slow and painstaking, but his few mistakes were crucial. In appearance he was short, almost dwarfish for sixteen, with stoat-like features and a bad skin. Where others of his age went about like exotic parakeets, with day-glo crests of hair and multicoloured tattoos, Damon's head was crowned with a Brylcreemed toque of an almost solid consistency, more like the result of topiary than combing, and his sartorial tastes ran to tracksuit trousers and an army surplus sweater. He aspired to running his own disco – he deserved the Queen's Award for the ambition least likely to succeed – and to this end he was saving the pittance I was allowed to pay him.

So I had Damon, Declan and the Little Men. I had two children entering the forbidden foothills of puberty. And I elected to stay at home. But now, as if to pay me out for my complacency, here was Dr Constantine Ghikas. In the antiseptic gloom of his Basset Parva consulting room stood the fly in my ointment, the spanner (oh delicious thought) in my works . . . the Greek in my marital woodpile.

In response to his urbane: 'Now what can I do for you?' I was strongly tempted to answer: 'Doctor, doctor, I'm suffering from an uncontrollable urge to tie your wrists with your stethoscope, to wrap my legs around your waist and impale myself on your Hellenic column . . . '

What I actually said was: 'Doctor, this is Mr O'Connell who helps me in the garden. He's cut himself on the shears.'

'I'm bleeding!' growled Declan. 'I'm soaked with it!'

He held out his injured hand, but Dr Ghikas had spotted the blood in his armpit and darted forward to inspect it, thinking perhaps that Declan had plunged the shears into his left lung. Lifting Declan's arm he peered enthusiastically at the rancid excess, smothering the grimace which momentarily contorted his features when his patient's foetid body odours hit home.

'Not there!' trumpeted Declan, nearly sandwiching the doctor's handsome aquiline nose between arm and chest. It occurred to me that one human being with BO might, without too much difficulty, inflict a slow and lingering death on another in just this way.

Dr Ghikas removed my ad hoc dressing from Declan's hand and examined the wound. His eyelashes were like thick, burnished awnings shielding unsuspecting females from the full cerulean allure of his eyes. The lashes were in piquant contrast to the otherwise rather ascetic cast of his features. His hands, holding Declan's calloused paw, were large, and elegant, and squeaky-clean.

'It's not serious,' he said, lifting the awnings and treating me to a blast from those heavenly eyes. 'The fleshy areas are always messy.' Ignoring Declan's expression of near-homicidal indignation, he went on, 'You did a good job. I'll just give you an anti-tetanus jab, Mr O'Connell, and you'll be right as rain.'

Declan shuddered seismically. 'Mother of God, da needle . . . ' he quavered prayerfully.

I saw, with grim satisfaction, that Declan was phobic about injections. As Dr Ghikas prepared a syringe I licked my lips, both with lust, and with relish at the prospect of the needle penetrating Declan's bristly and shrinking flesh.

Dr Ghikas returned, swabbed and punctured. With a faint glottal popping sound Declan fell to the floor in a dead faint.

Dr Ghikas and I both had Declan's blood, literally, on our hands. We stared apprehensively at one another across his inert form, like a couple of conspirators after a murder.

'That's interesting,' remarked the doctor, breaking the spell in a matter-of-fact tone. 'He seemed such a tough character.'

'He is, normally,' I said, 'but you seem to have found his Achilles heel.'

Dr Ghikas stepped over Declan's legs, discarded the syringe, and washed his hands again at the sink. Then he came back and crouched down by his recumbent patient.

'Please would you give me a hand?' he asked.

Together we hauled Declan – an unlikely Cupid – into a sitting position, and pressed his head down between his knees. The doctor's hand and mine touched where they lay on his stubbly neck.

Declan regained consciousness with ferocious suddenness. One moment he was a bundle of dirty washing, the next his head was up and pivoting wildly as he tried to get his bearings.

'Where am I?' he bellowed, his perturbation giving fresh zest to the cliché.

'It's all right, Mr O'Connell,' said Dr Ghikas, helping him to his feet and then to a chair. 'Plenty of people don't like injections. I'll get you some water.'

As Dr Ghikas changed the dressing, I caught Declan's eye, and saw there first the wild surmise, then the despairing realisation, that I had seen him at his lowest ebb.

When we were done, Declan scurried with indecent haste back into the waiting room, but I was in no such hurry.

'It was good of you to see us,' I said. 'I hope we haven't delayed you too much.'

'No, no, not at all. You did the right thing.' Dr Ghikas held the door for me. 'By the way, I must ask, aren't you Mrs Blair, our local author?'

'I suppose I must be.' This was a gratifying development. Not only did he know that I wrote, but that I coped with grisly accidents, too.

'My mother loves your books,' he said.

'I'm so glad. It's always nice to hear of a satisfied customer.' With truly spine-chilling facility, I added: 'A surprising number of men read them too, you know, but they usually say it's their wives who bought them.'

'Well, I don't have a wife,' he replied obligingly. 'But if I did I'm quite sure that yours are the sort of books that would stop dinners getting cooked and socks getting darned.'

I decided to overlook this charmingly chauvinistic view of

23

the wifely role, and to concentrate on the good news: he was single. No matter that I wasn't. I seemed to have left my conscience somewhere on the back of Declan's neck, where our hands had touched. I beamed. After all, he was Greek.

Declan was standing with his back to us, staring furiously at a coloured chart designed to assist in the early detection of breast lumps. The receptionist was watering the plants.

'Yes,' went on Dr Ghikas, warming to his theme, 'my mother's read lots of them. In fact, I wonder – would you consider it a frightful imposition if I brought a copy of your latest one over for you to sign?'

'Not at all!' I waved an insouciant hand. 'Do you know where I am?'

'I believe I do.' He gave me a look which could only be described as collusive. 'I think I've seen you out jogging.'

Better and better, my image was rounding out nicely. 'Yes, you may have done,' I replied, 'I go most days. But I'll just give you my address.' I took one of my posh calling cards out of my bag, grateful at last that I'd taken George's advice and had them printed.

'Excellent,' said Dr Ghikas, putting the card in his breast pocket. 'I'll drop in then.'

I took Declan home after that. So great was my sense of well-being that I even loaded his horrid mantis-like bicycle on to my roof rack. Bog's Gap was at the other side of the village, less than a mile away, so the mere fact of my driving him there was enough to underline his extreme feebleness. And I pressed home my advantage with a continuous stream of cheerful, patronising chat along 'you-should-put-your-feet-up-for-the-rest-of-the-day' lines.

At number twenty I reached the front door before him and described to his wife – a woman limp and pale as a net curtain – exactly what had occurred, in graphic detail.

I returned to the car buoyant in the knowledge that I had provided Mrs O'Connell with the wherewithal to subdue Declan, for perhaps the only time in their married life.

When I got home I poured myself a glass of wine and took it into the garden. I sat in the sun in a deckchair and Fluffy and

Spot, anticipating the opening of their respective tins, took up positions on either side of me, like bookends.

How odd that I should earn my living, and a handsome one at that, from describing females bouleversées by passion, but only at this late and unexpected stage be experiencing it myself. From the moment I had clapped eyes on Dr Constantine Ghikas there was no doubt that my every relevant orifice was gaping shamelessly open, ready to gobble him up like a venus flytrap at the first touch. So sudden and violent had my reaction been, that I still felt like two quite separate people in one skin, one of them a scribbling housewife and mother, the other a slavering post-pill predator who could eat family doctors for breakfast.

When Damon arrived at two I was still in the garden, on my third glass of wine. Twice, Fluffy and Spot had accompanied me back into the kitchen and twice had been disappointed. Their dejection was obvious, they were not accustomed to wait for lunch. My ministrations were terse and speedy, but usually punctual. Now, my face flushed with sunshine and Spanish red, I stroked and scratched them, and hummed soothingly with my eyes closed, but had so far failed to wield the tin-opener.

At last, hearing Damon's motor scooter, I roused myself and went indoors. I fed the pets and wandered into the sitting room, still carrying my glass. Damon was more than usually wan. He was changing the Hoover bag with the care of a surgeon performing a caesarian, but he still contrived to release gobbets of fluff all over the floor.

'Is everything all right, Damon?' I asked solicitously. 'Are you quite well?'

'I'm not exactly over the parrot,' he replied.

'Why is that?'

'The jobs people got me another house,' he said, 'just up the road. I been there this morning.'

'But that's good, isn't it?'

He shook his head. 'She couldn't handle it.'

'Sorry? Handle what?'

'Me. She's really into stereotypes, she wants some little old lady with a hairnet.'

25

'Really? Well perhaps you should wear a hairnet, Damon,' I suggested. 'You know, look the part.'

'I am what I am,' pronounced Damon, incontrovertibly, plugging in the Hoover. 'If other people can't handle it, that's their problem.'

'How right you are,' I said.

'What really makes me vomit,' went on Damon, 'is I just got past the hundred mark with my savings, now I've got this setback. I really don't need this.' He switched on.

I was feeling beneficent. 'I could take some more of your time, Damon,' I bellowed. 'With my husband away there's plenty of odd jobs need doing!'

'Trif,' said Damon. ''Scuse me.'

Clara got back at three-thirty, shortly before Damon was due to leave. A cultural gulf yawned between my daughter and my charperson. Clara was skinny, exquisite and supercilious, and viewed the working class as some kind of necessary evil to do with urban life, like public lavatories and litter, and therefore nothing to do with her.

She was in her final year at the primary school in Basset Magna. During term time her life was divided between this institution, where she queened it as the tallest girl in the school, good at games and brainy enough not to attend in class, and her pony Stu (a mare, despite her name) whom we kept in a nearby field with others of her kind.

Though Stu was costly to run and evilly disposed towards more or less everyone, I had to allow that it was only her squat equine form which stood between Clara and full-blown punk-hood. When I read in the papers about carefully nurtured girls from middle-class homes who nonetheless wound up as pop star's molls and worse (' ''He liked me in leather,'' says Brigadier's daughter'), it was Clara's haughty young face that I saw staring up from the page.

I was in the kitchen, making moussaka (my mind still running on things Greek), and Damon was washing the tiled floor in the hall, when Clara arrived.

'Hi,' she said, dropping her shoe bag, sweatshirt and lunch box to the ground like the spoor of some gigantic beast. 'Can I have some money for the shop?'

'For what?' As if I didn't know. George was against the practice of sweets-after-school, and it was his stern imagined look which usually stopped me in the act of giving in on these occasions.

She shrugged. 'Dunno . . . packet of Fangs.'

'What in God's name are they?'

'Please – go on.'

'No.'

She went to the breadbin and began making a sandwich. 'Has he done my room?'

I grimaced at her. 'Yes! Ssh!'

She leaned back to peer with exaggerated care at Damon. 'Ah, swabbing the decks, I see.'

'Clara!'

She folded the sandwich twice, stuffed the lot inside her pretty mouth and jerked her thumb in the general direction of outside.

'If you're riding remember your hat. And take that lot upstairs before you go anywhere.'

She scooped up the elephant droppings and sauntered across Damon's nice clean tiles and up the stairs. But I was saved having to make any apology on her behalf because the phone rang in the sitting room and Damon rushed to answer it.

He liked to practise his executive skills on my callers. Now he stood with the receiver hunched between ear and shoulder, a biro and memo pad at the ready.

'I think she may be a bit tied up,' he said, glancing at me as I stood waiting. 'But if you hang in there for a second I'll check her out.' He put his hand over the mouthpiece. 'It's your editor.'

As I took the receiver from Damon – it was warm and greasy like cooling bacon – I tried to picture Vanessa 'hanging in' anywhere, and found it impossible. Her brand of brittle Oxford effervescence would surely wither under delay.

'Hallo?'

'Hallo, Harriet – again!'

'Hallo, Vanessa.'

'Look, I'm sorry to disturb you a second time – '

'That's all right, I was only cooking.'

'God, you're wonderful. Look, is there the least chance you could come in here tomorrow? The sales people are dying for a chat with you, and also we've got our Australian representative over for a couple of days and I know he'd adore to meet you – you didn't meet Vince last time, did you?'

'I don't think so. What time would you want me?'

'Oh . . . ' she mused, 'twelvish? Then we can have a talk in the office and go out for a bite of lunch.'

I could not really quite reconcile the enormous amount of my time taken up – effectively a whole day – with the infinitesimal professional benefit to be gained from lunch with the Australian rep. Still, I was well trained.

'I'll be there at twelve.'

'Lovely! And Harriet . . . '

'Yes?'

'Any chance of a tiny peep at *The Remembrance Tree*?'

My brain whirred and clicked. 'I'd prefer not. I've had a bad day, you know, one domestic crisis after another, one never likes to show work after . . . ' I let the sentence hang in the air. You only had to feed Vanessa her cues.

'Not another word! I know I'm just a typical greedy editor. I honestly think you creative mums are *wonderful*. 'Bye now, you get back to your delicious cooking and I'll see you tomorrow. 'Byee!'

Having, as usual, patronised me to pieces, she rang off, doubtless to refine, package and process my remark about domestic crises for the benefit of the PR department.

During my conversation with Vanessa, Clara had departed for the stable, and Gareth had returned, in company, from Basset Regis comprehensive. As I entered the kitchen I was confronted by the broad, grey-flannelled beam of Brett Troye as he crouched over the portable snooker table. Other boys, also in the uniform of the comprehensive, stood about, acknowledging my arrival with small twitches of the facial muscles. Damon was on the sidelines, cycle clips on, crash helmet under his arm. Where Clara regarded Damon with icy hauteur, Gareth and co. simply accepted him, and he in turn blended easily into the background which this young male company provided. After all, Damon was of the same species, and the product of the same education. His few extra years and current status in our household only provided Gareth et al. with proof, if proof were needed, that there was nothing out there worth having. The kitchen was thick with the heavy excess energy of the 'lads': males of that awkward age when they have ceased to be little boys but are yet not quite young men.

I waited politely while Brett potted the pink, followed closely by the white. The sharp inhalations of admiration were at once drowned by jeers of derision.

'Suffer, Troye, you great wally!'

'Now look,' I said, squeezing and trying to take the floor. 'Don't you boys have any homework?'

This suggestion met with much eye-rolling and ponderously comic face-pulling.

'Come on, put this table away, please, and on your bikes all of you. Gareth, go up and get stuck in.'

This provoked a positive gale of coarse hilarity, but they put the table away, gouging only a small hole in the ceiling as they stood it on end, and not using any bad language. I surveyed the roomful of lusty pubescent male flesh that was the lads: water, water everywhere, nor any drop to drink. And since this morning the clear crystal fountain that was Constantine Ghikas had brought on a terrible, raging thirst.

The lads who did not belong to me – Brett Troye, David Lane and Daniel Lovejoy – left via the back door.

'Seeya,' said my son, product of a book-lined home. 'Autographs later, fans.'

He closed the door after them, said 'Shite,' and went to the front door to catch them on the way out.

'Hey, Lovejoy!'

'Yeah?'

'Shall I come up yours later?'

'Yeah, okay.'

'Up yours then!' More guffaws greeted this rapier-like sally. There were a few more 'seeyas', the gate slammed (I knew it would fail to catch and bounce open again), and Gareth closed the front door.

'Off you go then,' I said. 'And do it properly. No visiting and no telly unless you give it your full attention for at least an hour.'

Gareth grabbed my lapels and lifted me on to my toes in a spontaneous display of affection. Not for nothing was he known as the Steroid Kid; he was fully as tall as me and filling out at an alarming rate.

'Looking for hassle?' he enquired rhetorically.

'Just get on with it.'

He shambled off, and in a second or two I heard the thump and moan of the New Wave band whose caterwaulings habitually accompanied any of his brainwork.

Returning to my moussaka I bumped into Damon, whose weaselly presence I had overlooked during the eviction of the lads. He had put on his crash helmet and looked like a khaki ninepin.

'Oh, Damon, your money.'

'When you're ready.'

I gave it to him and he counted it with the brooding concentration of a riverboat gambler.

'When shall I come then?' he asked.

'Sorry?'

'The extra time.'

I remembered my offer, made in the rosy afterglow of my meeting with Dr Ghikas.

'I could use another afternoon,' I said cautiously.

'I'll be round Friday then.' He pocketed the money. 'Just let me know what needs doing, right.'

'I will.'

'I made some tea.' He jerked his helmet.

'Oh? Oh, thank you.'

'See you tomorrer.' And he was gone.

I realised that my unconsidered remark about George's absence had unlocked an unsuspected cache of chauvinism in Damon. Suddenly it was not I who was doing him the favour but the other way round. I only hoped that he would not interpret my feminine needs in any wider sense. I had already selected my candidate for that particular task.

*   *   *

Half an hour later I put the moussaka in the oven and the dog on the lead and called up the stairs to Gareth.

'Gareth! GARETH!'

The music was turned down. 'What?'

'I'm taking the dog out for five minutes.'

'Right . . . '

'Please don't have that thing too loud or you won't hear the phone if it rings.'

'Yeah, yeah.' The double affirmative implied both understanding and impatience. Music swelled once more, though not quite as loudly. I took Spot across the road to the ponies' field. It was a mixed pad. The two geldings with whom Stu shared stood morosely head to tail beneath a tree. Clara was by the fence, cleaning out Stu's hooves with a calm concentration that comes from being plugged into a Sony Walkman.

'Hallo, darling,' I shouted. But she might as well have been entombed for all the reaction my greeting provoked. I had a sudden vision of parents the world over ranting, beseeching, entreating, exhorting, while their offspring stared vacantly back, humanoid but uncomprehending, tuned in by wires and headphones to an alien culture. Even Declan, for God's sake, with all his faults, was at least in direct and ebullient communication with the rest of mankind.

Clara's eyes moved across me, but with no sign of recognition. She put down Stu's hoof and transferred her attention to the rear left-hand corner. Unfortunately she muffed the pick-up and Stu brought down her hoof – the size and consistency of a Le Creuset Marmite – on Clara's foot. My daughter gave a shriek of agony and ripped off the headphones the better to belabour Stu, who stood with a well-satisfied air, ears pressed back, thick hide twitching beneath the blows. The faint jangle of Frankie Goes to Holloway accompanied this clash of personalities. Spot pricked his ears appreciatively. I waited to be noticed.

When I was, I got the inevitable flack.

'God, it's agony!'

'Bad luck, darling, are you all right?'

'No! Is that all you can say, bad luck? She weighs an absolute ton!'

31

'She didn't mean to,' I offered, though without much conviction. Stu's surly delinquency was enough to test the faith of the most ardent hippophile.

'You don't seem very bothered, what if I've broken something?'

Because I knew she hadn't broken anything, I was able to see the potential advantages in this situation.

'I wonder if I should run you over to surgery?' I asked.

'Oh, Mummy,' said Clara. 'Don't be so ridiculous!'

Chapter Three

The next day I made the usual complex arrangements to ensure that the inner child would be satisfied and the house remain standing in my absence, and left to catch the ten-thirty to London. Just before going I cast my eye over Maria et ses amis, rehearsing my responses to the inevitable eager interrogation. I decided that vague but intelligent-sounding replies which begged the question were my best bet. Things along the lines of 'beginning to feel at home with it' and 'writing myself in' sounded suitably authorly but were profoundly non-committal.

On the platform of British Rail Basset Magna, I spotted a couple of familiar faces. One belonged to my neighbour Brenda Tunnel, the other to Robbo Makepeace, chairman of Basset Tomahawks YFC, of which Gareth was a midfield star. I too was on the committee and knew that at this time of year, with soccer about to go into temporary abeyance, fund-raising reared its ugly head. I did not want to spend my journey into town discussing discos and draw prizes with Robbo, so I gave him a cheery wave and fled towards the end of the platform with the purposeful air of one hell-bent on travelling in the last seat in the train. My headlong flight carried me straight into the arms of Brenda Tunnel.

'Hallo, Harriet! How's the writing going?'

'Okay, thanks,' I replied. 'Where are you off to today?'

'Oh don't worry,' shrilled Brenda, divining the reason for my question, 'I'm only meeting Trevor's mum off the train, she's coming for the day.'

'That's nice,' I said, with rather more warmth now that I knew the conversation would not extend beyond the next few minutes.

'She absolutely has to sit in the last seat in the train,' explained Brenda. 'She thinks then if there's a crash she'll be safe.'

'She may well be right,' I said. 'And how are things, Brenda?'

She sighed. 'Not too good. You know, with me and Trevor.'

'I'm sorry to hear that. Why exactly? You always seem so – '

'He doesn't like me working at the Wagon.'

'Oh dear. I see.'

'He's very jealous, very possessive,' said Brenda, with some pride. I looked at her in a new light. She was built, as I've mentioned, on a Wagnerian scale, resembling nothing so much as two hundredweight of nutty slack in a duvet cover. But on the plus side she had a good skin, nice hair and an extrovert nature. It was not wholly impossible to imagine the Wagon's habitués giving the spiel to Brenda.

On the other hand it was a good deal harder to cast Trevor Tunnel in the role of fierily possessive husband. He too was on the Tomahawks committee, a thin, strangely dejected man, much given to hackneyed ideological pronouncements which he dropped into the discussion with the forced and leaden regularity of constipated stools.

All in all, Brenda and Trevor were one of those couples whom it was especially hard to picture in the conjugal bed.

'Have you considered giving up the job?' I asked, since I was being placed in the invidious position of ad hoc agony aunt.

'I couldn't do that!' objected Brenda con spirito. She was a recent convert to feminism, and as with most converts, its tenets were law to her.

"Then you must convince Trevor that it doesn't constitute a threat,' I said, wishing the train would come.

'Being friendly with the customers is part of the job,' insisted Brenda. 'It's part of what they pay me for. And I flatter myself I'm quite good at it.'

'Right, of course, I see the difficulty,' I agreed. Mercifully, at this moment, the train appeared. 'Well, here we are! Have a good day with your mother-in-law.'

Brenda wrinkled her nose in what was intended to be a gamine expression of disfavour but which in a woman of her build resembled the snorting of a percheron.

Trevor's mother turned out to be tiny and wizened. Had both women been animals I would have half expected Mrs Tunnel senior to leap at Brenda's throat and drain her of red corpuscles.

I had a quiet journey. It seemed I'd successfully evaded Robbo, and I saw no one else I knew. I read the paper, but without taking in what I read. Rapists and rock stars, athletes and arsonists, pundits and personalities paraded meaninglessly before me; my mind ran on Constantine Ghikas. Like most married women my imagination had been unfaithful several times a week for the past ten years or so, but this was not tantamount to admitting that our marriage was on the rocks. On the contrary, it was a success. It worked. We understood each other, we liked each other, and, increasingly intermittently, we fancied each other. When our respective fancies coincided the earth still moved sufficiently to account our sex life a success. When they did not, each of us was quite prepared to accommodate the other in a spirit of sporting good fellowship. The very ease with which I had decided not to accompany George to the Middle East and the good humour with which he had left me, was one of the reasons I knew we were built to last. We had integral flexibility. Marriages like ours were not made in heaven so much as manufactured on earth for optimum durability, the product of careful planning and good will on both sides. George could be pompous, vain and high-handed.

But he was handsome, generous, and uncomplicated. And he was also unreservedly enthusiastic about my work, read what I wrote with genuine interest, and spoke of me with pride to others.

So I had always known that George and I would stay together. And in spite of occasional lustful musings I had never been tempted to put my body where my brain had been. Never, that is, until now.

I looked at the woman sitting opposite me. To my surprise she was reading, with every appearance of enjoyment, the weekly women's magazine in which the serialisation of my last book was currently appearing. When she laid the magazine down in order to dab her nose with a tissue I saw that she was well into part three of *Love's Dying Glory*. She continued, turning a page with an air of rapt involvement. Her breathing was adenoidal and a faint smell of eucalyptus emanated from her.

Dear reader, I thought, what would you do if you knew that the person facing you was the author of that stirring tale of wild passion? And again what if you knew that she was planning to lay her GP at the earliest possible opportunity?

The situation was quite titillating. When I got off the train at King's Cross I was in such a semi-erectile state that I suspected I had a funny walk.

Not funny enough to be unrecognisable, though, for just beyond the ticket barrier I was accosted by a breathless Robbo Makepeace.

'Harriet!'

'Robbo, hallo! Actually I'm in the most awful hurry.'

'That's all right,' he said, as if pardoning me for some embarrassing solecism. 'I just wanted to tell you there's an extraordinary meeting of the Toms committee on Friday.'

When, I thought, were the meetings not extraordinary?

'Okay,' I said, 'give me a ring and I'll try to make it.'

'It's pretty much a crunch situation, I'm afraid,' Robbo added weightily. 'We could finish up with no fupbore for the lads.'

'Fupbore for the lads' was the hallmark of Robbo's creed. In the face of squalid argument, calculated cheating and just about every other shade of unsportsmanlike behaviour, he persisted in the view that the 'Toms' existed to provide a competitive outlet for the stalwart British virtues of fair play, loyalty and team spirit.

'I will try and come,' I reassured him. 'And now I really must dash.'

As a result of my exchange with Robbo I arrived at Era Books a touch late. After the usual undignified wrangle about my identity with the security-conscious receptionist I rose in the lift to the second floor.

I emerged to find a small selection of Era's hypers, hustlers and harpies assembled to greet me in the lobby of the main office. Beyond them the PBI of secretaries and editorial assistants slaved away in a series of glass and plywood corrals.

The greeters comprised Vanessa; Christopher Lazenby, sales director; Marilyn Drinkwater, publicity; and Tristan Whirly-Birch, PR man extraordinary. There was about these slightly tarnished products of the public school system an air of gentility gone to seed, and nobility corrupted, such as may be observed in photos of Mittel-European royalty disporting in Paris nightclubs. Publishing seemed to eat gently raised and expensively educated young men and women for breakfast, and to regurgitate them in a still recognisable but spoiled form. It seemed odd that the scions of good families, especially the female ones, should be so possessed by the idea of publishing as an okay thing to do. It appeared to have the seal of uppercrust approval. The editorial office of Era Books sounded like nothing so much as a busy day at the Royal Show. And yet a more rancid hotbed of avarice, hypocrisy and moral turpitude would have been hard to find.

There was no doubt that these special characteristics found their apotheosis in Vanessa and Tristan, both skilled and viperish practitioners of the publishing arts.

Now Vanessa stepped forward and took my arm as if I were simple or infirm, or both. It was one of the many small ways in which she contrived to make me feel a hayseed.

'Bless you, Harriet,' she gushed through a miasma of Desert Breeze. 'How I wish all our authors were as obliging as

37

you.' She had a way of implying, or perhaps I just inferred, that my co-operativeness was somehow dull and demeaning.

She also invariably made me feel that my 'good' clothes, donned expressly for the occasion, were further evidence of my bucolic background. Not for her any special effort. In spite of the rolling acres in the shires which were her heritage, Vanessa exuded street-wisdom. Today, along with the inevitable laced boots and rolled-down socks, she wore a pair of scarlet long coms, complete with buttoned back panel for frostbite-free defecation. These were topped by a Fair Isle cardy slung round the shoulders, and a humbug-striped ra-ra skirt. She was parlously thin, and her blonde hair was teased away from her face in a style which suggested that her toe had just been stuck in a live electric socket. But she was just beautiful and well-bred enough to rise above the breathtaking nastiness of her toilette.

'Hallo, Vanessa,' I said. 'Hallo, Chris.'

'Hi,' said Chris. In this small gathering of the literati only Christopher Lazenby was not out of the top drawer. As befitted one who had to soil his hands with commerce, Chris was a rough diamond, with breakfast-food vowels, personalised jewellery, and the Zapata moustaches which had been all the go fifteen years ago but were now the stamp of the young exec. estates of Potters Bar and Borehamwood. He was also the only Eran who still admitted to enjoying business lunches. While others toyed with crudités and grilled sole, Chris slurped thick soup and wiped up gravy with bread. His backside strained against its chainstore trousering, and his fitted pink shirt parted slightly in the interstices between buttons, revealing a glimpse of well-filled gut.

'Morning, Marilyn.'

'It's so nice to see you, Harriet.'

Marilyn Drinkwater was a smart, but colourless, woman approaching that dangerous corner in her career when exciting potential becomes annoying garrulity. Her looks were of the pale pastel variety which are only attractive in youth. Now in her late thirties, she looked as if Brenda Tunnel's mother-in-law had spent the night clinging to her jugular.

'I hear you've been having a pretty hectic time at home,'

38

she remarked as the five of us set off in the direction of the conference room, Vanessa's hand still beneath my elbow.

'Yes, it has been, but then when isn't it?' I replied obligingly, and the Erans glanced at each other with warm, collusive approval – I was such a *nice* author.

Tristan, who had been silent till now, remarked: 'We think you're going to like Vince.'

'Do you?'

'Oh yes, yes,' they chorused.

'Then I expect I shall.'

In the conference room Tristan held a chair for me and I sat.

'That is an enchanting brooch,' he said, studying my left lapel. His proximity was as fragrant, fresh and deadly as a bunch of belladonna. His face was round and bland, his hair smooth, his collar stiff and his tie wide; all combined to give him a humpty-dumptyish appearance. He was said to have impressed the Great Man of Era Books almost at once with a publishing acumen quite staggering in a mere strip of a lad (Tristan was twenty-five). But the truth was he was so rich, so landed and so gentrified, and consequently so utterly without scruple, that he could have sold tonic wine in Jerez.

'Isn't it pretty?' I agreed. 'My husband gave it to me on our anniversary.'

This was the unalloyed truth but I only mentioned it for the effect I knew it would have on the Erans. All four of them assumed expressions of almost pained admiration.

'God,' said Marilyn in reverential tones, 'it's good to meet someone with a happy marriage.'

On the long wall opposite, the paperback cover of *Love's Dying Glory* had been pinned up, presumably as a compliment to me. It depicted Victoria Principal, Richard Gere and Al Pacino in Regency attire. Gere and Principal were locked in a muscular embrace while Pacino looked on with an air of saturnine disapproval. In the background was a galleon, apparently moored on the heads of some men fencing in frilly shirts, and a Moorish castle with a few date palms rising from the surf. All in all it was an excellent distillation of the work it was to enclose.

'Like it?' asked Vanessa.

'It says a lot about the book,' I said.

'That's what we think,' agreed Chris. He made a sweeping gesture with his left hand. The hand was adorned with digital watch, identity bracelet, wedding and other rings, and a Marlboro cigarette. 'We're putting your name over the title on this one, in red, and the title itself in the same red, but shiny. Like catches the light.'

'Nice,' I said.

'You haven't heard the half of it!' shrilled Marilyn. 'We have such plans for you.'

'Gosh.'

'My feeling is,' announced Tristan, 'that we need to play up your domestic circumstances more. It's incredible how you manage to write with the children about, and a houseful of pets and so on.'

'The children are quite big now,' I reminded her. 'It's not that difficult to write.'

'I still think it's a useful image,' he persisted, addressing the others now. 'We want more pictures of Harriet at home with her family and her animals.'

Amid the general murmur of assent I thought of Declan and Damon; of Gareth playing snooker and Clara wired for sound; of Fluffy and Spot and the misanthropic Stu; of Brenda and Robbo and (be still, my erogenous zones) of Dr Ghikas. And I was not sure that the sum of these disparate parts was quite the rural idyll which Tristan clearly envisaged.

'Will you have some coffee, Harriet?' enquired Vanessa. The plain, ruminating secretary raised her head above the foliage on the far side of the glass partition.

'Thank you, that would be nice.'

'Lucinda – some coffee please!'

The tapir ambled off to fetch refreshments, and as she went, Vince Priddoe arrived. He was a tiny man in a cream suit and a light blue roll-necked pullover. There was no hint of dangling corks, nor of tubes of the amber nectar thrust into the hip pocket. On the contrary he embodied the sporty quasi-California chic which every smart man was currently trying to achieve. I had little doubt that his diet was fibrous and fat-free, his body trim and at a peak of cardio-vascular fitness, his sex-life varied and caring, his mind expanded by frequent energetic social intercourse with minority groups such as authors and women (and sometimes, as now, both at once), and his leisure time spent productively.

Vince's hand when he shook mine was smooth, cool and tanned; his teeth when he smiled gleamed in capped splendour; and he smelled of the kind of unguents which are sold by Americans with Italian names who fly about in Lear jets. I felt like an unmade bed. I could not in a million years see myself on an author tour of the Antipodes with this paragon of self-fulfilment.

'Harriet – ' he gave my hand a little tug as if trying to draw water out of my mouth – 'let me take a good look at the woman who gives so much pleasure to so many people.' As an opening gambit this made my gorge rise. But I mumbled something suitably self-effacing and at Vanessa's instigation we took our places round the conference table. The tapir brought coffee, and I stirred in milk and sugar. Vince took his black, with pills, and asked in addition for a glass of water.

'And how about this,' he said, gesturing at the cover on the wall. 'That has to be the most striking cover of the year. Are you pleased with it, Harriet?'

'Oh, delighted.'

Vince turned to the assembled Erans. 'I think I just have to get Harriet over to Australia, they'd love her over there. Tell me, Harriet, have you ever been down under?'

'No, I never have.'

'It's a wonderful country, Harriet,' said Vince. 'It's a big country, and a wild country, and one you ought to see.'

'They read there, too, contrary to popular belief,' said Chris. 'The figures – '

'My countrymen,' announced Vince firmly, overriding Chris's interruption, 'have a tradition of plain speaking. They know what they like, Harriet, and what they don't like, and they let their preferences be known. I don't mind telling you I'm proud of that.'

'Admirable,' I said. It was clear that Vince Priddoe, with all his manifold virtues, was utterly without a sense of humour.

I became even more certain that my first visit 'down under' would not be undertaken in his company. As the others talked I let my mind return like a homing pigeon to images of Dr Ghikas – his tweed suit, his thick lashes, his lonely bed . . .

'. . . need at least ten days,' Tristan was saying. 'And I imagine that once Harriet has made arrangements to be away it doesn't make much odds whether she's away for two days or two weeks – would I be right, Harriet?'

In the space of a few minutes the Australian scheme appeared to have fleshed out alarmingly. I pressed the panic button.

'Normally you would be,' I said. 'But my husband's away for the whole of this year, which does complicate things. I very much doubt,' I added firmly, 'that a tour of Australia would be on.'

'Doesn't this husband of yours get leave?' asked Vince, quite testily. 'I mean – ' he looked at Vanessa – 'when exactly is the paperback publication date?'

'October – so exciting,' said Vanessa. It was now the end of May. Suddenly the summer seemed extremely short. I had a sudden vision of Constantine Ghikas, bollock-naked and with everything at the high port, walking backwards into the sea while I lay on Bondi Beach trapped up to my neck in sand. It was not comforting. But when it came to the manipulation of Erans I was a wily old fox.

'Australia sounds quite wonderful,' I said, wistfully. 'But I honestly couldn't abandon the kids for that long, much as I would like to. I really hate to let you down over this – '

'Nonsense! Nonsense!' they all cried obligingly. Vince looked baffled.

'Besides,' Tristan added, 'you're coming over to the Fartenwald Buchfest, remember, and that will be of tremendous value, even though it's only for a couple of days.'

'So you're coming to Fartenwald?' Vince brightened immeasurably. 'Well, that is good news. I shall be there myself, so I shall be able to try my powers of persuasion on you again.'

'You could try, Vince,' said Marilyn roguishly, 'but our Harriet is a family person, unlike most authors, and we wouldn't want her any different!'

Lord, how little they knew me. I shifted lasciviously on my hessian seat. My Bottom was without a doubt translated.

As they chatted, and I stared at the cover picture on the wall opposite, my thoughts elsewhere, my conscious brain noted one thing. Al Pacino was wearing a wrist watch.

I mentioned this at lunch which we took, fortuitously, at the Zeus, a Greek restaurant in Holborn. Vanessa tinkled mirthlessly.

'You noticed! Don't worry, we do know.'

'Super.'

'I should have pointed it out right away. There is quite a bit of touching up to do.'

'What's all this about touching up?' asked Chris, leering over a forkful of mixed dolma.

'The wrist watch.'

'What a prize fuck-up,' opined Chris.

'Language, Christopher,' rebuked Marilyn. 'There are ladies present.'

'Oh yeah?'

Marilyn turned to me. 'Harriet, I do need to get your biographical notes up to date. Tell me what I should know, there's a dear.'

The lack of changes in my life embarrassed me rather. And the change which had occurred was not mentionable.

'I'm a year or two older,' I said.

'You don't look it.'

'Thank you.' Little did she know that I was no longer the well-balanced and wholesome scribbling housewife so beloved of the Erans, but a lust-maddened virago hell-bent on adultery.

' . . . they're teenagers, surely?' she was asking. I caught her drift.

'No. Well one is, sort of, just. They're in between really.' I considered my children for a moment – Clara, even thinner, more lovely and more waspish than Vanessa; and Gareth, nearly as big, just as greedy, and potentially more foul-mouthed than Chris. What, in God's name, would they be like when they were teenagers?

'She's in a world of her own,' observed Vince. 'Where were you, Harriet, back in Tudor times, with the old lutes strumming there?'

'We're all dying to read *The Remembrance Tree*,' said Vanessa, as if for the first time.

'I endorse that,' said Vince. 'You know, Harriet, it would be a great help to our people in Australia if we had some idea what you've got in store for us. People like continuity, readers want something to look forward to.'

'Don't badger the lady,' said Chris, making a swiss roll of pitta bread and tsatsiki. 'We all know it'll be shit hot.'

'Oh, we know *that*,' agreed Vanessa, 'but just the same, a few titchy hints would be tremendous . . . '

'Yes, come on, Harriet,' echoed Vince.

As I launched into my by now finely tuned filibuster on the subject of *The Remembrance Tree*, I wondered why Vince should suppose that the constant repetition of my christian name would make him seem a nicer and more sensitive human being; when all it did was to confirm me in my opinion that he was an utter pillock.

Lunch wore on and the retsina went down. We became first convivial, then matey. The behavioural quirks of the Erans, of which I had been so stringently critical not an hour since, now seemed lovable little foibles. We're all pros together, I thought mawkishly. This is Life. By the baklava and Turkish coffee I was all set to spill the beans concerning Dr Ghikas. Only my well-developed sense of self-protection stopped me, and that in the nick of time.

I employed the time-honoured means of escape, and went to the loo. This involved running the gauntlet of the Zeus's kitchen passage, complete with Greeks in greasy aprons, and bins full of what might have been either rotting rubbish or the raw materials for moussaka.

The Ladies had curling lino and a holy picture. I stared at myself in the mirror (remarking as I did so that it did not suit me to drink, it made the tissues of my face dilate like a sponge under water), and told myself that at the moment, no matter what the temptation, there were no beans to spill. I must wait until matters had developed, which please God they would,

44

and then, with dalliance so to speak under my belt, I might drop it into some future conversation with the insouciance of the seasoned campaigner, and leave them all with their image of me in forlorn tatters about their ears. But for now, what would I be admitting to? Just unrequited lust, not a very edifying state for a middle-aged housewife and mother.

I went back to the table, where second coffees had been poured.

'Here she comes!' cried Marilyn. 'I hope you've got your diary handy, Harriet!'

In my dream I screeched 'Knickers!' at them, and pulled the cloth and everything on it from beneath their noses.

In reality I sat, rummaged in my handbag for my diary and said, with the cheery compliance of the well-trained author: 'Fire away.'

I got back to find Clara, astonishingly, in the kitchen with Damon. They were eating toast and peanut butter. Damon was sitting at the table scanning a copy of the local paper, and Clara was standing with her back to him on the other side of the room, waiting for the electric kettle to boil. They looked like an old married couple, and every bit as surly. From upstairs I could hear the pounding of heavy metal, an indication that Gareth, at least, was doing his homework.

'Damon!' I said. 'Oh God, of course, it's Friday today, I'd forgotten our new arrangement. When did you get here?'

'Two o'clock, like always,' he said.

'But Clara had the key, how on earth did you get in?'

Clara answered. 'He got in through that window on the stairs that you leave open for Fluffy.'

'Good grief.' I sat down at the table.

'It's a cinch, over the back-yard roof,' Damon enlarged. 'No prob.'

'Honestly Damon, I'm sorry to have locked you out, but I'm not at all sure it's a good idea for you to be breaking and entering when I'm not here.'

'He didn't do any breaking,' said Clara, truculently. 'I thought I'd just explained that.' Since when had she been Damon's ally?

'I didn't want to let you down. No way,' added Damon, rather touchingly.

'Well, that's very thoughtful of you, Damon. It's just that if anyone had seen you . . . '

'That's his look-out,' said Clara irrefutably.

'But it might give someone else ideas.'

'That's true,' conceded Damon. 'You should get window locks fitted, deffi.'

I seemed to be trapped in an argument I stood no chance of winning.

'Yes. Anyway, thank you,' I said weakly. 'Any chance of some tea?'

Clara poured me one and bonked it down in front of me like a waitress in one of those small-town-America films.

'Good day?' enquired Damon over the *Basset Bugle.* The situation was rapidly making me feel like a stranger in my own home.

'Yes, thank you, not bad.'

Clara had left the room, and now she came back carrying a note. 'This came through the letter box,' she said, handing it to me.

I unfolded it. It was a sheet from a medical prescription pad. On it, in horrific doctor's handwriting like a barbed wire entanglement, was written: 'Dear Mrs Blair, I called with my mother's copy of your book, but unfortunately you were out. Would you very kindly sign it for her? Her name is Anna. I'll drop in and collect it some other time. Many thanks – Constantine Ghikas.'

'Where's the book?' I asked Clara.

'What book?'

'There should be a book with this.'

'Hold it,' said Damon. 'Stay right there.' He went into the hall and returned with a fat brown paper parcel.

'Found it on the doorstep,' he explained.

I opened the parcel. Inside was the hardback edition of *Love's Dying Glory,* whose cover (mercifully) depicted nothing more than a sheaf of red roses with one or two fallen petals. No duellers in the surf, nor film stars in digital watches – in fact nothing whatever to be ashamed of.

'One of yours?' asked Damon. 'M-hm?'

I opened the book and glanced at the title page. In the same atrocious hand were inscribed the words: 'Dearest – I'm sure you'll like this. Many, many happy returns – Kostaki, November 1983.'

So he was her little Kostaki, was he? Phase one must certainly culminate in being invited to address him by this charming diminutive. I could hear myself murmuring 'Kostaki . . . oh, Kostaki,' as we embraced on some not-too-distant future occasion.

'I must go and make a phone call,' I said, abandoning my tea, and went through to the sitting room. This was directly beneath Gareth's room, and the harmonised pile-drivers of Status Quo were consequently more intrusive. I pressed my fingers to my temples and tried to collect my thoughts. I couldn't ring him at the surgery; on the other hand there were only ever two doctors on duty, so he might possibly be at home. But there again I had neither home address nor phone number. Surely, though, there could only be one Ghikas in Basset Parva?

I sat down by the phone. My right hand was just poised to lift the receiver, the left to dial directory enquiries, when it rang.

I nearly jumped out of my skin as though the phone, like a malign, many-eyed mollusc, had found me out in a disgusting secret vice. Which, if wishes were doctors, it would have done. I picked up the receiver.

'Hallo there!'

'Hallo . . . ? Sorry . . . ?'

'Telepathy – you were just about to call me!'

It was George. The chill shock of reality made me slump back in my chair.

'Hallo, George.'

'Don't get too carried away, it's bad for the blood pressure.'

'I'm sorry.'

'San fairy anne. Happy anniversary.'

'Oh God.'

'Shall I ring off and start again?'

His determined geniality goaded me into some semblance of civilised behaviour.

'I feel *awful*. I completely forgot.'

'Well I didn't, so I thought I'd ring and tell you that it don't seem a day too much.'

'How sweet of you.'

'Think nothing of it. How are you all? Kids okay?'

'They're fine. I've been in town today, at Era. Clara's eating toast in the kitchen and Gareth's doing prep.'

'What about you? How's the oeuvre coming along?'

For once I wished he wouldn't be so interested in my work. I'd answered enough questions about it for one day, and his well-meant enquiry just increased my sense of guilt.

'Lousy,' I said. 'Yesterday Declan fouled up the electrics and then cut himself on the shears, so I got next to nothing done.'

'He'll have to go.'

'No, no, he's invaluable really.'

'He's a walking bloody disaster area, with absolutely no regard for anyone else's time or work. Or patience. And you know it.'

This was bad news. If George decreed that Declan should be fired it would fall to my lot to do the firing and to suffer the consequent verbal flack. I shuffled back down.

'It wasn't his fault he cut himself, and it was quite nasty. I had to take him to the doctor. He's done a good job on the hedge,' I added, with the smooth mendacity of fear. 'By the way, did I tell you that Era are sending me to the Fartenwald Buchfest next month?'

'Are they? That's terrific. You'll enjoy that,' George assured me firmly. 'Will you be able to arrange it with me away?'

'Yes, it's only for three nights. I can farm the children out with the Tunnels, I hope.'

'Good!' There was nothing George liked better than news of purposeful activity. 'Good, good.'

We continued the conversation along lines of effusive mutual admiration for another couple of minutes, until George terminated it with a crisp 'I love you,' and rang off.

I sat there, limp and glum as a mackerel on a slab. The wind was well and truly out of my sails. Hearing George's voice had brought home to me the real enormity of my intentions with regard to Dr Ghikas. Unfortunately it had not put paid to them. I knew I would continue right on down the primrose path, but the going might become distinctly shitty.

Damon put his head round the door.

'I'll be off then. I done those window frames in the spare room.'

'Oh – thank you, Damon.'

'We could do with a drop more Sanifresh.'

'Rightie-ho.'

'Get the Meadowsweet if you can.'

'I will.' He stood there. 'Sorry, your cash.'

'You could give it to me Tuesday,' he said, without conviction.

'No, no, hang on.'

I located my bag and paid him. As he left, he lifted a hand to Clara, and she reciprocated. I should have been glad to witness this apparent breakthrough in my daughter's attitude to the sons of toil, but I wasn't. I felt only the gravest foreboding.

Chapter Four

On Friday night, galvanised into activity by my day with the Erans and subsequent conversation with George, I enlarged to some effect on Maria Trevelyan's relationship with the Hawkhursts, and with the spine-tinglingly glacial Richard in particular. It was the sort of thing I could do with my eyes shut, but the sight of those few well-covered pages lying beside the tripewriter bucked me up no end, and I spent the next hour cogitating on the right dedication for Constantine Ghikas's mother. In the end I plumped for the simple and dignified: 'To Anna Ghikas, with very good wishes from the author, Harriet Blair – Basset Magna, May '84.'

Saturday and Sunday dragged their heels. The weekend was the only time when I positively missed George's organisational flair. Without the prop of his inspired bossiness the three of us sank into a slough of sloth and mutual recrimination. In my case this was aggravated by the need, as I saw it, to hang about the house and garden in case Dr Ghikas called back for his book. But of course I should have guessed he would be far too considerate to trouble someone during their hard-earned leisure with anything so trivial.

I actually had to go out twice. On Saturday night I

attended a dinner party of stupefying tedium given by some friends the Channings, who misguidedly saw it as their mission to save me from the miseries of grass-widowhood. To this end they had twinned me with a whinnying wine importer whose only redeeming feature was that he far preferred the sound of his own voice to that of mine, thus absolving me from conversation.

On Sunday I took Gareth and Clara, under protest, to a barbecue in aid of the church roof. Everyone who was anyone in Basset Magna society was there, spreading the word about up-coming flower festivals, craft fairs, toy evenings and sponsored skips. The rector, Eric Chittenden, in whose garden the barbecue was held, presided over us with practised bonhomie, sausage in one hand, cider cup in the other, advising a select few of the existence of an acceptable sherry on the sideboard in his dining room. By the time we went home at three-thirty the children's morale had risen considerably under the influence of the fizzy infuriator, while mine had sunk to an all-time low.

On Monday morning the signed copy of *LDG* still lay on my kitchen table, a hostage to lust, but there had as yet been no word from Dr Ghikas. This morning I was going to need rather more than the Irish DJ could provide if I was to trouble the tripewriter. So when Gareth and Clara had left for their respective schools I put on my running kit.

Spot, alerted by this dreadful note of preparation, attempted to squeeze under the bed, but I was too quick for him.

'Walkies!' I cried threateningly, and clipped on the lead.

When kindly and admiring friends asked me why I ran, how I found the time, and what precisely the benefits were, I had my answer ready. It has changed my life, I would rhapsodise. I have so much more energy. I no longer have a weight problem, nor do I suffer from depression. I enjoy a sense of well-being.

These protestations shut them up, but they were not the whole truth. The plain fact was that running was so grim, so taxing and so unutterably dull that the rest of life gained by the comparison.

Also, it freed the mind wonderfully. I was a different being

51

to the one who had started jogging a year ago. Where once I had cowered behind haystacks and parked cars, smarting with embarrassment as acquaintances and tradesmen passed by, I now loped along in a world of my own, equally oblivious to wolf-whistles, jeers and greetings. And once I was out of the village and pounding the open bridleways, nothing short of a motor-cross rally coming in the opposite direction could have brought me back to earth.

Today I ran with the scowling doggedness with which I imagine men on oil rigs take cold showers.

I thought about Maria. Time now to illustrate the polarities of her complex nature as personified by blond, aristocratic Richard, and the swarthy under-gardener with his well-filled trousers. How to do it? I observed the flapping question mark of Spot's tail above the young kale. A hunt was always good value. Competing with the flash horsemanship of the Hawkhursts, and of Richard in particular, Maria would come to grief over a ditch. The first face she saw when revived would be that of the gardener, as he pressed a cup of water to her ashen lips . . .

The only trouble was, I couldn't keep Dr Ghikas out of it. Willy-nilly, his well-groomed golden head peeped from behind each yew hedge and arras; a specimen bottle gleamed dully amongst the stirrup-cups; his stethoscope whisked tantalisingly through the maze; his black bag lay, a seductive anachronism, in the Great Hall. I could not erase a mental picture of his elegant figure in period dress – the well-turned calf in coloured stockings, the face framed by an extravagant ruff. I began seriously to consider altering my synopsis to take account of a soulful and toothsome stranger from foreign parts.

So far gone was I in these fanciful musings that I failed to notice Spot, who had stopped dead in his tracks to investigate the mouldering carcase of a rabbit. His motionless form, rigid with ecstatic concentration, neatly chopped my shins just below the knee so that my legs remained on one side of him and the rest of me hurtled on its way into a heap of rotting sprout tops. I emerged dirty but unhurt, landed one or two well-aimed blows on the dog and squelched on my way, paying rather more attention to my route.

I had covered three sides of a rectangular circuit of about four miles, and was now approaching the road on which I would turn right for the home straight to Basset Magna. I put Spot back on the lead, and set myself the unprecedented challenge of covering the mile home in seven minutes.

After about a hundred yards I became aware of a car coming up behind me. I hugged the side of the road, mentally preparing myself for the buzz which no red-blooded motorist can resist giving a pedestrian on the open road. But it didn't come. The engine-noise of the car, a cheap and cheerful down-market puttering, remained steady about four metres behind my right shoulder. It seemed I was the unlikely focus of attention for a kerb crawler. The road began to slow down into the welcome dip which preceded the steep climb into Basset Magna, and I accelerated. The puttering rose a semitone or two and stayed with me.

Irritably, I veered on to the grass verge and stopped. The car – a jaunty green Fiat with its bottom in the air like a motorised wheelbarrow – drew alongside me and pulled up. The driver leaned across and pushed open the door on the passenger side. The face looking up at me, from beneath the brim of one of those adorable tweed fishing hats, was that of Dr Constantine Ghikas.

'Good morning,' he said. How suave he was!

'Good morning,' I replied. 'I tried to call you on Friday. I've signed your mother's book.'

'Thank you so much. It seemed rather rude just to leave it on the step, but then I didn't want to bother you at the weekend . . . '

'Not at all, absolutely . . . anyway, it's done now, so you must collect it.'

'Well, yes – look, should I insult you if I offered you a lift?'

The thought of climbing into the snug confines of that nifty little car went to my head like strong drink. My leg would be only inches from his own twill-covered thigh, brushing the trembling upright gear lever upon which his hand (the back adorned with a scattering of coppery hairs) now rested.

I leaned forward eagerly, the sweat breaking out on me

like sap rising in the spring. 'How very kind,' I said, 'I don't see why – '

It was at this moment that I became conscious of the smell arising from my perspiring body. The pile of nicely degrading sprout tops into which I had so recently ploughed was taking its delayed toll. The odour was not, unfortunately, indescribable. I could describe it quite accurately. It was as though I had farted. And no ordinary fart this, but a veritable empress of flatulence. A real five-star, blue riband, nostril-clenching knock-out.

I lurched backwards, head thrown up like a nervous race-horse.

'But I mustn't!' I squawked. 'I've just fallen over in something nasty, and I've got the dog with me, and your nice clean car – '

'I quite understand,' he soothed. 'Tell you what, shall I call in later this morning when I've done my house calls? I won't keep you from your writing, I'll just be in and out.'

Oh, be in and out, do, I thought. In and out, in and out . . . feel free.

'That's fine,' I said.

'It's most good of you.' He slammed the door, revved the engine and raised a hand in farewell. 'See you later!'

The green Fiat spluttered on its way, and I loped noisomely after it, with a light heart.

As I turned the corner into our road there were Brenda and Baba enjoying their regular tête-à-tête on the corner by my house. Seeing me coming they stood well back as if I were a bull elephant instead of a nine-and-a-half-stone house-wife.

'Morning!' I trumpeted obligingly. I was a friend to all the world now, and it especially behoved me to be civil to Brenda if I wished her to stand in loco parentis while I attended the Buchfest.

'Harriet, you make us all feel guilty,' tinkled Baba. She was lying in her teeth, of course. Baba was a tiny, trim, immaculate woman with a bijou, immaculate home, and two seraphic little boys with neat hair and shiny shoes. Her husband travelled in Scotch tape. Their house, garden and garage were in such a state of intensive maintenance that they seemed not just to have kept deterioration at bay but to have put themselves in credit for the next fifty years. And yet Baba and Clive continued to knock through, sand down and do up, to mow, hoe, edge, weed and plant, to wash and vacuum their family saloon and rake their gravel sweep. On the days the dustcart came round, Baba put out one black plastic bag, caught at the top with the length of wire supplied for the purpose. I generally put out three or four such bags, two of which would have been breached by Fluffy in the small hours to expose the tell-tale necks of wine bottles like the heads of vultures gathering at a kill. By their rubbish shall ye know them.

I stopped, and Spot put his nose up Baba's Country Casuals skirt.

'Whoopsadaisy,' said Baba.

'He likes you,' I said. I wondered if they could smell my special aura, and moved in a bit closer. 'How was your mother, Brenda?'

Brenda grimaced. 'Between her and Trevor I feel stifled, you know?'

'Ah, poor Bren,' commiserated Baba. I reflected that it would take a lot more than the stringy forms of Trevor and his bat-like parent to stifle Brenda, puffed out as she was with the hot and heady rhetoric of the women's movement.

'Pity she isn't with you today,' said Baba, 'I'm having a little coffee morning in aid of the Young Wives.'

'Yes . . . shame,' said Brenda.

Baba turned to me. 'How about you, Harriet? Nice cup of coffee and some hazelnut gateau about ten forty-five?'

Fortunately for my eternal soul I was able to answer with absolute truthfulness: 'Actually I'm expecting someone this morning.'

Baba treated me to a cutesy little smile. 'Lucky for some!' she twittered like the bird-brain she was. I pictured the inside of Baba's head like the front garden of a seaside boarding house: very miniature, laid out in tiny raised flowerbeds and dainty gravel paths, picked out with shells and gnomes, adorned with filigree trellises and teensy wooden haywains filled with dinky flowers. As anal and repressed a landscape as you could wish to see.

'Yes, I'd better get back,' I said, feeding her her next cue, 'or he'll catch me in the shower.'

As I jogged off I heard Baba's piping laugh. 'Chance'd be a fine thing, eh, Bren?'

In fact I had ample time to shower, change, and describe Richard Hawkhurst on horseback before Spot launched into his mega-wuff for total strangers and I saw the transport of delight parked by my front gate. I waited for Dr Ghikas to knock, and then allowed a further thirty seconds of exquisite anticipatory tension to elapse before I opened the door.

He stood with his tweed hat in his hands, smiling serenely at me over Spot's hysterically bouncing head. A pair of dark glasses peeped from the breast pocket of his light grey Norfolk jacket.

'Hallo,' I said. 'Sorry about the dog.'

'He's only doing his job.'

'I suppose so. Do come on in and he'll calm down.' I closed the door after him. 'Would you like some coffee?'

'That sounds wonderful – are you sure I'm not disturbing you?'

'No, not at all, I'm due for a break.'

'In that case – ' He placed his hat on the hall table, smoothed his hair and followed me into the kitchen. Fluffy was eviscerating a vole near the back door, and I opened the door and booted out both cat and cadaver in one seamless movement.

'Pets!' I cried. 'What can you do?' The buggers had really let me down.

'I'm very fond of cats,' said Dr Ghikas. 'We have one at home. Unfortunately, Nature red in tooth and claw, and so on . . . you can't change them.'

'You're so right.' I filled the kettle. 'Your book's there, on the table, I do hope what I've put is okay.'

He glanced at it. 'Marvellous. She'll be thrilled to bits.'

At that moment the phone rang, and I said 'Excuse me,' and went into the sitting room to answer it.

It was Tristan, anxious to impress upon me just how

'taken' Vince Priddoe had been with me, and how enormously they were all looking forward to seeing me at the Buchfest.

Because Dr Ghikas might be listening, I was not as brief with Tristan as I might otherwise have been.

'Of course I do appreciate the importance of the Buchfest,' I said loftily. 'But I am loth to take too much time away from *The Remembrance Tree* at present. I feel it's important, a much bigger undertaking than anything else I've written.'

Tristan must have been quite flabbergasted by all this which was, for me, a nearly unprecedented stream of unsolicited comments. There was a short, wary silence on the other end, before he said weakly: 'You are coming, though – aren't you?'

'I shall certainly try. In the meantime, you will see that that wretched watch comes off the cover of *LDG*, won't you? And I'd like to see the display material when it's ready.'

'Of course, no problem.' Was I mistaken, or did I detect a new note of respect in Tristan's voice? 'And please – we all of us here appreciate that writing comes first.'

I replaced the receiver with a profound sense of satisfaction. For the preceding few minutes, and for the basest possible motive, I had been the cool, authoritative, demanding lady writer of my fantasies.

Back in the kitchen, Dr Ghikas was perusing my noticeboard with his hands in his pockets. As I poured coffee, he said over his shoulder: 'I see your son is a footballer.'

'Oh yes, his world revolves around it.'

'Mine used to at one time. I'm still a keen soccer fan.'

'Really?' I handed him his coffee. 'Do you actually play?'

He shook his head. 'I've had a bit of cartilage trouble in recent years. But I still go to good matches whenever I can. Who does your son support?'

'Ipswich.'

'I've got a season ticket for Ipswich,' said Dr Ghikas. He sipped his coffee and I crossed my legs. 'Perhaps he'd like to come along with me some time.'

'What a simply terrific offer,' I enthused. Now was not the moment to worry whether Gareth, inflamed by the posh

57

seats at Ipswich Town, might besmirch the Blair escutcheon and wreck my chances with the doctor. 'I'm sure he'd love to.'

'I'll see what I can do then.'

We sat down at the table. He riffled through *LDG*, giving me an opportunity to admire again those luxuriant lashes.

I began to speak, made a noise like a rusty hinge, and cleared my throat.

Dr Ghikas looked up. 'Sorry?'

'I was going to say – I'll give your mother a copy of my new one when that comes out. If she truly enjoys them.'

'Oh, she does. And she does like to have a hardback, it's so much more satisfying.'

I could see Anna Ghikas in my mind's eye – a little dumpy, grey-haired figure in black, her face set in lines of profound and disapproving reserve, like the women I'd seen on our last holiday on Rhodes. But what of the Ghikas menage in Basset Parva? That was much harder to imagine. Did Constantine live with his mother, or she with him? Or had I just assumed they lived together?

Dr Ghikas was still riffling. 'They call you a romantic novelist, but it's pretty racy stuff,' he commented admiringly.

This reminder threw my picture of the tubby Hellenic matriarch somewhat out of focus.

'A certain amount of humping is de rigueur, I'm afraid,' I said. 'I do hope your mother doesn't find them too risqué.'

'Too risqué?' He laughed, revealing white, slightly crooked teeth, and an engaging cleft – it was too virile for a dimple – in his right cheek. 'Absolutely not. And anyway, as you obviously know, humping, as you put it, becomes perfectly acceptable the moment you dress it in period costume.'

I was conscious of a breakthrough having been made. I had, as it were, broken the loose talk barrier with Constantine Ghikas and had not found him wanting. He had revealed the unsuspected streak of asperity in his nature, like the dash of lemon juice, chilli or Tabasco which turns a delicious but bland dish into a taste experience.

'That's quite true, I'm afraid.'

He closed *LDG*. 'Time I was off.' He rose, unfurling his

length from the kitchen chair like a banner saying 'Eat Me'. I licked the condensation from my coffee from my upper lip.

'Thank you so much for the coffee, and for signing the book.'

Rather belatedly – I had been mesmerised by the very un-English snakeskin belt which he wore beneath the Norfolk jacket – I sprang to my feet. My God, he was going, the book was signed! Short of developing a chronic but non-disfiguring complaint and becoming a kind of bucolic Dame aux Camelias I could think of no way of getting to see him again. My own doctor was Donleavy, Grand Master of the Cervical Smear, and to change would be too obvious.

I watched, my brain whirring, as he put on his hat – what a seductive action that is, in the hands of the right person. Constantine Ghikas was that person. He slapped his Herbert Johnson titfer atop his head with Runyonesque élan, the brim shading his eyes, the crown cleft just so, like his cheek when he smiled. Lies rose readily to my lips and fluttered forth to settle on him like a net.

'I'm determined not to get dull while my husband's away this year,' (better to clear the air of that one), 'I'm planning a dinner party, would you like to come?'

'How very kind. When is that?'

More whirring and clicking. 'Saturday week. Not at all formal. Just a bunch of friends.'

'It sounds delightful, I'll definitely try and make it.'

This was a bit vague for my taste; nothing short of total commitment would do. 'I might drop a proper invitation through your letter box,' I said. 'Whereabouts are you exactly?'

'Oh – ' he felt in his inside breast pocket and handed me a card.

'Lovely, thanks.'

I saw him out. As he closed the gate behind him – and he amassed brownie points for actually activating the latch so that it remained closed – he asked: 'How is Mr O'Connell, by the way?'

For a second I was unable to match this august handle with Declan. When I did I realised I hadn't a clue how Declan was. So I lied in my teeth. 'A bit sore, but on the mend, I believe.'

'It's odd, isn't it,' mused Constantine Ghikas, 'as strong as an ox but simply wilted at the sight of the needle. I've heard about people like that but I've never actually come across one before.'

I smiled knowingly. 'Declan is an original in all kinds of ways.'

'A good worker, though, of the old school, I dare say?'

'Yes - yes, I suppose he is.' Now was not the moment to launch into my no-holds-barred dissertation on Declan's shortcomings.

'Goodbye then, and thanks again.' He doffed the hat briefly, climbed into the Fiat and made a getaway worthy of Starsky and Hutch. His driving bore all the hallmarks of the medical practitioner - it was fast, jerky, impatient and bloody dangerous. As I watched the car disappear from view I reflected that some forms of antisocial behaviour, such as illegible handwriting and reckless driving, were perfectly acceptable in a doctor. What a pity that screwing married female patients wasn't one of them.

Chapter Five

'Fupbore for the lads,' opined Robbo Makepeace. 'That's what we're here for. And the day we stop providing that is the day we should all pack up and go home.'

'The thing is though, Robbo,' said Eric Chittenden, who aside from his other pastoral duties was secretary of Tomahawks YFC, 'we also exist to maintain a high standard of football in the area, and if we can't do that I'm not sure I see the point. Quite honestly.'

'This is true,' agreed Trevor Tunnel. 'The Under Fourteens have been played off the park the last three Sundays, and if they lose their manager . . . ' Here a pregnant pause. 'No way.' A shake of the head. 'No way.'

'If I may intervene again,' said chairman Robbo, 'we are getting away from the central issue here. We are getting sidetracked.'

We all nodded. The Toms committee was always getting sidetracked. It was habitually to be found, wandering aimlessly, up shit creek without a paddle.

Tonight we were at least quorate. There were eight of us attending the extraordinary meeting of which Robbo had warned me at King's Cross the week before. Gathered in the umbrageous chill of the pavilion annexe were Robbo, Trevor, Eric and myself; plus the Atkins, Stan and Nita; unhappy Tanya Lowe, who belonged to things in order to escape her family; and Brian Jolliffe, until now manager of the Under Fourteens, whose resignation was the 'central issue' to which the chairman had just referred. We were a polyglot group, representative of church, laiety, farming, commerce, the arts (roughly speaking) and egomania. Of all these factions the last was the most significant since it was contained to some degree in all the others. The Toms committee would not have recognised a dispassionate debate if it had jumped up and blacked their eyes.

The Reverend Eric Chittenden was a bluff, handsome man who had received the call late in life. For twenty years he had successfully sold electronic components, and he now used the skills thus acquired on behalf of the Almighty. George, I recalled, had always mistrusted him, claiming that Eric's popularist style was the mark of what he termed a 'moral lightweight'. But George was alone in this. The regular congregation of St Cuthbert's in Basset Magna had doubled since Eric's incumbency, and even diehards who were still gagging on Series Three did not blench when the rector wore a safari suit to the church fête, nor when he took the previous night's episode of 'Dallas' as the basis for his sermon. He was universally popular, and this for simply doing as he pleased.

The fact that Eric was secretary, and not chairman, of the Tomahawks, was significant. Splendid fellow though he was, 'fupbore' was generally recognised to be the preserve of the working man, and the YFC's supremo was expected to have a social standing commensurate with the task. Other village activities might be run by the landed gentry and the silicone chip brigade on the principle of noblesse oblige. But fupbore was for the lads.

Besides being chairman of the Toms, Robbo was scoutmaster of the 2nd Basset Troop, and his wife Glynis was Akela of the cubs. I had no idea what Robbo did for a living. Whatever it was it was quite secondary to his role of involved and responsible member of the community. One of the highlights of his year was Remembrance Sunday when, in full quasi-military rig he strutted round the village at the head of a straggling squad of embarrassed teenagers, bawling unnecessarily at them to halt by the war memorial for the Act of Remembrance. So powerfully did this particular juju work on the susceptible Robbo that for a full two minutes his shoulders almost met behind his neck, his knuckles glinted whitely and his Adam's apple lurched up and down like a drunk trying to stand.

Glynis had a firmer grip on reality. As Akela she would detail her lieutenant, Baloo, to march at the front of the cubs, while she brought up the rear, moustaches quivering, lanyard bouncing, trefoil glittering like a malign supernumerary eye on the tie which traversed her bust. The great twin pockets of her uniform gave the impression that at any moment the buttons might fly open, the pocket flaps rise, and the muzzles of two laser guns appear, to rake the sniggering rank and file with withering fire.

Her sphere of influence did not end with the cubs. Glynis's name was spoken with awe wherever two or three were gathered together in the name of the scouting movement, be they the humblest brownies or the loftiest of Queen's Scouts. And we all knew that when the subject of the Toms' summer disco came up on the agenda, Robbo would volunteer his spouse as a bouncer, and would not be refused.

Trevor Tunnel was the hapless manager of the Under Tens, possibly the least sought-after task in the club. Stoically he escorted his rabble of nine-year-olds around the county, exhorting them to get their act together, begging their sheepish parents to support them, standing hunched and dejected on the touchline as all eleven players moved up and down the pitch like a swarm of red and white bees. Occasionally the Under Tens lost sight of the opposition striker altogether in the crush, and tackled each other by mistake, with scant regard for the rule book or even the dictates of common decency.

To keep Trevor in his place we assured him, often, that his was an important, nay a sacred, task. To him had fallen the stewardship of future Tomahawks stars. He, Trevor, was the custodian of infant talent, and no one else could hold a candle to him in this regard.

Privately, I thought of Stan and Nita Atkins as the Nutkins. Squirrelish, they were – little busy, sandy, chattering people who might run up your trouser leg when you weren't looking just to see if your knickers were clean. Under them the Under Twelves were enjoying a period of unprecedented success. They and they alone had got the tricky and time-consuming business of team managership sewn up, what with their camper-van, their cost-price confectionary and orange juice (Stan worked for a supermarket chain) and their nause-ating partiality. 'They're lovely boys,' Nita would opine winsomely, and while the rest of us might squirm we had to allow that her attitude got results. The Under Twelves were the pampered darlings of the club, trained to a near-robotic perfection, and enjoying the high morale maintained by the Nutkins' many incentives. Stan and Nita had no children themselves, which explained a good deal.

Of course, they had the best age group. At eleven and twelve the boys had learnt how to play football, and though keen, were still young enough to be tractable. At Under Fourteen, Gareth's stratum, they seemed to pitch headlong into that deep and featureless ravine between boyhood and teenagerdom, their voices yodelling and booming as they fell. They were all swank and wank, and prey to a slummocky lassitude which evinced itself in large-scale absenteeism. No wonder Brian Jolliffe had resigned: he had spent the last few months trying to claw his way from the bottom rung of the Basset Area Junior League with only ten men. Without Gareth – who, they told me, was a striker of no mean clout – the Under Fourteens would long since have sunk without trace.

At the top end of the club, the Under Sixteens were under the management of Eric Chittenden. No vague malaise dogged them. There was no doubt at all where they stood – just a whisker away from the juvenile courts. Eric's role was that of social worker. He did not have to concern himself with their performance: they won everything. What they lacked in skill and sportsmanship they made up for a thousandfold, as Eric had often remarked, in 'competitiveness'. Once changed into the distinctive Tomahawks' kit of red and white, like a pack of glowering, spotty Santas, they simply ground their fags beneath their boot heels and lumbered coughing and cussing on to the pitch, there to wipe the opposition off the park with their customary brutal ease. It was hard to concede that this menacing phalanx of acne'd Neanderthals had ever been the ineffectual lads of the Under Fourteens, still less the keen, bright protégés of the Nutkins. But they must have been. And it boded ill for the future.

I became aware of Robbo's gaze resting on me. ' . . . suppose we can rely on the ladies for that?' he was saying.

Tanya and Nita both looked at me as if they knew I had not been paying attention.

'Sorry, Robbo? I missed that.'

'We had reverted pro tem to the question of the disco,' explained Robbo patiently.

Stan put his hand by his mouth in a theatrical gesture. 'Thinking of her book,' he mouthed to the rest of the committee. 'World of her own!' Perhaps thinking that this sally had been a touch stringent, he attempted to soften it by bestowing on me a gigantic, hammy wink.

'Can we ask you ladies to handle the refreshments?' asked Robbo.

'Of course we will, won't we, girls?' chittered Nita, getting out her tiny well-thumbed diary and consulting it with much purposeful rustling.

'Shall we make a date to go to the cash-and-carry in Regis? I have Stan's card.'

'Count me out,' said Tanya, who never made the slightest pretence of enthusiasm for the Toms or their works. 'I'll be there on the night, but days I'm over the abbatoir.' We nodded understandingly. Tanya was crucial to the smooth running of the fat-rendering plant. Her dedication to this grisly occupation was further evidence of the awfulness of her family.

'You and me then, Harriet?' said Nita.

'Perhaps we should decide what to give them first,' I suggested, not to be outdone in the triviality stakes, but Nita was ready for that one and parried it neatly with: 'Oh, we don't want to take up committee time with that, do we? Why don't you and I have a little get-together on the food some day soon . . . ?'

I pictured Nita and I perched like gigantic bluebottles on a pile of monster cheese and chutney sandwiches.

'Okay,' I said.

'Now then.' Robbo was portentous, lifting his agenda-sheet and pursing his lips to show that once more we were going to address ourselves to the central issue.

A tremor of consternation went round the pavilion annexe, a squirming of backsides on slatted benches, an exchange of speaking looks, a determined scrutiny of finger-nails and trouser knees. We knew that once more the thorny question of the Under Fourteens managership was coming under Robbo's hammer. Brian Jolliffe, Bunterish and impassive, was the architect of our discomfort.

'I have to say it,' said Robbo, saying it. 'The Under Fourteens are a key group. If we have to abandon running a team in this age group my feeling is that the whole club will be placed in jeopardy.'

We sighed wretchedly. This was not a position with which the club was unfamiliar. Threat of dissolution hung over it always. We few, we happy few, had the task of keeping it going. The Toms were hugely popular, membership swelled horrifically each season, it towered above us like a mushroom cloud and if we failed in our duties the fall-out would be terrible. And yet there was Brian Jolliffe chickening out, apparently without remorse.

And who could take his place? Stan, Nita and Trevor were in the clear, full of rectitude, their consciences Persil-white. Even more a man apart was Eric, both secretary and manager. Robbo, as chairman, was automatically exonerated from further duties. That left Tanya and I, who as women were quite out of the question. Never had I been more thankful for the chauvinistic cast of my fellow committee members.

But who did that leave? Mentally we counted and assessed and found ourselves lacking. Our feelings toward Brian Jolliffe grew less and less kind.

'I must ask you once more, Brian,' said Robbo, enjoying the atmosphere of courtroom drama which now swirled about the annexe, 'to reconsider. You've been doing a great job with those lads – '

'Balls!' retorted Brian with such vehemence that it was obvious he'd been building up to this explosion for some time. 'Absolute ruddy bollocks! You said – Eric said – at the beginning – they've been played out of sight for months – '

'That was me said that,' interposed Trevor, Eeyore-like.

'I don't give a monkey's who said it,' went on Brian, 'it's true! I've been knocking myself out trying to motivate those lads, but I might as well have been playing the fucking arse-flute for all the good it's done. They just don't seem to care and now I'm bloody sure I don't either!' I regarded Brian with new respect, impressed by the frankness of this outburst. But others, I sensed, were not so admiring.

'Now then, Brian,' said Eric, slipping naturally into the role of mediator and advocate, 'you mustn't take anything that's been said as a personal criticism of you. You don't have a thing to reproach yourself with.'

'I know that! I've been telling you that!' squawked Brian, quite purple with fury. He closed his eyes, as if taking a grip on himself. 'No. No – I'm sorry, but let me put it this way, I know when I'm beaten. They don't turn up, they're scruffy, they don't get stuck in – ' he turned to me – 'Your Gareth's an exception, I may say. But the rest! I turn out weekend after weekend, Monica's got a list of jobs as long as your arm for me to do – '

'Sounds like a blessed release!' quipped Stan, but Brian did not hear the joke, let alone see it.

'And what happens? Sweet F.A., that's what!'

'Sweet F.A!' Stan looked round at us, hell-bent on restoring our sense of humour. 'How very apt!'

Brian continued on his elephantine way. 'I started out with all good intentions, you all know that. I believe in this club. I thought the Under Fourteens could do well. They began all right. They played super against Cheveley Wildcats last September,' here a little frisson of nostalgia went round as we recalled those palmy days, 'but since then it's been downhill all the way. They've beaten me, and I don't mind admitting it. Someone else can have a go and sodding good luck to them!'

He folded his arms and sat back. The rest of us continued

to look at him for a moment, in expectation of a reprise, and when none was forthcoming re-fastened our stares on to Robbo. Eric sat with his hands clasped on the minute book, head bowed. I suspected he was tuning into The Boss to see if a higher authority could salvage something from this adminis-trative holocaust.

'Well,' said Robbo, 'Brian has said his piece. Obviously we can't pressurise him to stay on. It only remains for me to thank him for his stalwart work with the lads, and to ask for any nominations or volunteers for this vital job as Under Fourteens manager.'

He glanced round dully, knowing there would be no bids. And we stared back with stuffed-animal eyes, all trying to prove, through impassivity, the justice of our claims to immunity.

'I appreciate,' went on Robbo, to fill the yawning void of unhelpful silence, 'that we all have busy lives, and most people here are already doing worthwhile and time-consuming jobs within the club . . . but I beg you to wrack your brains for anyone – even someone not at present a member – who might be approached about this.'

There was another long, blank silence. 'It goes without saying,' said Trevor, 'that a good working knowledge of the game is vital. You can't win a team's respect unless you can do what you ask them to do.'

What, I thought – must one be able to pull one's finger out, to get stuck in, to stop acting like a flipping woofter? Was this why Trevor himself had so signally failed to imprint his authority on the Under Tens?

'No question,' agreed Stan Nutkin. 'The boys look to the club officers to set an example, both as players and as human beings.'

The sheer irrefutable triteness of this assertion left every-one duly speechless, but it was in the squirming, burning silence that followed it that I had my idea. An idea which so perfectly married need with desire that it quite took my breath away. I warmed my hands on it for a second or two before presenting it to the assembled company.

'I think I know someone who might fill the bill,' I offered

tentatively, and was at once the focus of rapt and grateful attention.

'Who would that be, Harriet?' asked Robbo in measured tones.

'Dr Ghikas, the new doctor over at Parva.'

This threw them. Their expressions of slavish relief froze, their smiles became bloodless and their eyes glassy.

'I don't know him, I confess,' said Nita, piqued no doubt by my rapid acquaintanceship with this substantial local figure. 'We've always had Dr Salmon.'

'I only met him recently,' I confessed – I could afford to be magnanimous. 'He's an extremely nice person, and a football enthusiast. He played regularly himself till a few years ago. Being new to the area he might like to get involved in this kind of local activity.' God help me.

'Well!' Robbo looked round for endorsement, but went ahead anyway. 'I must say, this does sound hopeful.'

'We mustn't count our chickens, though,' warned Trevor. 'The doctor may feel it's early days for this kind of commitment.'

'Look,' I said, the very embodiment of sweet reasonableness. 'I'll try him if you'd like me to, but if you think it's inappropriate . . . '

'Harriet,' said Eric, lifting a hand, 'you have our blessing.'

'You go and ask,' said Tanya Lowe. 'I'm on his list and I wouldn't mind a look at him before I go there with my legs.'

I was still trying to work this out when Stan leaned towards me.

'Excuse me for raising this – but the doctor's Greek, isn't he? I mean . . . well, how Greek is he?'

'You'd never know,' I said truthfully. 'Fair hair, blue eyes, BBC accent. He actually seems rather more English than you or me.'

'Fair enough. I'm satisfied, then,' said Stan.

'Perhaps before we put all our eggs in one basket we should know if there's anyone else that anyone can think of?' enquired Robbo with the overexcited air of a man who believes he's struck gold. Everyone shook their heads.

'Then can we officially ask you, Harriet, since you know the doctor, to make an approach on the club's behalf?'

'Of course.' You bet your life you can. I could almost see the Fates, like a cluster of benign maiden aunts, beaming down at me from the ceiling of the pavilion annexe.

Outside, sated with drama, we went our ways. Only Tanya Lowe came up to me as I unlocked my car. She was accompanied by her dog which had been tethered outside during the meeting. It was a vast, blubber-laden labrador, like a walrus with corners. Fodder for the fat-rendering plant if ever I saw it.

'You'll be at this disco, then,' she said.

'Looks like it.'

'You ought to get that doctor to come along, then we can all get to know each other.'

'Yes – yes, that's not a bad idea, Tanya.'

'Good luck with him, anyway,' she said. 'We could do with somebody new.' How right she was.

'Good night, Tanya.'

'Night. Heel, Sukey,' she added, as she and the canine abomination waddled off into the dusk.

I got home in fine form, chased the children away from the television and into bed in record time, and then went to the study and sat down at the tripewriter.

In the days following my last meeting with Dr Ghikas I had advanced Maria's story quite substantially, and had now reached a key scene between Maria and the under-gardener. The hunt had gone well, and had served to establish Maria's dual fascination with her haughty cousin and his muscular employee.

I switched on the tripewriter and began writing immediately.

Maria stopped in her tracks, the roses forgotten. The turmoil in her breast showed itself in a haughtiness she did not feel.

'What are you doing here?' she enquired, icily.

The young man stood lazily before her. His sleeves were rolled up to reveal strong, brown-skinned forearms. Maria was unsettlingly aware of his brute strength, now in repose, but which might be summoned up at any instant. The sensation of feminine frailty that this awareness gave her was both frightening and exhilarating.

'Working,' came the reply, not without a hint of sarcasm. 'And you, miss? Picking roses, I see.' His dark eyes rested on the few long-stemmed yellow blooms which she held in her hand. Maria's heart beat fast, her mouth was dry. He took a few steps towards her and was now standing impertinently close, his broad chest and shoulders only inches from her face.

'Please,' she faltered. 'Let me pass.'

He waited a moment, towering over her. She could not look up at his face, which she knew would most assuredly mock her.

'Pray step aside.'

After what seemed an eternity he stood back and she went on her way with as much dignity as she could muster. Her head was high, but the yellow roses trembled in her hand, and there was blood in her palm where she had squeezed the thorns.

I sat back and re-read these paragraphs. In doing so I realised with a shock that I had written all of them on automatic pilot. I had not, in the whole of this key emotional scene, made one conscious decision about what to put next. The realisation was profoundly depressing. With sudden energy I attacked the tripewriter once more, and wrote:

Abruptly she dropped the roses and rushed back to where he stood, still watching her with sardonic detachment. Before he could prevent her she stuffed her hand down the front of his trousers.

'This', she whispered as she worked, 'will show you who's boss, you great hairy muscle-bound yob.'

Feeling much revived I switched off the tripewriter and went to bed, there to read the introspective musings of a proper author.

Chapter Six

I now had two excellent, bona fide reasons for calling on Dr Constantine Ghikas. There was the invitation to my putative dinner party (for which he was as yet the only guest); and I was official representative of Tomahawks YFC, in the matter of the Under Fourteens managership.

This last appeared a slightly less wonderful scheme in the cold light of the following day. After all, if Dr Ghikas was not willing to take on the managership, where would that leave me? As an interfering female who wasted no time in trying to off-load unpleasant tasks on to unsuspecting newcomers.

I took the idea out for a short walk at breakfast time. Gareth had just completed his second bowl of Brekabix swamped in milk and granulated sugar, and was addressing himself with scowling concentration to the sports pages. Clara was on her third slice of lightly toasted refined carbohydrate.

'What is it,' I mused, then realised I had not captured my audience and added more loudly: 'Tell me, Gareth, what is it with your team in the Tomahawks? Why have they gone to pieces so?'

'Mm . . . ?' Gareth tilted his head slightly but did not take his eyes off the paper. 'Dunno.'

I persisted. 'I was at the football committee meeting last night. Did you know that Mr Jolliffe was resigning as manager?'

This secured his attention. 'Ace,' was his comment. 'Who do we get?'

'That's not very charitable, Gareth,' I said. 'Poor Brian was at his wits' end, he says he couldn't do a thing with you – not you personally, but as a team – and he has tried very hard.'

'Jolliffe's a plonker, Ma. He couldn't organise a fart in a bean factory.'

Clara, usually unmoved by her brother's jokes, let out a high-pitched cackle of laughter. It was one of those rare moments when I wished George was around. There would have been no farts in bean factories if he had been at the breakfast table, reading the FT and eating muesli with goat's milk yoghurt.

I wound myself up determinedly. 'I think that's a rotten thing to say, Gareth. And you may change your tune when you hear that you may not "get" anybody as you put it. The team may have to be disbanded.'

'Nice one, Ma,' said Clara, spreading more toast.

Gareth's jaw dropped, and his eyes goggled. Why are lads so devoid of subtlety? Everything must be writ large and dished out with a spade.

'Flipping heck!' he exclaimed. 'That's a bit steep, isn't it?'

'You either want to play decent soccer or you don't,' I retaliated. I sounded awfully like Robbo; I very nearly let slip a 'fupbore'. 'But anyway, there is one slim chance of salvation, and it's down to your mother to do something about it. So I shall expect to find your room tidy when I go up there.'

'Sure. Go on then – who is it?'

'Dr Ghikas from Basset Parva – ' I caught Gareth's expression of despairing derision – 'and before you start rubbishing him out of hand, let me tell you that he's been no mean footballer in his time.'

'Footballer? What, when was this, back in the baggy shorts?'

'You really are childish sometimes, Gareth.'

'Isn't he?' agreed Clara. 'He really is.'

For this shaft she received a shin-cracking kick beneath the table which galvanised her into leaning across and grabbing her brother's hair.

'I've got nits!' bellowed Gareth. She at once released him.

'You are revolting.'

'You haven't, have you?' I asked anxiously. Keen though I was for excuses to visit the surgery, I did not feel that an infestation of headlice constituted the gateway to passion.

'Of *course* not.'

'In any case,' I went on primly, 'you'll be extremely lucky if anyone agrees to manage you lot, with your track record. Tell that shower you play with to pull finger, why don't you. Dr Ghikas is a very busy man, and he has a season ticket for Ipswich. I'm sure he'd much prefer to sit in a comfortable seat and watch decent soccer than to freeze on some God-forsaken recreation ground encouraging you lot!'

'Thank *you*,' said Gareth with ponderous sarcasm. But I had seen the look of avarice cross his face at the mention of Ipswich, and I left this point to do its work without further underlining from me. So wrapped up had I been in my final blast at Gareth that I had not noticed Clara leaving the room. By the time Gareth had assembled his school bag and sports kit and gone, she had still not reappeared. I looked at my watch and called, but there was still no response. She should have left, in order to visit Stu en route to school.

I went back into the sitting room. Breakfast TV burbled in the corner. Samantha Clack, blushing and bridling in an angora jumper with koalas on it, was making some hackneyed pronouncement about fashions in swimwear. There was something about TV 'personalities' (oh most vile misnomer) which set my teeth on edge. They seemed so smug and safe, insulated from reaction and retaliation, on a constant drip-feed of mindless admiration from people who mistook exposure for importance. And saints preserve us, here was Fred Cluff, cuddly and avuncular in roll-neck and tank-top, saying that if all women looked like Samantha they would not need to worry about the style of their swimsuit. The saccharine tone of this exchange was enough to make you gag.

'I'm going, I'm going,' said Clara, who was not in fact going but kneeling on the floor on elbows and knees with her bottom in the air, writing something.

'For goodness' sake,' I said, 'switch off that twaddle and get going, you'll be late.'

'No I won't.' Clara rose with maddening slowness, folded the piece of paper on which she'd been writing, and put it beneath a vase on the windowsill. Then she scooped up her PE bag off a chair and offered me a coolly tilted cheek.

' 'Bye.'

The moment I heard the front door close I went to the window and removed the paper from beneath the vase. I experienced not the tiniest twinge of guilt, for Clara was so scornful and secretive that only the most rigorous surveillance could ascertain what she was up to.

It was a list of song titles, quite blameless in itself, but for one thing. In the top left-hand corner was written the word: 'Damon'. My suspicious nature went into overdrive. Only a few days ago Clara had barely acknowledged Damon's claim to be a member of the human race, and now here she was writing him billets doux on the subject which was, after horseflesh, closest to her heart. What the hell was going on?

I replaced the piece of paper and went back to the kitchen. Tomorrow was Thursday, Damon would be coming in the afternoon. I would watch him and Clara closely. And perhaps Gareth would have some inside information. With lists on my mind I sat down at the table with notepad and biro. Beside me sat Spot, eyelids drooping, keeping slumber at bay on the off chance I might whip a marrow bone from beneath my jumper, or take him for a nice slow walk in the woods.

I wrote: *1. Take invitation to C. G. Ask about soccer* but almost at once crossed it out. This was the plum, the juicy reward for completing the other, less appetising tasks.

I started again: *1. Write to George.* This was crucial, after the poor showing I had put up on our wedding anniversary. The closer I came to my adulterous objective, the nicer (at a distance) I would be to George.

2. Ask Bren. Tun. about kids, Buchfest.

3. Ring Nita re disco.

Number three was a nice tactical point. To relieve a Nutkin of the initiative was to draw its sting. 'Nita!' I would say. 'I've drawn up a list of what we might need. Why don't you pop round for a coffee and we can discuss it?' The thought of her frustration was exquisite. I was just about to reinstate 'C.G.' at the foot of the list when the phone rang.

'Harriet? Nita Atkins here! No time like the present, I thought, so I've drawn up a bit of a list of basics I think we'll need for the disco, and another of optional extras, funds permitting. Any chance you could pop in this afternoon and we can chat about it?'

I swear she must have been able to hear my teeth grinding.

'Harriet?'

'Yes.'

'Oh, you're still there, I thought I'd lost you! How about it?'

'Um – yes, I suppose I can drop in. I take it you'll be in all day?'

Nita deflected this thrust with a brief: 'Goodness yes, I've got to finish new loose covers for the settee before the weekend!'

I did not – *I would not* – ask her what pressing and peculiar circumstance required that the settee be recovered before the weekend. I had seen the Nutkins' settee and it was unimpeachably clean, neat and plump, like its owners; a paragon among settees, tastefully sprigged and braided, its crevices innocent of mouldering detritus, its arms neither greasy nor threadbare.

'See you later then,' I said. I put the phone down and went back, with much recourse to the copulative adjective, to the kitchen table. Never mind, if I called on Nita in the early afternoon I could go on to Basset Parva from there. Mid-afternoon might be a good time, doctor-wise, falling as it did between house calls and evening surgery, and I might well find Constantine Ghikas at home.

I went up to the study and did a couple of hours at Kersey House, assiduously deleting my aberration of the previous night. I then completed another work of romantic fiction, in the form of a letter to George. At two o'clock I left, posted the letter and went to call on Nita.

Her settee was certainly unclothed, quite indecent in plain white cotton, like a nun in her underwear. But there were plenty of other seats in the Nutkin household. From the sunlit pine kitchen wafted the aroma of a nourishing casserole, prepared by Nita to welcome Stan on his return from the Betabise depot at Basset Regis.

'Bless you, Harriet!' said Nita, furnishing me with coffee and home-made butter-crunch bikkies. 'I'm rushed off my feet at present, it's a case of finding a spare moment to catch up on these things.'

'It must be.'

'Stan and I are having a gang of country people round on Saturday,' she confided. By this I knew that she meant people dressed not in Burberrys and flat caps, but in leather waist-coats, chaps and stetsons. Among their many interests the Nutkins numbered country music, and were often to be seen decked out like Annie Oakley and Wyatt Earp, heading for venues as far afield as Maidstone and Basingstoke to share this esoteric pleasure with dudes of like mind.

'We love it,' she went on. 'We're going to have a real down home evening. My brother's bringing his original Box Car Willie.'

'Wonderful,' I agreed. So this was why the settee was to be recovered. Perhaps Nita's plans for its refurbishment included a saddle and sheepskin noseband.

'About the disco . . . ' I suggested.

On her list, Nita had catalogued, as basics: crisps, bread, cheddar, chutney, marge, sausages, lettuce and salad cream. Oh, and salt. Her optional extras included such delicacies as peanuts, pickled onions and crudités with dips. The disco would need to be loud.

'Any comments, Harriet? Any suggestions?'

'No – you're so much better at all this than me,' I said grandly.

'Well then, what about the shopping?'

'Whenever you like.' I utterly refused to join in her display of hectic busyness.

Nita proposed a day and time and I agreed. 'And now,' I said firmly, rising from the bandy-legged reproduction chair which Nita had but recently re-upholstered in avocado Nulon, 'I must be off. I have to be somewhere in – ' I glanced at my watch like an Olympic track coach – 'fifteen minutes.'

'It's all go, isn't it?' chuckled Nita, hoisting me neatly with my own petard. 'Never a dull moment!'

She came with me to her front door, complete with dimpled glass and leaded fanlight, and stood on her tiled porch, by the brass carriage lamp, to wave me gaily on my way.

As I snarled out of the Nutkin driveway, blipping the accelerator for maximum disturbance of the gravel, I wondered why it was that women like Nita, who would never dream of serving bangers and Branston at their own board, knew instinctively that they were just the thing to serve to the proletarian masses at any social gathering at the village hall. I was sure that the yodelling sharpshooters and cowgirls assembled chez Nutkin on Saturday night would feed like fighting cocks on the rare and delicate dishes which were now so many lumps of coloured concrete in Nita's jumbo freezer.

I was filled with fear and loathing for the Nitas and Babas, with their boarding house brains, their cash-and-carry cards, their full diaries and clean carpets.

In my irritation I drove so fast that I was in Basset Parva in six minutes flat, and only narrowly missed running down the octogenarian post-lady of whom the village was justly proud.

I slowed down. The address on the doctor's card was The Rickyard, Fore Street. It turned out to be a house I had often admired, and which, when it came on the market just after Christmas, I might have been tempted to buy myself had it not been snapped up by Dr Ghikas.

I turned into a gentle 'U' of drive, encircling an island of lush grass and hydrangeas which contrived to appear both well cared-for and unforced.

The house itself seemed to be snoozing in the afternoon sunshine. The front door stood invitingly ajar, and most of the sash windows were open. A marmalade cat paced in a measured way towards me, then suddenly lay on its back and writhed voluptuously, asking to be tickled, just like its owner (I hoped) soon would.

There was no sign of the green Fiat, but outside the garage

stood a svelte Honda Civic in a coppery brown like an Ambre Solaire bottle. As I got out I took a peep inside, looking for clues. The seats of the Civic were upholstered in an oyster suede-look fabric, of the sort which would not have lasted a week beneath the calibre of passenger I normally carried. On the front seat lay a Barbra Streisand tape and Yves St Laurent silk scarf. Neither car, nor tape, nor scarf fitted in with my picture of the Ghikas household. I did hope that I was not going to find the doctor and a beautiful, wealthy female patient exchanging confidences over Earl Grey tea in what I did not doubt would be a William Morris drawing room.

I went up to the front door. There was an old-fashioned bell-pull and I gave it a tug. A melodious, distant chime sounded in the house. As I waited I glanced down at myself. I had changed out of shorts and singlet into a longish printed cotton skirt and an embroidered blouse, pretty and demure enough to satisfy even the most exacting and old-fashioned mama.

The marmalade cat ran past me into the house with a proprietorial air. I began to feel slightly ill at ease. The house exuded a lazy confidence and effortless chic which I would have mistrusted in a woman and which was no more comforting in bricks and mortar. Purple clematis curled in airy profusion round the door, honeysuckle massed by the wall, lilac and rhododendron vied in shades of purple, bees hummed and butterflies hovered –

'Come in!' A woman's voice came faintly from the far side of the house. 'Come through the gate and round – I'm in the garden!' To the left of the house was a wooden gate. I went through it and along a narrow path between shrubs to where the back garden opened out, sunny and idyllic.

A woman came towards me. She had on a huge, brightly printed cotton square which she had wrapped about herself, sarong-style, and the halter-straps of a yellow bikini showed against her smooth, tanned skin. She was small, trim and graceful. Her short hair was swept back in a style both chic and boyish. She was of at least a certain age, but she wore her years with such dash it was impossible to pinpoint their exact number. She was, in fact, the human embodiment of the

Honda Civic I had admired in the drive – sleek, coppery and aerodynamically perfect.

Behind her on the lawn, in the shade of a large chestnut tree, stood a white wooden lounger with red and blue cushions. On the lounger lay an open book, face down, and next to it on the grass a tray with a jug and tall glass. The whole picture was one of ease and self-indulgence, but with none of the sluttishness which generally attends these states.

I at once felt hopelessly declassé in my flowered drapes and homely flat sandals, but the woman smiled charmingly.

'I'm so sorry not to have come to the front door, but I was in a state of undress when you rang.'

'No, *I'm* sorry,' I burbled, 'for disturbing you when you were enjoying the sun. Actually I was looking for Dr Ghikas . . . ' I stared about me with a wild surmise, as if he might be hiding amongst the flowering shrubs.

'He's out at a home delivery, I'm afraid,' said the woman. 'Can I help?'

'Um . . . ' I was tongue-tied. For one thing I had no idea whom I was addressing. I clutched my dinner party invitation like a child on an adult errand.

'I'm his mother,' she said, as if reassuring me as to her credentials, 'if you want to leave a message.'

To say my gast was flabbered would be the understatement of the decade. I could not have been more stunned if ET had sprung from the branches of the laburnum and shaken me by the hand. And not just stunned. Bouleversée! Apalled!

'How do you do, how nice to meet you,' I murmured weakly. 'I'm Harriet Blair – '

'Oh, but what a coincidence, how lovely!' she cried. 'I'm just re-reading one of your marvellous books and enjoying every page. I can't tell you how thrilled I was to receive that signed copy of your new one, I shall simply treasure it . . . come and sit down. Would you like a glass of iced coffee?'

I followed like Big Foot or the Incredible Hulk as she opened another chair, patted the seat invitingly and picked up the jug.

'I'll just go and get some more and another glass. Don't go away, it's so delightful to meet you . . !'

She wafted off towards the house and I sat there, pole-axed by the unexpected. Where, oh where was the dumpy Greek matron clad in all-concealing black, ready to protect her son tigerishly from the predations of loose women? I had taken such care to dress appropriately. I had organised my face (unmade-up), my hair (smooth and clean) and even my armpits (unshaved) to suit with this imagined parent. I had been prepared to win her over with my wholesome charm and good manners. But now it was perfectly plain that Mrs Anna Ghikas could outcharm me, even on a bad day. She was twice as smart, a lot better-looking, and I could not even dismiss her as small-minded since she would obviously prefer to read a book in the garden than to dust her furniture.

Hopelessly fazed I watched her come back, and pour us both iced coffee.

'Kostaki,' she said pleasantly, 'will be so sorry he missed you, but unfortunately confinements wait for no man. All the same, I can't say *I'm* sorry, because it gives me a chance to talk to you on my own.'

'I'm glad you like the books,' I said.

'Like them? I love them – they're the most tremendous fun!' Thus she paid me a nice enough compliment, while unmistakably implying that mine were bubblegum books, enjoyable but insubstantial. She was right, of course, but with a genuine grudge against her I felt happier.

'When I last saw Dr Ghikas I invited him to a dinner party next week,' I explained. 'But I said at the time that I'd give him a proper written invitation, otherwise these things sometimes get forgotten, don't they?'

'How sweet of you.' She took the invitation. 'I'll make sure he gets it. Do tell me, are you working on another book at present?'

I told her what there was to tell concerning *TRT*, and she prompted me with occasional perceptive, interested questions. Affirmed, so to speak, as a person of consequence, I became more daring.

'Please don't think me nosey,' I said, 'but Ghikas is a Greek name, and surely you – '

'No, but my husband was,' she replied, reading between

the lines. 'I'm as British as Yorkshire pud.'

The mere mention of this homely dish emphasised how very unlike it she was, and I was sure she knew it. 'I met and married Spiridion when I was working in Greece between the wars. But Kostaki was educated at Winchester and St Andrew's.'

'I see,' I said.

'Kostaki and I bought this house jointly.' she went on gaily, 'when he knew he was coming to work here. But I'm just a long-term visitor, I wouldn't dream of asking a man to share his home with his poor old mother,' she laughed engagingly. 'Spiridion died a few years ago and I've been rather a gypsy ever since.'

The more she rattled on, the more punch-drunk I became, and the more glad that she was not a permanent fixture at The Rickyard.

'I'm a marine archaeologist,' she said.

If I'd been punch-drunk before, this piece of information practically had me out for the count. I had always thought archaeologists, whether marine or lubberly, to be whiskery persons with rope sandals and grit beneath their nails.

'My work is my passion,' she went on, 'especially now Spiro's not here. One old wreck hauling up another, so to speak.'

I was dazzled. For one wild moment I fancied that if I had said to Anna Ghikas: 'I want to lay your son, and as soon as possible,' she would have made the spare bedroom instantly available.

I croaked something about old wrecks being far from the case, but she was off and running now.

'I shall be going to Turkey soon. People keep telling me I should give it up at my age, but it's like everything, if you still have the taste for it, why not?'

'Oh quite.' I eyed the body beneath the sarong. 'Do you actually dive?'

'Not seriously, alas, not any more. I just correlate the information and the bits and pieces as they come up.' Brought to the surface of the wine-dark sea, I had no doubt, by a squad of burnished young men in infinitesimal bathing trunks.

'How do you like Basset Parva?' I asked, to get away from this unsettling picture.

'We love it,' she said. 'Everyone's been so kind.'

I bet they have, I thought, groaning inwardly. The social gatherings of Parva were notorious for the accompanying jingle of latchkeys hitting the ground. And it was extremely doubtful that the indolent executive wives of the village would share Declan's violent prejudice against the Greek doctor.

'I love this house,' I remarked, desperately. 'I've often admired it.'   .

'Would you like to see inside?' she asked at once. 'Do! But please excuse the dust, it's the fine weather.'

We wandered across the lawn and went in through the french window. The interior of The Rickyard was, of course, exquisite, a tasteful, confident hotch-potch of eclectic furnishings and hangings and pictures and objets trouvés. And, as she'd predicted, dust.

'Kostaki's a tidy devil,' remarked Anna Ghikas, 'but he has to suffer me when I'm here.'

She escorted me through the house, discussing its age and merits, enlarging on the provenance of this and that, unembarrassed by the graceful chaos of her surroundings.

'This is his study,' she announced. 'I'm not really allowed.'

She was right, he was tidy. In complete contrast to all the other rooms the study was neat, the floor clear of clutter, everything in its place. I poked my head in and gazed about, but there were no dead giveaways and I was just about to withdraw when she brushed past me and picked up a photograph off the desk.

'I'll just show you this, it's my husband.'

If I'd been expecting some swarthy, dwarfish Greek with a walrus moustache, like the head waiter at the Zeus, I was again disappointed. Spiridion Ghikas, leaning against an open-topped MG in a T-shirt and shorts, was a tall, slim man, of film-star good looks. Moustache there was, but it was the merest scimitar of black on his upper lip, enough to make his teeth gleam extra white as he grinned into the camera. His hair was black, and ruffled as though he had just been towelling it after a swim. He was definitely the thinking woman's under-gardener.

'He's awfully handsome,' I said.

'Oh yes,' she said dismissively, as though it went without saying, 'and with all the contingent faults. Conceited, woman-ising, puerile and utterly delightful.'

'When did he die?'

'Six years ago. But we weren't living together. I'm afraid we did not provide Kostaki with good role models for marriage and parenthood.'

She did not sound in the least repentant. As we went back downstairs I tried to re-focus on Constantine in this new light. For some reason the knowledge that he was the fruit of this hotheaded sporadic union was not comforting. The severe little lady in black would have been much easier to handle.

As we reached the hall the front door opened wide and Constantine arrived.

'Well?' asked Anna Ghikas. 'What was it then?'

'A boy, ten pounds! I thought that kind of thing went out with crinolines. Hallo . . !'

He beamed at me amiably enough, but his remark about the baby served to remind me that he had spent the last few hours staring up some other female's vaginal passage.

'I'm just off,' I cried, in a positive ferment of conflicting urges. 'The children will be home from school. I just brought your invitation to dinner next week.'

'Must you dash?' asked his mother.

'You can stay for five minutes, surely?' echoed Constantine. But my mouth, like Maria Trevelyan's, was dry, and my heart was pounding, and these disabilities entirely incapaci-tated me.

Smiling wildly at no one in particular I headed for the door, then remembered my other reason for coming and flung over my shoulder: 'By the way, I've been asked by our local boys' football club to make an approach to you.'

'That does sound tempting,' said Constantine, almost flirtatiously.

'Oh – no – I'm afraid we're in dire need of a manager for the Under Fourteens, and after what you said I thought perhaps – I hope you don't think it presumptuous – '

I was not doing awfully well, but he was Olympian in his poise.

'That sounds rather fun. I'll take it on if I've got time. When do they play?'

'At the moment they have training on Saturday mornings and matches on Sunday afternoons, and then of course there are monthly committee meetings . . . ' My voice tailed off as I realised how supremely unappealing it all sounded.

'Tell you what,' said Constantine, 'I'll think it over and let you know when I come to dinner.'

'Super. Really. Thank you so much.'

On this singularly un-cool note I left. Mother and son stood in the doorway watching me starting and stalling the car before finally screeching out into the road. As I drove home, fiery with humiliation, I imagined them discussing me in the hall. I swore that the next time I met Constantine Ghikas I would be dressed to kill and to hell with reputation.

Chapter Seven

Having procured Constantine Ghikas as the centrepiece for my dinner party I set about arranging everything else around him with considerable care. I decided that in order not to scare him off, nor to arouse the suspicions of anyone else, I must invite either three or five others so there would be no implied 'pairing'.

I settled on Linda and Mike Channing, to whom I owed hospitality, and who regarded the task of taking me out of myself as a sacred trust; and my good friend Bernice Potter who would connive at any scheme of mine, no matter how nefarious.

The Channings accepted at once, overjoyed at this evidence of my emergence from purdah. I hadn't seen Bernice for a while so I decided to call on her and invite her in person.

Bernice was actually married, but she socialised on her own because her husband Arundel did not care for that sort of thing. Arundel was an academic of the most rarefied sort, who only made forays into the world of real people in order to further his career. According to Bernice she had married Arundel because he had been the only man to date who'd been able to dominate her. And he had married her (also according to Bernice) because she had been the brightest English student around at the time, and had enormous breasts.

Since the first flush of their passion, things had changed, with the exception of Bernice's mammaries which were still of outstanding size and quality. Bernice did nothing with her First, except write obscure and quite unpublishable erotic verse, and she very soon ceased to be dominated by Arundel. It just wasn't in her nature. Within a year of their marriage she was laying down all kinds of conditions which Arundel, still hypnotised by her upper chest, meekly accepted. One of these was that she would not give up her friends and her social life no matter how much he disapproved of them, and only if she could indulge both without criticism was she prepared to attend academic gatherings. The bargain was struck.

The Potter menage in the university town of Barford consisted of: Bernice; Arundel; and Arundel's father, Barty, a lecherous septuagenarian who acted as their de facto secretary, answering the phone with much coughing and hawking, and sedulously supervising the contents of the drinks cupboard.

I hadn't seen Bernice for four months, since before George left, but I knew that didn't matter. She never expressed the least surprise at seeing me, and always approved whole-heartedly of everything I did.

Barty answered the door. He wore a drooping grey cardigan, made still droopier by the presence of his teeth in his left-hand pocket. He was a flaccid, damp old man, all of whose juices seemed perilously close to the surface.

On seeing me he grinned gapingly and popped the teeth back in with a gloop and a click.

'Hallo, my dear, come on in, do, you're quite a stranger round here these days . . . '

I slithered past Barty into the hall, dancing about on the balls of my feet to avoid the physical contact of which he was so fond.

'Is Bernice about?' I asked.

'No sooner said than done, my dear,' said Barty, getting in a quick pat on my bicep. 'Just you stay there and I'll find her for you.'

He shuffled off. 55 Tennis Court Road, Barford, would have done nicely as the old dark house in a 'B' feature horror film, and Barty was even more exactly suited to the role of loathly butler.

But Barty's clammy aura was swiftly dispelled by the arrival of Bernice in a turquoise velour tracksuit, pink and turquoise leg-warmers and fuchsia trainers. Her dark, frizzy hair was caught up with a length of puce double-knitting wool. In fact Bernice was a double-knitting sort of woman – warm, heavyweight and loose. She would have been fat, but for the size of her bust, which had the effect of scaling down the rest of her.

'Ripping!' she exclaimed in her Angela Brazilish way, embracing me mightily. 'I do love the way you just bowl up after months of silence, the same as ever.'

This remark held no trace of rancour. 'I've come to invite you over, as a matter of fact,' I explained as I followed her into the kitchen.

'Super!'

Barty was at the sink, filling the kettle. He turned as we came in and grinned goatishly.

'Coffee, girls?'

'That's all right, Barty,' said Bernice. 'I'll do it, you run along.'

'I don't know how you stand it,' I murmured, watching him sashay away.

'What?'

'Him. Barty. A repulsive old man with the hots for you, always on the premises and usually with his teeth out.'

'Gosh, you're so acerbic, you are a *scream*!' hooted Bernice, spooning granules and pouring water. 'I look on Barty as one of the perks of marriage to Arundel. My wish is his command, which can't be bad.'

'Perhaps not.'

We sat with our coffee at the huge, cracked deal table, and Bernice lit a cigarette. She dressed like Jane Fonda, but her body-consciousness was rather less developed than the late Brendan Behan's.

'So!' She blew smoke at me and wriggled her shoulders

expectantly. 'How are things in the world of pulp?'

'Pulpy. Look, Bernice, would you come to dinner next Saturday?'

'Delighted. Why?'

'You assume there's an ulterior motive.'

'I'd be bloody disappointed if there wasn't. What are friends for?'

I sighed. 'You're right, of course. I'm hopelessly stricken with someone, and the dinner is stage one in my master plan.'

'But you don't want to seem too obvious, so you need another spare woman.

'Would you mind?'

'Mind? A buckshee spread just for providing a cover story? I just want to know what brought all this on.'

'A thunderbolt,' I said, and went on to explain about Constantine Ghikas. Bernice listened in rapt silence until I got to the bit about his mother.

'Don't like the sound of her, dear,' she said. 'Good God, the woman's probably living off his immoral earnings.'

'I'd pay!' I said. 'I swear I'd pay if I could only just – apart from anything else, it's uncomfortable. I need to get it out of my system.'

Bernice shook her head. 'Doesn't work like that. If you think that, surfeiting, the appetite would sicken and so on you couldn't be wronger. You'll be like a junkie, gasping for it.'

'I'm gasping for it now!' I shrieked, and then bit my tongue as Barty ambled in.

'Got everything you need, girls?' he enquired.

'Nearly everything,' replied Bernice. 'And what we haven't got you are in no position to provide.'

'Don't bet on it, my love!' cackled Barty, melting once more into the gothic shadows of the front hall.

'You shouldn't encourage him!' I whispered ferociously.

'Fiddle-de-dee!' said Bernice. 'He's all talk and trousers. At that age he needs a bit of cheering up.'

'Anyway,' I went on firmly, 'you'll come.'

'You couldn't keep me away, dear.'

'How's Arundel?'

'Corrupted at last. Hoping to break into television.'

I could not imagine Arundel as a media-pundit, and told her so.

'It all goes to show nobody's perfect,' she agreed. 'But he's busy justifying it on the grounds he'll reach a wider audience. Something you know all about, of course.'

Bernice never disparaged my work, but a person would have had to be of singular integrity to have shared the past twelve years with Arundel and still retain a balanced attitude towards popular fiction.

'Yes,' went on Bernice, 'he's quite swept away with the idea of dishing up a spoonful of erudition along with the soap.'

An unpleasant thought suddenly occurred to me. What if Arundel, as part of his new expansionist policy, should decide to broaden his social horizons, too?

'I say,' I began, 'I don't suppose he's going to want – '

Bernice shook her pony tail. 'No, no chance. I shall be free as usual to watch you manoeuvring your prey into the corral.'

'It may not work,' I warned.

She rolled her eyes. 'What, an umarried doctor? And a Greek to boot? I'm only amazed he hasn't ravished you already!'

I didn't know how to convey to Bernice that Dr Ghikas was not the swarthy, ouzo-soaked Lothario of her imagination. I was saved having to try because we heard Arundel talking to his father in the hall, and a moment later they both entered.

It's interesting that two people can be very alike, physically, and yet one may be handsome or striking while the other is plain or even downright repellant. Such was the case with Potter père et fils. Neither was tall, both were thin. Both had high foreheads, prominent noses and deep-set eyes. Yet whereas in Arundel the sum of these parts was an appearance of high-caste asceticism, a sort of chilly allure, in Barty they constituted the shifty, loose-lipped ferret-face of the proto-typical dirty old man.

Arundel treated Barty like dirt, but as no one, Barty included, seemed in the least put out by this I had stopped allowing it to offend me. Arundel was a generally charmless man, but his father's unlovely presence in his life seemed a mitigating factor. Anyone who could tolerate so embarrassing a parent as a permanent house-guest couldn't be all bad. I suspected that what bound them together was their shared passion for Bernice. I pictured them hanging on, one to a tit, like Romulus and Remus.

'Cup of coffee, son?' asked Barty.

Arundel kissed his wife. 'Thank you.' He extended a cool, stiff hand to me. 'Hallo, Harriet, what brings you here?'

'She's invited me to dinner on Saturday,' said Bernice, 'to participate in an evening of lust and licentiousness.'

'Good,' said Arundel absently.

'I hear you may be on the telly,' I said.

'It's possible.' Arundel took a cup of tea from his father and the two of them sat down at the table with us so that we looked like a rather ill-matched bridge school. 'I'm thinking about it.'

'Fame at last,' cackled Barty, slurping tea. 'Eh, Bernice, watch the old man on the box? Seen *you* on the box, love,' he pressed my arm confidingly, 'when they did that thing about roe-mance. I thought you came out of it very well, I won't hear a word against your books.'

This seemed to me to be my exit cue. Bernice came into the hall with me, her arm round my shoulders. I wondered at her ability to remain so separate from the other people in her life. She scarcely worked, she had no children, the desiccated plants and dust-dulled knick-knacks at 55 Tennis Court Road bore witness to her lack of domesticity, and yet there was no trace of demeaning dependence in her character. Cat-like, she had the air of bestowing the largesse of her presence on the lesser mortals who peopled her surroundings.

'Hey,' she said now, 'I'm looking forward to this. What will you cook, aphrodisiac nosh of some kind? Shall I bring a pud?'

'No, that's sweet of you but don't bother,' I said quickly. Bernice's puddings were sludgy, amorphous, and a hundred per cent proof. I couldn't even imagine her transporting such a concoction to my house, sloshing and slapping on the passenger seat of her rust-flaked station wagon, filling the car with combustible fumes.

'Cheerio then,' she said, kissing me. 'And good luck. It's so terrific to see a clever woman giving in to her natural urges.'

On the way home, I considered this remark, and found it lacking. If it had been me who was being pursued, then I would have been giving in to my natural urges. But – and I was old enough to find this undignified – it was I who was in pursuit. I did not even know whether the slightest reciprocal interest had been aroused in my quarry. I wondered, not for the first time in this cataclysmic week, if I had gone completely barmy.

My house, when I got back to it, teemed with life. Declan, right hand still heavily bandaged, was pushing the motor mower back and forth on the back lawn like the Grim Reaper. The snooker table was up in the kitchen and Gareth and Brett Troye were engaged in a needle frame. I could tell it was serious stuff because they both stood staring at the table as if the secrets of the universe were inscribed on its green baize surface.

'Homework?' I asked automatically, ever the doting parent.

'Hang on,' said Gareth, and then, to Brett: 'I'm going for the brown.'

I stood patiently while he executed the shot successfully and then shaped up for a further stab, the butt of his cue resting on the windowsill next to my Crown Derby cream jug.

'Watch out,' I suggested.

'Hang on,' said Gareth again.

I stepped forward, prepared to be trenchant. 'I've hung on once – have you done your homework?'

'We haven't got any,' supplied Brett, since the Master, brow furrowed and tongue protruding, was lining up on the red.

'Surely,' I persisted, 'you have some reading or something.'

'Nope, we surely haven't.' Gareth, successful again, straightened up and chalked the tip of his cue with a practised air which froze my blood. Wasn't the ability to play snooker the sign of a misspent youth? And here was my first-born, the fruit of my loins, perfecting his decadent arts right here in my kitchen.

'Then we'll find you some!' I snapped. 'Put this away now. And Brett, you run along home.'

'Come off it, Ma!' complained Gareth, managing to be both hectoring and whiney at the same time, a talent peculiar to lads.

'I will not. Goodbye, Brett. Gareth, go and read a book for an hour.'

'Blimey Ma, who've you been drinking with?' was his mordant retort.

'Just get on with it.'

He spotted a chink in my armour. 'Give us a hand with the table, then, Brett's gone.'

I was ready for him. 'Isn't Damon here?'

'Yeah.'

'Right, he can give you a hand before he goes. Beat it.'

He went upstairs, his door closed, and the pounding of heavy metal shut me even more firmly out of the filial consciousness.

Looking out into the hall, I saw the Hoover by the sitting room door, and heard voices murmuring faintly on the other side. Still in combative mood I marched across and went in.

Damon and Clara were sitting on the floor near George's expensive Japanese sound centre, with George's equally expensive record and tape collection spread about them. Clara held a notebook and pencil. As I entered they both looked up with identical expressions of dumb insolence, though my daughter's, from being habitual, was more complete.

But it was Damon's appearance which swept the suspicions clean out of my head and left me speechless. He had undergone a metamorphosis. Gone were the baggy tracksuit trousers and khaki pullover. His runtish form was now tricked out in a style known as 'preppy' and which can look quite fetching on hunky young Americans with big shoulders and perfect teeth. Damon wore a red checked shirt with a button-down collar, a heather mixture tweed jacket (it was now June), beige twill trousers, red socks and white canvas shoes. In deference to these clothes he had also had a haircut, which was a pity because his glistening pompadour had been his finest feature and without it he seemed even slighter and more weaselly. I noticed for the first time his prominent ears. All the clothes were a shade too big. The overall effect was bizarre, and strangely menacing.

'Damon?'

He got up, while Clara busied herself gathering up the tapes and LPs.

'Hallo there,' he said. It was truly appalling.

'What exactly are you doing?'

'Sorry.'

'Have you finished the house?'

'I got to get in the kitchen.'

'Don't let me stop you.' I held the door open for him. 'And when you've done in there bang on Gareth's door and help him put the snooker table away. Please.'

'Will do.' He made a forelock-touching gesture and skipped nervously past me.

When he'd gone I pushed the door to and rounded on Clara.

'Whatever were you doing?' I asked. 'He comes here to work for me, not to play records with you. I thought you hated him,' I added uncharitably.

She shrugged. 'He's all right.'

'Never mind that. You make sure you put your father's things back carefully, I've no intention of covering up for you if there's any damage when he comes back!'

'Okay, okay, no need to get your knickers in a knot.'

'I'm not! And clean out those caveys, they're beginning to smell.'

'Sure . . . '

She wafted past me and out into the yard. I wondered why the hell I couldn't make the disparate elements of my life hang together and centre on me, as Bernice seemed to do with material at least as unpromising. Sweating with irritation I went into the kitchen and ignored Damon as I boiled the kettle and brewed tea, staring out of the window at Declan. Compared with those inside the house he seemed a paragon of straightforwardness and dependability. And had he not been the instrument of my first meeting with Dr Ghikas? For Declan's tea I chose the mug bearing the legend 'You're just champion' (it had a footballing connotation), and cut him a slice of the fudge cake I should normally have reserved for next of kin.

'How is the hand, Declan?' I enquired genially, as he balanced the mug on a fencepost and addressed himself to the cake.

'Mending.'

'Lawn looks nice.'

' 'Twould look better if you got yourselves a decent mower, so it would,' he asserted, spraying me with a shower of dark crumbs like John Innes potting soil. 'These fiddly diddly tings is okay for a postage stamp, but they're not man enough for a roddy great patch like this of yours.'

Accustomed as I was to the general tenor of Declan's conversation, I knew better than to judge his remarks by content. It was quantity that counted, and by this criterion he was being outstandingly sociable.

'Perhaps when my next book comes out,' I said gaily, 'we'll get you one of those super ones you sit on and drive around.'

Declan grunted. 'It pays to get a decent mower, so it does.'

'Of course. Well – ' I pressed my palms together and smiled warmly at him. 'Keep up the good work. I have to slip out for a few minutes, but the children are in.'

'The boy plays a helluva lot of billiards,' said Declan disapprovingly.

'He's doing his homework now,' I countered. 'And Clara's cleaning out her guinea pigs.'

'Not before time.' He handed me his empty plate. 'Have you seen the other feller?'

'No – that is, who?'

'The little feller, the one does your work for yer.'

'Damon.'

'That's the feller!' Declan rolled his eyes. 'Mother of God, what a sight.'

'He's smartened himself up,' I said, doing it to annoy.

'Is that what you call it? Lord bless and save us, what a figure of fun.'

I looked at Declan. His squat figure was dressed in a pair of dungarees with only one strap; a ragged Fair Isle pullover, gigantic oiled-wool socks, presumably to protect his feet from the soaring summer temperatures; and the sort of boots which could have housed the old woman with too many children. All in all he looked like someone in a glass house who'd just heaved a ruddy great rock through the window.

He gave me back the tea-mug. 'You watch that girl of yours,' he said darkly. 'He thinks he's Jesus Christ Almighty in them ridiculous togs.'

I took the plate and mug back to the kitchen, which now glistened wetly in the wake of Damon's ministrations with squeezy mop and cloth. He was buckling on his crash helmet in the doorway. The snooker table had been put away.

'See you tomorrow then,' he said.

'Yes.' I stared at him, trying to read his expression, or better still his thoughts. But his narrow face peered out from the encircling helmet like a rodent's from its hole, and I could deduce nothing from its look of beady-eyed vacuity.

'Perhaps,' I suggested, 'it would be better if you didn't wear those smart new things to work. I'd hate them to get spoilt.'

'Keen, eh?' He looked down at himself. 'Don't worry.'

And with this futile advice, he left.

I fed Fluffy and Spot, told the children I was going out for five minutes, and headed up the road in the direction of the Tunnels'. This seemed an eminently appropriate moment, with maternal feeling at an all-time low, to ask Brenda if she would put the children up while I attended the Buchfest. I knew at once that all was not well at 'Trevenda' when I saw the heirs to the Tunnel empire loitering in the front garden. Even more than most modern children, Jason, Nigel and Michelle looked ill at ease in the great outdoors. Now they stood in the centre of Trevor's York stone patio like three threatening, outsize garden gnomes, androgynous in jeans, trainers and navy body-warmers.

'Hallo, Jason,' I said, addressing myself to the eldest one, who attended the comprehensive with Gareth. 'Is your mum in?'

'Yeah.' Was I mistaken, or did a sly look pass between the three of them?'

'Go round the back,' suggested Michelle, all helpfulness, 'she's in the kitchen.'

I went down the path at the side of Trevenda, and through the high wooden door which admitted me to the rear of the house. I soon realised my mistake, but the knowledge that the three young Tunnels would be smirkingly awaiting my return caused me to hold my ground.

Brenda was in the kitchen all right, but she was not alone. Trevor was there too, and they were engaged in a row of operatic proportions. Or at least Brenda was, blackguarding her husband con spirito, against a background of stupendous bangings and clashings.

I peeked timorously round the corner and in at the window. Interestingly, Brenda, for all her superior fire-power, both verbal and physical, and her new-found emancipation courtesy of the Wagon, was washing up, while Trevor stood just behind her right shoulder looking hangdog. The crashing emanated from the sink, where Brenda's Winter Wonderland dinner service was standing up manfully to the most vile mistreatment. Brenda herself was puffing and tossing her head like a Suffolk Punch.

'I'll do as I like!' she shrieked, making the draining board quake beneath a vast, fluted flan dish. 'I don't just exist through you, I'm an individual, with an individual's rights and preferences! So sod you, Trevor Tunnel, you're not telling me what to do!'

Indeed he wasn't. I had rarely seen even the lugubrious Trevor looking so cast down.

'Cool it, Bren,' he advised forlornly, but his wife chose this moment to vent her feelings by lifting a sauceboat – of the old-fashioned kind, with drip-saucer attached – and hurling it through the window above the sink and into the garden. It missed my profile by centimetres and ploughed lip first into the polyanthus.

'Oh God, oh God!' wailed Brenda. 'God help me!' I really admired her brio. 'Call yourself a man?' she enquired rhetorically of the hapless Trevor. 'You're no good to me, and you never will be!'

A door slammed and a quick peek through the shattered window revealed that she had left the room. That left only Trevor, who would certainly not be in the market for acting as messenger to his wife.

But as I turned to go I was caught in a pincer movement. Trevor emerged from the back door to retrieve the sauceboat, and Jason opened the passage door behind me.

'Find her, did you?' asked Jason.

I blushed fierily, for after all he knew how long I'd been there; it must be perfectly plain to him that I'd been no more than a common voyeur and eavesdropper.

'Er – '

But Trevor saved my embarrassment by being a thousand times more discomfited than me. Standing there with the muddy sauceboat held in both hands he at once launched into a torrent of self-excuse.

'Oh – Harriet – so sorry – what can I do for you? Just took the afternoon off to be with the wife for a change, you know . . . she's a bit overwrought – I'm really sorry you had to hang about like this – '

Jason sniggered and pushed past me.

'Take a cup of tea to your mother, Jason,' ordered Trevor.

I began to back up the passage.

'Please don't give it another thought,' I yelped, 'I only dropped in for a chat with Brenda, another time'll do, I can see it's a bad moment – ' I suddenly thought of something which might cheer him up. 'I spoke to Dr Ghikas, by the way, and I think he may be willing to help out with the Toms – '

'Trev-argh!' bellowed Brenda from an upstairs window. Trevor glanced up fearfully.

'I'd better go,' he quavered.

'And me. 'Byee.'

As I scuttled away, past the sniggering Nigel and Michelle, I heard Brenda scream: 'Don't you call me overwrought, you slimey turd!' and there was another explosive crash as she heaved a second missile – a teasmade, perhaps, or digital clock-radio – through the bedroom window. And this time it was Trevor who called on his Maker.

Chapter Eight

A few days before the dinner party I received a royalty cheque from Era Books, and bought myself a dress, and Declan a motor mower of the sort advertised on television, which is said to cause the neighbours agonies of envy as they watch the manicured green tramlines unrolling behind it.

'What's that for?' asked Clara when she saw the dress. She had been uncharacteristically amiable since last Thursday when I'd caught her with Damon, so it was clear she had something to hide. On the Friday they'd ignored each other completely which, far from allaying my fears, made me even more suspicious. Just the same, it was pleasant to have Clara so amicable, whatever the reason.

'I've got people to dinner this Saturday,' I said, 'remember? You're going to the roller rink with the Langleys, it's Sabina's birthday.'

'Oh yeah.'

'Mrs Langley said you could spend the night.'

She shook her head. 'No thanks. They've got a smelly toddler.'

'Dominic's a dear little boy,' I said, perjuring myself.

'He pongs and he comes into Sabina's room in the mornings and gets into bed with me.'

'Tell him to get into bed with Sabina. Come on, darling, you go to the Langleys, it'll be much more fun than here, with the place full of grown-ups.'

I could see her weighing up the pros and cons of further argument. The cons won, which made me even more certain she was up to something.

'Okay.'

'Thanks.'

'Put the dress on, let's have a dekko.'

It was purple silk, short and loose with elbow-length sleeves and a deep V-neck. At Boutique Meridiana in Basset Regis I had really fancied my chances in it. Eager to show my daughter that there was life in the old bitch yet I pulled off my balding Levis and Barford Athletic Club T-shirt and slipped the purple silk over my head.

We were both standing plumb in front of the wardrobe mirror, and were able to see simultaneously what kind of figure I cut, and it was not encouraging. I removed my blue towelling socks but that just revealed the ghostly pallor of my feet and ankles on the end of my well-weathered jogger's legs.

'Bloody hell,' I said.

Clara tweaked at my wild hair. 'Get yourself a perm.'

'I don't want a flaming perm!'

'Okay, okay. Anyway, it'll be all right on the night. With a few bits and pieces.'

'Hm. Like a carthorse in brasses.'

'It's a trif colour.'

I wasn't born yesterday, I knew what she meant. I dragged off the dress and stuffed it back in the wardrobe, desperately trying to remember why I'd bought it in the first place. I had wanted something different, something brilliant and dashing that Constantine Ghikas would remember. The girl in Boutique Meridiana had draped beads round my neck and a green cummerbund round my middle and pronounced me a knock-out. Well, I would do the same, dammit. With the cunning accessorising so warmly advocated by the women's magazines (and, on this occasion, by Clara), I would be a knock-out once again. Perhaps.

Despondently, I stared out of the window. A child on a pony

101

rode by and I watched listlessly. Oh, to be eleven again. But as the pony's rolling, rotund backside disappeared round the bend in the road the scales fell from my eyes. I turned, but Clara had gone.

'Clara! Cla-ra!'

'That's my name . . . ' Her voice came faintly from her room. I stamped through, still in my underwear, knocked as the caring parent should, but walked in without waiting to be asked. She was lying on her bed pasting fresh cuttings into her Badness album.

'Clara – I've just seen another child riding Stu. It looked like Sabina.'

'That's right.'

'Oh – you know about it, do you? Is she competent? I didn't even know she rode.'

Clara shrugged. 'She told me – '

'Does her mother know she's out on your pony, alone?'

'I dunno. That's her problem.'

'It's not at all a good idea to let Stu out unaccompanied like that. She's not a beginner's pony, she has a very hard mouth – what if something happened? No more lending, is that clear?'

'Don't fuss, Mummy, and anyway I haven't – ' She stopped so abruptly and expressionlessly that for a moment I thought I'd imagined she was going to add something.

'Haven't what?'

'Nothing.'

'Haven't what?'

'I haven't lent her. I've hired her.'

'Clara!' I experienced both shock and admiration in roughly equal measure. 'You can't do that!'

'Well, I have.'

'Don't be pert with me, young lady!' I threatened, towering over her. 'What on earth would Mrs Langley say if she knew?'

'She doesn't know. I mean she knows Sabina's riding, but she doesn't know she's paying.'

'How much are you charging, for goodness' sake?'

'Seventy-five pence an hour. It's great value.'

I sensed a shift in emphasis to throw me off the scent. 'It must stop now, do you understand? Now this minute! What do you need the money for anyway?'

'I'm saving up.'

'For what? A racehorse?'

She hesitated. 'Some equipment.'

'You'll have a rise in pocket money in September, wait till then. In the meantime there are some jobs you could do for me which I'll pay you for. But for God's sake stop hiring out that pony! Get over to the field now and tell Sabina. And you can tell her you'll stay on Saturday, while you're about it.'

She got up off the bed and went. I followed her on to the landing, but the sound of Gareth and his cronies coming in at the back door reminded me I was in bra and pants and I retreated into the bedroom.

I'd only just scrambled back into jeans and T-shirt when Gareth walked in, with Brett Troye in close attendance.

'You might knock!'

'A thousand pardons.'

'What do you want anyway?'

'Brett told me the scouts are having a wide game and night camp on Saturday, okay if I go?'

It looked as if Dame Fortune, just for a change, was smiling on me. 'Yes, of course. What does it entail, this wide camp?'

'Oh . . . ' With permission granted, the effort of explaining the event to me was too great. 'We roam around the village finding things, with the cubs as well, and then after Makepeace – '

'*Mr* Makepeace to you.'

'He does bangers and dampers in his back garden.'

'How very kind of him.'

Gareth and Brett exchanged glances and smirked. Thank God I hadn't had the purple silk on when they arrived.

'I've got people to dinner on Saturday,' I said grandly, 'so that will fit in nicely.'

'Right.'

The lads withdrew, and as Brett went downstairs I heard one of them say, 'Ay've got people to dinnah!' and burst into squeaky guffaws of suppressed mirth.

103

Because I was already in the granddaddy of a bad mood I compounded it by launching into a grand tidy-up. In my house, even with the meticulous George absent, and in spite of the efforts of Damon, The Mess was like the star of some old, bad, black-and-white horror film: a malignant, ever-growing entity which might be temporarily pushed back, but which within days was oozing and creeping once more from its lair to enfold room after room in its whiskery embrace.

All Damon and I could do was to keep it at bay. And even then it continued in its underground form, lurking as slut's wool beneath the beds, mouldering as apple cores in the hearth and neglected shards of bone in the dog's basket, clinging in sticky rings beneath the sauce bottles in the kitchen cupboard.

I was powerless against it, or so I felt. This resulted in my ignoring The Mess until it reached monumental proportions, and then conducting, as now, a hate blitz which left the house in a state of shrinking, quaking nakedness, smarting from an onslaught of household bleach which must have dispatched even the remaining one per cent of household germs. And which left me slumped over a g. and t., reflecting gloomily that Jeffrey Archer and Wilbur Smith did not have to waste perfectly good working time prizing chutney jars off shelves with a knife, and gagging over the debris beneath the fridge-freezer. It was during these immediate post-blitz dolours that I felt most keenly my mediocrity as a writer. Was it any wonder that I did not set the *NYT* best-seller list alight? That the only reviews I got were those appearing in list form in August, damned for ever under the heading 'Holiday Reading'? That intelligent women like Anna Ghikas found me 'tremendous fun'? I was bogged down. The housewifely fantasies in which I dealt, the Tudor studs and Regency ravers, were so much part of my everyday consciousness that they seemed to sip coffee with me at breakfast, to rustle alongside as I jogged the bridleways, to parade and posture in the bedroom as I read *Cosmopolitan* and drank cocoa. Only days ago had I not written a complete sequence without making a single conscious decision?

The depressing fact was that I came from the tail-end of the generation who still saw themselves as homebodies who managed to do a job with the energy that was left over, rather than vice versa. It was not George's fault, God knows he had always encouraged me, and if I were to be left alone tomorrow I should still have been able to make a more than adequate crust from the historical hotbeds that were my stock in trade. No, it was my own self-image (as a *Cosmo* reader I was acquainted with the psycho-speak) which was at fault. If I was to change as a writer there had to be a fundamental change in me. Which might very well begin with Constantine Ghikas. Who knows but that a few snatched hours of illicit passion might unleash new fires in me, both literary and carnal? With the house barren and subdued and the children skulking in their respective bedrooms I once more took out the purple dress and held it against myself. My optimism returned. It was different, and that was what I was going to be.

On the night of the dinner party, the absence of both children enabled me to get off to a flying start. I was far less anxious about the meal, which consisted of tried and tested foolproof dishes, than about my own toilette, to which I devoted a considerable time. Having given Damon the Friday off, I had retained him for this evening to do the washing up and make coffee. It was soothing, as I painted my face and subdued my hair, to hear him Hoovering the sitting room and setting out ashtrays in an otherwise empty, tidy house. It gave me the entirely spurious impression that I was a lady of leisure. In an ideal world I might have wished that Damon was a stylish 'exquisite' such as might have come my way in the city, who would have advised me on face-packs and made mouth-watering hors d'oeuvres for the dinner table, but failing that he was still sufficiently unusual and now, in his new persona, clean too, to be a conversation piece. As I was putting on mascara there was a knock at the door and Spot, who had been lying under the bed generating a fresh harvest of slut's wool, exploded forth and hurtled down the stairs slightly too fast for his skin, which seemed to slide back and then sharply forward.

In the mirror I saw that I'd applied a row of black dashes, like exclamation marks, over my left eye. As I wiped them off I heard Damon's voice making greeting noises and Bernice's tooting and blasting like a traffic jam.

'Yoo-hoo!' she called. 'I'm coming up!'

She came into the bedroom with Spot orbiting her legs, now in a state of abject apology.

'Wow,' she said, plumping down on the bed. 'And double wow.'

I stood up, straightening the beads and smoothing the cummerbund. 'Do you think so? Honestly? I mean, if you didn't know me, what would you think?'

'I'd think you were Basset Magna's answer to Joan Collins.'

'She's fifty.'

'You can't have everything, dear.'

Bernice herself was dressed in a trouser suit like those worn by the exponents of judo. The jacket had no fastening, but was secured, if it could be said to be secured at all, by a black tie around the waist. I was sure the colour of the belt had nothing whatever to do with Bernice's proficiency in the martial arts, and wondered if after all it had been a good thing to ask her. She could have given half her breast-weight to me, and still have had the edge.

'You don't look so dusty yourself,' I said.

'Thank you, you reckon?' She bounced up and struck attitudes in front of the mirror. She wore open-toed red sandals and her toenails were painted.

'Drink?' I asked.

'My dear, I could murder a Scotch and dry.'

We went into the kitchen, where Damon was opening packets of nibbles with his teeth. For his evening's duties he was accoutred like a poor man's Shakin' Stevens in a mint-green jacket, with the same checked shirt and twill trousers, and a green knitted tie. Bernice placed her hand on his left shoulder and peered over his right.

'How super to have help,' she enthused, apparently oblivious of the effect her upper chest against his shoulder-blades was having on Damon. 'And aren't you looking suave, Damon!'

'Yeah,' agreed Damon, in a strangulated voice.

'Isn't he,' I echoed, handing her her drink to put him out of his misery.

'Do you want all these nuts out?' he squeaked, holding up the packet.

'No, just a bowlful. And some black olives, they're in the fridge.'

Bernice took a slurp of her Scotch as we went over to the sitting room. 'Heaven! Arundel is so against spirits. Now tell me what we've having – fetta? Tarama? Moussaka?'

'Cold cucumber soup, roast lamb with herbs, lemon syllabub, Stilton.'

'Sounds *simply* delish. You have no idea how nice it is to be let off my cooking. I get worse, you know. I must train Barty to cook.'

I was appalled. 'Bernice, you *musn't* – think of it.'

'Why ever not? Cooks don't have to be pretty, they just have to cook.'

'But what about hygiene? I mean, Barty . . . '

'So? We get Barty's peck of dirt, and I get to sip sherry and watch TV. A perfectly acceptable deal, *I* reckon.'

She took a large handful of cashews from the bowl which Damon had placed next to the sofa, and poured some of them into her mouth and some down the front of her jacket.

'Where are the dear little ones?' she asked, munching. 'Did you finally immure them in the Regis bypass?'

'Clara's away for the night and Gareth's with the scouts.'

'What bliss,' she said, without malice. Bernice quite liked my children, but she had a well-developed appreciation of the child-free state.

Of course, everyone was late. And because Bernice had been early we were finishing our second stiffener by the time the next knock sounded. Damon had been shuffling in and out as we talked, and nibbles of all sorts now stood invitingly about, while Peggy Lee breathed hospitably from the sound centre. The stage was set.

'Off you toddle,' said Bernice.

It was Constantine. Second stiffener or no I was quite unprepared for the dazzling beauty and elegance of his appearance. I had not seen him for more than a week and it was gratifying to note that the reality outdid the memory. In white jeans and a pale blue sweatshirt he appeared almost gilded, his hair gleaming and his skin the colour of honey on the comb. In one hand he carried a bottle of German white wine and in the other a bunch of freesias, dewy fresh, which, if he had bought them in the veggymart in Regis that morning must have cost him upward of ten pounds.

'Oh . . . !' I cried winningly as he handed them to me. 'They're gorgeous! Does anything smell lovelier than freesias?'

He sniffed the air and smiled engagingly. 'Your cooking, perhaps?'

'And wine – you have gone to town.'

'Coals to Newcastle, I'm sure, but you can always lay it down for another time.'

This mention of laying down made my pulses race. I caught him looking over my shoulder into the kitchen and there was Damon, green and angular, watching us.

I handed him the freesias. 'Damon – would you put these in water and put them on the table?'

'Is that the footballer?' asked Constantine as I led him to the sitting room.

'I'm sorry?'

'Is that your son? The one who's keen on soccer?'

'Oh, gosh, no, that's Damon, my charperson.'

'Ah, right . . . !' There was a discernible note of relief in the poor man's voice and I realised how close the Toms had been to losing their potential Under Fourteens manager.

'My two are out this evening,' I explained. 'With other people,' I added, in case he should think me the kind of parent who turned eleven- and thirteen-year-olds out into the night just because she had a few friends in.

We went into the sitting room. Bernice stood centre stage, grasping the bristling Spot by the collar. Of necessity this public-spirited act involved leaning forward, so Constantine's first impression of my friend must have been of two majestic and untrammelled boobs on the verge of escaping from a flimsy jacket.

'This is Bernice Potter,' I said.

'How do you do!' cried Bernice. 'No hands! Harriet, shall I put him somewhere?'

'I'll shut him in the yard.'

I dragged Spot away, and when I came back Bernice had taken it upon herself to furnish Constantine with a drink. He turned as I came in.

'I was just saying, I'm awfully sorry but there is a slim chance I might have to take a call tonight. I'm standing in for Doctor Salmon, it was the only night he could get tickets for *Lucia* at Covent Garden and I could hardly refuse.'

'No, of course not.'

'I gave the switchboard your number, I hope you don't mind.'

'Not in the least.'

'The unacceptable face of general practice, eh?' said Bernice.

He raised his eyebrows. 'Actually no. I think the anti-social hours part of general practice is of inestimable value.' Oh, so did I, so did I. 'It's the one part of our job which rescues us from being just a clearing house for the hospitals. I'm afraid I'm idealistic about the role of the GP in the community,' he added with a disarming smile. This was not such good news.

'I wish there were more like you about the place,' sighed Bernice. 'I come from Barford, and I couldn't even tell you what my doctor looks like. Not that I'm ever ill, actually . . .'

She was enlarging on her robust state of health when there was a knock at the door and I went to answer it.

If Bernice and I could be said to have laid a foundation, then Mike and Linda Channing already had the footings up.

'It's only us!' carolled Linda. Only? 'I'm sorry if we're late, we've been to a swill at the Mathers, do you know them?'

'No.'

'Lucky you,' said Mike. He kissed me warmly. His breath was a humid tide of Glentrivet. He left his hands on my shoulders and looked me up and down. 'You're looking dishy.'

'Thanks.'

'Doesn't she?' agreed Linda. 'Very Raj Quartet.'

'Is that what it is?' Mike put his arm round me and gave my spare tyre a jostle. 'I call it Being Sexy.'

'Well, you would!'

All this was entirely good-humoured, in fact they went off into gales of quite unjustified mirth. I took their orders for drinks and allowed them to go unattended to join the others, ricocheting off one another as they went along the passage to the sitting room.

Damon was sitting at the table, smoking and reading *New Musical Express*. The freesias were in a mayonnaise jar in the middle of the table.

'Damon!' I hissed. 'Put that out, for goodness' sake, I don't want the place stinking of smoke when we come through to eat. And put those flowers in something nicer – a champagne glass will do.'

He folded the paper and put it in his pocket, then rose and shied his fag end into the sink where it sizzled like an angry snake. I took glasses for the Channings from the cupboard, and passed a champagne glass to Damon for the freesias.

'I shan't really need you again till later,' I told him, 'if there's anywhere you want to go.'

'Gotcher.' He pointed two fingers at me like a six gun, it was all most disconcerting. 'I'll nip round the Wagon.' The publican at the Wagon and Horses was famed for his 'ask-no-questions' policy towards under-age drinkers. But it was the practicalities rather than the ethics of the situation which concerned me.

'You're working tonight, remember, Damon. Only a little drink.'

'Gotcher,' he said again. He plonked the glass of freesias on the table. Before opening the back door he paused to turn up his collar and shoot his unshootable cuffs. Then Damon, his Marlboros and his *NME* were swallowed up in the dusk.

I checked the food, poured the drinks and went back to my guests.

Mike and Linda were holding court, quite drowning 'The Fool on the Hill', a track I particularly liked. Bernice looked bright and startled, Constantine politely attentive.

Mike took his glass, swigged and continued with scarcely a pause: 'You can imagine, can't you, the good lady and myself arriving in Tenerife simply covered in these appalling spots – you know, people edging away from us on the plane, customs waving us through with ashen faces – '

'Not a pinch or a nudge to be had from the airport

Lotharios!' This was Linda, taking up the tale. 'We thought of suing the Heathrow catering people but quite honestly I think they did us a favour. We sprinted through immigration like rats up a drainpipe.'

'Were they frightfully itchy?' enquired Bernice. I did hope no one was going to ask Constantine to diagnose the Channings' spots.

'No, not really,' said Linda, looking at Mike for confirmation. 'Just bloody unsightly. You should have seen us next day though – picking each other over in the hotel room like a couple of chimps. Social grooming they call it on the box, don't they – '

'Except that in our case it had distinctly antisocial connotations. It's extraordinary actually,' Mike assumed a loftier, more serious tone, 'there's nothing alienates one human being from another as quickly as a skin complaint. Connotations of dirt and contagion – in our case quite unfounded, I might say . . .'

I saw Constantine's pleasant, interested smile, and his civility made me wish Mike and Linda would disappear up their own anuses. In an attempt to break the conversation down into two smaller ones I went to stand next to him and said quietly: 'Everyone has a horror story about flying, don't they? It's the most dehumanising form of travel.'

'Absolutely. It has the advantage of speed, and that's all.'

'But even that's overrated!' exclaimed Mike, determined to play Circulating Man. 'The time one gains on the actual flight is all lost again with the endless farting about at the various termini – '

'And those inevitable go-slows by foreign air traffic controllers,' added Linda enthusiastically. 'I don't think I've ever had a stop-over at Rome when the organ-grinders haven't made us circle for an hour!'

Bernice, God bless her, was quicker off the mark than I to put a stop to this dangerous line of talk. After all, Athens was notorious among airports, and the Channings would doubtless be able to corroborate general prejudice with a highly coloured and much embellished account of their own experiences there.

'I won't have anything to do with it!' announced my

friend. 'Arundel and I went on a dig in Cumbria last summer and it was absolute bliss.'

'How intriguing,' said Linda. 'Did you find anything remarkable?'

'Good heavens no! Arundel was for ever going spare about old smashed-up pieces of this and that, but in the main I just lay behind an Iron Age fortification and got the *most* superb all-over tan.'

Mike finally moved in on her. It had only been a matter of time. He was a man whose stated preference in a social gathering was for 'knees-under and leg-over'.

'I do love your suit,' said Linda to Bernice, spiking her husband's flattery guns with practised ease.

Constantine turned to me. 'It seems to be a modern trend on these occasions for the women to look superb and the men to dress like football coaches.' This reminded me of something, but before I could ask he went on: 'Yes, I'll take on your Under Fourteens with the greatest of pleasure. When will I have to start?'

'Thank you so much!' My mood positively soared. 'That is marvellous, I'm sure you won't regret it. And you won't have to do anything before next season, obviously.'

'But I feel I must do something,' he said, with an enchanting air of earnest good intention.

I just had to indulge him. 'That's no problem. There's a seven-a-side tournament at the end of the month. If you were to come along to that I could introduce you to the others and you could see the boys play.'

'That sounds fine.'

'I'm afraid,' I added, with assumed diffidence, 'that managers are automatically on the committee.'

'No problem, I'm an old hand at committees. Turn up, look keen, keep quiet.'

'What's this?' asked Mike, tearing his gaze away from Bernice's gaping judo jacket, 'houses of ill repute?'

'Committees,' said Constantine, 'and how to survive them.'

'God, don't mention committees,' said Linda, whose law degree and fluent French had secured her a role in the 'cabinet' of a noted Eurocrat. 'They've roped me in to be part of something called Euro-Encounter.'

'Sounds like a malfunction of the waterworks, doesn't it?' said Mike supportively.

'What is it exactly?' asked Constantine.

'That's the forty-thousand-franc question. We're going to meet quarterly in various one-horse places au continent, to bore each other sockless during the day and wreck our livers at night.'

'Take no notice,' said Mike, 'she loves it.'

'I'm sure I should,' said Bernice.

'Yes,' agreed Mike, 'let's talk about *you* . . .'

'I must go and look at dinner,' I said.

Constantine made to follow me. 'Anything I can do?'

'No, but do come along and talk if you want to.'

He followed me to the kitchen and studied my noticeboard – again – while I basted the meat, shook the salad dressing and put out the cucumber soup with trembling hands.

'So how do you like Basset Parva?' I asked, the sparkling conversationalist.

'What, professionally or socially?'

'Um . . . socially, I suppose.'

'It's fine. It's a nice village and there's a lot going on.' So he'd noticed. 'I could be out every night if I chose. But there's some disadvantage to being an unmarried doctor in a small community.'

'Oh, I'm sure! Of course, there must be!' Conditioning and training made me eager to agree, to uphold the necessity for spotless integrity and moral probity even as I gasped at my own stupidity. Hadn't I expressly invited this unmarried doctor in order to vamp him, to make him as mad with lust for me as I was for him? And yet here I was acting the champion of conventional morality. I hacked wildly at the baguette in an access of frustration, but he didn't seem to notice.

'That's why it's so nice to come over here,' he said. 'I feel less watched.'

'Quite!' I agreed. 'Now I think I'm ready, I'll go and tell the others.'

Bernice, Mike and Linda were standing gazing up at the

row of my previous titles on the top shelf of the bookcase. From their expressions it was impossible to guess at their reactions to *Castle of Dreams, The Flight from Love, Rose of Autumn* et. al., but as I entered Bernice greeted me with:

'Ah, here she is. Superwoman. The Caped Hostess. All this and dinner too. We were just commenting on your general versatility and brilliance.'

'Good,' I said. 'Dinner's ready.'

During dinner I had the sensation of things getting out of hand. For a start, I was tight. When nervous I drank fast, and the effects were delayed and catastrophic. Mike and Linda had been oiled to begin with and were now so well lubricated they were like a couple of cakes of soap – you couldn't grab hold of them. Crazily they slithered and swooped from one anecdote to the next, spilling salt, sending slivers of tomato and Spanish onion cascading to the ground to be sniffed and rejected by Fluffy, helping themselves to wine and periodically over-filling glasses and shouting 'whoops'. Their mood was infectious. The tenor of the party became one of febrile hilarity. Bernice's judo jacket sagged invitingly. Constantine's expression became a lot less polite. I caught Bernice's eye and treated her cleavage to a withering look. Obligingly she tweaked it, and it parted again.

During the syllabub the phone rang and I answered it.

'Is Dr Ghikas there?' asked a female voice, elderly and genteel.

'Yes, he is. Who is that?'

The voice frosted over. 'I was given this number by the surgery.'

'Just hang on – ' I put my hand over the mouthpiece. 'Constantine, it's for you.'

'Thank you – sorry about this.'

'Take it in the bedroom if you want to, top of the stairs and facing.'

I waited until I heard him lift the receiver, then put mine down and went back to the table.

'Poor bugger,' said Mike. 'Who'd be a doctor, eh?'

'I would,' said Bernice. 'You never see a doctor on a bike.'

114

'Oh yes, but *darling*,' protested Mike, 'what a life. Ghastly surgeries full of snotty kids and haemorrhoids and thread worm – '

'That's the nurse,' I corrected him. 'The nurse does thread worm.'

'Glad you told me that!' said Mike and we all laughed merrily.

'But fancy being on call at the weekend like this,' said Linda, in her best seriously-though tone. 'Like running a shop.'

We pondered this simile, and then Bernice said: 'He's gorgeous, though.'

'Oh *yes*,' agreed Linda. 'Tasty, tasty!'

'Don't be ridiculous,' I blustered, in the overemphatic way of the woman with the bad conscience.

'Never you mind, girl,' said Mike, putting his arm round me. 'Your secret is safe with us. A little field work, eh? A little research? And why the hell not!'

Constantine came back into the room and sat down in his place.

'That was quick!' observed Linda. 'Not terminal then?'

'No. She quite often rings me up.'

'Ah, hypochondriac is it . . . ?' asked Mike with the air of one versed in medical lore.

'No,' said Constantine, 'just elderly and on her own.'

This cast something of a blight. But Mike Channing on the outside of three g. and t.s and a bottle of Beaujolais would have been proof against an arctic blizzard.

'There was a young lady of Parva,' he declaimed, 'who had an affair with her farver. She said, "Callow youth is so rough and uncouth, but Farver in Parva is suaver!" '

We all laughed immoderately, especially Mike, who had tears coursing down his cheeks. Constantine laughed in a slightly stupefied way as if he couldn't believe his eyes and ears. He had long since started covering his wine glass with his hand to preclude topping-up and I did hope the rest of us didn't seem too disgusting.

'How about a game?' asked Mike. 'Would anyone like to play a game?'

'God, Mike, really . . . !' said Linda, 'I'm sure they don't.'

'I do!' said Bernice predictably.

'Good idea,' agreed Constantine, more surprisingly.

Mike looked at me. 'Harriet?'

I was overcome with a mild sense of hysteria. 'Sure, sure, why not . . . ?'

'Attagirl!'

While I put on the kettle for coffee Mike herded his little flock back into the sitting room and began outlining the game.

As I stood there gazing into space and wondering where it would all lead, the back door opened and Damon came in.

'Perfect timing!' I cried. 'We've just finished and you can make the coffee. Four large spoonfuls in this jug, and don't forget to bring a strainer, out of this drawer.'

'Oh yeah. Right. Will do.' He removed his jacket and hung it on the back of one of the chairs. In my well-refreshed state I felt almost maternal towards him but when I smiled – benignly, as I thought – he shied away as though Count Dracula had treated him to a leer dripping with gore.

'Where are your kids?' he asked, as if to remind me of my respectable matronly status.

'Out,' I explained. 'Thank you, Damon, this really is a great help.'

' 'Sorlright, I got nothing on,' was his reply.

Back in the sitting room, a short reprise from Mike gave me to understand that the game involved a man carrying a woman from point A to point B with various prescribed parts of her body touching the ground at all times.

'But who's the arbiter?' asked Bernice. 'I mean who says which parts?'

'We all write down different parts on bits of paper and put them in a hat or a bin or something, and someone makes a selection before each go,' said Mike. 'It's easy-peasy.'

'What's the object of the exercise?' asked Constantine, the last rational voice on earth.

'Just to do it!' replied Linda. 'Because It's There.'

'Well, not quite, darling,' said Mike. 'It will be over a set course and against the clock.'

116

'I see,' said Constantine.

'Rightie-ho then!' cried Bernice. 'What are we waiting for? Give me a pencil and paper, someone.'

I fetched both from the study and we all scribbled busily. Linda touched Constantine on the arm. 'Be careful, won't you, doctor,' she said. 'I don't want to end the evening with a prolapse.'

'Heaven forfend,' he murmured, deep in thought.

When we'd finished writing Bernice screwed up the bits of paper and put them in a vase, while Mike rummaged through George's tapes and put on Francis Albert.

'Songs for Swinging Naughty Bits,' he announced.

'There's a fly in this ointment,' observed Bernice. 'We're not an even number.'

'I could take two,' offered Constantine gamely, holding his glass of Perrier like a badge of office.

At this moment Damon came in with the coffee tray. Bernice rose from her chair with the suggestion of a lurch, and more than a suggestion of the swinging naughty bits to which Mike had but lately referred.

'Put the tray down, Damon,' she ordered. 'You *shall* go to the ball.' It was evidence of how drunk I was that beyond a slight peck of mild surprise I accepted this solution with equanamity.

'Could you lift me, Damon?' asked Bernice reflectively, looking him up and down. He was by three or four inches and twenty pounds the smallest person in the room, and not in rude health.

He eyed her back. 'Doubt it. I could try.'

Bernice waved a dismissive, imperious hand. 'For fuck's sake,' she said, 'it's nineteen eighty-four. I'll carry *him*.'

'Sure, fine, right, okay,' said Mike, impatient with the delay. 'Now who's going first?'

'You're the expert, you go first,' I said. 'You and Linda.'

'May I know where I am to be carried?' asked Linda.

'I hereby declare this fireplace point A and the front door point B,' said Mike. 'Any queries?'

'That's hellishly difficult,' complained Linda, taking off her shoes. 'We're all going to get wedged in this doorway.'

'That, petal, is where the skill comes in. The course is there and back, against the clock. Okey-dokey, allons-y!' He thrust his hand into the vase and brought it out clutching a bit of paper.

'It says here, left elbow.' He held the paper up for the rest of us to see. Then he scrutinised his wife, like a removal man assessing an awkward piece of furniture – a harp, a grand piano, a large and elaborate desk – and finally rushed her, in one movement turning her upside down with her head on the sofa, and wrapping her ankles round his neck. This manoeuvre afforded the rest of us an uninterrupted view of Linda's underwear, which consisted of plain white pants and flesh-coloured tights with a sturdily reinforced gusset. It must have occurred to us all simultaneously that if this evening Linda were to be struck down by the number 6 to Basset Regis she would have nothing whatever of which to be ashamed.

We also noted that Linda's legs were good right up to the top, were free of cellulite and broken veins, and had recently been subjected to the bikini wax which is the stamp of the well-organised woman.

I glanced at the others. Bernice, thank God, was re-organising her jacket to withstand the rigours of the game; Damon was tying his shoelaces; and Constantine was looking on with complete detachment over his glass of water. Linda's crotch, it appeared, held no interest for him. I dare say he saw too many in the course of his work.

To be fair to Linda, as Mike hoisted her about, hauling on her right arm and bending her left like a piston, elbow first, to the ground, she exhibited the most admirable British sang-froid, such as enabled many a spunky Victorian lady to travel through uncharted mountain wastes 'With Mule and Note-book'.

'All right down there?' asked Mike.

'As well as can be expected.'

'Ready, timer?' Constantine nodded, waving his left wrist. 'We're off!' They moved off, soixant-neufing it down the hall (Mike having negotiated the narrow doorway with consummate skill) like some elaborate monster from the mists of mythology.

We fell about. We all thought each other so perfectly splendid, so amusing and attractive (this with the possible exception of Damon) that it would have taken a disaster of cataclysmic proportions to shake our convivial mood. That disaster was coming, we could not know how soon, but for now, like the sun-kissed hedonists of that long Edwardian summer, we continued to laugh like drains.

The Channings, as befitted the experts, completed their circuit in a nippy thirty-two seconds, without mishap. Linda regained the vertical with more dignity than she had a right to, her well-cut coiffure falling back into place at once and her colour returning to normal in less than a minute.

'Thirty-two seconds to beat!' cried Mike. 'Right, Bernice, you ready?'

'Sir!'

'You?' Mike looked at Damon.

'Guess so.' I had to admire Damon's calm – his 'cool' I suppose he would have called it – and could only suppose it masked a kind of inertia panic. The situation in which he found himself was so totally foreign to him that his stunted verbal and facial vocabulary had not the wherewithal to express an appropriate reaction.

Mike drew a piece of paper from the vase. In the declamatory tones of a fairground barker he called out: 'Buttocks! Buttocks are trumps!'

'Buttocks, schmuttocks,' said Bernice airily. 'Sit down, Damon.'

Damon sat.

'Take your shoes off,' Bernice instructed, 'and lock your ankles round my upper thighs. Then we clasp wrists and ankles and Bob's your uncle!'

Damon had no uncle Bob. He was a hopelessly inept pupil. Perhaps his ghastly assumed phlegm had meant suppressing his powers of rational thought – never all that great – as well. Also, as his work for me had indicated, he was assiduous but cack-handed. It took a full three minutes for Bernice to get a grip on him, and he on the situation, and they subsequently failed to complete the course.

Bernice and Damon locked together looked like one of the

unlikelier illustrations from the *Karma Sutra*. His day-glo socks sprouting from beneath her ample bottom, her black belt tickling his ever-reddening nose, encapsulated exactly what is meant by the term culture clash. His peg was square and her hole round, and even had there been the remotest possibility of the one coming into contact with the other, no conjunction would have been possible.

'Let me get you a drink, Damon,' I said, as he staggered stiffly in from the hall, where Bernice had summarily dumped him.

He croaked something affirmative and I fetched him a can of Pils from the fridge. He sat on the sofa, staring glazedly in front of him, nursing the can on his chest and taking occasional gulps from it. I didn't like the look of him. It was hard to imagine what it was like for a culturally deprived seventeen-year-old of limited experience to be carried upside down by a woman of Bernice's build and background at a dinner party of his employer's.

'Our turn, I believe,' said Constantine. He placed his hand on my shoulder and left it there. In any man not so patently a gentleman it would have been a frankly flirtatious gesture. I wondered if I felt hot and sweaty through the purple silk.

Mike put his hand in the vase and drew out a bit of paper.

'It's a real bugger!' he cried. 'Right knee!'

'Perhaps,' I said sportingly, 'I'd better take my tights off.'

'I know,' said Constantine. 'You put your left foot in my trouser pocket.'

'Steady on,' intervened Mike. 'Not allowed. All perks must be incidental. Feet in pockets are out.'

Bernice and Linda cackled with laughter. Damon sank still lower on the sofa, the can of Pils almost obscuring his face.

'Very well,' said Constantine. 'Back to the drawing board.'

In the end we solved the problem by these means: Constantine laced his fingers behind my back, and I draped my left leg over his arm; I bent my right leg so that the knee brushed the ground, and he grabbed my foot with his fingers and held it up. I had not been in such acute discomfort since I'd played Long John Silver at boarding school, but I was heedless of it. Anaesthetised by lust I dangled there, my face bobbing not six inches from Constantine's fly, his tantalising scent in my nostrils, the pre-shrunk denim which covered his narrow hips brushing from time to time my fiery cheek.

'Ready?' asked Mike. 'Then go!'

With the cheers of the onlookers ringing in our ears we set off. It was a kind of torture by promixity. The more exhausted we both became, the tighter I had to clasp Constantine's belt at the back, and the more firmly my face was pressed against him. It would have taken only the slightest reciprocal pressure, the merest twitch, the smallest suggestion of engorgement, and I should have cast caution and sportsmanship to the winds and wrestled my partner to the ground. But as we bumped and dragged along the hall like a murderer and his victim no one would have guessed at these salacious fantasies.

By the time we turned at the front door – where Mike, acting as invigilator, bounded round us, studying our technique – my joints were screaming in agony, but this was as nothing beside my agonies of frustration. I reflected that this might well turn out to be the closest I ever came to unveiling the secrets of Constantine's inner leg, for this ludicrous parody would probably put him off for good.

'You won! Twenty-eight seconds! You won, you jammy buggers!' cried Bernice, as we hurtled with a final turn of speed back into the sitting room.

Then several things happened simultaneously. We collapsed on the floor, still locked in our position, my face now entirely smothered by Constantine's crotch; the uncurtained windows were suddenly piled with staring faces, mostly young, male, and wearing expressions of astonished glee; and Damon was extravagantly sick.

For a brief, half-stifled moment I twisted my head and rolled my eyes and took it all in. Then I closed my eyes once more and concentrated desperately on what was surely going to be my first and final clinch with the Greek doctor.

Astonishing how quickly the euphoric effects of alcohol and

lively social intercourse are dispelled by embarrassment. From a tableau which in its peculiar nastiness must have resembled a sort of white-collar gang-bang (or, given my position, gang-blow), we resumed our separate and relatively respectable identities with lightning speed. Constantine ministered to the gagging Damon (whose indisposition, it was all too luridly apparent, was attributable to the merging of pork scratchings, rum and coke, and ice-cold Pils); Bernice flew to the kitchen for detergent and cloth; Mike Channing changed the tape; and Linda poured cold coffee with a trembling hand. An imperious knock sounded on the front door, and the wall of grinning faces moved away from the window. I stuffed my tights behind the sofa cushion, slipped on my shoes and marched, with grim robotic calm, into the hall.

On the doorstep were as unwelcome a group as in my wildest nightmares I could have envisaged. At the head of a tight phalanx of smirking lads in green shirts – the 2nd Basset Scout Troop – stood Glynis Makepeace, clad in the armour of light: badges, belt, beret, lanyard, whistle and woggle. Just behind her was Nita Nutkin in a broderie anglaise peasant blouse and red gingham pinafore. The contrast between the two was startling, but for one thing – they wore identical expressions of tight-lipped disapproval.

'Well, hallo!' I squeaked. 'Hallo, Gareth!'

'It's unfortunate,' said Akela, and I knew she considered the misfortune to be entirely hers, 'that we have to disturb you when you've got company.'

'Not at all.'

'We have a problem,' she boomed, calling the meeting to order. 'Baloo has come to grief.'

A nervous tic fluttered in my right cheek. 'Good heavens.'

'He's at our house, the poor thing,' chittered Nita, getting in on the act. 'Stan's got him on the sofa right now.'

'I suspect it's nothing but a wrench,' said Glynis in an accusatory tone. God help Baloo if he was found to be malingering. 'We've taken all the usual first-aid precautions, but it had best be looked at.'

'Probably.' I was beginning to get their drift.

Glynis's eyes swivelled alarmingly as she watched Bernice

nip across behind me on her second journey to the sink with the bucket and the bottle of Kleeneze.

'I believe,' said Glynis, 'you have the doctor here? Dr Kikarse?' She enunciated a version of Constantine's name with elaborate distaste.

This had to be a rhetorical question, since only minutes before she had seen Constantine and me intertwined in a kind of human sheep-shank on the sitting room floor.

'We rang the surgery exhange from my house,' explained Nita, 'and they gave this number for the doctor on call, and your Gareth said – '

'Yes, yes.' Murderously, I scanned the faceless horde of scouts for my son. 'The doctor is here. Why don't you come in for a moment?'

They surged past. Akela, disfavour made flesh; Nita, bright-eyed and curious, hoping no doubt to stumble on a sparsely clad gigolo snorting cocaine from an apostle spoon; the scouts, all agog for a fresh glimpse of the sink of depravity which was my home; and after them a dozen or so tiny cubs who (I prayed) must have been far too short to see anything through the sitting room window.

'If Dr Kikarse can spare a minute,' said Akela, 'Anita can escort him back to her house, and I will accompany the troop to my garden for refreshments. 'My husband,' she added, 'has gone on to start a fire.'

'Has he?' I said. 'Just hang on for a second, will you?'

I went back to the sitting room and closed the door behind me. My guests, and Damon, had assumed a sort of studied casualness which would have fooled no one. The twin stenches of semi-digested alcohol and Kleeneze had combined to produce an atmosphere like one of the larger London Gents.

Each clasped a cup of cold coffee and they were listening to Tom Lehrer. The screeches of appreciative laughter emanating from the sound centre contrasted sharply with their expressions of introspective gloom.

'What's up?' enquired Mike, perking up no end at my arrival. 'Anything we can do?'

'Not really. Constantine, it's you they want.'

'What? Me?' He stood up with indecent haste. 'Who?'

'There's a patient for you at the Atkins' House,' I said.

'What, another? Mr and Mrs Atkins? I was there last Saturday too.'

'It's not actually them – '

'No, it wasn't last time,' he explained enthusiastically, 'it was one of their guests. Got tangled in a lariat, and in struggling to free himself knocked over a pot of hot barbecue beans all down his legs. Fortunately he was wearing – '

'They're waiting for you in the hall,' I said. 'Rebecca of Sunnybrook Farm, and Akela.'

'I'm coming. By the way,' he added on the way out, 'I don't know how Damon got here this evening, but he certainly shouldn't be in charge of anything on wheels.'

'Oh, I'll run my partner home,' volunteered Bernice, slapping the whey-faced Damon on the knee. 'One lift's much like another, eh Damon?'

He moaned weakly.

Out in the hall Constantine was all practised solicitude.

'We meet again, Mrs Atkins. How is Mr Hickock?'

'Oh fine, absolutely fine – we must stop meeting like this!'

'Absolutely. Now what's the trouble this time?'

Akela stepped forward. 'My Baloo has incurred a wrench.'

For a moment I could see Constantine mentally riffling through a hundred medical textbooks. 'Sorry?'

'One of the cub leaders,' explained Nita. 'His ankle.'

'Take me to him, Mrs Atkins,' said Constantine. Then Nita bore him, his bedside manner and his little black bag off into the night.

'Work of moments,' said Akela scornfully. The cubs and scouts had retired into the kitchen, and now she flung open the door to reveal them pre-empting the bangers and dampers with bowls of cereal.

'Troop – out!' she commanded, and they obeyed like lambs, adding at least ten bowls and spoons to the existing washing up.

'Troop – to Jubilee Close – forward!' rapped Akela. I watched with grudging admiration as the 2nd Bassets shuffled off. She certainly had the problem of discipline licked. I wondered if a tie and forage cap would help me, but concluded that without Glynis's many natural advantages I should simply appear ludicrous.

I closed the door after them, and leaned on it for a second, a broken woman, before going back to the others.

It was eleven o'clock and my beautiful, well-planned dinner party now resembled nothing so much as a brisk evening at Vine Street Police Station – an uneasy melange of drunks, casualties, loose women and under-age offenders. And to top it all Constantine had been taken from me, carried away on a tide of malign circumstances against which it had been bootless to struggle.

Someone had replaced Tom Lehrer with Clara's Badness album, the monotonous, sardonic flavour of which was perfectly suitable for the terminal stages of a disastrous social occasion.

Bernice leapt to her feet, chest aquiver.

'Right, I'm off! Damon, on your feet, your carriage awaits.'

'Bernice!' I wailed. 'Don't go – I need you!'

'No you don't!' she replied. 'Damon needs his kip a lot more, don't you, Damon?'

Damon responded with a damp, wavering snore. Bernice hauled him to his feet.

'Where does he live?'

'Scargill Cuttings, Basset Regis. You'll have to ask him the number. I say Bernice, are you sure – '

'Sure as eggs. Thank you, my dear,' she kissed my cheek, supporting Damon on one arm, 'for a gorgeous dinner. I shall be on the blower anon.'

I saw them out, and watched them go, listing and tottering like a couple of amateur caber-throwers, through my front gate.

Mike and Linda Channing had taken on the appearance of fixtures and fittings, blending in to the background to see what might transpire.

I sank down in a chair with a groan.

'Jolly enjoyable evening,' said Mike. 'Plenty to drink, bit of rough trade ' I supposed he meant Bernice and Damon –

'raided by scouts, next best thing to being raided by the Bill. Pity you've lost old Kildare, though.'

'Yes.' It was a pity all right. I'd almost certainly scared off the one person I wished to attract, and prematurely ruined my reputation in the process. Vividly I recalled Nita Nutkin's smug, beady-eyed curiosity, and Akela's formidable disapprobation as she shielded her tender charges from contamination.

'I think I'll shoot myself,' I said.

'Oh, don't do that,' said Linda. And added 'How's George?', thus producing like a rabbit from a hat the one remaining topic guaranteed to speed my decline.

'Don't ask her that,' said Mike, leaning over and poking his wife in the ribs. 'She might tell you.'

'What about the book?' went on Linda, displaying the impervious tenacity which was such an asset in her work. 'How's that coming along?'

'Slowly and painfully.'

'If you want my opinion,' said Linda, 'which I'm sure you don't, *I* think you're due for a shake-up. A change of tack. A whole new thing.' And as if she hadn't mouthed enough banalities for one evening she added: 'I reckon there's a different Harriet in there somewhere, just struggling to get out!'

I finally burst into shrill, hysterical laughter.

By midnight it was apparent to me that Constantine was not going to reappear. Gareth had returned, blackened and dyspeptic, from his alfresco supper in Jubilee Close, and gone to bed. The Channings, sensing that the evening's diversions were at an end, finally left.

I went into the kitchen. Due to his forced participation in the game, Damon had done very little washing up. I was confronted by a greasy battlefield of leftovers and remains in the centre of which Fluffy crouched, licking the butter with his eyes closed.

I opened the back door and lobbed him out. I then released Spot from the back yard, gave the guinea pigs some French bread and celery, and locked up.

I took off the purple silk and replaced it with my towelling dressing-gown while I cleaned my face, but I was still too despondent to go to bed. Instead I went to the study and sat down at the tripewriter. As a seductress I might be a non-starter, but Maria Trevelyan was about to make up for all that.

The plot of *TRT* was progressing smoothly along conventional lines. Now, nearly halfway into the book's total length, it was time for Action. Civil war raged. Kersey House was under siege from the Parliamentarians. Maria, with her 'low dark stature' and tomboyish nature, was the obvious choice for an undercover job. Attired as a lad, she would slip out of the house during the hours of darkness, and carry a message to the King's men at nearby – I glanced at my bookshelf – Bradbury. Without more ado I set the scene: Maria lit fitfully by candle-light as she struggled into the garb of a boy, assisted by the Hawkhursts' faithful old nursemaid, Martha. No sweat.

. . . *with the breeches scarce half on, Maria heard a sound at the door. Before she could cover herself, it opened, and there stood the tall figure of Richard Hawkhurst. He was, as always, elegant, and in one hand he carried a goblet of wine. In the flickering candlelight she saw that his pale, aquiline features were animated by the sardonic smile she had come to hate.*

Martha would have gone at once, but Maria caught her arm

'No, goodwife, remain. What is the meaning of this intrusion, cousin? Is it not enough that we have the enemy at the gate, without there being no sanctity in a lady's bedroom?'

At this he threw back his golden head and laughed aloud, a hollow mirthless sound which bounced mockingly off the walls of the shadowy chamber and made the candle flame gutter.

'Not so prim and shrewish, madam, it does not become you! Martha, you may leave us.' Ignoring Maria's protests he stood aside to let the old woman pass, and closed the heavy door behind her.

Face aflame, Maria struggled with the stiff belt, painfully conscious of Richard's amused gaze upon her as he leant lazily against the wall. Finally she had fastened the heavy buckle and stood, legs astride and hands on hips, her eyes sparkling with anger.

'Well, Sir Richard?' she enquired. 'I hope that I pass muster as a boy?'

At once she wished she had not spoken thus, for sarcasm was

Richard Hawkhurst's stock in trade, there were no words which he could not take and twist into a barb to wound his adversary.

'Why yes, cousin,' came the reply. 'You make an excellent lad. The appearance you have achieved, and the manners you have from nature.'

At this most piquant juncture I distinctly heard a knock at the front door. It was a very soft knock, but my visitor's attempt at discretion was wrecked by Spot, who exploded from beneath my bed, hurtled scruff-first down the stairs and cannonaded into the front door on a rip tide of hysterical baying.

I looked at my watch. Who on earth went around knocking on the doors of solitary females at one a.m.? Beasts, that was who.

I went into Gareth's room, the window of which afforded a view of the front door. My son stirred and groaned, his sleep troubled by Robbo's bangers and dampers. He was the snoring refutation of the scouts' motto, Be Prepared.

I peeped out. Down below by the front door stood a tall figure in a broad-brimmed black hat, like an advertisement for Sandeman's port. I could not think of a single person of my acquaintance who affected such a hat.

I went back to my room, selected a high-heeled shoe and crept down the stairs. Spot's baying had settled down into his impersonation of Hitler addressing a rally. Out in the yard the guinea pigs joined in, tooting and hooting, perhaps hoping for some Stilton with their celery. I caught sight of myself in the hall mirror. The shoulders of my dressing-gown were spattered with purplish spots from my last attempt to dye my hair. My face, wild-eyed, glistened with Grecian Dew. I looked like a wrapped leftover.

'Who is it?' I quavered.

Well of course, my putative assailant would at once have identified himself: 'It's the Mad Beast of Magna, missus, come to dismember you and stuff the bits in the freezer. Mind if I come in for a mo?'

'It's me!' came the hissed reply.

'Who?'

'Constantine! I just had to – '

I opened the door. There stood Constantine Ghikas,

beneath a black, wide-brimmed hat of the kind worn by the officers of the fifth cavalry, if film directors are to be believed.

It was wonderful to see him. But not, I feared, so wonderful for him to see me. My earlier euphoria had been shed along with the purple silk and green cummerbund. I was now at a low ebb, both socially and sartorially.

'Come in,' I said. 'Sorry I took so long, I saw the hat.'

He removed it and dropped it on the hall chair. 'Mrs Atkins gave it to me, you know what she is.'

'I'm not sure that I do.'

'You know, country and western and so on.'

'Oh, that.'

He took the shoe from my nerveless grasp. 'Were you going to brain me with this? Nasty.'

'I suppose it would have been.'

'Look, I only dropped in to thank you for a pleasant evening, I'm so terribly sorry to have got you out of bed – '

'You didn't, I was working. A cup of tea, now you're here? Or coffee?'

I was getting back into gear. After all, I had Constantine to myself at last, in the small hours, and I was 'but scantly' clad. Faint heart never won fair lay.

We went into the kitchen. 'Sorry about all this,' I said airily. 'But Damon was too poorly, and I decided to do it tomorrow.'

'Don't apologise,' he said. 'It's I who am sorry for having to break up such a delightful evening.'

'You couldn't help that,' I said, filling the kettle. 'And there's always a next time.'

I set out mugs and spoons, jingling with suppressed lust. All of a sudden his hand came down over mine, pinning it to the melamine worktop. And I hadn't even heard him coming up behind me.

'I'm glad you said that,' he murmured. His face was so close to mine that I could feel his warm breath drying the Grecian Dew. But in God's name, what had I said?

'About the next time,' he supplied obligingly. 'I should be very disappointed if there wasn't one.'

This remark was like a pint of neat alcohol pumped straight

into my bloodstream. I went from wrapped leftover to Ginger Rogers in a single bound. This could well be It, girl, I told myself.

I turned to look up at him, as steam from the kettle wreathed about us.

'You're so – ' he began.

And then the phone rang.

I was all set to ignore it in true movie-queen style, but Constantine leapt back and bounded across the kitchen as if subjected to a high-voltage electric shock. He was clearly programmed, good doctor that he was, to answer the phone immediately, especially in the wee small hours of the morning.

'Bound to be for me,' he said, and picked up the receiver. Even at a distance of some six metres I could hear the penetratting wail of panic on the other end. Another deserving patient, no doubt. I clenched my fists. At that moment I could cheerfully have put the sufferer out of her misery with a blunt instrument.

'It's for you,' said Constantine. 'Your daughter.'

'What?'

'Your daughter wants to talk to you.'

'She can't.'

'You tell her.' He gave the receiver a little shake, like someone encouraging a donkey with a carrot.

I went over and took the phone from him. 'Yes?' I snapped, through bloodless lips.

'Mummeee! I want to come home! I had an awful dream!'

'Don't be silly, Clara, have you any idea what time it is?'

'No, but I – '

'It's twenty past one in the morning. Will you please go back to bed.'

'No!'

'Clara – ! Go and fetch Mrs Langley.'

There was a sputtering exchange on the other end, and Lydia Langley came on the line. She sounded as she always did – harassed, amiable and resilient.

'Harriet, I'm so awfully sorry about all this, but she went on and on about talking to you and I just couldn't say no in the end, I thought the little mite would have a fit.'

130

'Give her a sandwich,' I said. 'She'll be okay. But you've been disturbed at this ungodly hour – '

'Oh, not to worry about that,' said Lydia. 'Dominic's never had an unbroken night's sleep in his life.' (She referred to the smelly toddler whom Clara so disliked.) 'In fact he's the cause of all this, he went and climbed into bed with your Clara and gave her a fright, the little monkey . . . '

I could hear snifflings and squawkings in the background, children's voices raised in dispute, a man's snarl of irritation.

'Oh God,' I said, 'is poor Barry awake too?'

'Oh, don't worry about him,' laughed Lydia. 'He's a real owl, he's just making a nice jug of cocoa, we'll be right as rain in no time. We'll pop Clara back in the morning!'

As she said this I felt a hand touch my shoulder, and looked up to see Constantine about to leave, putting his bloody silly hat on, opening the front door with exaggerated care and delicacy, raising a hand in understanding farewell. Desperately I flapped an arm at him, but of course he was far too well brought-up to stay when my maternal withers were being wrung.

'Thank you, Lydia, you are a brick, thank you so much,' I gabbled, and hung up. But already I could hear the Fiat starting up, and as I reached the gate it shot tangentially from the kerb and bunny-hopped away.

I went back into the kitchen. The teapot stood ready. A residual ribbon of steam rose from the kettle.

With a roar that would have shamed all seven samurai I lifted the teapot (£7.95 at Close Seconds) and hurled it into the sink.

The sink being half-full of murky water, the pot failed to break. But a shower of brown and oily droplets flew to join the hair-dye on my towelling dressing-gown.

Chapter Nine

I woke next day with a mood of deepest indigo and a head like a bucket. Church bells rang, papers arrived, Clara came home and (displaying admirable discretion) went out again. Even Gareth lumbered downstairs while I lay in my bed like a marble effigy, with Spot at my feet and Fluffy on my chest, trying to forget. Only two people could possibly have cheered me, and one of them rang up.

'Morning, campers!' said Bernice. 'It must have been a good do last night, I've got a mouth like a fell-runner's crotch.'

'Hallo. Did you get Damon back safely?'

'But of course. I even had a brown ale with Damon's dad, so put that in your pipe and smoke it!'

I was impressed. 'What's he like?'

'Like Barty only not so pretty.'

'Struth.'

'How about you? Anything good happen after we left?'

'Nearly.'

'Only nearly, shit! Did he come back then?'

'Yes.'

'And?'

'And he seemed really keen, but then the phone rang.'

'Look,' said Bernice severely. 'Nobody who's really keen gets put off their stroke by the bloody phone.'

'They do if they're doctors. And anyway, it was for me, and while I was talking he left.'

'I don't know,' said Bernice in an exasperated tone, 'I really don't know. So what next?'

'Well,' I said. 'He's going to be manager of Gareth's football team, so that's something.'

'Is it? I wouldn't know.' There was a brief, gloom-filled silence. 'Tell you what, why don't we meet at the Hideaway one day this week?' She named the luxurious women's health club of which she was a member. 'We can swim with our sisters and talk dirty to our hearts' content.'

'All right. Yes, good idea, I'd like to. I've got to go into Era some time anyway, so I'll try and combine the two.'

'Oh for God's sake *do*, don't squander five quid going into town purely for pleasure, *whatever* you do,' said Bernice, sarcastically. 'Haven't you got some unpleasant elderly relative you could visit at teatime, too?'

'Piss off.'

'Shall we say Wednesday?'

'Why not.'

'Eleven o'clock then, Wednesday, the Hideaway. Perhaps you could manage a rather more action-packed instalment by then.'

'I'll try. 'Bye.'

I felt better for having made this arrangement. And my depression lifted still further when, as I was getting dressed, I heard the letter box click, and subsequently arrested Spot in the act of defending me from a handwritten note, black ink on grey paper.

'Dear Harriet,' I read, or rather deciphered. 'Just the briefest of lines to thank you for an enjoyable evening. The next time of which we spoke need not be long – I shall of course attend the soccer tournament, and Mr and Mrs Atkins also mentioned a disco . . . I do hope your little girl was all right in the end. My thanks again, yrs Constantine.'

I read and re-read this communication, trying to extract

from it that which I wished to find. But it proved tantalisingly elusive. The tone of teasing neutrality seemed to promise something and yet to deny it. I began to realise that Maria's reaction to Richard Hawkhurst was more firmly rooted in reality than I'd supposed. Could it be, I wondered, pulling on my running gear, that all those cold eyes, sardonic smiles and flaming cheeks were not clichés, the jargon of pulp, but actualities? And was I suffering from them right here in Basset Magna in 1984? But he had touched my hand, spoken warmly of there being a next time, said: 'You're so – '

So what, exactly, I wondered? So irresistible? So alluring? So handy in the kitchen? So obtuse? That one word was the missing link which might have moved our relationship (if we could be said to have a relationship) on to a different plane.

Positively buzzing with hypotheses I ran out of the front gate at exactly the wrong moment and found myself moving against a steady current of the faithful, off for their weekly fix of plain man's religion as pedalled by Eric Chittenden. Conspicuously, almost insultingly ungodly in my satinised briefs and Snoopy singlet, there was no alternative but to brazen it out with a turn of speed and a carefree wave as I zig-zagged between the soberly clad churchgoers.

Fortunately, as I passed Trevenda, a useful escape route presented itself, for the Tunnels rarely troubled their Maker, and there was Trevor creosoting his side gate. Seamlessly I cornered and jogged up their path, as if that had been my express intention all along. Three sets of closely drawn curtains on the first floor showed that Jason, Nigel and Michelle were still, mercifully, asleep. Of Brenda there was no sign.

'Trevor, good morning!' I cried, whisking through the half-open gate and nearly weatherproofing the both of us. 'Is Brenda about?'

'She's still upstairs,' said Trevor. Carefully he set down the can of creosote, with the brush resting across it, and pushed the gate to behind him. He had a large wad of lint strapped to the left side of his head, and over his ear, and looked distinctly peaky, but he managed a small smile.

'You're looking very sporty, Harriet,' he said. 'How many miles today?'

'I don't know yet, I've only just left home. What happened to you?'

He touched the wad gingerly. 'I walked into something.'

I considered that he'd fielded that one quite nicely, considering.

'Is Brenda still asleep?'

'No, no, no, I'll give her a shout.'

He went past me, and in through the back door. 'Come in, why don't you,' he offered, and I stepped over the threshold into the kitchen. Trevor did not shout, but went upstairs, having first removed his shoes, and I surveyed my surroundings. They presented a picture of serenity. The window was mended, the draining board clear and wiped, the Winter Wonderland all safely housed in cupboard and on shelf. The soothing aroma of beef browning in the oven wandered lazily through the air.

Trevor re-entered. 'If you'll excuse me,' he said, 'I'll leave you to it and get back to my gate.'

'Of course.'

Close on his heels came Brenda, in a navy boiler suit and espadrilles. I was sure she had chosen navy for its supposed slimming qualities, but unfortunately it was impossible to ignore the resemblance to Churchill.

'Brenda – was I disturbing you?'

'I was having a sort out,' she said, not answering the question, but she looked perfectly calm and I did not anticipate any airborne sauceboats.

'I came to ask a favour, actually,' I explained. 'I did call the other day but – '

'I was fighting with Trevor!' she finished, triumphantly.

'Oh, I wouldn't say . . . '

'I would! Trevor told me you'd been when I was taking him to surgery. He was embarrassed, but I said what for? If there's one person in this village who knows about expressing emotion, it's Harriet!'

'Well, I – '

'It's so damaging to suppress anger, isn't it, Harriet? Damaging and unhealthy for a relationship. That's the trouble with Trevor, he's frightened of his own anger.' She'd been

135

reading again. 'I lost my temper, I admit it. I threw things and shouted. I felt I was justified, you know? But now I feel one hundred per cent better!'

Undeniably, the contrast between Brenda, bright-eyed and boiler-suited, and Trevor, ashen and afflicted, was striking. I wondered if Brenda would have felt quite so chuffed if Trevor had rounded on her and broken the fluted flan dish over her head. Still.

'So what can I do for you?' she asked benignly.

Since she was in such a good mood it seemed pointless to beat about the bush. 'I have to go to a book fair in Germany at the end of the month,' I said, 'and I wondered if you could possibly see your way to putting up Gareth and Clara for three nights. It will be term-time, they can always go home for a bit after school, Clara will want to ride her pony and Gareth can do his homework, it's just a case of – '

'Of course! Say no more. They can come here, my three will be thrilled to bits!' I had leave to doubt this. The closest I had ever come to seeing the junior Tunnels thrilled was when Jason had framed me a few days ago. All the same, their reaction to the arrangement was unimportant. What counted was Brenda's co-operation, which it appeared I had in full.

'That's sweet of you,' I said. 'I'll leave a key with them. There's just one other thing.'

'You only have to say, Harriet.'

'My gardener will come on the Thursday. I don't suppose you could just pop down and see he's all right, about mid-day?'

'I'll do more than that, I'll take him something in a thermos,' said Brenda.

'He's not awfully sociable,' I warned. 'But he cut his hand working for me the other day, and since I don't stamp his card or anything I don't want to take any risks.'

'Just leave the whole thing to me.' Brenda went to the oven and opened the door, exposing a vast chunk of spluttering topside. 'Don't worry about a thing,' she added through the belching steam. 'You just have fun at the fair.'

As I jogged on my way I reflected on what I had come to think of as the Brenda syndrome. To be hurling sauceboats one day, to be queenly and obliging the next, that was surely the sign of being what the French call 'heureuse dans le peau'. Whereas my skin this morning, both actually and figuratively, felt like an old army blanket that had been left out in the rain. Brenda had invoked me to poor Trevor as the high priestess of self-expression, than which nothing could have been further from the truth at this moment.

But as I hit the bridleway, exercise began to have its usual therapeutic effect, and my spirits rose. It was a fine morning and there was plenty to look forward to. As Constantine had pointed out, there was the soccer tournament next Saturday, and the Toms disco not long after. The eager excitement with which I anticipated these two events was evidence of my altered state. B.C. – Before Constantine – I should have gone to almost any lengths to avoid them. And in three weeks' time there hovered the Buchfest, an entirely unknown quantity, but at least representing three days away from home at Era's considerable expense. Who knows what might occur between now and then? As I became increasingly aerobic so my head swirled with fantastic possibilities.

More immediately, I should have a pleasant day in London on Wednesday, the first half spent with Bernice in the Hideaway, the second spent with the Erans as they apprised me of my programme at the Buchfest. By the time I got home I was positively benign, and took Gareth and Clara to the Wagon and Horses for lunch where we ate microwaved pasties and drank gaseous shandies in the garden, without a single twinge of conscience.

By Wednesday morning I was inordinately glad of something positive to do which would take me out of the house. Forty-eight hours of relatively undisturbed work had advanced *TRT* wonderfully but had left me feeling like an O, and a jittery one at that. I had forgotten (after fourteen years of marriage, one does) just how detached a state is that of being in love, or lust. One exists only through the lust-object. One may be busy, but one is never involved. Every other activity is transcended by the overwhelming desire to fuck.

It was a hazy, promising morning as I drove to the station, and I daydreamed. In spite of the entirely carnal nature of my feelings for Constantine, these daydreams comprised a sort of soft-focus rustic idyll. There was I, in dirndl skirt and artfully disarrayed peasant blouse, gambolling through waist-high corn bright with poppies . . . and here was Constantine in flowing white shirt and skin-tight trousers, bounding in hot pursuit, his usually well-groomed hair flopping all over the place, his arms flung wide . . . When he caught up with me, which he did with very little difficulty, we embraced and sank to the ground, to be hidden by the corn, the fluttering surface of which supplied, like the waves of the sea, the necessary implication. In my daydream we were careless of the prickly and insect-infested discomfort of our surroundings, and no irate landowner apprehended us for flattening his crops. It was all amazingly like *LDG, TRT* and the rest. I should have had a large, red 'L' pinned to my backside.

Pleasantly preoccupied, I drew up at the crossroads between Magna and Parva and waited for a loaded tractor to pass. When it had done so I was confronted by Dr Salmon in his burgundy Mercedes estate, turning right off the Parva road, on two wheels.

Spotting me he braked noisily, straddling the dotted line, and rolled down the window.

'Hallo, Mrs Blair!' He spoke loudly over the strains of Pagliacci.

'Morning, doctor.' I revved the engine nervously. I felt as though I were up before the Beak. Thus conscience, and so forth.

'My young colleague Dr Ghikas told me he saw a patient of mine the other day, Mr O'Connell.'

I broke out in a warm dew of relief. 'Yes, he cut himself on the shears, but he seems quite all right now.'

'I only mention it,' went on Dr Salmon chattily, as another motorist swerved round him like an angry hornet, 'because the poor chap is absolutely terrified of injections, and it was rather bad luck for Dr Ghikas having to cope with that without prior knowledge.'

'He coped splendidly,' I said. 'I was full of admiration.'

'Good, good . . . ' Dr Salmon blipped the accelerator as if to move on, changed his mind and added, 'Didn't ruin your evening on Saturday, did it, my having to hand the torch to Dr Ghikas? Not too many calls I hope?'

'No, that was fine.'

'Excellent, excellent!' He wagged a finger at me. 'Not too many days off now, Mrs Salmon is looking forward to your next yarn!'

I revved again, urging him to be gone. A gigantic container lorry had pulled up in the centre of the road, signalling right, the driver glowering down from his great height with the menacing confidence that comes from superior size.

Dr Salmon glanced in his mirror, said, 'Infernal ruddy juggernauts,' and shot away on a wave of recitative.

I slunk left in the lee of the lorry and spent the rest of the journey to the station practising mature and dignified speeches of self-extenuation in my head.

Bernice was waiting in the foyer of the Hideaway, off Lancaster Gate. She was a member of the club and this permitted me to use the place a maximum of once a month at preferential rates, as her guest.

For a morning's expensive mortification of the flesh, my friend wore yellow cheesecloth harem pants and a white cotton top conspicuous for the absence of much of what is usually there. Her hair encircled her head in a huge bushy cloud. On her feet were gold and purple Turkish slippers with curled-up toes.

'Hail, friend!' She enfolded me in her huge, cuddly, feather-bed-like embrace. 'What's new?'

'Nothing, I'm afraid, I haven't seen him. But he did send a note.'

'He's awfully polite, isn't he?' she said mournfully.

'I think that's charming,' I retaliated stoutly, though actually I shared her misgivings.

'You're a fool to yourself, Blair,' said Bernice without rancour. She surged over to the desk where sat the Hideaway's receptionist, a smooth, foal-like girl in a white overall and childish white sandals.

Bernice laid her bust on the counter like a challenge. 'Mrs Potter and guest for two hours, my dear,' she announced.

'Right you are, Mrs Potter,' said the girl, glancing at Bernice's membership card, and giving her a beige leather book in which to sign her name. Her voice was soft and remote, her face expressionless. It was hard to accept that she and Bernice were of the same species, let alone the same gender. It occurred to me that if I could only steer Clara through her schooldays without mishap she would be well suited to this type of work.

'Just carry on through,' she murmured. 'Enjoy yourselves.'

The foyer of the Hideaway was like one of those upmarket futuristic fitted kitchens – white, shiny, glacially antiseptic. But once Bernice and I had stowed our clothes in lockers and changed into voluminous towelling robes, we entered a very different environment. The decor of the club proper was designed to persuade careworn females that they had been lifted from their mundane worlds of work and family by a benign omnipotent hand, and set down on an island paradise in the Caribbean. Murals depicted azure sea and silver sand, lianas drooped from the ceiling and palms and hibiscus sprouted from artfully disguised pots on the floor, finches cheeped and fluttered in glass enclosures. The only thing missing from this idyllic picture was the presence of an indigenous tribe of delicious and suggestible young men who would be seen and not heard. But it was the raison d'être of the Hideaway to provide a womanly haven, serene and secure from the predations of male swine, and one can't have everything.

We headed first for the jacuzzi. This was Bernice's favourite spot because, she said, it was like being touched up by an octopus. We got in and sat down with our backs against the side. Our companions in the pool were a scaly, weatherbeaten woman in bifocals who was reading F.R. Leavis, and a breathtaking white-skinned redhead who sat motionless, head back and eyes closed, responding, I reckoned, to the octopus.

'Ah . . . ' sighed Bernice. 'This is the life. Who needs sex?'

'I do.'

'Well, in that case you really must come on a bit stronger to your bashful intern.'

'He's not an intern – '

'Don't nit-pick. On your own admission you let him slip through the net the other night. I can scarcely credit it.'

'It's all very well,' I said plaintively, 'but I do have to be a little careful. After all, doctors can be struck off.'

'That's his problem, not yours.'

'And I am a married woman.'

'*That's* your problem, certainly. But then who started this whole thing?'

'Bernice, it hasn't started.'

'That's an extremely nice point. It's all up here, you know,' said Bernice, tapping her temple with her forefinger. 'He knows you're married, the worst thing he can do is turn you down. If he goes along with you then his reputation's his affair.'

'I suppose so.' I raised my feet off the bottom of the pool and watched them bobbing on the surface like a couple of ghostly hands. The F.R. Leavis lady looked at us from beneath her shaggy eyebrows. I was sure she would have been a lot more shocked to be sharing the jacuzzi with the author of *LDG* than with an unscrupulous adulteress.

'Now I'm going to give you some advice,' said Bernice.

'Thank you,' I replied humbly.

'It's your environment as is holding you back,' she went on. 'It's all those kids of yours – '

'I – '

' – and those droves of benighted wildlife, and that one-horse place you live in with all those cross-eyed villagers, and those awful people who work for you – '

'Now look – '

'No, *you* look! Take a bloody good look. I mean what does someone like Damon do for a girl's body image. When you see him wiping the worktops does it make you feel like a pampered female animal? Does it? Or like one no-hoper employing another?'

'That's hardly the point!'

'Pardon me, but I think it is!' cried Bernice, who now had

the full attention of both scaly-skin and the redhead.

'And your books – I mean there's nothing the matter with them, but they don't help, and in that rural slum of yours there they are all the time reminding you of who you are.'

This was too much. 'Steady on,' I said, 'I like them doing that. In my rural slum, as you put it, they are one of the very few self-affirming factors!'

I was pleased with this. I could almost feel a ripple of sisterly appreciation emanating from Scaly and Red at this brave talk of self-affirmation.

'Yes, yes, yes, yes,' snapped Bernice dismissively. This was the first time in all the years of our friendship that there had been even a breath of criticism from her, but she was really making up for lost time. 'I know all that, but they're just trappings, it's all trappings, keeping you in your place. And il dottore, too, for that matter. What you need, both of you but especially you, is a bit of anonymity. Escape the mental and material clutter. Cut the cackle. Just be two free spirits on a foreign strand or whatever.'

She sounded just like one of my books. 'Oh, you mean a dirty weekend.' From the corner of my eye I caught the redhead nodding encouragingly.

'Something like that,' said Bernice.

'And how exactly do you propose I set about arranging it?' I enquired. 'Just breeze into surgery with an Awaybreak for two in Brighton clutched in my sweaty hand and suggest he keeps me company?'

With a leviathan-like slurp, Scaly rose from the pool, reclaimed her robe and flip-flops and stumped off.

'Oh dear,' I said.

'There you go again!' bellowed Bernice. 'What the hell does it matter what she thinks? You're just one more naked punter in here, dear, so what's to lose?'

'Quite right,' put in the redhead.

'Thank you,' said Bernice, and turned back to me. 'Don't ask me how to do it, you're the one who's paid to cook up plots. Use your ingenuity, work it out. I mean aren't those disreputable publishers of yours sending you anywhere, or anything?' She must have read something in my face. 'Of course they are, they're always packing you off on to these ghastly pop music programmes so that you can plug between discs, and so on, you see I know all about it!'

She had struck a chord, I had to admit. It was not the first time that the Buchfest had occurred to me as a possible trysting-place. But even were I to succeed in getting Constantine to Fartenwald the possible pitfalls were legion.

'They never let me out of their sight,' I said. 'It'd be like trying to touch each other up under the noses of half a dozen chaperones.'

'Fiddle-de-dee,' said Bernice. 'There's nothing like a hotel for illicit liaisons, I've read all about it in books.'

The redhead gave a tinkling laugh, said 'Good luck!' and left. Her body was absolutely flawless and temporarily distracted us so that we sat, like a couple of female Marats in the quivering water, gawping enviously.

'Okay,' I said at length. 'I'll think about it.'

We moved on via gymnasium, massage and swimming pool, to the sauna. This was occupied by some very old, probably rich, scrawny ladies from a north London garden suburb. They seemed so stringy and desiccated and so exaggeratedly tanned that I was sure further loss of moisture would result in their turning into wizened husks on the benches. But they cast a look of waspish disdain in the direction of us well-larded people, so the mistrust was mutual.

In the boiling steam and enforced languor of the sauna Bernice and I conducted a more sporadic and desultory exchange than the one we'd had in the turbulent waters of the jacuzzi.

'Arundel's got that telly,' said Bernice.

'He's pleased?'

'He affects indifference, but you know Arundel, vain as hell.'

'What programme?'

'Ummm . . . ' Bernice shifted on the slats with a squeak and a slap, like a juicy steak being turned on a barbecue. 'Can't remember the name. Some arts thing . . . culture for the horny-handed.'

'He doesn't mind that?'

'You must be joking. Think how brilliant he'll look against a background of cartoonists and break dancers and paperback hacks. Saving your presence. In fact,' she continued dreamily, 'I think we are both entering a new phase in our lives. You are about to become a mistress, and I am going to be a glittering media hostess, my board graced nightly by producers, casting directors and rising young actors . . . '

I glanced at Bernice's stupendous bosom and reflected that if the young actors were not already rising they certainly would be when they dined chez Potter.

'Yes . . . ' she mused. 'And Barty will buttle.'

After the sauna we had a cool shower, got dressed, and wound up in the club's health food bar, munching manfully on wholewheat quiche and sipping flat cider. The tropical motif had here been carried to extremes, with triffid-like vegetation on every hand to trap the unwary diner, and a miniature aviary full of glum parakeets who sat pecking their plumage and dropping the occasional faeces on to the sawdust below.

'Who's a pretty boy then?' enquired Bernice rhetorically in passing.

'Cut the crap!' came the response, quick as a flash. 'Peace sister,' added another, more in keeping with the Sapphic tone of our environment. The flat cider, though unpalatable, proved stronger than one might have thought, and over an hour we systematically replaced the fluid and calories that we had shed in the previous two. Glancing about us and giggling we spotted Scaly (still reading Leavis), Red, and the desiccated grannies, all tucking in to their brown pastry with a will.

'You know,' said Bernice, 'every time I come here I hope to be propositioned by another woman, but it never happens.'

'If you're so keen, why don't you take the initiative?' suggested the flat cider airily.

'Yes . . . ' my friend eyed me speculatively. 'Perhaps you and I should give it a go. After all, we know each other already, so we could cut out the chatting up. Absolutely ideal really, and no risk of pregnancy.'

'You're forgetting something,' I said, putting my hand on her shoulder. 'I don't want to.'

'That's right, you don't. I knew there was a hair in the custard,' said Bernice.

It was in this mood of free-ranging sexual reference that we finally strolled out into the sunshine and made our farewells. Bernice's last words to me were: 'Get him on neutral ground – then go for it!' I pondered this in the cab en route to Southampton Row. It was indubitably sound advice, but nowhere near as easy to implement as Bernice made out.

At Era Books I found Tristan sitting in the lobby holding wool for the normally hostile elderly receptionist, Vi. His presence absolved me from the usual burden of proof as to my identity, but such was Vi's sway that Tristan arranged her wool carefully over the back of a chair before coming to my side and bestowing a glancing, antiseptic kiss on my cheek.

'Sorry,' I said, assuming naturally and involuntarily the role the Erans had created for me. 'Am I late?'

'Late, Harriet? I very much doubt it – I don't know when we said.' He meant this to be soothing, but I found it infuriating, with its implication that the arrangement so carefully made was of no real consequence.

I glanced crisply at my watch. 'Two-thirty,' I said. 'So actually I'm not.'

'Of course not,' agreed Tristan. He took me by the arm, as do smiling TV hostesses with the bemused participants in game shows, and steered me to the lift.

'We're going to use the boardroom as it's not in use at the moment,' he told me. 'The others are waiting there.'

We stepped into the lift and stood side by side, looking towards the door and slightly upwards as one does, for some reason, in lifts.

'You're looking especially glamorous,' said Tristan, 'what have you been doing?'

I ignored the somewhat backhanded nature of this query, and told him about the Hideaway.

'That does sound absolutely lovely,' agreed Tristan. 'But isn't it chock-a-block with the anti-depilation lobby?'

This remark was beneath contempt and I forebore to answer it. 'Have you had lunch?' he added, steering me out of the lift.

'Yes, thank you.'

'Because we could always send out for something. Can't have our star author fainting from hunger on the premises.'

'She won't.'

We entered the boardroom. Vanessa, Marilyn and Chris were clustered at the far end of the conference table, smoking and smirking and exuding that air of indolent, privileged secrecy peculiar to publishers who are cooking things up.

Now they rose to greet us, still wearing the tail end of their smirks. Chris leapt forward and put his arm round my shoulders, almost setting my hair on fire with his cigarette.

'Hallo! Hallo! Hallo!' they chorused.

'Come and take a pew,' said Chris, 'and we'll tell you what we've got planned for you.'

I took my seat, and Marilyn spread my programme and itinerary out before me with all the pride and care of a head waiter serving up the specialité du chef.

It was an impressive document, bristling with headings, sub-headings, names, dates and times. If Marilyn's document was to be believed I would not have a moment to call my own at the Buchfest, but I knew better than to take it at face value. Though I had never been to Fartenwald before, I was familiar with its reputation, and I understood the working methods of the Erans. When Marilyn wrote of working breakfasts with American editors, of consultations with Swedish agents, drinks with Danes and dialogues with Germans, of meetings over coffee and exchanges over tea, of dinners with the literati at which I should be the still point of a turning universe – when Marilyn referred to this glittering array of appointments I took it with a generous handful of salt. I knew, and the Erans knew I knew, that my presence at the Buchfest was all that was required, and the rest was just so much Dream Topping. Authors at book fairs were de trop, and for Era Books to be transporting me thither at vast expense would be seen for what it was – a gesture of grandiose optimism, or the politics of desperation, depending on one's point of view. The word would be bruited about over the à la carte menus of an evening: 'They must think a lot of Harriet Blair . . . either that or they paid an arm and a leg for her last one . . . '

'As you see,' said Marilyn, 'we're putting you up at the Fartenwald Dynamik, as befits your status.'

'That's right,' said Vanessa. 'The rest of us are slumming at the Rumpel Inn on the wrong side of town.'

In this matter too I had a firm hold on publishingspeak. My bestowal at the Dynamik was another exercise in conspicuous expenditure. And they were only too happy to return, at the end of a hard day's hyping, to the steins and sauerkraut of the Rumpel Inn where they could discuss their triumphs and disasters free from my inhibiting authorial presence.

'Wonderful,' I said. 'What fun, I shan't know myself!'

The Erans beamed. I could almost hear them relaxing. I was, after all, such a nice author. There had been a teeny hiccup in my behaviour a week or so ago, when Tristan had thought he detected a note of rebellion in my telephone manner, but that was all over and forgotten now, they could see that. I was so obviously grateful for the little treats they were meting out, and so ready to repay their investment with the breezy hard-working charm so often remarked upon by journalists in the better provincial newspapers.

At this moment the boardroom door opened and there before us stood the Great Man of Era Books.

Now I have said that the rank-and-file Erans were almost exclusively out of the top drawer. But no such accusation could have been levelled at their leader, whose origins were in society's shoe locker. Despite his Croesan wealth, his customised Roller, his half-dozen fully serviced luxury homes and his Cheltenham Ladies' College wife, the Great Man was quintessentially common. No officer he, he had come up through the ranks (from the sales force, to be precise) and he allowed no one to forget it. No matter that what he knew about books might have been comfortably inscribed on the head of an Asprey's swizzle stick, he had forgotten more about hiring and firing than the rest of them would ever know.

He was a small, strutting, red-faced bantam-cock of a man with a penchant for the sort of three-piece suits worn by the male Tamla-Motown groups of the late sixties. God knows what his exclusive Savile Row tailor must have suffered in making these monstrosities, with their nipped-in jackets and

147

cropped, double-breasted waistcoats, but the GM had one for every day of the month, usually embellished by a watch chain and a foulard tie of striking and expensive vulgarity.

His thatch of hair and tepee-shaped eyebrows were white, with a strange yellowish gloss, as though stained by the smoke of a thousand Havanas. Though there was never officially a breath of scandal about the GM, it was rumoured that he liked uniforms, and that the CLC wife (who was rarely on public view) was obliged to strut about their mansion in Denham dressed as a member of the Hitler Youth.

The GM was habitually accompanied by a middle-aged Girl Friday, known as the General Fucktotum, who wore strictly tailored suits which made her look like a nurse in the summer and like a traffic warden in the winter, so there was probably some truth in the rumour. Today, in striped seersucker, with a watch pinned to her lapel, she hovered behind the GM's left shoulder like an anxious ward sister showing a crusty consultant round minor gyni.

'Good morning, all you happy people,' said the GM, infecting each tainted vowel and elided consonant with his despised authority. 'What are you doing with my Mrs Blair?'

The conference table quivered beneath the combined weights of the Erans as they shot to their feet. But I remained seated and smiled placidly up at the GM. He treated his top management like the naughtiest class in the school, but he approved of me.

'We're presenting Harriet with her programme for the Fartenwald Buchfest, sir,' gabbled Tristan.

'We're so thrilled that she's agreed to come,' added Vanessa.

'It's going to make all the difference in the world to our paperback promotion,' said Marilyn, and then added hastily: 'Not that there's any doubt it will do wonderfully well!'

'That's right,' agreed Chris. 'Amazing. Sir.'

'It's all very exciting,' I cooed graciously, and was rewarded by the warm waves of gratitude and relief which eddied round me.

The GM laid a solicitous hand on my shoulder.

'Where are you putting Mrs Blair up?' he enquired.

'At the Dynamik,' said Tristan, whose turn it was to speak. 'You know it, I believe, sir.'

'Very probably I do,' said the GM. 'Look after her properly now. Mrs. Blair,' he leaned over and looked into my face, 'besides being a lovely lady, is the mainstay of our fiction list.'

The others all bellowed with laughter in endorsement of this amusing and perceptive remark.

'Mrs Blair will be very comfortable at the Dynamik,' put in the Fucktotum in her efficient, colourless voice. 'It is the best hotel in Fartenwald, sir.'

'I'm delighted to hear it,' said the GM. 'Only the best will do for our star author.'

'Well, thank you,' I said. 'I'm really looking forward to it.'

Another burst of febrile laughter, the GM and I clearly had a double act of which to be proud. Now he bent over me again and murmured sibilantly in my ear: 'My wife tells me you're getting a touch racier these days.'

'Is that so?' I trilled, straight out of the knife box. 'What about my books?'

At this they all laughed so much I feared for their safety, and the GM gave a cold-eyed, approving smile.

'The research is rather taxing,' I added daringly, carried away by my success. I thought the Erans would have a seizure.

In the wake of all this bonhomie, Tristan asked: 'Were you looking for anyone in particular, sir?'

'No, laddie, I came to present my compliments to Mrs Blair.' The GM was notoriously bad at remembering the names of his employees. It was his chief weapon in the class war.

'Will you be coming to Fartenwald, sir?' enquired Chris.

The GM glanced at the Fucktotum, who shook her head. 'I may very well do,' he said capriciously, 'not that it's any concern of yours. You just get on with selling my best author's book.' And with that, the GM gave me a final bone-crunching clap on the shoulder, and left.

For a full minute we all sat and talked nonsense to one another in case he was crouched outside with his eye to the keyhole, spying on us. But when the tapir entered with coffee, revealing a coast that was clear, Chris lit a Marlboro with a trembling hand, and spoke for us all when he said: 'Shit a brick. The man's a sadist!'

That evening as I sat at the tripewriter, there seemed a special appositeness in what I wrote. For I was dealing with Maria's flit, clad as a boy, to the Royalist camp at Bradbury, and I kept thinking of the GM's lady wife, stretched out on her calfskin chesterfield in khaki shorts and knee socks, thrilling empathically with my heroine.

Moonlight, cool and mysterious, I wrote, *bathed the gardens of Kersey House in silver light as Maria slipped from the kitchen door and moved softly in the shadow of the wall, around the house. A sudden burst of coarse male laughter and singing, perilously close, reminded her of the extent of the danger. The Parliamentarians were sitting round their fires, carousing, celebrating a victory which must in truth seem already theirs. Their cannons were trained on the graceful towers of Kersey, their well-fed soldiery had but to wait until starvation brought low the proud and haughty Hawkhursts . . .*

Maria bit her lip. She would not fail them. She would not fail Richard. Her chance of escape lay through the kitchen garden, and out by the old oaken door in the stone wall beyond. It would be a blind spot for the enemy, shielded as it was by a tall hedge of laurel. Once past there, she must walk boldly and put her trust in her new identity . . .

So lost was Maria in these fearful musings that she did not, till it was too late, see the tall figure which barred her way. Then suddenly her wrist was held, her arm bent agonisingly behind her, a rough hand covered her mouth, and a familiar voice snarled in her ear:

'And what have we here, pray? Some clever young pup as wants to bat his pretty eyelashes at the Roundheads and get a coin or two for it? You need a lesson, tyke, and I'm the man to give it to you!'

And with this cavalier talk of treacherous arse-banditry I switched off the tripewriter and went to bed, feeling surprisingly chipper.

Chapter Ten

The days between my trip to London and Saturday, rich with the promise of the soccer tournament, passed in a haze of happy anticipation. Two distinctly encouraging developments had emerged from my meeting with the Erans. For one thing, the GM would not be present at the Buchfest; and for another, I should be staying alone at the grand and luxurious Dynamik. So provided I could persuade the Erans that I was too exhausted in the evenings for anything but the lightest and most workmanlike dinner, the hours of darkness would be mine to do with as I pleased. I took these to be omens, and my heart was consequently light.

The minor domestic irritants which would normally have used up a quite disproportionate amount of my energy, both mental and physical, scarcely affected my pulse rate. Did Gareth need new football boots before Saturday if he was not to suffer total public humiliation? I bought him the best Regis Sports had to offer, plus some machine-washable shin pads. Did Clara wish to enter for the local gymkhana, and to remind me of my responsibilities in that respect? I bearded the viragos of the saddlery in their den, procured tail bandages, stirrup leathers and sheepskin numnah, and furthermore booked the notoriously unreliable blacksmith, Terry Billings, to attend to Stu's hooves some time in the next week. Did Damon want the Friday before the gymkhana off, because he and his new sound system had been hired for the occasion? I gladly granted it, and even congratulated him on this entrepreneurial coup.

Brenda showed up on Thursday, to introduce herself to Declan, as she put it. Before taking her into the garden I summoned Gareth and Clara and told them of the arrangement I had made concerning the book fair. In the face of these fascist tactics, and Brenda's wall-to-wall boiler suit, they were, understandably, the embodiment of sullen, silent reproach, but it would have taken a wholesale insurrection and bloodshed to put me off my stroke today. I left them to their mutinous scowling and bore Brenda off into the garden where Declan was trawling the pond with a lawn rake.

As we approached he lifted the rake, laden with a noisome tangle of rank, black weed, leprous tennis balls and corroded dinky cars dating from Gareth's infancy, and shook it in our faces like a cantankerous Neptune.

'Will you take a look at this?' he growled unnecessarily. 'It's a wonder anything lives down there with all this bloddy rubbish!'

'You're obviously doing a super job, Declan,' I said. 'The fish won't know themselves. I just wanted to introduce you to my neighbour Mrs Tunnel. She'll be keeping an eye on the place when I'm in Germany at the end of the month.'

'Hallo, Declan!' said Brenda, extending her hand democratically, and being ignored for her pains.

'Germany, is it?' he said. 'What do you want with Germany?'

'I'm going to a book fair,' I explained.

'It's one of the drawbacks of being a famous author,' said Brenda. 'Having to go off and leave your family to stay in expensive hotels abroad.' She meant it as a joke, but to Declan it was deadly serious.

'How long will you be gone for?'

'Only three nights. The children will stay at Mrs Tunnel's, they'll feed the pets, and the dog will go to my friend in Barford.' I hoped I was not traducing Bernice, but she had always accommodated Spot in the past and I assumed she would do so again.

'Yes, I'll be popping down with a flask of something tasty,' said Brenda. 'And you must tell me what kind of cake you like,' she added winsomely.

Declan hurled his forkful of sludge on to the ever-growing pile behind him and eyed Brenda. He had very few facial expressions, ranging from surly to homicidal, but now I saw one that was new to me, and I could not quite define it. If I had not known Declan so well I might almost have taken it for – but that was unthinkable.

His features settled back into their customary misanthropic folds. 'What about him?' he asked, jerking his chin in the direction of the house. 'Mr Val Bloddy Doonican there?'

'Oh. Yes,' I said. 'Brenda, there is Damon, the lad who cleans round for me. I'll tell him just to come on the Thursday, shall I? Perhaps he could collect the key off you. It would be helpful if he could tidy up a bit while I'm away . . . '

Throughout this dissertation I was conscious of their separate gazes resting upon me, Declan's full of scorn and suspicion, Brenda's sisterly and enthusiastic.

'Of course!' she cried. 'Just leave the whole operation in my hands. We'll run a tight ship, won't we, Declan? We'll prove that she's entirely dispensable.'

Again that furtive, unsettling expression flitted like a sewer rat across Declan's face, before he grunted his agreement and returned to the pond.

'Quite a character, isn't he?' said Brenda as I walked her to the gate.

'Yes. Yes, he's certainly that.'

'What about the other one? Your cleaner?'

I was just about to say that I didn't think a formal introduction would be of any value, when the window of Gareth's room opened and a large rag-weave rug, obviously intended to be draped over the sill, flew out and landed on Brenda's head, bearing her to the ground.

'Oh dear,' said Damon, looking down on his heaving handiwork. 'Naughty one.'

153

I was still smirking about this as I got ready for the soccer tournament on Saturday morning. It had taken all Brenda's new-found womanly poise not to give Damon the rollocking of a lifetime and disparage him for the inept, adolescent rat fink he undoubtedly was. Instead she had shrugged off the rug, bidden me farewell and strode off up the road as if being dive-bombed by carpets was an entirely unremarkable occurrence, and it was left to me to choke down my laughter and reprimand Damon as best I could.

It was a fine morning for the seven-a-sides. My responsibilities were few. As a committee member without portfolio I had only to display interest by showing up. Besides, I was official sponsor to Dr Ghikas, Great White Hope of the Toms.

In George's absence, I planned to take a bottle of his best claret to donate to the raffle. I knew that the bottle would probably be won by some philistine OAP who would have preferred milk stout, and who would in all probability hand it back in favour of the economy-size drum of ant powder. But the gesture was in keeping with my mood.

The first match was due to kick off at one. Gareth set off for the recreation ground on his bike, a substantial packed lunch in his saddlebag, at ten-thirty.

'You'll be awfully early,' I admonished. 'What on earth will you do?'

'Practise our skills,' said Gareth.

'Well, don't get worn out before you have to play,' I said lamely. What really concerned me was the amount of time that my children spent beyond the reach of my surveillance. I felt, rather vaguely, that I should be supervising them better, but on the other hand their independence and frequent absences from home were among their most endearing features.

'You want us to practise, don't you?' said Gareth slyly. 'I mean you don't want us choking in front of Dr Ghikas, do you? He might change his mind.'

Having sent home this shaft, he pedalled off at break-neck speed. I recalled the scene that my son had witnessed through the window the night of the dinner party, and reminded myself to be careful.

Clara was still at the kitchen table, consuming slice after slice of white toast and pilchard paste. She ran on the sort of fuel that would have made less robust systems silt up and grind to a halt in days.

'What are your plans for today?' I asked.

She shrugged. It was her star gesture. Only when she had set the tone of the exchange with this maddening hunch of her shoulders did she venture speech. 'Riding.'

'Well listen, I shall be round at the football over lunchtime, do you want to join me there for a picnic?'

She looked at me as if I'd suggested a course in old-time ballroom dancing. 'I don't know,' she said. She pronounced it like 'Ivanhoe'.

'Clara, you have to eat!'

'I can make a sandwich here, Mum.' The use of my handle was, I knew, intended to be conciliatory, and I accepted it as such. After all, I didn't really want her with me.

'Okay, but be good now,' I said. 'And if you need me you know where I am.'

'Right.' She sounded suddenly, curiously brighter, as though she had emerged victorious after complex negotiations, though our exchange had been cryptic to a degree. I looked at her more closely.

'Please be sensible.'

She widened her eyes. 'Did I say something?'

I decided, just for once, to take her on her face value, and went upstairs to prepare myself for Constantine on the touchline.

When I arrived at the rec at twelve-thirty I had taken considerable pains to look as though I had taken no pains whatever. I was, I fancied, tousle-haired, fresh-faced, and casually dressed in primrose yellow running shorts and matching T-shirt, and yellow and white trainers without socks. I had abandoned a handbag in favour of a straw holdall which would carry the equipment for maintaining this look throughout the day, plus provisions, and the bottle of claret.

The nerve centre of the operation was Robbo Makepeace's tent and caravan, positioned to one side of the village hall. In the hall itself were various subsidiary attractions such as the raffle, the soi-disant Crazy Horse Saloon administered by the Nutkins (frankfurters, bridge rolls and the inevitable beans), tea, coffee and squash courtesy of Baba Moorcroft, and a crèche run by the rector's wife, Dilly Chittenden. The crèche was like a cake stall in reverse – it filled up within half an hour of the start – and already Dilly, a cheerful well-turned-out blonde, was barely visible above a heaving swarm of infants.

As I entered the hall to deliver my bottle I noted that everything was proceeding, if not according to plan, at least according to precedent. The visiting teams of Under Fourteens were dotted here and there on the rec like colourful groups of Halma men, being subjected to pep talks by their managers. Squads of rival parent-supporters setting up camp round the periphery eyed each other with ill-disguised fear, loathing and contempt. The host team were still in the changing room with Brian Jolliffe, whose swan song this was. Robbo was testing the public address system with a series of sounds like a rogue elephant. Eric Chittenden, wearing his clerical collar to pre-empt the inevitable accusations of cheating which would be hurled in the heat of the moment, was marking out the results board under the icy gaze of the opposition secretaries.

In fact he was not the only one in uniform. The occasion seemed to have brought out the role-player in several people. In the Makepeace caravan I spotted Akela, whose job it was to deal with injuries and complaints (though all but the most serious tended to melt in the heat of her gaze) and she too was fully whistled and woggled. In the hall, when I entered, it was hard at first to see anything through the pall of smoke from the Crazy Horse Saloon, but as I grew accustomed to the atmosphere I discerned Stan and Nita, both dressed like the chorus in *Oklahoma!* Or at least, Nita was, but on mature reflection Stan looked more like Bob Hope in *Paleface*, with bulbous sheepskin chaps and an oddly high, domed stetson.

I waved to them, to Dilly and to Baba, and made my way to the raffle table, presided over by Tanya Lowe. Sukey lay beneath the table, licking her anus with mournful, heavy-lidded relish.

'Hallo, Tanya,' I said, 'I've brought something for you.'

She took George's claret and glanced at the label. 'Somebody'll enjoy a glass of that, I shouldn't wonder,' she said doubtfully.

The other prizes ranged from bath salts, through ant powder and hand cream, to tonic wine. The claret, when set down amid these more plebian offerings, had the awkward look of a Tory candidate canvassing a council estate.

'How did it go with the doctor?' she asked.

'Fine,' I replied. 'He's coming today. And he will manage the team next season.'

'What's he like?'

'Oh . . . ' I shrugged airily. 'He's okay. I mean – '

Fortunately I was prevented from perjuring myself further by the arrival of Tanya's son, Lance. Lance Lowe, at the age of sixteen, was like some hideous heavy in a low-budget Western, complete with premature beer-belly, home-rolled cigarette, cuban heels and lumbering, Mitchumesque walk. Like all baddies, he was usually to be found at the centre of a flotilla of runtish acolytes, anxious to be walked over rather than sought out for arbitrary punishment. Today, ominously, he was alone. Beneath the table Sukey growled.

'Hallo, son,' said Tanya.

'Going to buy some tickets, Lance?' I asked.

'Nah.' He surveyed the prizes on display. 'Daht it.' I felt for poor Tanya. No wonder she turned up at all the committee meetings. But even her look of despairing supplication was not enough to keep me at her side when Constantine might already have arrived.

'Cheerio, Tanya,' I said. 'See you later.'

Outside things were getting under way. The Tomahawks had finally emerged from the dressing room and were about to play on pitch one, that nearest the village hall. Robbo had temporarily abandoned the public address system to arbitrate in a dispute near the results board. Brian Jolliffe stood on the touchline with his bucket, sponge and first-aid box, and Trevor Tunnel, all in black less heavily bandaged than when I'd last met him, was about to referee.

I saw Gareth and waved. Someone waved back, but it was not my son. It was Constantine Ghikas, dressed predominantly in white, hallmark of the single and childless person. He looked, though not angelic, like an angel. And I felt like a soul in purgatory, clamouring at the gates.

'Well,' he said, as I went over to him, 'you look as if you ought to be on the pitch instead of watching.'

'I'm not sure how to take that,' I said.

'You look delightful,' he assured me. 'All that jogging pays off, take my word for it. Now tell me,' he went on smoothly, saving my blushes, 'is your boy playing here?'

'Yes, this is the Tomahawks, in red and white,' I explained. 'And that's Gareth, in central defence.'

'He's a tall boy.'

'Yes, he's very mature for thirteen. I hope he's going to do me credit.'

'I shouldn't worry . . . ' Constantine placed his hand, for a fleeting moment, between my shoulder blades, where it seemed to scorch a hole in the primrose T-shirt. 'After all, I shall be a servant of the club, shan't I? Rather than the other way round.'

In the event, the match was one of those draws after which the opposition (Byefield Badgers) asserted with vehemence and some justification that they had been robbed. The Badgers were all over the Toms for ninety per cent of the game, scored one blinder, and peppered the cross bar with chances. But at the eleventh hour, as a result of a scuffle in the goal mouth which Trevor was powerless to untangle, they suffered an own-goal and had not been able to redeem themselves in the remaining minutes of the match.

'Well?' I asked Constantine, as the two teams moved contentiously off the field. 'What do you think of them? Of course that's not the full team.'

'Gareth is a useful player,' he said. 'No, I really mean that. And the other big boy . . . the one with the moustache – '

'Brett Troye.'

'No, honestly? He's not bad, either. The rest are so-so.'

At this moment Robbo bustled up, clasping Eric round the waist as if he might at any moment try to escape.

'Would it be Dr Ghikas? The name's Makepeace.'

'How do you do, Mike,' said Constantine.

'Sorry? No, Makepeace, Robbo Makepeace, how do you do. And this is Mr Chittenden, our rector, who is also secretary of the Tomahawks.'

'Eric, please,' said Eric.

'Eric,' said Constantine.

Trevor, perspiring and agitated, joined us from the pitch and wrung Constantine by the hand.

'Trevor Tunnel,' he gasped. 'You'll have to excuse me, I walked into something.'

'Of course,' said Constantine.

We stood round him like a barber shop quartet with our heads on one side, waiting, as it were, for the nod.

Robbo rubbed his hands together. 'Well, doctor,' he said, with an air of gleeful anticipation. 'Can we take it that your presence here is a positive indication that you will be joining the club next season?' His eyes flicked to me. 'Harriet here said she would approach you.'

'Oh, she has,' said Constantine, 'and she was most persuasive. I'd be delighted to help out if I can. I've just been acquainting myself with the talent.'

Robbo's eyes rested for a second on my exposed upper thighs. I saw an uncharacteristic lewd joke rising from the long-forgotten depths of his mind like a leviathan, and stepped in quickly to deflect it.

'I think Dr Ghikas feels we were rather lucky there,' I said. Over their shoulders I caught sight of Brian Jolliffe, a picture of dejection, sitting on the steps of the hall. 'Badgers should have won.'

'Perhaps, perhaps,' said Eric. 'But it's a funny game, football.'

This was the cue for a positive hail of clichés.

'That's so true,' said Robbo. 'Live a hundred years, you'll never understand fupbore.'

'It's one thing out here,' said Trevor, a shade pettishly, 'and quite another in there. Quite another.'

'But this is the game's great charm, isn't it?' said Constantine, joining in with a will, 'it's unpredictability? It's not always the best man who wins, that's part of the fascination. I freely admit that football's a passion with me.'

'Oh, doctor . . . !' said Robbo, shaking his head and clasping Constantine's shoulders, much affected. 'You don't know what that does to me, hearing you say that. Fupbore!' He looked round at the rest of us. 'Greatest game in the world when it's played right. And it starts here – ' he thumped his left pectoral with the side of his fist. 'If it's not here – ' more thumping – 'you can't appreciate fupbore, and you can't play it.'

'And that goes for all of us,' said Eric, looking faintly embarrassed.

'Don't run off with any ideas, doctor,' said Trevor. 'That wasn't such a bad game those boys were playing, looked at from my position.'

'Nor from mine, I assure you,' said Constantine suavely. 'The talent is there, without a doubt. And I'm sure they've been soundly coached,' he added tactfully. 'But the thing isn't quite jelling.'

I smiled appreciatively. I knew all about things not jelling. He was using the same terminology that I employed when the Erans asked to read my book. It sounded okay, profound even, but it meant nothing.

'All I can say is, doctor,' said Robbo, having said a good deal, 'it's really good to see you here and welcome you to the club. I'm sure I speak for all of us when I saw how much we look forward to working with you, promoting good fupbore in the area. I hope our lads put on a reasonable show for you – they're good lads really, but they need motivating.'

'Yes, we shall have to see what we can do,' said Constantine.

'Will you join us at our end-of-season family disco next Saturday?' enquired Eric. 'It's usually a good evening.'

'I'm planning to come. Thank you.'

'Excuse me,' said Trevor. 'I'm on.'

This was the signal for our group to disperse, with more hand-wringing and shoulder-clasping. You'd have thought Constantine had just personally rescued the entire club from immolation.

'Golly,' he said as we walked away. 'They do take it seriously.'

160

'Having second thoughts?'

'No, not at all. Commitment's the thing, isn't it?'

'It sounds right, yes.' I felt an incipient giggle contorting my face, but feeling that levity at the club's expense might queer my pitch I quickly smothered it, and said: 'Shall we see where the Tomahawks are playing next?'

From the fixtures board we ascertained that the Toms would be next but one on pitch two. This was on the far side of the rec, on a gentle downward slope which meant that from the village hall only the top halves of the players were visible. Beyond the pitch the rec was bordered by a row of weather-warped cypresses, planted by the parish council some years ago to protect the playing field from the biting wind which hurtled each winter across the flat farmlands of Barfordshire, direct from the Russian steppe. At this time of year that part of the rec would be a pleasantly secluded sun trap.

'Shall we walk round and sit in the sun?' I suggested. 'I brought a picnic.'

'Did you really? What, enough for two?'

'Certainly.'

'That sounds wonderful. I was just thinking it was Mrs Atkins's hot dogs or nothing.'

'No contest,' I said, a shade uncharitably, but fortunately he laughed.

Down on the south side of pitch two it was hot and virtually unpopulated except for a linesman with his back to us. We sat on the grass and Constantine accepted a chicken leg and a mugful of Valpolicella. Badgers and Cougars got under way, but we didn't pay them much attention.

'Tell me,' said Constantine in a conversational tone, 'do you miss your husband?'

I nearly choked on my pepperami. 'Sorry?'

'Your husband – do you miss him?'

Now this was undoubtedly the moment at which the woman practised in the arts of extramarital coquetry would have been ready with some amusing quip, both ambiguous and alluring, with which to wind in the fish. Sadly, I was not that woman.

'No,' I said.

'Ah.'

'I mean,' I continued, in an awkward rush of elucidation, 'you asked if I actually missed George and I – '

'Said no.'

'Yes.'

'Perfectly straightforward.'

I glanced at him. He wrapped his chicken bone in his paper napkin and licked his fingers. Then he picked up his beaker of plonk and very delicately removed a small insect from its surface with his finger and thumb. I had the unnerving experience of not only not knowing the score, but not having the foggiest whose court the ball was in.

I took refuge, as I so often did, in food, and rummaged in my holdall.

'Would you like some cherries? Or a yoghurt?'

'Cherries sound nice.'

As Badgers and Cougars changed ends, I placed the brown paper bag on the grass between us and we helped ourselves, in silence. My silence was the hot-cheeked, dry-mouthed one of the totally tongue-tied, his the serene and contemplative one of the man in charge. Occasionally, as the final action-packed minutes of the match were played out before us, our hands met in the bag, fingers scrabbling and feeling for the fruit, prising the ripe ones off their stems and carrying them to our mouths. Some of the cherries were over-ripe and bruised, exuding a good deal of sticky juice. It was impossible, surely, for him to ignore the resemblance between the cherries and those parts of the body with which our fingers might otherwise have been engaged?

We ate the cherries and stared unseeingly as whistles blew, flags were waved, fouls declared and free kicks awarded. As we ate, we blew out the stones, which soon formed a ragged line in front of us – the asterisks, as it were, which in the past I had used to such good effect in my novels – his a little further away than mine.

The match ended and Badgers, Cougars and attendants moved away over the rising ground towards the administrative nucleus, while the rogue elephant trumpeted instructions. We were left alone.

162

'The other night,' said Constantine, 'when I came back, after the dinner party . . . '

'Yes?' I barked.

'I can't pretend my motives were entirely polite.'

'Weren't they?' I was overtaken by a dizzying sense of absurdity. We were still neither of us looking at the other, but eating cherries at a terrific rate and blowing out the stones like machine gun fire. Even at this moment of delicate sexual tension I could not help thinking that the inevitable loosening of our respective bowels might pip us, so to speak, at the post.

'You don't behave like a grass widow,' he said. 'You're so – '

I caught my breath. This was it, he was going to supply the missing link.

'So – tempting,' he concluded.

It was, like the rest of him, perfect. I could not have dreamed up an ending to his sentence which more smoothly married flattery with expediency. The word 'tempting' projected on to me the luscious, passive availability of a cream cake . . . and in the same way portrayed him as the helpless victim of a powerful, but inert, allure. We were both, by virtue of that word, innocent flotsam tossed on a wild and raging sea of lust.

'Thank you,' I said.

It never occurred to me that it might not be a compliment. And any doubts were dispelled, galvanically, by the feel of his hand slipping inside the elasticated waist of my running shorts, beneath the clinging edge of my St Michael briefs, and between the cheeks of my backside, until it rested beneath me, his long, knowledgeable fingers exploring, gripping and probing as they had not two minutes since in the bag of cherries.

I sat motionless, a human shishkebab, all thought and feeling concentrated on my skewered cunt. I pictured his finger, as on a TV screen, like one of those enchanting little rodents so beloved of David Attenborough, bustling about its cross-sectioned burrow, fitting as snugly as a cock in a condom.

'Golly,' I squeaked, like Merril of Mallory Towers on hearing she's been voted most popular girl in the school. 'Steady on.'

163

'Don't worry,' said Constantine. 'I shall.'

I closed my eyes. He continued with his deluxe four-star internal examination. I remembered, swooning, the appearance of his hand, muscular, tapering, scrupulously clean. Undoubtedly he must have handled, in the course of his work, the private parts of innumerable thirty-five-year-old women, and remained unmoved. Those same fingers which now had me reeling on the turf of pitch two like a thing possessed must have probed a hundred vaginal passages, kneaded breasts without number, conducted foraging parties round many a shrinking cervix . . . had plunged the hypodermic into Declan.

'Please . . ' I gasped politely. My head was beginning to go back, I couldn't remain sitting much longer, and his breath, too, was now coming thick and fast. Coming, coming, coming . . . The rogue elephant announced that Tomahawks would now play Cheveley Wildcats on pitch two.

'Yes?' replied Dr Constantine Ghikas, belatedly.

'I can't - '

'Hold on - '

'My God - '

'Just go with it - '.

'But - '

'You can do the same for me some time - '

'Oh - !'

The scarlet and white phalanx of the Tomahawks appeared over the rise like an Apache raiding party, and behind them came their old rivals the Wildcats, in a bilious livery of purple and yellow. As all twenty-two thundered towards us I reached a tumultuous and bumpy climax on the hard summer turf, and was still riding its eddying wake as they clustered round the ref for the toss.

It seemed incredible that they could not see what was going on. Surely I was scarlet, my eyes bulging like cue balls, my knees quivering and my pelvis threatening to bore a hole straight through to Australia? But no, the game began, Gareth even managed a small wave, the linesman was charging back and forth in front of us as if nothing had happened. Never had I watched a game of soccer with such concentration. But as we sat there watching Cheveley take the ascendancy, so we were both conscious of a small noise behind us. I was washed up on the dry land of reality with a sickening thud. We both glanced over our shoulders, and as we did so Constantine removed his hand with exquisite delicacy from my knickers.

We were just in time to see, beyond the grim ranks of the parish council evergreens, the yeti-like back view of Lance Lowe, lumbering stealthily away. From one pudgy hand swung the half-empty bottle of George's treasured claret. Out of nowhere, there came into the forefront of my mind the closing lines of a popular verse. 'You can tell a man who boozes from the company he chooses . . . and the pig got up and slowly walked away.'

Taking our cue from the pig, Dr Constantine Ghikas and I rose, and set off round pitch two, in opposite directions.

Talk about post-coital triste. If anyone had apprehended me as I plodded behind the Wildcats' goal I should first have brained them with the half-full bottle of Italian red, and then burst into hysterical tears. As it was I paused for a second while a goal-kick was taken, and there was Constantine, a solitary figure in sparkling white, apparently gazing back at me from the opposite end of the pitch, through the Tomahawks' net. The obvious metaphor was too much for me, and I emitted a loud honking sound which in *TRT* would have been described as a choking sob.

The Wildcats' goalie, all of thirteen, glanced over his shoulder.

'Bless you,' he said.

Chapter Eleven

The first few days of the ensuing week were the purest purgatory. Constantine and I had spent the remaining hours of the soccer tournament staying as far apart as was commensurate with our roles of committee member and manager-to-be. He behaved with absolutely spine-chilling poise (though I noted, with some small satisfaction, a grass stain on the seat of his white jeans), whereas I was a quivering, knock-kneed wreck. The suspicion that Lance Lowe might have been watching us was almost too horrible to bear, so I pushed it to the back of my mind, there to fester like an unattended sore. Guilt at the enormity of what I had done, or at least allowed to happen, hovered over me like the smoke from the Crazy Horse Saloon, and there was no opportunity to smooth things over with Constantine, for the others now took possession of him and even bore him off for a drink at the Wagon when the tournament was over. Greenhorn that I was, I could not decide whether digital sex on the touchline constituted the start of something big or the end of a beautiful friendship.

I was not to remain in ignorance for long. Wednesday was the date agreed on by Nita and myself for our trip to the Regis cash-and-carry, and from these inauspicious beginnings there sprang a sequence of events which was to leave me in no doubt as to which way the wind blew.

We set off at one-thirty in the Nutkins' camper-van, and spent a good hour at the cash-and-carry discussing the relative merits of different brands of crisps, and meticulously counting the pickled onions in catering-size jars. Or at least Nita threw herself into these calculations with a will, while I pushed the trolley and endorsed her conclusions. Much as I disliked the feeling that she had a hook in me after the night of the dinner party, I could not afford to ignore it, particularly after the events of Saturday.

'Toms did well on Saturday!' she remarked, scrutinising monster drums of frankfurters in brine. 'You must be pleased, Harriet, putting up a good show for the doctor.'

'What?' I felt the proverbial chilly moisture beading my brow.

'Gareth and the other lads – they did well for the doctor. Middle of the league, weren't they?'

'Oh – yes, I believe so.'

Nita selected two tins of the frankfurters and moved on to the giant flagons of ketchup. I trundled rebelliously in her wake.

'He's a charmer, Dr Ghikas,' she said. 'We had a little accident on our country evening, you know, and he couldn't have been more obliging, really entered into the spirit of things.'

I remembered the hat after Baloo's accident, but didn't like to mention it, since for me to have seen it he would obviously have had to call on me in the small hours.

'Will he be coming to the disco?' asked Nita.

'As far as I know.'

'I'm definitely booking a dance!' She hunched her shoulders and gave me a cheeky, confiding little smile. 'Now then – a nice piece of mild cheddar and some spreading marge . . .'

It was a quarter to three when we eventually parked the van outside my front gate. I was to take charge of the non-perishables, while Nita would take the rest home to store in her freezer. As we opened the back of the van, the Ghikasmobile drew up behind us, and Constantine put his head out of the window.

'Afternoon, ladies!' he called. 'Need a hand?'

'I should say so!' cried Nita. 'Lovely!'

He got out. He was in his shirtsleeves. I definitely needed a hand. His.

'Hallo, Harriet,' he said cheerfully, branding me once more between the shoulder-blades. 'I say, what have you been doing, getting supplies for the fall-out shelter?'

'Food for the disco,' explained Nita. 'You are coming, aren't you?'

'You couldn't keep me away. Are you unloading everything here?'

'No,' I said firmly. 'Just the bottles and tins.'

I opened the front door and the three of us brought the stuff in and piled it on the kitchen table.

'Anyone for a cold drink?' I asked when we'd finished.

'I'd love to, but I must tootle off,' said Nita. 'Everything to do and no time to do it, same old story!'

We came to the gate and saw her off in the camper-van, and then I turned to Constantine.

'Cheerio. Thanks for the help.'

'Don't I get the cold drink?'

'Yes – sorry, yes of course, if you'd like one.'

We went back into the kitchen. The presence of Fluffy and Spot, and the distant tootings of the guinea pigs, all soliciting for food, somehow served to underline the absence of humans. We were very much alone.

I had assembled squash, lemon slices and ice cubes, and was running the cold tap when he grabbed me.

Now, Erica Jong has immortalised the zipless fuck – that free and easy congress untramelled by the formalities of courtship or foreplay – but I had never thought to experience it myself.

Which all goes to show how wrong you can be. Within literally seconds of Constantine's clasping me round the waist, we were at it like an animated cement mixer, rattling, rolling and pounding against the door of the fridge. Even in the considerable heat of the moment I found myself thinking that

he must have done this kind of thing before, to have perfected such astonishing legerdemain with regard to women's clothing. For my afternoon with Nita I had been wearing tight jeans and a belt, a long-sleeved T-shirt and a waistcoat. For the purposes of casual intercourse I represented a sartorial Alcatraz. But if I was Alcatraz, he was the Bird Man. My God, I thought to myself, if this is his pitch with riveted jeans, my yellow elasticated jogging shorts must have looked like the gates of the Perfumed Garden flung wide.

Such had been my (albeit latent) anticipation, and such his own speed and enthusiasm, that the entire coupling, with satisfaction on both sides, took less than five minutes.

On disengaging, we both sank to the floor where several ice cubes were melting rapidly, to form an icy puddle. In the sink, the cold tap was still running busily.

'Heavens,' I gasped. 'If the four-minute warning ever comes, I'll know who to send for.'

'That's right,' agreed Constantine chattily, giving my cheek a huge lick like a calf with a block of sea salt. I had pulled up my pants but my skin-tight jeans still hobbled me neatly round the knees. My waistcoat was off, my T-shirt round my neck, and my bra undone.

'Just look at me,' I said.

'I am.'

'You took me by surprise.'

'Did I?' He sounded genuinely amazed. 'I must say I thought we'd dealt with the necessary preamble.'

It was then that I finally realised that I was into a whole new ball game.

I waved goodbye, not without certain misgivings, to Bernice's polite and bashful intern. I had been uneasy in my role as predator; my unease was at an end. I had thought that I knew my subject but, as my friend would have said, I couldn't have been wronger. A delightful, but distinctly dangerous future stretched ahead.

He put his arm round me and kissed me. All his caresses were characterised by an extreme incisiveness.

'I can't tell you,' I mumbled, 'how worried I've been since Saturday . . .'

'Oh, really . . . ?' He pushed his hot, wet tongue so deep in my ear I thought it might come out the other side. 'Why on earth was that?'

'Um . . . well . . . you know, it was all a bit unexpected . . . and then that boy might have seen us . . . '

'What boy?'

'You know – the fat one – he was sitting behind us all that time.'

'Oh, really? Good experience for him.'

He planted his open mouth firmly over mine, at the same time clasping a breast in either hand. I was completely transported. If a second helping was on offer I could very easily stand it. What with his enveloping muscular warmth, the now tepid puddle of melted ice beneath us, and the smooth, chill surface of the refrigerator at my back, I was in an agonisingly acute state of sensory arousal, goose pimples in some places, perspiration in others, extreme readiness everywhere.

We had just slithered, murmuring and squelching, into a more orthodox position when I heard the gate click shut and open again, and this sharp douche of reality reminded me that it was about the time that Clara came home from school.

But if I had envisaged being the fearful, cautious partner, leaping up and leaving my lover in a discarded heap on the floor, I was wrong again. As with answering the telephone, protection of his status must have been as natural to Constantine as breathing. With the same lightning speed with which he'd jumped me in the first place he shot to his feet, adjusted his dress, flattened his hair and was at the sink filling a glass, leaving me to get my act together as best I could. Crouched over and clutching at my jeans I hobbled like a frantic Quasimodo to the downstairs cloakroom.

As I did up fastenings and peered at my new-style cuckolding self in the mirror, I heard Constantine talking to Clara in the kitchen. And the best of British luck, I thought.

But when I joined them, they appeared to have struck up an immediate rapport.

' . . . so you'll be there too?' he was asking genially, leaning back against the sink and sipping his drink, relaxed as you please. He wasn't even flushed.

'Yes,' said Clara. 'Mummy doesn't like discos, but I do.'

'Why don't you like them?' asked Constantine.

'Too noisy,' I grunted. I seemed to have lockjaw.

'Sign of old age, Ma,' said my daughter.

Constantine drained his glass and set it down on the draining board, smacking his lips. 'That was most welcome. I must be off.'

'Must you?' I asked.

'Yes. Duty calls.'

'Thank you for – ' I flapped a nerveless hand at the mountain of provisions on the kitchen table – 'lending a hand.'

'Not at all. Goodbye, Clara! Glad I was passing at the right moment.'

I opened the front door for him. My legs were like a couple of those infernal frankfurters in brine, damp and bendy.

'See you soon,' I said. 'And thanks again.'

Without even checking on Clara he leant over and sucked my neck.

'My pleasure,' he said. And went.

Back in the kitchen Clara was taking a jug out of the fridge. 'Yuk!' she complained. 'The milk's slopped all over everything, and it wasn't me that slammed the door.'

I opened my mouth to make some extenuating remark, but even as I did so she put down the jug, bent over and picked up my waistcoat from where it still lay on the floor.

'This is all soggy too,' she remarked, dangling it from finger and thumb and then lobbing it in my direction. 'And you're *always* telling me not to drop things wherever I take them off!'

'Sorry,' I said.

When I woke next day I was just a great big silly smile on legs. So rapid had been the turn of events the previous day that I'd scarcely had time to appreciate their implications, but now that they had sunk in I was so elated I was practically airborne. I found that I was spattered with bruises, and there was a red mark on my neck, but far from feeling any discomfort I glowed rosily all over as if I'd been given a good rubdown with a rough towel. I was so benign and relaxed that I did not once quiz

Gareth about his homework, nor did I apprehend Clara for going to school in jeans.

There was no doubt now that there would be no shame in asking Constantine to come to Fartenwald for at least part of the time. Indeed, it appeared there was no shame, full stop. I felt as if I'd been running a race in the dark, thinking myself last, and had suddenly burst into daylight and crossed the finishing line as winner. It was heady stuff. And as Bernice had predicted, I was like a junkie, gasping for it. The next occasion could not come too soon for me.

Fate, it appeared, was colluding with me, for while we were eating breakfast, American paperback copies of one of my earlier works, *Flight from Love*, arrived in the post. Or to be more precise the postman bellowed 'Parcel!' and lobbed them over the gate, in order to avoid a close encounter of the canine kind.

I opened the package on the table, and took out a couple of copies.

Gareth immediately took one and scanned the front cover.

'Erk,' he said. 'Bo Derek meets Godzilla.'

'Don't be silly,' I said automatically, but in truth the cover wasn't too good. I seemed to remember the story was a latter day version of the fable of Beauty and the Beast, and the somewhat literal transatlantic interpretation featured – well – Bo Derek and – '

'Who's the bloke in the background?' asked Gareth, through cereal. 'A pirate?'

'A sea captain,' I said. 'Sholto Macfadyen.'

Clara took a copy. 'Medallion Man,' she offered, and began riffling through the pages.

'Looking for the dirty bits again?' said Gareth.

'There are no dirty bits,' I reproved him.

'Pull the other one, Ma,' said Gareth, 'it's got a synthesiser on.'

Clara began reading the blurb on the back. 'It says here, ''Katrina – a woman of two worlds, a woman divided, a woman torn between passion and honour, love and pity. Katrina – two men loved her until death. And you will never forget her.'' God.'

'Yes, well . . . ' I mumbled. There was no defence for paperback blurbs. I just hoped that the reading public was man enough to accept that publishers have a jargon of their own, like estate agents, which properly interpreted does no one any harm.

'Who gets her in the end then?' asked Gareth. 'Godzilla or the ugly one?'

'I'm not telling you,' I said.

'For Pete's sake, Ma, I'm not going to *read* it.'

'Sholto gets her.'

Clara pushed her chair back with a screeching sound. 'And they lived happily ever after at Knot's Landing.'

'Out!' I cried, brandishing a copy of *FFL*. 'Out, out, out! And Clara, put Stu in the loosebox, the blacksmith is supposed to be coming.' I would not have thought it possible for my morale to rise any higher, but on taking a further, undisturbed look at *FFL*, it did so. I was a writer, and here was the solid, irrefutable, printed proof. The phrase 'latest bestseller' was balm to my soul. I had a body of work, and today it had grown by one more volume. These few cubic inches of paper and coloured cardboard were my passport to the real world, my claim to an identity beyond that of involved village matron.

What's more, *FFL* would be my passport this morning to The Rickyard, Fore Street. Thoughtful soul that I was, I should take a signed copy over for Constantine's mother. I glanced at my watch. But not just yet. A little later, and surgery would be over.

I zoomed upstairs and assaulted the tripewriter. The under-gardener – his name was Jamie, the working classes always used diminutives – in the process of giving Maria the good hiding she so richly deserved, had discovered that she was not what she seemed.

'God's blood, 'tis a maid!' he gasped, as Maria's thick dark hair cascaded down her back, and her all-too-womanly body sprang to meet his rough hands as they ripped the leather waistcoat. ' 'Tis Miss Trevelyan!'

'That is so!' hissed Maria, glad of the darkness that hid her burning face, and the tears of humiliation which stung her eyes. 'And you are too quick to strike, sir, when it is your safety that I seek!'

'My safety?' She heard the bafflement in his voice now, and his

173

hands, which had gripped her shoulders like a vice, became gentler. 'How so?'

'I am dressed thus to pass by our enemies unnoticed, and to carry word to the King's men at Bradbury. Thanks to you we might both have been killed! Now will you let me pass?'

She was trembling with fury, but as she tried to wrench free of his grasp and to catch up her flowing hair, he held her more firmly and then drew her close against him, so that her heart, like a captive bird, pounded against his.

'By all that's holy, you have spirit, Maria Trevelyan . . . ' he whispered as his hard, demanding mouth came down on hers.

It was all over bar the shouting. Only the fridge was missing. I didn't even bother with the asterisks. And then Maria was on her way, much emboldened after this mid-flight refuelling, leaving Jamie to button his flies in the shadow of the house.

I put on the yellow shorts and top which had proved so successful at the weekend and went downstairs. Declan was in the garden, hoeing, but feeling that an exchange with him might tarnish my excellent spirits, I simply shouted that I was going out for a while, and set off on Gareth's racing bike, with the copy of *FFL* clipped to the back. The hard, narrow seat of the bike bore a quite striking resemblance to those parts of Constantine with which I had intimate acquaintance, and as I dismounted and tottered to the front door, I conjured with his address . . . The Prickhard, Fore Play . . . Ah me, but the creative imagination was a wonderful thing.

On this occasion Anna Ghikas answered my ring almost at once. She wore designer jeans and a white collarless shirt. I experienced again that slight twinge of inferiority, but comforted myself with my secret.

'Hallo!' she cried, opening wide the door in the most welcoming way, 'Come in and have a glass of wine – I am.'

'Are you sure? I'm not disturbing you?'

'From what, my dear?' she tossed over her shoulder as she led me into the living room. 'No, I'm off on the old wreck trail in Turkey the day after tomorrow.'

A wine box stood on the table among piles of books and papers. The marmalade cat sat on the window seat in the position George called 'shouldering arms', washing itself.

'You're in the middle of packing up,' I said.

'Yes, and how nice to get an excuse to stop.' She fetched a second glass from the corner cupboard, and furnished us both with a shot of Medium White Table.

'Kostaki tells me he saw you the other day.'

'Yes.'

'At the football, wasn't it? I'm awfully glad you got him involved in that, he'll enjoy it and it will keep him out of mischief.'

'It's very good of him.'

'He likes to keep his hand in.'

'I noticed that.'

'Come and sit down.' She led me out on to the patio and we sat down.

'I thought you might like this,' I said, handing over *FFL*, inscribed more informally this time: 'To Anna, from Harriet, with love'.

She took it with an expression of delight. 'Oh, look at this, how simply gorgeous! And you simply couldn't have brought it at a more opportune moment. I absolutely devour books when I'm working. All those long hours in the tent, usually with some obscure affliction of the digestive tract. *Flight from Love*, what fun, and the American edition, too! But your covers don't do you justice, do they?'

'You're polite to say so.'

'No, no, no, your books are nothing like so obvious as their covers suggest.'

'Thank you.'

'Kostaki's not here, I'm afraid,' she went on, setting the book aside and displaying an unnerving awareness of where my true interest lay. 'But he usually turns up around lunchtime.'

'Oh, I'm not hanging about getting under your feet,' I said firmly. I could wait. Just about. 'I just cycled over to give you this. When did you say you were off?'

I could remember perfectly well, but it was still nice to hear her say it again. I was beginning to see The Prickhard in a new light, as the empty, private pleasure palace, child-free and pet proscribed, in which Constantine and I might rattle fridges and assault posture springing to our hearts' content. I felt positively affectionate towards Anna Ghikas.

I rose and held out my hand. 'I do hope your Turkish expedition will be a success,' I said warmly.

'Thank you, my dear. The tricky part is the raising of the mast.'

Only for some, I thought. 'Please get in touch when you get back,' I said. 'Perhaps I'll have another book for you by then.'

I pedalled back to Magna with a light heart and a damp crotch. The slight delay in the making of my arrangements was actually rather titillating. I did not go straight home, but cycled instead the extra hundred yards to Stu's field, to see if Terry Billings had arrived.

To my surprise his orange Ford Anglia with the foam rubber dice in the rear window was parked by the stable door. Of all the Little Men, Terry was the least reliable. Only the severe dearth of blacksmiths in the Basset area made it possible for him to remain in business. Not only was he unpunctual, but cross-eyed as well, which you would have thought was a serious defect in a blacksmith. I lived in the not entirely frivolous expectation of seeing a horse pass by with a horseshoe nailed to its knee.

Terry was a stout, middle-aged Teddy boy in whom a slim and sultry James Dean struggled to get out. Even now as I parked my bike and approached the loosebox I could hear Eddy Cochrane delineating the 'Three Steps to Heaven' at full blast over the roar of the calor gas fire and the clash of hammer on nails.

I peered over the half door. Stu was tied up facing me. At her far end was Terry, his mouth full of nails.

'Morning, Terry!' I shouted.

He made a circular motion in the air with his free hand. Stu, less welcomingly, laid back her ears and bared long yellow teeth at me.

'Everything okay?' I bawled.

'Yup.' Terry banged home a final nail and turned down the transistor. His large, mauve-tinted spectacles were pushed to the top of his head, so that which Terry himself referred to as his 'stiggertism' was on plain view. I wondered what had originally attracted Mrs Billings to her husband and concluded that perhaps the whole thing had been a mistake and he had been looking at someone else.

'Getting the old girl straight for the gymkhana, then?' asked Terry.

'That's right.'

'She's a good old girl, this one,' he remarked, giving Stu a punch in the flank. 'Never gives me any bother.'

'Good,' I said.

'Old donkey down the road the other day kicked me glasses clean off me face,' confided Terry, lifting the glasses off his head to emphasise the point. 'Eighty pound these cost, to correct me stiggertism, and the old bugger booted 'em right in the air.'

I was impressed. 'And they weren't broken?'

He replaced the glasses on his nose. 'Nope. 'Oof got me on the way down, but the glasses was all right.'

'What a relief. Did you need stitches?'

His eyes swivelled wildly for a moment, as though I had mentioned trepanning.

'Nope. Bit of TCP put me right.'

'Wonderful. Now what do I owe you?'

The last thing Terry said to me was that he would see me at the gymkhana but I did not stop to wonder why, after years of absence, he should suddenly take it into his head to attend.

That evening, with the house and garden orderly in the aftermath of Damon and Declan, and the children absorbed in liquidating aliens on the home computer, I rang the Ghikas number.

Anna Ghikas answered the phone. 'Yes?' Faintly, in the background, I could hear the strains of some exquisite, elaborate violin music.

'Hallo again, it's me, Harriet,' I said boldly and casually. 'Is Constantine by any chance there now? I've got a message for him from the football committee.'

'Yes, he's here. I'll get him.' She put down the receiver and I heard her call: 'Kostaki! For you!'

She picked it up again. 'He's coming. 'Bye-bye, my dear.'

'Have a good trip.'

There was a pause, fiddles twiddling away like billyo in the background, then footsteps on the wooden floor.

'Hallo there.'

'It's me.'

'I know.'

'Look,' I babbled, all of a dither at the sound of his voice and my own temerity. 'It's nothing whatever to do with football. I have to go to a book fair in Fartenwald in Germany the week after next. They're putting me up in solitary state at the best hotel in town – '

'Good idea,' said Constantine. 'Now when would that be?'

'I'm going for three nights, Tuesday, Wednesday and Thursday.'

'I'm sure I could make those . . . ' he said in the slightly detached voice of a man consulting a diary. He really had missed his vocation. 'Or at any rate a couple of them. One has to make time for these things.'

'Fantastic. I really – '

'I think you're frightfully efficient.'

'And still tempting?'

'Absolutely.'

'I can't *wait*.'

'We'll have to see what we can do. It'll be a pleasure. Cheerio.'

As high as a kite on success and anticipation, I telephoned Bernice and brought her up to date.

'You jammy devil!' she said admiringly. 'I never thought you had it in you.'

'I never thought he had it in him!' I said. 'I mean he really called my bluff. He's completely shameless!'

'God,' sighed Bernice. 'Here's me, only very slightly married and let off the lead practically every other night, and what happens? Zilch. Zippo. Zero. And there's you, with all those kids, and nosy neighbours and – '

'Okay, okay, don't start that again.'

'But it's true! There's you with just about every disadvantage known to woman, and you land a single, foreign, shameless doctor! I mean what sort of odds would you be given on that?'

Pretty long, I thought smugly to myself as I poured myself a gin and tonic and put my feet up in front of the Beeb. Pretty damn long!

Chapter Twelve

The Basset Magna gymkhana was an annual event which brought out the worst in man, woman, beast and child. Instigated by Squadron Leader Reg Mather, DFC (rtd) as a festival of equitation for children under fifteen, to foster the joy of participation rather than the vulgar glee of winning, it had deteriorated in the ten years since its inception into a wholly predictable exercise in crude one-upmanship. Fine nuances of breeding, both human and horsy, were there for all to see, and for the cognoscenti to relish. Those entitled, by virtue of their caste, to wear green boots and Harry Hall body-warmers, no longer did so; and those whose children's ponies had been bought with the tainted money of advertising or estate agency wore them without realising that they gave themselves away. On the other hand it was the ad execs who could afford the really high-class show ponies which their offspring were usually (and *quite* predictably, sighed the gents) unable to control.

But it went without saying that neither group won anything. No one from the Basset vicinity did. Keen though the locals were to do well, they stood no chance when the semi-professional hoi-poloi from the outlying areas rolled up in gigantic horseboxes a-rustle with rosettes, their shamelessly unhorsy parents opening minibars in the backs of their Jags and Range Rovers, and playing Demis Roussos on their stereos. There was generally a preponderence of boys among these hard-nosed usurpers, scuttling the widely held myth about girls and horses, and contributing to the alternative myth that when the male of the species turns his hand to something he will usually become proficient at it. They rode ponies a shade too small for them, with an elbow- and leg-flapping bravura which was chilling to see. The ponies slithered between bending poles and round flags as if made of treacle, and screeched to a halt on the finishing line, nostrils dilated, as their riders vaulted off and won yet another rosette and fifty pence. Despite mutinous mutterings among the locals about 'pot-hunting', it was impossible to disregard the expertise of these outsiders who spoke of 'gymkhanering' as others might of shopping or weeding, as something they did with take-it-or-leave-it regularity.

The day of this year's gymkhana dawned fine and hot. Clara left the house early in order to plait Stu's mane, which gave the latter the look of a surly, equine Boy George. Clara herself wore jodhpurs and Gareth's school shirt and tie. At least, I reflected, you could not easily categorise my daughter. She herself was so naturally disdainful and aloof, and her mount so obviously plebeian, that they made a piquant twosome. Clara carried with her an Adidas sports bag containing her daily ration of white bread and processed cheese, and those items necessary to transmogrify herself and Stu into the Lion and the Unicorn for the fancy dress that afternoon.

Shortly after his sister's departure, Gareth left, bound for the same destination and clad in his scout uniform. By ancient usage the 2nd Bassets acted as menials at the gymkhana. Actually, they did most of the work on the day, for the stewards proper were mostly local parents keen to get a vicariously horsy finger in the philhippine pie. None of them wanted to appear a slouch, so while the awful people who had brought the pot-hunters lay about reading tabloids and drinking tequila, the stewards infiltrated the various arenas and collecting rings, wearing responsible expressions and getting underfoot.

The scouts, on the other hand, took up a position perched on the rails in front of the secretary's tent, and made frequent forays into the main arena to rebuild shattered courses, catch erring ponies and carry off injured riders. They had one great mental advantage over all the other locals: they saw riding as a sport indulged in exclusively by girls for obscure and perhaps unmentionable reasons of their own. This prejudice meant that they had only scorn and contempt for the imported wally-woofters who were prepared to stoop to a female sport for their own self-aggrandisement, and they jeered and barracked the pot-hunters in a manner of which BP would have heartily disapproved.

Determined, like Clara, not to be categorised, I arrived at the gymkhana wearing a resolutely unhorsy black sun-dress and sandals which absolutely precluded me being pressed into service as a steward at the last minute. I felt as though my recent activities must be branded across my rump in letters of fire: THE GREEK DOCTOR WAS HERE. But my smug self-obsession was partially dispelled when I observed a mesh of wires swinging from tree to tree around the periphery of the field like lianas in a rain forest, and remembered Damon's pivotal involvement in the day's proceedings. Given a three-acre field and sixty-odd adolescents on horseback, only a mega-man with the patience of Jove, the wisdom of Solomon and the lungs of King Kong could remain in control without an efficient public address system. And this year it was Damon's turn to instal the equipment.

I experienced a small twinge of anxiety. If anything went wrong I should have to bear at least part of the responsibility. It was I, after all, who had provided Damon with the wherewithal to purchase his equipment in the first place. The gymkhana clearly represented a dry run for the mobile disco, and I was not sure what Damon might not do to further his expanding business interests.

In the secretary's tent I spotted Lydia Langley, with Sabina at her side, dispensing tickets for the various events. I felt I owed her an apology.

'Hallo, Lydia,' I said, going round her side of the table and automatically beginning to tear tickets off a roll.

'Good morning, good morning,' replied Lydia in her bracing, but slightly absent manner. 'We've already seen your daughter. And your son.'

'Good, good,' I intoned, catching it from her. 'Look, Lydia, I'm awfully sorry about the other night. About Clara. She's not normally like that.'

'Glory be, who cares?' said Lydia. She wore a white Aertex shirt, cotton print skirt, ankle socks and sandals. Her daughter Sabina peeped balefully at me from behind a tangled curtain of hair.

'And incidentally,' went on Lydia, 'Clara has been kind enough to offer Stu to Sabina for the trotting and potato.'

'Oh?' It only took a split second for me to see what lay behind this. The hiring racket had been shut down by me, and Clara owed Sabina. 'Super.'

'Entre nous,' said Lydia loudly, 'I think Clara has other interests today – ' she clapped her hands – 'Will you *please* stop that and form an orderly line!'

So Lydia had chucked the grenade and run for cover behind her administrative duties. As I emerged from the tent my darkest suspicions were confirmed. Damon was emerging arse-first from beneath the tail-flap of the chief steward's dormobile. Watching him with close attention was Clara, her arm through Stu's reins. Not twenty metres away behind them stood the scarred orange Anglia of Terry Billings, with Terry getting out of it. Damon saw me first as he scrambled to his feet.

'Morning,' he said. 'Okay?'

Clara jumped as if shot. 'Hallo, Mummy.'

'Shouldn't you be participating in something?' I asked crisply.

'No, it's the leading reins first.'

Terry joined us and at once gave Stu a tremendous clout round the ear.

'Lovely bit of weather for it,' he remarked.

'What brings you here, Terry?' I asked.

'That's my future partner,' said Damon.

'Who is?'

'I am,' said Terry.

'What?'

' 'Is partner.'

I was still digesting this information when Squadron Leader Mather leaned out of the cab of the dormobile and said: 'All ready down there? Okay if I get the show on the road?'

Damon put his nicotine-stained thumb and forefinger together, signifying the absolute acme of readiness. 'Fire away, Major.'

I was conscious of almost palpable tension, but in fact the amplification was fine. The squadron leader announced that the first event in the main arena would be the Leading Rein Ride and Run, and we could all hear him without either straining or being deafened.

I breathed a sigh of relief. 'Well done, Damon. Is this all your equipment?'

He shook his head. 'Bit of their old rubbish, bit of my stuff.' He spread his hand and rocked it. 'Interface is the iffy part, know what I mean?'

I hadn't the remotest idea what he meant, but I nodded sagely. My first objective was to separate Clara from the 'other interests' at which Lydia had hinted so darkly.

'Why don't you,' I said, without the trace of a question in my voice, 'go and offer Sabina a practice ride on Stu?'

'Okay.' She addressed Damon: 'See you.'

'Seeya.'

I watched her go, then glanced back at Damon who was back on all fours pointing out something on the underside of the dormobile to Terry. I did not care for the cut of Damon's jib this morning, especially his air of having confidential business with my daughter.

'You're obviously very tied up,' I said weightily, 'so I'll leave you to it.'

The main arena was filling up with mounted pre-pubes and their tight-lipped parental squires. I sat down on a straw bale at the bottom end of the ring, partly to gloat. This end was where the smaller children fell from their ponies with the monotonous regularity of windfall apples, and had to be scooped up and replaced to the accompaniment of ungentle tweakings and recriminations from their parents.

184

Dilly Chittenden and Lydia Langley's husband, Barry, were both bottom-end stewards on this occasion. Dilly had been a good company wife when her husband worked for Astec Electronics, and now that he answered to a Higher Authority she kept up the good work. Today she wore white jeans and a matelot shirt, with gleaming white plimsolls. She was a walking invitation for every horse in the place to drop one in her path.

'Well done, Dilly,' I said. 'I chickened out this year.'

'But Harriet, you do so *much*,' said Dilly. 'And Ricky' (the rector) 'tells me you're the saviour of the Tomahawks too!'

'Not exactly – but I was able to provide them with a saviour.'

'Dr Ghikas, yes, I saw him with you at the tournament. He looks absolutely ideal.'

'Yes, doesn't he,' I said.

'Belt up, you two,' said Barry. I expect he still held it against me that Clara had kept him up all night. 'They're starting.'

Event after event unfolded before us. Pre-pubes fell, and howled, and were re-seated; parents lodged official complaints with Squadron Leader Mather, or snarls of unofficial protest with rival parents; Barry Langley was barged by a Shetland and had to be replaced; Dilly's plimsolls took on the appearance of something unsavoury dredged from the mouth of the Thames; around the periphery of the field the beginning of the pre-prandial happy hour was signalled by the chink of glasses underpinning the blare and honk of continental crooners.

It was quite pleasant, sitting with the hot sun in my face and nothing much to do, being goosed by errant stalks from the straw bale and knowing that my children were fully and blamelessly occupied. The Crazy Horse Saloon was in operation again, a lot less noisome in the open air, and I bought myself a hot dog with double fried onions.

I was so relaxed that it only gradually dawned on me that the scouts, Gareth included, had homed in on a target for their insults. This was an especially large and uncouth boy from the pot-hunting contingent, an embryonic Lance Lowe if ever I saw one, sitting abaft a squat, wall-eyed palomino. In the equine pulchritude stakes this animal came even lower down than Stu, but had the low carriage and scuttling gait of the proficient gymkhana winner.

The boy, whose age, I estimated, lay somewhere between Clara's and Gareth's, had an exceptionally low forehead and a shadow on his upper lip. He wore a nylon *Star Wars* T-shirt, and from the greasy cuffs of his too-small jods there emerged grey woolly socks and trainers. No serious entrant was smartly turned out. He did, however, sport a crash helmet of the most formidable kind, complete with chin strap, as if to warn rivals of his intentions.

The heckling, when I picked it up, had already reached the 'Fall off, fatso!' stage. The squadron leader was stifling these taunts by the simple expedient of leaning out of the sun-roof of the dormobile and striking the relevant miscreant over the head with his walking stick. But it was patently obvious that the 2nd Bassets on the scent and in full cry were not to be so readily put off. Their behaviour had even impinged on the consciousness of the pot-hunting parents, for a woman in salmon velour and orange mules, with a fruit-infested cocktail glass in one hand, came up to the ropes on the left of the arena and began shouting. 'Thass a good boy, Kirk, you show 'em! Don't you let 'em get to you, Kirky!' and other encouraging remarks.

I noticed with trepidation that the next event was the Eleven to Fourteens Potato Race, and that Clara was leading Stu into the ring with Sabina Langley on board. The fat boy was also taking part in the first heat, and in consequence the jeers from the scouts, and retaliatory exhortations from the salmon woman (who had now been joined by a fat, hairy, heavily tanned man in shorts and a necklace), were hotting up. Stu, ever receptive to atmosphere and not, at the best of times, requiring much to get her dander up, laid back her ears and rolled her eyes horribly. Clara cuffed her and said something which I was extremely glad I couldn't hear.

I did wish that it was not Sabina's turn to ride. I did not doubt her competence, but she lacked my daughter's cold fire. There she sat, her matted pre-Raphaelite mane drooping from either side of her hard hat like the ears of an Afghan hound, her hands resting limply on Stu's withers. She did not look like a girl about to imprint her authority on the proceedings. And this with the ever more feverish crossfire of scouts and pot-hunters, the participation of the menacing Kirky and the absence from the ring of Sabina's father, who was still drinking sweet tea in the St John's ambulance tent.

Dilly glanced over her shoulder at me. 'We're in for some fireworks, by the look of things!' she remarked happily. 'What an awful-looking boy that is, surely he can't be under fourteen? I'd be simply terrified to go in the ring with that!'

'Yes,' I agreed, 'so would I.'

The squadron leader announced over the public address system, which was holding up well, that due to a dearth of entrants for this particular event, this was not a heat, but the final.

I groaned. That was all we needed. A lot was at stake, and all concerned knew it. From the tail of my eye I spotted Damon and Terry smoking and conferring behind the chief steward's dormobile. At least that aspect of the day was proving unexpectedly hitch-free.

The half-dozen entrants lined up at the top of the field where Robbo was starter. He was flustered, poor man, by the unseemly conduct of the 2nd Bassets, and by the absence of Akela who had taken the cubs camping on the marshes north of Barford. Still, he did his best as always, requesting fair play and sportsmanship and encouraging the ponies and their riders to form something approximating to a line.

When his arm came down, it was the signal for a positive storm of encouragement and invective from both sides of the ring. From Gareth I distinctly heard a cry of 'Kill, Stu, kill!' and from Salmon and Shorts answering bellows of 'Go it, Kirky boy, show 'em what you're made of!'

They thundered down the field towards the furthest poles, upon each of which a King Edward balanced precariously.

'Hell's bells,' said Dilly, and ducked beneath the rope, 'this is where I get off.'

Even if Sabina was not competitive, Stu was. With the bit firmly between her teeth she reached the first potato at the same time as Kirk and Sabina was just able to grab it as her mount cornered on two legs and set off on the uphill return journey to the blue plastic bucket where the potatoes had to be deposited. By the bucket Clara bounced up and down, fists clenched in an agony of frustration, under Robbo's watchful gaze.

Three of the competitors missed the bucket altogether and had to dismount and take a second stab at it. Of the remaining three Kirk and the ashen-faced Sabina were out in front and neck-and-neck, with Stu perhaps marginally ahead. The difference in styles was most striking: Kirk crouched low over the palomino's neck, whip flailing; Sabina was a mere passenger, grey-lipped and hollow-eyed, hanging on to the pommel for dear life. I was awfully worried about her, but my anxiety was tempered by glee at the distinct possibility that she might win.

'Give 'im some stick, Kirky darlin'!' yelled Shorts. 'Show the bastard who's boss!'

'Come on, Sabina!' I cried, rising from the straw bale and brandishing a fist. 'Do it for Magna!' It was all most diverting.

'You don't care, do you, Harriet?' asked Dilly admiringly.

By the time they turned at the start to fetch the final potato, there was a small but discernible increase in Stu's lead. The scouts were already jubilant, in premature expectation of a famous victory, and quite a crowd of pot-hunting parents had assembled on the other side, jaws rotating and glasses slopping, to urge on their champion.

And all might have been well had not Clara, carried away by the élan of Stu's performance and probably wishing to show the assembled throng that she was the true owner, lifted her crop and given Stu a tremendous thwack on the rump as she rounded the bucket.

She had displayed hubris, and tragedy followed. Stu, not understanding the spirit in which the blow had been dealt, was very properly affronted by this shoddy treatment. She reared, spun round on her axis, and as she came down, depositing Sabina nose-first in the mire, lashed out with her back legs and caught Kirk's palomino a thunderous blow on the flank. The palomino squealed and leapt in the air and Kirk flew like a human cannonball over the ropes and almost into the arms of Salmon and Shorts. Even then the squadron leader, veteran of many such occasions, might have salvaged something, had not the iffy interface to which Damon had lately referred chosen this crucial moment to freak out.

The squadron leader, mildest of men, and not given to raising his voice, came over the airwaves like Jehovah on a bad day: 'JUST KEEP QUIET, EVERYONE, AND SETTLE DOWN!' he advised in a voice with all the calm and moderation of a 747 crashing on take-off. 'IF WE'RE ALL PERFECTLY QUIET AND SENSIBLE WE CAN SORT THINGS OUT IN NO TIME – '

He must have realised, poor man, that something was amiss, but not what. Instead of shutting up, or switching off, or both, he did neither, but lost his usually well-maintained composure and snapped at Damon: 'IN GOD'S NAME, MAN, WHAT THE BLAZES IS GOING ON HERE?'

'SPOT OF BOTHER, MAJOR,' confided Damon, fortissimo.

'SPOT OF BOTHER?' barked the squadron leader. 'WE'RE SHOT TO BUGGERY!'

'STEADY ON, GRANDAD,' advised Terry, whose presence, in all the bedlam, I had forgotten. 'NO NEED TO GET OUT OF YOUR COT.'

'STARING RUDDY IMBECILES!' said the squadron leader. 'CAN'T YOU DO SOMETHING?'

'ACTCHERLY, YEAH,' said Damon. 'I GOT SOME INTERLUDE MATERIAL.'

Too late, I realised what he meant. An eardrum-rending avalanche of pop music poured forth from the speakers to bludgeon into a quaking pulp those of us who were not already deafened. Everything in George's teak cassette-cabinet had been grist, it seemed, to Damon's mill.

Every animal in sight shot several feet in the air as if electrocuted, galvanised by the torrent of unspeakable noise which spewed from each one of the half-dozen amplifiers around the meadow. Squadron Leader Mather's festival of equitation had been transformed, at a stroke, into the kind of lavish pandemonium which Hollywood whizz-kids spend millions trying to reproduce for the silver screen. Ponies reared, bucked, kicked and bolted on all sides as though some hippophobe poltergeist had let loose a swarm of angry bees. From the pot-hunting camp whole quiches whizzed through the air like disintegrating frisbees . . . poles and potatoes hurtled skywards like giant exclamation marks . . . shrieks and oaths rose faint and distorted from amongst the horseboxes . . . pre-pubes stumbled and wailed amongst the debris like children recently orphaned in war . . . cocktail shakers and thermos flasks zoomed here and there like little Exocets to plummet, as often as not, into the piles of warm horse manure dropped in extremis by the panic-stricken animals. At the top end of the main ring, where a row of hitherto docile moorland ponies had been tethered to a rail, the fence was simply peeled from the ground like elastoplast as the ponies berserked in unison . . . family groups, blamelessly munching sandwiches on straw bales, were upended en masse, their mixed assortment of legs waving in the air like bizarre plants in a tropical breeze.

As Dilly Chittenden and I clung together with the holocaust raging round us and Art Garfunkel rendering 'Bright Eyes' as he had never done before, I achieved eye-brain co-ordination for just long enough to notice one thing. The chirpy green Ghikasmobile was bouncing over the turf towards the ringside and Constantine, as perfect a picture of dégagé amuse-ment as I had ever seen, was looking about him, with one bare, suntanned arm resting on the open window. I found time to wonder, in my agony, whether he had ever before attended a gymkhana, or whether he supposed such an event always comprised horses wreaking wholesale havoc while humans took cover from a heavy flak of flying hardware and airborne picnics. Art Garfunkel roared his last, but the baton was immediately taken up by a voice – Damon's, though strangely altered by the assumption of a nightmarish mid-Atlantic twang – babbling inanities at breakneck speed and at the same shattering volume.

'WELL, ALL YOU MIDSUMMER MUSIC LOVERS! SUNTIME FUNTIME'S REALLY HERE! AND IF YOU WANT THE BEST, I MEAN THE BEST, SOUNDS FOR YOUR PARTY, BARBECUE OR DISCO, DISCO-OPERATIVE HAS THOSE SOUNDS! FIFTIES ROCK AND BALLADS, SIXTIES RHYTHM AND BLUES, SEVENTIES FUNK AND REGGAE OR THE NOW! CHART-TOPPERS, WE'VE GOT 'EM ALL . . . !'

Yes, I thought murderously, and most of them mine and

George's. I'd had enough. Because I was the only person present in a position to understand what was going on, I was also the first to make a positive move to end it. I disengaged from Dilly and charged, hands over ears, towards the squadron leader's dormobile.

At the rear I found them, Damon and Terry, the authors of our misery, crouched together like black and midnight hags over a gently steaming knot of wires. As I towered over them, purple in the face and mouthing inaudible invective, I saw Damon lift a pair of pliers, grasp one of the wires and give it a savage tweak.

There followed a serpentine hiss, a sulphurous stench and a series of sounds like a firework display over the public address system, terminating in Damon's reverential: 'SHIT A BRICK . . . '

Then, silence. Or at least what passed for silence to our deafened ears, but was actually the muted sound of ponies kicking hell out of family saloons and pre-pubes having hysterics.

'Damon,' I thundered. 'What have you done?'

'Bit loud, eh?' he conceded. 'Bit of a dodgy connection there.'

'How could you? It was awful! Awful!'

'Just got away from us for a moment. It's cool now.'

The 'us' reminded me of Terry. I turned the harsh searchlight of my attention on to him.

'Terry, for heaven's sake, what happened?'

'Hallo again,' said Terry, his eyes swivelling wildly behind the eighty pound giglamps. 'Ole girl did all right there.'

I wondered for a moment to whom he was referring – Sabina? Clara? – but then realised that of course it was Stu he was talking about. In the chaos and uproar of the last few minutes I had completely forgotten about the race but Terry, as ever, had a firm grasp on the essentials. My fine fury seeped away. It was altogether too late to impress upon Damon the dangers inherent in employing a partner who could inspect his nose for blackheads without the aid of a mirror. My blood congealed when I thought of Terry, more accustomed to

191

banging large nails into dinner-plate-sized hooves (and that mainly by instinct), bringing his talents to bear on a mass of delicate electrical wiring.

The squadron leader appeared, whey-faced, at our sides, his mouth thin as a stray hair on a bowl of porridge.

An awful sense of responsibility came over me. It was my son who had led the barracking . . . my daughter who had struck the fatal blow . . . my pony who had kicked Kirk's . . . and my employee who had reduced this years' gymkhana to a haymaking shambles.

'Everything under control, Reg?' I asked.

The squadron leader very properly ignored this enquiry.

'There are injured people out there,' he said, extending an arm in the direction of the main ring, but never taking his eyes from Damon's face, 'panic, confusion, damage, and mayhem.'

'Could be worse then, Major, right?' said Damon, treading the rim of the volcano like a blind man.

'Ole local girl did all right there,' asserted Terry. Makes a change.'

'I think,' said the squadron leader evenly, 'that both of you should pack up your palsied equipment and leave. For your own and everyone else's safety.'

'Pronto!' I cried, unscrupulously shrugging off all taint of shared responsibility and aligning myself with the establishment.

With justifiably poor grace Damon and Terry began reeling in their blackened wires and cables. The squadron leader and I turned, with awful apprehension, to view the scene in and around the main ring.

'Well,' said Reg Mather. 'At least things seem to be quietening down.'

It was all relative. The scene which met our eyes resembled the battlefield after some bloody and terrible rout. The ponies who had recovered were grazing on the spoils of war, in the form of lumps of paté de la campagne, poppyseed rolls and pork pie; those who had not were still careering and cat-jumping around the perimeter of the meadow, reins flying and stirrups flapping, with their owners in pursuit, screaming

192

and cajoling by turns. Around the arena itself, scouts, stewards and members of the public grouped, milled and re-grouped amongst the debris with an air of distracted good intention. At least three people, though, were taking positive and effective forms of action. These were Clara, whom I saw riding the disgraced Stu out of the top gate at a brisk trot; Gareth, who was giving first aid to Sabina Langley with what I considered to be excessive zeal; and Constantine, who was moving from child to wailing child, in my direction, presumably checking for fatalities and distributing words of comfort and advice as he went.

'Grrnnyash!' The squadron leader emitted a strange explosive sound indicative of strong emotions forcing their way through a tiny chink in the armour of iron control. 'Who the hell is this johnnie?'

'This,' I said, as Constantine reached our sides, 'is Dr Constantine Ghikas. Constantine, this is Squadron Leader Mather, the organiser of the gymkhana.'

'How do you do,' said Constantine. 'Is it normally like this, or did I just strike lucky?'

I had an idea that Reg Mather would regard this levity with the keenest disfavour, and stepped in quickly to deflect it.

'Something went wrong with the public address system,' I explained.

'Oh?' Constantine spotted Damon and Terry with their wires in the background. 'Ah.'

'How fortuitous that you were here, doctor,' said the squadron leader, 'I'm really afraid we may have some serious injuries.'

Constantine shook his head. 'I've had a look round. Mostly shock and bruises, the St John's people are doing a good job.'

Reg Mather put his hand to his brow and squeezed his temples. 'In all the years that I have been organising this event, such a thing has never happened before.'

'Why don't you go and get some tea?' enquired Constantine sympathetically. 'There's nothing you can do for the moment, I'm sure.'

'What a good idea,' I agreed enthusiastically.

'Perhaps you're right. Then perhaps in a few minutes we could consider a fresh start.'

'Absolutely.'

We watched the poor man stumble away in the direction of the tea tent.

'Your Gareth is being a perfect gentleman and a model scout,' remarked Constantine.

I glanced over at Gareth, who was now clasping an apparently recovered Sabina round the waist and assisting her to walk.

'Hm.' I grunted gracelessly. 'I don't think somehow that his actions are as selfless as you imagine.'

'I should jolly well hope not, at his age,' said Constantine. 'Speaking of which, do you fancy a walk?'

He escorted me to the far corner of the field where a mighty spreading oak tree provided shade and shelter for the portaloos. There was no one about and he placed himself between me and the rest of the field and laid my hand on his gratifyingly rigid crotch.

'You look gorgeous in that dress,' he said. 'So wonderfully inappropriate.'

'Is that a compliment?' I murmured.

'A fact.'

'I don't think – '

'I'll be at the hotel in Fartenwald. We can do it in the lift.'

Shakily, I responded in kind. 'Only if the bar's too crowded.'

'That's right,' he said.

As we walked back to the ringside I realised, with an awful thrill, that there had been no joke intended.

That night Maria, cheeks still flushed from her encounter with the peremptory Jamie, reached Bradbury, there to be dealt with exceeding roughly by the Royalist troops. Until, of course, they discovered she was not what she seemed, when they dealt with her even more roughly and with many cries of ' 'Sblood, 'tis a maid!' and 'You go first, Sir Murrayne!' She came through all this with her usual aplomb and was finally manhandled before the King's general, who took wine with her and told her she had put up a damn fine show and must surely be the best man the Hawkhursts had got. I, too, sailed through these scenes with my customary fluency. It was a piece of piss. The only problem was restraining Maria from jumping the rude soldiery before they jumped her. My heroines were traditionally spirited when roused, but not accustomed to take the initiative, sexually speaking. Hidden fires was the watchword, and at present, if I wasn't careful, Maria would be roaring up every chimney in sight to the consternation of my regular readers. Regaining my presence of mind I bedded her down, tired, well content, and blamelessly alone, in a spare tent, with a guard outside to protect her from the importunings of the rank and file. It only remained for the handsome, frosty-eyed camp surgeon to examine her for any injuries she might have incurred during her mission . . .

At the Toms' disco, Constantine was a 'succès fou'. In fact, it was enough to make you sick. While he preened in the limelight, doing all the things which *I* had primed him to do in order that the Tomahawks would take him to their collective bosom, I myself was obliged to remain in the shadows, both literally and figuratively, behind insurmountable barriers of junk food.

Constantine turned his considerable hand to everything from rock 'n' roll to robotics, and with partners as diverse as Baba Moorcroft and Akela. He put himself about to a quite uncalled-for extent. Indeed, in his efforts not to single me out for preferential treatment, I considered that he was subjecting me to positive discrimination. I ground my teeth as Nita Nutkin was whirled away from my side in a flurry of leatherette fringes and given the Ghikas treatment to the strains of Dolly Parton's 'Here I Go Again'. For two interminable hours he never came near me. Even the male members of the Toms' administration were not overlooked, for Constantine closed the first half of the disco by persuading Eric, Robbo, Stan and Trevor to join him in Greek dancing. As a display of Zorba-style male pride this exercise left something to be desired, for Trevor had no sense of rhythm and kept involuntarily sabotaging the ensemble, so that the five of them bobbed and jerked crazily and threatened to dislocate each other's shoulders. But it served to establish beyond a shadow of doubt that the doctor was a good chap at a do, and the very man to raise the Tomahawks Under Fourteens to the uttermost pinnacle of the Basset League where they belonged. He even handed out the end-of-season awards with an air of unimpeachable benign respectability which I found almost unbearably titillating.

The only thing which saw me through this long night of sexual frustration and insane jealousy was Damon's appearance as DJ. It was horrific enough to have to sit through that hideous 'suntime funtime' routine again. But here was Damon, his self-confidence apparently undiminished by the events of the previous Saturday, decked out in a lemon suit of some hessian-like fabric, strutting and gryating in the flashing lights like a demented banana, exhorting us all to boogey on down to his great sounds.

This alone might not have been sufficient to distract me from my main preoccupation, but a further and crucial dimension of horror was supplied by the arrival of Clara on the stage, wearing her pink bermudas and off-the-shoulder T-shirt, and acting as a kind of ornament-in-residence, posturing and clicking her fingers, mostly with an expression of studied vacuity, but occasionally flashing Damon – Damon! – a collusive smile.

'Isn't that your Clara?' yelled Nita.

'Yes!'

'Mature for her age, isn't she?'

'They all look like that nowadays!' I bellowed, glad that the necessity of shouting made it impossible to detect a tremor of uncertainty in my voice.

'And there's your Gareth!' observed Nita. 'Seems to be enjoying himself!' I peered into the Dante-esque melange of bodies and spotted my son cavorting enthusiastically around a near-motionless Sabina Langley, like a cannibal with an oven-ready missionary.

'All having a great time!' repeated Nita complacently.

At this juncture Stan, who had been on the door, interposed himself between us and the ghastly prospect of my children's rampant hormones. He wore the gear he considered suitable for discos, that is to say a powder-blue cardi-coat, tattersall check trews and Hush Puppies.

'Hi, Stan!' I cried. 'Having a groovy time?'

'About eight-thirty by my watch!' he replied. 'And watch out for alcohol!' he howled, his cravat rippling over his agitated Adam's apple.

The problem was a perennial one. Drink other than coke or squash was not sold at the Toms family disco, though adults could bring a bottle of wine if they so desired. But the fifteen- and sixteen-year-olds under the auspices of Lance Lowe brought alcohol and fags, and set up a supply depot on the edge of the football field, where ragged clouds of cigarette smoke could be seen rising from behind a palisade of six-packs and cooking claret. Apoplectic with frustration, the committee would watch their older charges make regular sorties from crowded hall to fuel dump, have a swig and a puff, and return suitably refreshed and swaggering to the fray. Not that most of them had much to look forward to inside, for most of the girls of the same age were battle-hardened veterans of many such occasions, well beyond the reach of their peers, and content to shuffle in a cold-eyed group with their cronies and ogle (usually) the disco operators.

At nine o'clock, following Zorba's dance, Damon took a break from his exertions and there followed a twenty-minute interval during which the loos filled up and fresh supplies of parental bouncers came to the door as insurance against the expected insurgence of bikers from Regis.

Now, for the first time, Constantine came into the kitchen. He had broken into a light sweat on the dance floor and looked especially tasty with his hair clinging damply to his brow, and his tie loosened and askew. Nita had gone to get some fresh air with Stan, and I was sitting perched on a stool eating crisps and turning curling sandwiches over the other way to straighten them out.

'Hallo,' he said. 'How am I doing?'

'Beautifully.'

He came and stood next to me, slipping his hand down

inside my dress and massaging my bare back. Salt and vinegar crisps floated unheeded to the ground like autumn leaves.

'Stop that,' I said.

'Why?'

'I like it.'

'There you are then. Hallo, Nita, I was just trying to persuade Harriet here that a little glass of wine on duty is something she owes herself. You both do, how about it?'

As Nita beamed and bridled and said yes, I reflected for the umpteenth time on Constantine's ability to cover his tracks at a moment's notice. In the second that it had taken Nita to cross the threshold the touch of his hand on my back had subtly changed from a lover's feverish caress to the amiable, asexual pat of a social acquaintance pressing me to a drink. It was quite chilling.

' . . . I'll go and fetch it from my car,' he said, and went.

'Isn't he lovely?' said Nita.

'He's okay,' I said. 'A bit smooth for my taste.'

'You know your trouble, Harriet?' chuckled Nita, the woman of the world. 'You're too fussy!'

Constantine returned with a bottle of Betabise Tafelwein under each arm and Stan, Robbo and Eric in close attendance. Plastic cups were handed round and generous measures poured. Constantine himself had a coke.

'You're not having one, doctor?' asked Robbo.

'You forget, Robbo,' replied Constantine, who was by this time well into christian names with all concerned. 'I'm not a local like the rest of you. I have to drive back to Parva after this and it's more than my job's worth to be breathalised.'

'You're so right,' said Robbo, taking a deep draught from his own cup. 'Just not worth it for a man in your position.'

'And let me tell you,' put in Stan self-importantly, 'I know this wine, it's one of our top sellers, and it has quite a bite in spite of its gentle appearance.'

Quietly, almost gingerly, Eric put his cup down on the draining board. 'Well,' he said, 'so far so good. Everyone seems to be enjoying themselves, and no trouble so far!'

'Is there usually?' enquired Constantine, and everyone immediately shook their heads vigorously.

198

'Of course not!' said Nita. 'But you can't legislate for unpleasant elements from outside the village, can you?'

Eric peered through the serving hatch into the murk of the main hall. 'It's really thinned out. Always amazes me where they all go to in the interval.'

This reminded me of something and I excused myself, reluctantly, and went through the swing doors into the lobby of the village hall. Aside from Trevor, Tanya Lowe, and the bouncing fathers there were Damon and Clara and a few others, eating blobs of orange-coloured expanded polystyrene out of a plastic bag. The whole group surveyed me with the utmost phlegm and the hectic urgency of my arrival now looked ridiculous. I tried to give some point to it by elbowing my way to the Ladies but this was chock-a-block with sharp-haired little girls crowding the mirror and I retreated almost at once, to find that Gareth and Sabina had joined the group. So at least everyone was where I could see them.

'So, Damon,' I said, feeling like an early Victorian explorer trying to communicate with primitive tribesmen. 'You're a fully fledged disco-owner! I don't suppose you'll be needing to clean my floors for much longer.'

Damon chewed ruminatively on the curry-flavoured polystyrene and treated me to a slight lowering of the eyelids which I took to signify assent. It was noticeable how he had grown in stature in the estimation of his peers since this new venture. Though physically he could not compare with the massive, singlet-accoutred functionaries of the usual disco, there emanated from him a spurious but undeniable air of savoir-faire which acted on the teeny-boppers like strong drink.

'Is Terry with you tonight?' I asked.

'Yeah,' said Damon. 'But no worries. It's cool.'

'He's a roadie,' explained Sabina unexpectedly.

'What's that?'

'Does the heavy stuff, Ma,' said Gareth. 'Why don't you stick to things you know?'

This seemed like sound advice. I looked at Clara. She wore that utter facial blankness which is the special property of the female pre-pube on the defensive.

'I think we should get started again,' I said. 'We have to pack up at eleven, you know.'

'Okay,' said Damon. 'Don't get your knickers in a knot.'

I was still smarting under this one when I re-entered the kitchen, and gulped down the rest of the Betabise special as if it were unpalatable medicine. Constantine at once replenished my cup. Eric was telling a story harking back to his Astec Electronics days.

' . . . I had to dance with this woman for the rest of the evening as part of my company duties. It was a very confusing experience for a red-blooded young executive, I can tell you, like embracing an Ali Baba basket. She was held in by so many bones and struts I thought everything might suddenly succumb to the pressure and pop out of the top! As it was, one of the uprights in her bodice worked its way free and began to advance upwards in the direction of my right nostril – ' He demonstrated with his finger. His audience was hysterical. 'It wasn't funny, I don't know what you're laughing at. I mean, imagine Yours Truly, painfully green and horribly ambitious, too polite to tell the chairman's lady that her whalebone is sticking up his nose . . . '

Our appreciative hoots and cackles were drowned by the resumption of the disco, belting out something cacophonous at a volume which set up a species of molecular reaction in the plastic coke bottles on the hatch so that they droned and vibrated like tubular bells.

Under cover of this aural onslaught Constantine put his arm round my waist and whispered, deep in my ear: 'Let me take you away from all this . . . '

It was what I'd been waiting to hear all evening, but now that he'd said it, I was programmed by my environment to respond like a good committee lady.

'But I'm on duty!'

'Now then, you two!' shrieked the ever-vigilant Nita. 'Put each other down. Doctor, you're wanted on the door!'

I saw at once the advantage of being totally overt. 'He's going to have a dance with me first!' I yelled, and literally dragged Constantine on to the floor. Nita, poor unsuspecting cow, was paralytic with mirth.

'Enjoy yourselves!' she mouthed.

We joined the throng, writhing and cavorting like good 'uns. Where we infiltrated a group of teenagers they would part like the Red Sea, leaving a small but discernible no-man's land around us, filled with a disparaging atmosphere of hostility and pity in about equal parts. I sensed that most of this was directed at me, a parent, and not at Constantine who had expended considerable energy on establishing himself as a bit of a card. It occurred to me yet again, as I toned down my gyrations, hypnotised by the suggestive lurching of my partner's pelvis, that I was way out of my depth.

I was, however, happily and randily ready to drown. So happy and randy, in fact, that I did not notice we had homed in on the storeroom until the handle was boring a hole in my back.

'What goes on in there?' asked Constantine, executing a couple of quick twirls and a shimmy just to confirm what was on offer.

'Storeroom!' I bawled.

'Sounds okay to me!'

'Don't be ridiculous, it's full of stuff!'

'Not that full, I bet!'

'It'll be locked!'

In response to this Constantine steered me smartly out of the way and tried the handle, which gave, as everything did, to his touch.

'See?'

I remembered that Robbo had taken folding chairs from the storeroom earlier in the evening, for the people on the door.

'Shall we?'

My answer was immaterial, since he had already herded me into the crowded gloomth and was closing the door after us.

It was rather as I imagined being back in the womb – the small, enclosed, airless place, the hot, moist promixity of another's vital organs, the muffled heartbeat of Disco-Operative. Apart from folding chairs the storeroom was jam-packed with gear belonging to Dilly Chittenden's playgroup. Boxes of Lego and bricks, small tractors and rocking horses, dolls, bears, playdough in polythene bags, garages and dolls'

houses stuffed with tiny plastic people staring at us from their
little windows like crowds at a coronation. There was no room
for even the most rudimentary considerations of comfort, but of
course this did not bother Constantine. On the contrary, it
seemed that the more inhospitable the setting the more sexual
energy he drew from it, and, to my continuing surprise, from
me.

So it was that with a trike balanced on my head, my
shoulder-blades grinding into a shifting stack of farm animals,
and one foot pedalling wildly on an errant felt-tip pen, I
achieved in record time yet another glorious, if not lyrical,
climax, in the knowledge that upwards of a hundred people
were no more than four feet away on the other side of an
unlocked door. It made Maria's nocturnal union with the
under-gardener look pretty small beer.

Unfortunately, as Constantine withdrew his head from
beneath my skirt my legs gave way and the tricycle which I had
been inadvertently supporting during our dalliance crashed to
the ground behind me with a hideous jangle of metal, bringing
with it a shower of tiny cows, horses, pigs and farmers' wives.

'Shit!' I cried. 'What the hell shall we do now?'

'March out and look good,' he replied. I knew now that he
meant exactly what he said, but even so the speed with which
he opened the door and strode back into the hall took my
breath away. I stumbled after, smoothing my skirt, and
hearing, with dismay, a final carthorse drop from its folds as I
did so. But, of course, he was right. The crush of perspiring
children and their watchful parents were not interested in us,
nor, apparently, did they even notice us emerging from the
storeroom. And the sound of the falling carthorse, though it
seemed like the crack of doom to my guilt-sensitised ears, was
completely lost in the din of Disco-Operative at full belt.

Constantine threw himself back into the swing and in this
manner we made our way back to the kitchen.

'I've brought her back, you see,' he yelled at Nita, who
was counting the takings.

She wagged a finger at him, then pointed at me. 'I saw the
two of you diving into the storeroom!'

I flushed, burned, sweated and turned to ice in the space

of about a second, I swear, but Constantine was composure personified.

'Yes!' he replied. 'Your turn next, Nita! No, actually I wondered if there were any roller skates, so that the youngsters could have a roller-disco competition! But no! Perhaps another time! Another dance, later?'

He waltzed off to join the others on the door and I took up my position once more at Nita's side. She was shaking her demi-wave with an air of amused indulgence.

'What a lad he is . . . !' she reflected, pinching a pile of fifty-pence pieces. 'He's got an answer for everything!'

I crossed my legs. I'd have plaited them if it had been physically possible to do so.

'Yes,' I said, 'hasn't he just?'

Chapter Thirteen

I travelled first-class to Fartenwald. I knew this was not only to enhance my image as an author who basked in Era's high esteem, but also to separate me from any Eran stragglers who might be on the other side of the curtain.

After the organisational marathon of the past few days I was looking forward to the three-hour flight for a spot of shut-eye, attended, perhaps, by lubricious, anticipatory dreams. But I hadn't bargained for the ceaseless ministrations of the first-class stewards (I'm Gary – Cruise Me), who waved steaming cloths with tongs, plied drinks, newspapers, menus and canapés, and enquired continually after my comfort. I hadn't had so little peace since I was in Barford General having Clara. Every time I closed my eyes to conjure up Constantine rampant in the lift of the Dynamik, my arm would be gently touched as if by some kind, firm nanny and yet another salver of glistening rolled vine leaves – not a happy choice in view of my erotic preoccupation – would be passed under my nose. Erans notwithstanding, I began to long for the cramped slave quarters at the rear where I might have hunched up and dozed off without interruption.

I fancied that I had left matters at home in good order. The dog I had taken to 55 Tennis Court Road, where tempers were a little strained. Arundel did not care for animals and had obviously attempted to put his foot down over the matter of Spot, whom Bernice always took in and spoiled horribly in my absences. But the days were long since gone when Arundel's foot had inspired any respect in Bernice. By the time I got there she had taken the offensive and was telling Arundel con brio that if she couldn't do a little thing like looking after a friend's dog, then things had come to a fucking pretty pass and what the hell *could* she do? Barty and I stood in the hall, united in our role as non-combatants, with Spot between us, lips drawn back in an amiable grin, tongue lolling, sublimely unaware of his key status.

After about five minutes, during which Barty inspected his dentures and treated me to gummy, conspiratorial leers, the protagonists emerged. Arundel came first, sweeping past us on an icy wave of extreme pique. His aquiline nose, with its curved, fastidious nostrils, seemed clenched with disfavour so that he resembled a human Concorde. As the front door slammed behind him Barty, Spot and I quaked in his slipstream.

Then came Bernice, the complete antithesis of her husband. She was flushed and expansive, warmed both by the heat of conflict and the satisfying afterglow of victory.

'Bollocks to him!' she remarked genially. 'Hallo, darling Spot. Barty, take Spot to the kitchen and give him some of that cold goulash, there's a dear. And you – ' she pinched my cheek affectionately, 'get you to your doctor, and make sure you have something worth reporting when you come back.'

'Coffee madam? Mrs Blair, coffee?'

I started violently and found Ricky (or Julian, or Denzil or Gary) hovering over me with a coffee pot.

'Yes – thank you.'

Ricky poured coffee with many flourishes, whirled a bonbon dish of bittermints out of thin air and moved on, like a priest taking communion to the sick. I stirred in my whole packet of brown sugar as a V-sign to Basset Magna and all its work, and fell back on my reflections.

Brenda had called round, a zealot in the field of neigh-
bourly responsibility, to speak of the children's gastronomic
preferences, and what time they normally went to bed. I said
over and over again that they would eat whatever was put
before them, and go to bed when they were told, the earlier the
better, while my offspring stood just behind Brenda looking
daggers. As Brenda had burst forth from my front door, still
uttering cries of 'savoury flans!' and 'chips with everything!'
she walked, literally, into Declan, who was engaged in uproot-
ing the dandelions that edged the path from door to gate.

'Look where you're going, wumman!' he said.

'I'm so sorry, Declan,' cried Brenda, quite girlishly. 'I
never saw you there!'

She had then sidled past him with much exaggerated care-
taking, hunching her shoulders and sucking in her stomach in a
manner that was a direct repudiation of everything the
women's movement stood for. As she sashayed through the
gate I caught once more on Declan's face that look which had
disturbed me before. But yet again it was gone before I had
time to analyse it.

But now, to hell with all of them! I was finally on my way,
and not one of the poor fools I had left behind me in Basset
Magna had the remotest idea what I would be getting up to at
the Fartenwald Dynamik. Airborne over Europe, with Ricky to
attend to my every need, I was gloriously incommunicado. I
felt that kind of detached euphoria which accompanies the first
stage of drunkenness, before the vomiting sets in. I seemed to
myself to be astonishingly brave and clever and witty and
attractive –

'Mrs Blair – leekyewera?'

I started violently, nearly slopping my half-drunk coffee.
Ricky's co-steward, Dirk, was there, with pad and ballpoint
poised.

'I'm sorry?'

Dirk was a Scot with a nasal, Miss Brodie-ish way of
enunciating words, so as to give them several supernumerary
syllables.

There was the merest suggestion of a pained sigh.

'Berrandeeah, Mrs Blair? Hooeeskeeah, Hejambooeeah?'

The linguistic fog had lifted for a split second, long enough, thank God, for me to understand the question.

'Why not?' I said, rhetorically. 'I'd like a small cognac.'

'A smarl coeneearc and hoo-aye not . . . ' intoned Dirk. He scribbled briefly and moved on, to inflict his strangulated vowels on someone else.

My brandy arrived, and I took from my handbag the densely packed itinerary which Era had sent me. I was to be met at Fartenwald airport by Tristan, who had been in situ for two days prior to the Buchfest in order to oversee the setting up of the Era stand. He would take me by car to the Dynamik where the itinerary proclaimed first, tersely, 'Tea. Briefing', and then, more obligingly, 'Evening free'. Constantine and I had agreed to meet up at the hotel this evening so that we could in all honesty respond to enquiries by saying we 'ran into each other at the same hotel'. I did not even know what flight he was arriving on. The delicious chanciness of the whole arrangement had me squirming in my seat. The prospect of three nights in a four-star hotel, unencumbered by my dependants, would alone have been enough to fill me with rapture, but when Constantine was added to the brew it became heady stuff indeed. I could only conclude that my particular Lares and Penates had decided it was my turn for some fun. And by God I was going to have it!

Thanks to Era's generosity in the matter of first-class travel I actually stepped off the plane feeling fresher than when I'd got on. I fancied I looked every inch the successful (but approachable) author. With the Buchfest in mind I had bought a dashing, mannish trouser suit in cream linen, beneath which I wore a white silk camisole. Not wishing to be let down by shoddy accessories (a dreadful eventuality which magazines continually warn against), I had also purchased a (mock) snakeskin clutch bag and cream low-heeled pumps. The slight tan I had acquired through regular jogging, watching soccer and attending the gymkhana was much enhanced by this ensemble and for once I felt that I should not be outshone by whatever eccentrically modish rig-out Vanessa might be affecting.

As is so often the way, at the same moment that I thought

of Vanessa, I saw her. I had just reached the meeting area at Fartenwald, and was casting about for Tristan. The tourist-class passengers were milling about behind me and there, amongst them, was my editor, talking animatedly to (I could scarcely believe it) Constantine Ghikas. Completely taken aback, and not a little miffed, I hastily looked away again and bumped straight into Tristan.

'Whoops,' he said, clasping my shoulders, 'steady on! We don't want our best author breaking a leg before you've even started.'

'Sorry, I just . . . '

'You look spiffy. Had a good trip?'

'Very good, yes, wonderful,' I babbled. 'I've never flown first-class before.'

Tristan's bland, smooth face assumed its customary expression of unctuous complacency. I was such a hard-working author, it was a pleasure for Era Books to provide me with lovely treats in return. I glanced nervously over my shoulder.

'Seen someone you know?' he enquired, beginning to guide me in the direction of the exit.

I glanced back again, still undecided what my answer should be, but unfortunately this time Vanessa caught my eye and waved gaily, lifting Constantine's nerveless hand as she did so like a boxing ref with a new champ. She was obviously trying to tell me something.

'There's Vanessa,' I said.

'Really, old Nessa? Oh, yes – Nessa!'

Vanessa began to elbow her way through the crowds towards us, dragging Constantine after her. He did not appear flustered by this treatment, but accepted it with his usual good grace. He was so bloody gorgeous in every respect that all my erectile tissues stood to attention just looking at him.

Vanessa wore little baggy shorts like a nappy; sandals with thongs that criss-crossed to the knee; and a white T-shirt so startlingly backless and loose that it threatened to slip right off her narrow shoulders and reveal her naked torso. She looked amusing, stylish, predatory – and young. My heart plummeted down through the white camisole and cream trousers and came to rest somewhere beneath the incipient blisters caused by my too-new shoes.

'Well,' said Tristan, 'the clans are gathering. Hallo, dear,' he said, kissing Vanessa on both cheeks. 'How's you?'

Sloane and Drone roared with self-congratulatory laughter while Constantine and I stood on either side like a pair of fire-dogs, pop-eyed and ostensibly detached, wondering what the hell we were supposed to make of each other.

Vanessa swung round to address me, catching me in the eye as she did so with an errant spike from her sun-ray hair-style. Unfortunately my nose always goes out in sympathy with my eyes, so while mascara poured down my cheek, snot poured from my nose, and I rummaged, snuffling like a hedgehog, for a tissue in my clutchbag.

Vanessa, all 'Vent Desert' and lip gloss, was unmoved by my plight.

'Surprise, surprise, I found a friend of yours!' she cried.

'Oh - so you did,' I responded vivaciously, dabbing and wiping and wondering if I looked like the pirate king with one black eye and one bald one.

'Hallo - er - ' I wasn't sure how Constantine had seen fit to quantify our relationship. Should I address him as 'doctor'? or 'Constantine'? Or 'old thing'? Or gaily, perhaps, as 'sexy' or 'hotlips'?

Fortunately Constantine himself came to my rescue, poised as ever. Leaning across he planted a friendly kiss on my zebra-striped cheek and said: 'Harriet, this is so delightful. Vanessa was telling me all about the book fair on the way over, and how you were going to be in Fartenwald - and now it transpires we're going to be in the same hotel. We'll be able to have dinner together if these slave-drivers will let you.'

Hearing his name mentioned, Tristan chimed in. 'Of course we will! Tristan Whirly-Birch, Era Books, how do you do. Harriet's entitled to her free time, and it's nice to know she won't be on her own.'

This, at least, was said with sincerity, as the presence of a friend from home with whom I could have dinner would allow the Erans to roister at the Rumpel Inn with clear consciences.

We set off, an ill-assorted quartet, in the direction of the main exit. Vanessa told Tristan what Constantine's name was, Tristan repeated it all wrong, and Constantine smilingly corrected him. I felt a terrible sense of let-down, that my first encounter with my lover at Fartenwald should be in the company of the chief Erans. But Constantine, never one to let the shining hour pass by unfilled, set about elaborating on his alibi.

'I quite often come to Fartenwald, actually,' he said, addressing us all. 'A friend of mine from my medical school days teaches at the Institute here. On this occasion it's a bit of a busman's holiday for me – he's asked me to sing for my supper.'

'What *are* you going to do?' asked Vanessa, bright-eyed with specious curiosity. 'Give liver transplants to foreign publishers?'

'Why not, if the price is right?' replied Constantine. 'What a Japanese editor would call foleign lights, perhaps . . . '

When the hilarity following on this gem had subsided, he added: 'No, he wants me to speak at a seminar on pre-conception care.'

'Pre-conception?' said Tristan. 'Whatever will they think of next?'

'I think it's tremendous,' offered Vanessa. I smothered a smirk. Pre-conception care, indeed.

Tristan summoned a cab out of the ether as only old Etonians can, and said over his shoulder: 'I just hope if the GM comes that he won't get overexcited. He has such bloody bizarre notions about books.'

After a brief, painfully polite wrangle over who should sit where we piled into the taxi, with Tristan in the front to direct operations and the rest of us in the back with me in the middle. Constantine's thigh was hard and hot against mine, his face cool and polite as he listened to Tristan.

' . . . he will insist on taking command, and sending us off on these wild goose chases, armed with blank cheques, to buy the *most* impossible books. He veers wildly between dry-as-dust tomes on ancient cultures, or feverish soft corn . . . '

' . . . known to get quite beside himself over female prison warders,' went on Vanessa, taking up the theme with enthusiasm, 'and nurses, of course. He once tried to get us to bid a hundred thousand for a book of American health statistics, just because there were lots of photos of ward sisters and whatnot.'

'Well, we all know what they say about nurses, don't we?' asked Tristan rhetorically. 'But then Constantine would know at first hand?'

'Who, me? I'm afraid I've led a very sheltered life,' said Constantine blandly, with admirable composure. He was fantastic. 'Tell me,' he went on, 'do you intend doing much serious business this week, or is it just for show?'

The gentle retaliation in this remark was not wasted on the Erans who at once reorganised their features into expressions of pained reflection, to show that beneath the glitz they were sensitive, committed people who loved their work.

'It all depends what you mean,' said Tristan warily. 'There won't be that many deals signed, sealed and delivered, very little cash actually changing hands. We're mostly here to see and be seen, but not just for show as you put it.' Vanessa shook her head in vehement repudiation of the very idea. 'No, it's a lot more than that. It's a market place, we're all displaying what we've got and seeing what others have to offer.'

'I'm with you,' said Constantine, and pressed his trousered leg ardently to mine.

'This is why Harriet's going to be so invaluable to us,' explained Vanessa. 'She's our window dressing – you don't mind me calling you that, do you, Harriet? – and of course she'll go round talking to people about *Love's Dying Glory*, and *perhaps* even *The Remembrance Tree*.'

'Is that your new one?' asked Constantine.

'Mm,' I said.

'She's being awfully secretive about it at the moment,' said Vanessa.

'Maybe you can prise something out of her over the roast venison tonight, Constantine?'

'I shall certainly try,' said Constantine, smiling at me.

'Aha! Constantine will be our mole!' cried Tristan.

I did wish they would stop using his name all the time. It

211

had been *weeks*, for God's sake, before *I* plucked up courage to 'Constantine' him.

At this point the taxi driver, who had until now been no more than a pair of shoulders and a crew-cut, burst into life like an actor who has waited a long time for his one line.

'Here is Dynamik!' he announced, as if warning us against dullness.

We disembarked, and the driver got our bags out of the boot. As Tristan fiddled with Deutschmarks, the driver enquired: 'You for Buchfest?'

'Ja,' said Vanessa.

'Books I like,' he went on expansively. 'Sornbirds, Princess Tisey, Lice – '

'Lice?' said Vanessa. 'Nichts verstehen.'

'Vitch off you bitchess iss my muzzer? Lice!' explained the driver, getting quite pink with the effort of making his point. Tristan, for once, looked baffled.

'Shirley Conran, perhaps . . . ?' offered Constantine diffidently.

'Ja, ja!'

'Oh, *Lace*, ja,' said Vanessa.

From Tristan's expression I deduced that he had given up trying to work out percentages in Deutschmarks, and was anyway far more anxious to put a stop to the driver's effusions. He handed over a handful of cash with expense-account abandon, our cases were taken by a doorman dressed in bottle-green breeches, white stockings, a frogged jacket and a cockaded hat, and we followed him to the reception desk.

Our business there completed, Constantine said: 'I must make myself scarce, I think. Shall we meet for a drink later, Harriet?'

'That would be lovely.'

'Six-thirty, then, in the bar?'

Flanked by the Erans I watched him go, like a drowning man watching the lifeboat being carried away on a current.

'Some tea?' suggested Tristan. 'We can just fill you in on what you'll be doing, then we'll leave you in peace to settle in.'

They assisted me to a table in the main lounge, walking on

212

either side of me like nurses in a mental hospital. Over tea they explained what I already knew from our previous meeting and the itinerary: that I had many appointments with important foreign publishers, the most crucial among which were the Americans, who might well be knifing each other for the rights of my book but who still needed buttering up; that for some of the time I should be on the Era stand, displaying myself rather like a tart in her window on the Reeperbahn, ready to pull in anyone who showed the remotest interest in my wares; and finally that I should be expected to eat and drink enormous quantities at other people's expense in order to impress them with the literary merits of *LDG* and *TRT*.

'I'm absolutely certain,' said Tristan, addressing Vanessa across me as though they were a couple of proud grandparents with a tiny grandchild, 'that Harriet's presence here is going to make an enormous difference to the Cosmos paperback campaign. She's so good at this sort of thing, everyone'll be eating out of her hand.'

'I don't know about that . . . ' I murmured.

'It's true!' shrilled Vanessa. And then, more confidentially: 'I'm relying on your dishy medical adviser to squeeze the details of *The Remembrance Tree* out of you, you know . . . '

'Yes, well, we shall have to see,' I replied.

Eventually they declared that they would have to go – it was approaching the happy hour at the Rumpel Inn – and I went up to my room. My case was there, the bed was turned down, and the lamp lit. On the table was an ice bucket containing a small bottle of courtesy champagne, and a bunch of freesias, ribbon-tied and bearing a card. I picked up the card and read: 'See you soon – K.'

For the intervening hour I feverishly prowled my suite. Such was my state of readiness that I fancied I had one of those bottoms like an inflated Victoria plum, which afford untold interest and amusement to the spectators at any monkey-house.

I had a bath, of course, assiduously using the many commodities provided by the Dynamik – bath oils, powder, shampoo, soap, body lotion and a deep-pile towel for each part

213

of my body – and managed to lie motionless for about five minutes in the steaming water.

The Dynamik was a grand, baroque, old-fashioned hotel which had been brought up to date by the simple expedient of tacking on as many modern conveniences as possible to the existing building. The decor of my suite ran to streaky velvet, knobbly chintz, a four-poster and a magnificent, if threadbare, Persian carpet. The bathroom had a bath with griffon's feet and many mighty pipes coiling and writhing in all directions like pythons at an orgy. The sitting room was furnished with massive, dark chairs, and two paintings depicting scenes in a boar hunt, with appropriate Teutonic gloom and ferocity. Amongst all this sombre grandeur the twenty-four-inch colour telly, digital phone, teasmade and teak minibar stood out like punks at a dowagers' tea-party.

I wasted another couple of minutes deciding what to wear, but my two dresses were still rather creased from the suitcase, and I decided to stay with the cream suit which was new and expensive and unlike anything he'd seen me in before.

At twenty past six I sprayed myself liberally from the cut-glass atomiser of Dynamikwasser, thoughtfully provided by the management, and then realised I probably smelt like every chambermaid in the place and tucked a freesia in my button-hole to adulterate the scent.

Finally, at twenty-five past I took up my snakeskin clutch bag and my room key, and ventured forth to meet Kostaki – had he not signed himself 'K'? – in the cocktail bar.

The corridor outside my suite had that air of hushed, thick-piled, well-insulated secrecy which is the special character-istic of the old-fashioned hotel. I felt that the Dynamik, like a wordly but well-bred aunt, would guard the naughty secrets of her youthful patrons while never losing her own elegance and dignity.

There wasn't a soul in sight. The long vistas of the second-floor corridor, with its many doors, and firedoors leading on to other corridors, were like the landscape of a dream. I might have been the only person in the hotel. My footsteps were as silent as a cat's as I went along to the lift. And, like the cat in the popular verse, my arse was wreathed in smiles.

214

I pressed the button and waited, the scent of Kostaki's freesia in my nostrils. The lift was unmodernised, a giant of wrought iron and dangling chains like the spaceship in *Alien*, and it was a long time coming. But in retrospect I should have been grateful for the wait. For, when the lift gradually bumped down in front of me, there, behind the elaborate grille, like some mercifully rare primate in captivity, stood the GM of Era Books.

'Well, if it isn't Mrs Blair,' he remarked smarmily.

'Good evening . . . ' I mumbled weakly. There was no escape. The GM had already opened the doors for me, but since I had failed to move from the spot they began to close again.

'Allow me,' said the GM and interposed his rolled-up copy of the Era catalogue between the doors. They snapped irritably for a moment, deprived of human flesh, and finally drew back once more.

'Going down, are you?' he enquired, unaware of the question's ghastly aptness.

'Yes,' I mouthed.

And now a strange thing happened. In those soundless, timeless, apparently motionless moments that we were suspended between floors, the GM and me, he spoke just three words, each one an unmistakable verbal ogle.

'*Love* . . . that . . . suit,' he said.

I swear I have never heard three innocuous syllables imbued with such labia-withering lust. The word 'suit' was given a grisly and pointed emphasis. I was reminded, in that fell instant, of his legendary predeliction for uniforms, but the reminder came too late. It was plain that my dashing, mannish outfit had stirred old fires. So not only was the old bugger here, large as life and twice as formidable, but I had succeeded, instantaneously and involuntarily, in taking his goatish fancy. It was a mercy we had only two floors to travel. I cast him the briefest of maidenly glances in acknowledgement of the compliment, but it was quite enough to remark his narrowed eyes fixed on me, and a distinct dew beading his brow and upper lip.

We arrived, with a bounce, on the ground floor. I pulled

back the grille and burst through like a rabbit flushed from a thicket. The vast marbled foyer of the Dynamik stretched away on all sides, dotted with smart people in nonchalant attitudes. I must have presented a striking contrast as I stood there staring wildly about me with my clutch bag grasped before me in both hands like a rounders bat. I had just established the where-abouts of the cocktail bar and was poised for flight, when the GM arrested me.

'Mrs Blair . . . allow me to buy you a nice drink.'

'A nice drink?' I squealed, rounding on him as though he had suggested some act of unspeakable depravity.

'Certainly, it would be a real pleasure.'

He pursed his lips as if reading a tempting menu. I was appalled. Where, oh where were Tristan and Vanessa when I needed them? Roistering at the Rumpel, free from the loathly attentions of the GM, that was where. Had they deliberately misled me? This couldn't be happening!

'I'm meeting a friend!' I squawked. 'I'm late already!'

'Then I'll buy you both a drink,' he replied, taking my arm and propelling me across the marble wastes. 'I can't bump into my star author and not buy her a drink, now, can I?'

We entered the aptly named 'Jaeger (or Huntsman's) Bar'. It was done up in a quasi-Mayerling style, complete with glassy-eyed stags and boars fixed to the walls, guns in cases, and giant pike suspended among petrified weed. I thought wretchedly that perhaps Constantine and I could enter into the spirit of the thing and have our very own suicide pact, right here. We could impale ourselves on some tusks before I met a fate worse than death impaled on the GM's well-travelled prick.

At last! – there was Constantine, looking heart-stoppingly handsome in blazer, cotton trews and a crisp white shirt. His face was in profile to us, his elegant hands encircled a tall, frosty glass of lager.

'There he is!' I cried, literally wrenching free of the GM's grasp.

'CONSTANTINE!'

Such was my agitation that at least a dozen heads turned, but Kostaki's, thank God, was among them, and he smiled and rose to meet me, apparently not in the least put out by my swaggering escort.

I scuttled to his side and turned to face the GM, feeling safer now that I was aligned with my inamorato.

'Constantine, this is a very important person – ' I introduced the GM – 'and this is Dr Constantine Ghikas, a friend of mine who just happens to be staying here – ' As soon as I'd spoken I felt that my choice of words gave me away, but the GM was far too vain to notice. He clasped Constantine's hand in both of his.

'Nice to meet you, doctor. Nothing to do with the book fair, are you?'

'No, no, quite separate, apart from knowing Harriet.'

'Lucky you! Now then, what will you have? Mrs Blair? Gin and tonic, barman. Doctor, what's your poison? And a lager. Sure you won't join me in a proper drink? Say no more.'

Constantine offered me his stool and I perched on it, with the two men on either side, like the female element in some bizarre vocal group. A sudden, vivid and hysterical picture of the GM rendering Da-Doo-Ron-Ron forced a grunt of manic laughter from my lips.

Both men turned to me at once. 'I'm sorry, dear,' rasped the GM, 'I didn't quite catch that . . . ?' He laid a hirsute beringed paw on my knee.

'I was about to say – I didn't realise you would be here,' I replied, waggling my knee energetically from side to side.' 'Tristan said – '

'Ah – ' said the GM with great satisfaction, taking his hand from my knee in order to tap the side of his nose with his finger, 'you see I don't always tell young Whirly Bird everything. It does them all good to be kept on their toes. But I'll probably only stay over tonight and tomorrow. I got to be in Anchorage the day after.'

'I see.' I forebore to ask what dark byways of the book trade took him to Anchorage. Anchorage was basically good news. Except that if he had only one night at the Dynamik he might feel compelled to favour me with more, more immediately, than he would otherwise have done.

While Constantine took up the Anchorage question I

pondered my predicament. I was on an extremely sticky wicket. My favoured status with the Erans had till now depended on my idyllically happy married state, my stability and maturity, etc. So I could hardly repel the overtures of the GM by revealing that Constantine was my lover. On the other hand my respectable married status would not in itself be enough to deter the GM from his fell purpose, since canoodling with him would be regarded as a girl's finest hour. How bitterly I regretted all the times I had signalled a special relationship, and made it plain that I considered myself on his wavelength while the others dithered and wavered! I had set myself up for this as surely as if I'd invited him to my room.

' . . . my mother is a tremendous fan,' Constantine was saying, 'but I haven't read any myself yet.'

They had progressed from Anchorage to *TLT* in double-quick time.

'You're missing something,' opined the GM, taking the opportunity to lay a far-from-avuncular hand on my shoulder. 'Mrs Blair is the mainstay of our fiction list.' I wished he would stop referring to me as a mainstay, it suggested something stout, functional and unglamorous, like a corset. 'It's pretty unusual, you know,' he went on, 'for authors to come along to book fairs.'

'Now why is that?' asked Constantine with polite interest.

'They're more of a hindrance than a help,' explained the GM. 'They get hysterical at the sight of all that competition. Not our Mrs Blair, though. She's a game girl – a real thorough-bred.'

He lifted his glass in my direction, his eyes surveying me over the rim as he did so like a couple of snipers focusing on their target. I couldn't stand much more of this.

I turned to Constantine, holding him with my glittering eye. 'What time did you book the table for?'

'Well, actually I hadn't – '

'Then I think we might as well go ahead if it's okay with you, I really should get an early night.'

'Don't worry,' said Constantine, 'it's only – '

I whipped round and addressed the GM. 'It was so nice meeting you. Thank you so much for the drink. Goodbye.'

I slid down off my stool and marched off, hoping Constantine would follow. He seemed to be taking his time, and I thought for one horrible moment that the GM might wind up having dinner with us, but in the foyer Constantine caught up with me.

'Steady on,' he said, taking my arm. 'What got into you?'

'He's not supposed to be here!' I hissed. 'He said he wasn't coming!'

'So? He obviously thinks the world of you,' said Constantine soothingly.

'That's just it!' I darted a look over my shoulder and dragged Constantine behind a pillar. 'I think he's taken a fancy to me!'

'It could be the making of you.'

'I don't want to be made! I don't need to be made!' I moaned, and laid my forehead on his shoulder. 'Or at least, only by you.'

'That's my girl . . . ' I felt Constantine's gratifyingly instantaneous response. But it occurred to me that while a hotel lobby might be Constantine's idea of the perfect spot for making whoopee, the pitfalls inherent in such a site were legion, and I'd had all the anxiety I could take for one evening. Gently, I pushed him away.

'Dinner,' I said.

As it was barely seven o'clock we were the first in the dining room, and the head waiter gave us a look of thinly veiled contempt, as if we might order fried bread and strong tea. But by the time Constantine had murmured God knows what bullshit in his ear about me, and my literary standing, and our relationship, he was all indulgence and obsequy, showing us to a table in the corner, admiring my freesia, and presenting us with vast morocco-bound menus, Constantine's with prices, mine without.

'Struth,' said Constantine. 'That's several Deutschmarks per prawn.'

'Don't worry,' I said. 'I'll pay and we can put it on my bill for Era.'

'Are you sure?' He looked quizzically at me over the top

of the menus. 'Won't that jeopardise your status as the Perfect Author?'

'I don't much care if it does,' I announced daringly. 'I reckon I need danger money for staying in the same hotel as that old billygoat, anyway.'

'You've persuaded me.'

We ordered, and I began to relax. The dining room of the Dynamik was huge and opulent, with ten-foot swags of ruby velvet curtain, six satellite chandeliers surrounding one gigantic one, and the ceiling itself elaborately painted with obese deities dressed in wisps of tulle. Everything was thick, and heavy and rich, from the damask napkins to the dense pink carpeting. In the centre of each table stood an arrangement of waxy gardenias.

'Nice here, innit?' I sighed.

In response, my escort removed one of his shoes and placed his stockinged foot on the seat of my chair, between my legs, feeling my crotch with his toes. The cream tablecloth reached to the ground on all sides so this manoeuvre was completely hidden from view.

'I don't like that suit,' he said conversationally.

'Well, I'm sorry,' I said in a voice that was especially clear and firm, to prevent it spiralling off into a squeak, 'but he does. He's got this thing about masterful women and uniforms and so on.'

'Hmmm . . . ' mused Constantine, digging as deep as the cream linen would allow. 'I wouldn't mind a uniform, but with legs like yours you should put them on show. You'd look good in one of those sexy hussar outfits the girls wear in American high school bands. Gold braid and stilettos.'

'You think so?' I said, my knuckles whitening on the arms of my chair, 'Well, I could hardly wear that at the Buchfest. Whereas this is . . . um . . . eminently suitable . . . '

'It is, of course,' agreed Constantine soothingly. 'And anyway, we'll be taking it off soon.'

The wine waiter, tall and glacial like a Norse warrior, arrived at our table, and Constantine perused the list at leisure, meanwhile stepping up his foot activity. As I tried to suppress what must have looked like a savage nervous tic I became seriously worried lest the constant friction of nylon on linen should cause a spark, and give a whole new meaning to the phrase 'flaming desire'.

The first course arrived, and we ate. All the food, to my fevered gaze, had the look of engorged private parts, which might at any moment rise off the plate and plunge into one or another of my bodily orifices, to make me the first woman ravished by a king prawn in the dining room of the Dynamik.

All through the meal we scarcely spoke, but concentrated on our activities above and below the plimsoll line.

'Look,' I croaked, over a passion fruit sorbet which swivelled lubriciously in its dish whenever I put the spoon to it. 'I have this awful feeling he's after me.'

'You forget,' said Constantine, 'you're with *me*. I shall protect you.'

'Yes, but you're not officially with me, you're just a friend from home who happens to be staying here, remember? And I'm the mainstay of his perishing fiction list . . . '

Constantine sat back in his seat, ostensibly to give me an appraising look, but actually to get more of his foot on to my seat.

'I see no mainstay,' he said. 'I see an absolutely gorgeous woman with a fevered imagination and a husband in Riyadh.'

We got to coffee. Or at least, he got to his, and I twice slopped mine between saucer and lips, and finally abandoned the enterprise altogether.

'Liqueur?' he enquired.

'You must be joking. Let's get out of here!'

Constantine put his shoe back on and rose from the table. I allowed him to come round and move my chair for the simple reason that I doubted my ability to stand unaided. The Norse warrior strode over and asked if we had enjoyed our dinner and Constantine, gripping me firmly round the waist, said that it had been excellent, and would they please put it on my bill. I felt that I might just as well have been consuming sawdust and iron filings for the past hour for all the gastronomic pleasure the meal had afforded me, though there had been compensations.

We strolled lopsidedly to the door, only to encounter the

GM, coming the other way. Constantine at once managed to make his encircling arm seem chivalrous and polite, rather than the indispensable support it undoubtedly was. He really was frightfully good at these subtle, self-protective changes in coloration.

'Hallo again,' said the GM. 'Good meal? They generally do you very well here.'

'It was first-rate,' said Constantine.

'Mrs Blair?' I was not to be let off. 'Everything to your taste, my dear?'

'Absolutely.' I had the impression that if I'd expressed any reservations the GM would personally have stir-fried the chef over a brisk flame.

'I hope you enjoy yours,' said Constantine. 'Good night.'

The GM's 'Good night' was still in our ears when Constantine said, in a perfectly normal voice: 'Your room or mine?'

'Ssssh!' I glanced over my shoulder, the very embodiment of guilt.

'Yours then,' he said.

Contrary to plan he eschewed the lift, for which there was a queue, and we went up the stairs which were broad, shallow, and gently spiralling. The walls were hung with sepia photographs of Old Fartenwald. Heavily moustachioed city fathers and their cruiser-class fraus gazed implacably down at us as we tottered and groped our way to the second-floor landing. Here, the groups of corpulent burghers gave way to massive oil paintings of the countryside around Fartenwald which, if the artist was to be believed, consisted of crepuscular pine forests and the occasional crumbling Schloss whose owners, I imagined, would be martyrs to lycanthropy. There was no one about. Constantine grasped my bottom urgently.

'Which way?' he asked.

'Number 106.'

As soon as we entered my suite we collapsed on the floor, and Constantine once again demonstrated his prestidigitation with women's clothing. He brushed aside the cream trouser suit with almost disdainful ease, and such was our mutual readiness and enthusiasm that the only problem was ensuring

222

that neither of us pre-empted the fun by popping our corks early. My head thudded rhythmically against the door, and I pictured, inconsequentially, the shiny plastic DO NOT DISTURB sign swinging on the handle just inches away.

Some time later we had made it – literally – to the bedroom, via the bathroom, the goose-pimply chintz sofa, and several metres of Persian carpet. As a lover Constantine was ardent, rough, rapid and expert, but making love with him, though thrilling, was about as lyrical as taking part in a three-legged race and presented roughly the same problems – those of synchronisation. The trick – which I was mostly too far gone to master – was to anticipate those moments when we were likely to peak together, and make the most of them. I wondered if the other women who had graced his life had had this turbulent sensation of being assorted ladies' garments in a front-loading washing machine.

Eventually, we slowed to a halt. Our respective top halves were shunted beneath the four-poster, so that anyone coming upon us might reasonably have taken us for a couple of car mechanics unable to unwind. Constantine was, of course, the first to regain his composure.

'Shall I get us some drinks?' he enquired, his urbanity untarnished by our bizarre and cramped circumstances.

'Thanks.'

He grabbed the edge of the bed and shot himself out and on to his feet in one enviably athletic movement. When I could hear him at the minibar in the sitting room I wriggled forth rather less gracefully, removed what remained of my clothing and put on my dressing-gown. Naively, I had been into Barford and bought two svelte and slippery nightdresses for my stay in Fartenwald, which I knew now, beyond a shadow of doubt, that I should never wear. I had omitted, however, to bring the rest of my night attire into line with the nighties and was in consequence stuck with the stained towelling. If I were ever to need proof that I was not a habitual cuckolder, the dressing-gown would provide it. It had been recently washed, but this had only the effect of reducing the spots of hair dye and greasy water to a uniform grey. Also, every time it was washed the sheer weight of the garment caused serious droopage in the cuffs and hem, so that I looked like an overgrown female version of Walt Disney's Dopey.

All this I was taking in in the large and ornate mirror, and I had just decided that it really would not do, when Constantine re-entered, stark naked and carrying two glasses of champagne and a dish of stuffed olives.

'Ah,' he said, handing me my glass. 'A metamorphosis.'

'Yes,' I agreed glumly. 'It's called reverse evolution. Butterfly into caterpillar at a single bound.'

'Rubbish,' he said, proffering the olives. 'I like all your different personas. It's exciting.'

He was, as I've said, naked, and there was every evidence that he was telling the truth. We were just drawing closer and about to take a deep draught from each other's glasses in the approved romantic manner, when I heard a knock at the door.

We froze. 'Who the hell can that be?' I whispered wildly. 'Didn't you put the sign up?'

'Yes, but it may have fallen off early on.'

I recollected with horrid clarity my head pounding the door. He was probably right. The knock came again, a brisk rat-tat.

'Perhaps it's just one of the hotel staff,' I ventured.

'Very probably. Go on ' Constantine flopped down on the bed and rested the olives on his chest. 'I'll just wait here.'

I went through into the sitting room, straightening the rug with my foot, and picking up several stray garments which lay on the floor. These I threw into the bathroom as I went by, and closed the door.

Why it came as a surprise to me I shall never know, but when I saw who my visitor was I was so thunderstruck that I stood with my jaw on my chest and allowed him to swagger past me into the room.

'Good evening, Mrs Blair,' said the GM. 'Fancy some champagne?'

He stood in the middle of my room, hugely pleased with himself, grinning like an ape and swinging a bottle of bubbly from one hand. He wore a beaded kaftan in a dizzying mixture of primary colours. What *I* did (fool!) was to close the door and murmur: 'I was just going to bed.'

'Shall we call it a nightcap then?' he suggested. 'Got some glasses?'

I was summoning the breath to say no, but he had already spotted the minibar, and was bearing down on it with awful resolution.

'I honestly don't want a drink,' I protested as firmly as I could. 'I just want an early night.'

'Then you shall have one, Mrs Blair,' replied the GM who, in spite of the kaftan, was continuing to address me as though he wore a three-piece suit, 'you shall most definitely have one.'

There was no ignoring the awful implication in this promise. As he set about the champagne cork I muttered 'Excuse me a moment,' and dashed into the bedroom, closing the door after me, and leaning back on it like a fugitive in a bad film, only this was for real.

Constantine lay on the bed, sipping his drink. The now empty dish which had held stuffed olives had slipped down on to his stomach where it lay like a beached coracle in the lee of his stupendous erection. He was grinning all over his face and was obviously well turned on by my predicament.

'You can laugh!' I hissed. 'What the hell shall I do?'

'Well, you can't bring him in here,' said Constantine. 'Because I was in here first.'

'Stop being so bloody facetious and *keep your voice down!*'

'Have a drink with him and send him on his way. You can do it.'

'But he's after me . . . !' I wailed weakly.

'So am I, aren't you the popular one?'

'Oooh . . . !' I moaned now, in black despair. It was clear I could expect no help from this quarter.

'Mrs Blair?' The GMs voice, tortured into ˎ terrible coyness, came from the other side of the door. 'Not shy, are you? May I come in?'

'No!' I spun round and pressed the door hard with both hands. 'I'm coming out!'

'Attagirl . . . !'

'Damn you!' I mouthed at Constantine.

'Good luck!' he mouthed back.

With head high and knees knocking, like an aristo going to the guillotine, I opened the door and went back into the sitting room.

What confronted me there was more grotesque than anything I could have conjured up, even in my worst night-mares. The GM had discarded his robe and now stood before me as a hideous parody of Richmal Crompton's William. Working from the top down, he wore: a small concentrically striped cap; a silk tie patterned with his own initials; a cellular vest; the kind of shorts usually associated with guerilla warfare in the tropics circa 1950; sock-suspenders; socks; and Gucci slip-ons.

The effect of this ensemble with his hectic complexion, cockerel features, and Havana-tinted hair was nothing short of macabre. My blood, which not half an hour since had been thundering round my erogenous zones like the APT, froze.

'Matron!' he lisped. 'Oh, matron – I want a drink!'

Matron? I was quite sure the GM's early education had been the responsibility of some lowly urban Mixed Infants, but obviously the boarding-school fantasy was a powerful one.

'I am not matron,' I said, as firmly as I could. 'I am Harriet Blair, author, wife and mother.'

'I love you, matron,' said the GM winsomely. 'You've got nice boobies.'

Things were progressing a lot more rapidly than was comfortable. He took a step towards me and I slid, cobra-quick, to the side. I spotted the champagne and glasses on top of the minibar. At least a drink might keep booby-talk at bay for a few more minutes.

'I'll give you a drink,' I said soothingly, 'and then you must get back to bed and go to sleep.'

'You'll come with me, won't you, matron?' he asked wistfully. 'You'll give me a lovely good-night cuddle?'

'Now then, here we are.' I handed him his glass, taking care to keep the minibar between him and me. My discomfiture was not aided by the fact that Kostaki, I knew, would be laughing like a drain in the bedroom, and no doubt getting off on the whole thing, too.

I picked up my own glass and took a huge gulp.

'Drink up,' I ordered sternly. 'It's bedtime and you shouldn't be in here.'

Unfortunately, my severe tone reinforced my fantasy-status.

'Have I been a naughty boy?' whined the GM craftily, moving in.

'Yes! No! KEEP AWAY FROM ME!' I bawled, and was rewarded by a distinct darkening of the scholastic cheek, and swelling of the shorts. He would have me, as the saying goes, coming and going. If I didn't put up some sort of a fight I was just a sitting duck, but if I did I would whip his passion into a white heat.

We stood there, staring at each other over our champagne glasses, each trying to anticipate the other's next move. Frantically I tried to imagine how one of my own intuitive, spirited heroines would deal with such a contingency. Why, with a toss of the head, a flash of the eye, and a swift uppercut to the assailant's jaw, at the very least. But not only was such behaviour quite out of keeping with my droopy spotted towelling, I also had a shrewd suspicion it would constitute an invitation to rape.

'Dear matron,' he breathed, fawningly. 'Don't be cross. I'm wild about you.'

He advanced towards me with infantile, pigeon-toed steps, and an expression of simpering lechery which made my gorge rise. His limp torso rose above his shorts in a series of false crests . . . his pectorals quivered menacingly beneath the cellular vest . . . his bewattled neck all but concealed the knot of his customised tie . . . his eyes gleamed lecherously beneath the dreadful cap. I was absolutely panic-stricken.

'Give us a cuddle, matron . . . I'll be good as gold, I promise.'

He put down his champagne glass, and now he made a sudden lunge, arms outstretched, across the top of the minibar. I lurched back, but not quite in time to prevent him grabbing my dressing-gown tie, which obligingly came undone and remained in his grasp as he nose-dived over the bar. So now, if I was to preserve, at the very least, my dignity, I had to hold the two sides of my dressing-gown together, leaving only one hand free to fight off the GM.

He looked pretty helpless, upended like a beetle with his skinny shanks waving in the air and the now-prone champagne bottle dripping down the leg of his shorts, but his cunning was devilish. As I reached behind me for the vase of freesias – the nearest available blunt instrument – I realised with horror that the GM had actually wrapped my dressing-gown belt around my ankles so that I was effectively hobbled, his prisoner. And what was more, he was using the belt as a lever to pull himself up, at the same time nudging his head beneath my skirts. I could feel the peak of his beastly cap creeping up my shins, and hear his stertorous breathing. I made a final, galvanic snatch at the vase, but missed it, and only succeeded in removing the freesias, with which I helplessly belaboured the GM's rump as I crashed to the ground. Cold water poured on to my face from above. The time had come for the cowards among us, if not to stand up (which was out of the question), at least to be counted. I blew out a spout of water, took a deep breath and yelled: 'HELP! KOSTAKI, HELP!'

I was nothing if not lily-livered. At that moment any threat to Constantine's reputation was as nothing beside the prospect of further intimacy with the madcap of the remove.

I should have known my lover would display admirable presence of mind. Any man who can screw a married woman witless (and fully clothed) against her own fridge freezer in under five minutes, and be able to make conversation with her daughter two minutes after that, has to be pretty much on the ball.

At the same moment that the abrasive lip of the GM's cap made contact with my shrinking cunt, Kostaki opened the bedroom door and strolled out, cool as ice, and dressed in shirt, tie, Y-fronts and, miraculously, a stethoscope.

'Oh, thank God, get him off me!' I howled.

Kostaki raised a soothing hand, walked over to where we lay grovelling in a puddle of champagne and flower water, and tapped the GM sharply on the seat of his shorts.

'You, boy!'

I felt the cap freeze; remain motionless for a few seconds;

and then, mercifully, begin to withdraw.

'Just what do you think you're doing, boy?' asked Kostaki as the GM sat up, dangerously suffused and somewhat sheepish.

'Giving matron a cuddle,' responded the GM meekly, as I struggled with the knot round my ankles and freed myself.

'Stand up when you address me!' rapped Kostaki. The GM stood up. I did the same, and retired, open-mouthed, to the safety of the sofa, wrapping my dressing-gown tightly round me. Bernice was never going to believe this.

'Giving . . . matron . . . a cuddle?' The GM writhed visibly beneath the sarcastic amazement in Kostaki's voice. 'Let me tell you, you little oik, that no gentleman cuddles a lady in that way! Do you understand? You have shocked and offended poor matron, and I want you to apologise to her at once, and get to bed. I shall deal with you in the morning.'

The GM staggered to his feet, looking ludicrously cast down. I could almost find it in me to feel sorry for him. I just hoped that dawn would bring forgetfulness along with the hangover he so richly deserved, otherwise he might well decide that the best form of defence was attack, and he was not a man one would choose for an enemy.

He removed the cap and stood before me, eyes lowered. 'Sorry, matron,' he mumbled.

'Don't let it happen again,' I said severely, beginning to enjoy myself.

'No, sorry, matron.'

Kostaki handed the GM his kaftan. 'Now put this on and cut along to bed. You haven't heard the last of this.'

He watched, with a display of haughty opprobrium that was staggering in view of his Y-fronts and bare legs, as the GM put on his coat of many colours, and then held the door as he left.

But the GM had one shot left in his locker.

'Matron . . . ?'

'What is it?'

'Your botty's nice, too.'

'OUT!' Kostaki pointed the way. 'Out of my sight, boy, and not another word!'

Laugh? We nearly died. Kostaki simply slid down the door to land in a shuddering heap on the floor, while I writhed on the sofa in an absolute agony of mirth, fuelled by hysterical relief.

'Oh Lord . . . give me strength . . . !' gasped Kostaki, crawling across the carpet towards me, tears streaming down his face. 'I've never seen anything so funny in my life . . . ! Old fish-face . . . the ink monitor rampant . . . and you, matron! Oh Christ . . . lying like a trussed turkey in a pool of water, hitting him with those bloody flowers . . . it was priceless . . . !'

'Well, what about you?' I cackled, pointing. 'If you could see yourself! What on earth did you put on that stethoscope for? I mean . . . ' I collapsed, unable to continue.

Kostaki lifted the end of the stethoscope and peered at it. 'What, this stethoscope?'

'Of course that stethoscope!'

'I've forgotten now . . . oh yes, I thought it might give me a spurious air of – of – '

'Of *what*?'

'Of authority!'

This was too much and we fell about once more, reeling and hooting and clutching ourselves until our guts ached with laughing.

When we had finally recovered, Kostaki clambered with his last remaining strength on to the sofa, slung my legs over his shoulders, and carried on where the ink monitor had left off.

'Hey . . . ' I protested unconvincingly, holding his ears as though steering a go-kart, 'I thought you said no gentleman ever cuddled a lady in this way . . . '

'That's right,' he replied, looking up momentarily and smacking his lips. 'But I never said I was a gentleman.'

Chapter Fourteen

In the overseas hall of the 29th Fartenwald Buchfest the next day, I was greeted by Vanessa in a state of high excitement.

'You're *never* going to believe this, Harriet,' she said, as she frog-marched me down interminable avenues of coconut matting to the Era stand, 'but the Big Cheese *was* here last night, the sneaky old bastard, *and* staying in the same hotel as you!'

Outwardly, I may at that moment have looked like a thirty-five-year-old authoress in a Liberty-print shirtwaister, but actually, I had turned to a pillar of salt.

'Golly . . . ' I began, hoping that some appropriate remark would simply rise to the surface and materialise. But fortunately Vanessa (in a gymslip, pop-socks and plimsolls), was too full of her news to wait for my reaction.

'He looked in here half an hour ago,' she babbled on, 'looking *simply* shot at, and said he was glad to see us all getting on with the job, but he was sorry he had to catch a flight to Anchorage. Can you imagine? Not a word of censure, not a single query. He was quite unlike himself. I wondered if the Dynamik had given him food poisoning. Are *you* all right?'

'Oh yes, perfectly.'

'Did you see him at all?'

'No! No, I didn't. I just had a quiet dinner with Constantine, and an early night.'

'*Lovely*,' agreed Vanessa.

The Era stand was alongside the back entrance to the overseas hall, a key position, and there was Tristan, standing before a vast blow-up of the *LDG* paperback cover, his head on a level with Victoria Principal's crotch. In the labyrinth of chipboard ante-rooms at the back of the stand I could see Chris Lazenby, Marilyn, the Fucktotum (in a hat) and the tapir Lucinda, going about their diverse business with the representatives of foreign publishing houses whom they had sucked in.

Spotting us, Tristan beamed, and raised a hand in welcome. He wore a natty dark suit and a carnation in his buttonhole, all of which created the impression that he was a bridegroom, and I a bride, being escorted up the aisle to his side.

'Speaking of your dishy doctor friend,' added Vanessa confidentially, 'he was round here early, too. He said he had some free hours and found the book fair so fascinating he might stay for a bit. You could have lunch with him if you like.'

This was below the belt. Kostaki and I had agreed, in a muted exchange over the breakfast buffet, that we would maintain a more-than-safe distance during the working part of the day. We were both a little punch-drunk after the events of the previous night and I, in particular, was wary of the movements of the GM, who was not in evidence in the dining room. And yet here was Constantine brushing aside the terms of our agreement and turning up, so to speak, in the lion's den.

But I was still slightly light-headed with sexual excess and sleep deprivation, and quite unable to exercise rational thought. So I mumbled something non-committal as we fetched up on the stand and Tristan kissed me warmly on both cheeks.

'Hallo, Harriet, don't you look nice?'

'Thank you, I bought it specially.'

'Look who's here!'

It was, of course, Kostaki, looking fresher than any man

had a right to after what we'd been through, and obviously well in with the Erans.

'Good morning,' I said, a little dully.

'Hallo!' said Kostaki. 'Hope you don't mind, but I'm free this morning, and I've never been to a book fair. How about some lunch?'

'Hang on,' I said. 'Aren't I supposed to be lunching with Clarion Paperbacks?'

Tristan patted me on the back. 'Take Constantine along, if you want to. It doesn't do any harm to appear sought-after.'

'I suppose not.' I sounded about as vivacious as a Dalek. The trouble was that being so close to Constantine reminded me with embarrassing clarity of our recent activities, so that it was actually difficult for me to stand with my legs together. I wondered how on earth I was going to get through my schedule with him constantly in the background, nudging my libido.

'I *must* show you something,' said Vanessa. 'The GM did have one brilliant idea!'

'Did he?'

'You know how he disapproves of drinking on the job – ' He did? I dared not look at Constantine – 'well, he's organised this dear little rest-room for us, with tea, juice, coffee, bikkies, fruit, not to mention comfy chairs for top-level discussions and so on. Isn't that sweet of him?'

She pushed open a door at the back of the stand and there, to be sure, was the rest-room, exactly as she'd described it, right down to the easy chairs, and the fleece of an acrylic sheep on the floor.

'Very nice,' I said. 'Very cosy. How thoughtful.'

'A marvellous idea,' concurred Kostaki enthusiastically over my shoulder, and as I turned and caught his eye I knew, without a shadow of doubt, what he had in mind.

When I eventually hobbled back on to the plane after two and a half days at the Buchfest, I was quite disproportionately pleased to see Ricky, Denzil, Julian and Gary waiting for me in the first-class cabin with hot cloths poised and canapés a-sizzle. They were exactly what the doctor (proverbial rather than actual) ordered – personable, solicitous, soothing and, most importantly, gay. I gave myself up like some weary old dog to the titbits and the gentle fussing, snoozing and waking as required, not at all the fractious subject I had been on the journey out.

I had never, I calculated, worked so hard, nor slept so little. My eyes felt like pissholes in the snow, my head like a bucket, my feet like raw steak and my cunt like Damon's shammy leather after a hard day on the downstairs windows. When I'd first invited Kostaki to join me in Fartenwald I had never in my wildest dreams anticipated such an intense period of sustained and imaginative fucking. The missionary position was to him what the tin-opener is to haute cuisine – beneath contempt. I had been spun round, upended, sucked, bitten, straddled and pummelled, often in quick succession and nearly always under the riskiest possible circumstances. And in between I had done my bit for Era Books like a good 'un, though God knows it had not been easy extolling the merits of *LDG* and *TRT* to earnest young Americans while Kostaki loitered nearby with a gleam in his eye and a lump in his trousers.

I functioned, book-wise, on automatic pilot. I smiled bleakly when Tristan and Vanessa congratulated me on my unflappable good nature. What did they expect? I was shagged to a ravelling. I was as likely to lose my temper as I was to win the Booker Prize. I acted laid back because I was laid back (and usually had been, not long before). There had been no respite between hyping and humping.

Constantine had left Fartenwald on an earlier flight, having already run his afternoon surgery extremely close, and not wanting to arouse suspicion among my Eran minders. To the last he had looked elegant and entirely composed, even to the extent of giving us a breakdown of the fictitious seminar on pre-conception care which he had supposedly attended for a few hours on both days. I realised that I was observing my first genuine, twenty-four-carat dual personality. No one would have guessed from Kostaki's outward appearance of conservative doctorly decorum the boudoir decathlete that lurked, grinning and grabbing, just beneath the surface. Vanessa had even been prompted to remark, with ill-concealed pique: 'Same old story. The really pretty ones are never interested. And he never even managed to grill you about *The Remembrance Tree!*'

It was the closest I came to spilling the beans and ramming them down my editor's skinny throat. But I restrained myself, and took comfort from the fact that the rest-room sofa on which she now perched with one lanky leg tucked beneath her was the same upon which Kostaki and I had scaled dizzy heights of erotic pleasure not two hours since while she and Tristan addressed a confused contingent of Malaysian publishers on the stand outside.

Sitting in the plane in a trance of exhaustion I had the not unpleasant sensation of having been burned at both ends. In spite of my extracurricular activities I had done Era proud. I had impressed Clarion Paperbacks, New York, of my basically serious literary intent, while reassuring them that there would be no watering-down of love scenes; I had stormed the language barrier to coax a smile from sullen Henni Lundquist of Finland, and had dutifully consumed macrobiotic salads and mineral water with Vince Priddoe while acting heartbroken over my inability to get to Australia this year; I had let slip tantalising and carefully worded hints all over the overseas hall about *TRT*, and I had endlessly struck the difficult balance between optimistic confidence and graceful modesty. I had, in short, been a model author: two-faced, freeloading and mendacious. And Era were well pleased with me.

It was late afternoon when I drove back into Basset Magna from the station. A sunny afternoon, with summer rising, and I was in the best possible spirits. The new Harriet Blair had emerged, with a vengeance, in all her carnal glory, sex-drive in top gear and cruising and Dame Conscience well and truly put in her place. With my return came faint, wraithlike thoughts of George, but everything was so neatly compartmentalised in my head that they did not fully impinge on my consciousness. Until, that is, I opened the front door and found a letter from my husband on the mat.

I picked it up and took it to the kitchen table where

someone had thoughtfully placed the rest of my mail. It was all bills and village circulars apart from one other, forwarded by Era.

I sat down. The house was extremely quiet. There was a smell of detergent and furniture polish; everything was unnaturally tidy. In fact my home had an air of wary and rebellious subjugation like an urchin scrubbed up for a party and told to sit still and in silence until it was time to go. Of course, Damon had been, and Brenda was probably retaining my children until she saw I had returned and had time to recover from my exertions.

Trepidatiously, I opened the letter from George. It was mostly news of unexceptionable tedium, full of *longueurs* about on-site conferences and labour difficulties. He had left the interesting bit till last.

' . . . You know,' he wrote, 'I said I should try and get back for a few days in the near future? Unfortunately that may not be on now, as I have to spend a few weeks in the Med on a small job for the bosses in London. Obviously my Arab masters won't be too pleased if I then take leave as well! I'm so sorry, darling, but it can't be helped. Please enjoy yourself, I should hate to think of you sitting at home every night watching "Dallas" with the children. I'll keep in touch, and let you know if there's a chance I can get away. Hope the writing goes well, and you have a good time in Germany at the book fair. Much love as ever, George.'

I put the letter back in its envelope. A few weeks in the Med? Poor George, my heart bled for him, how awfully tough to be sent to the Med, where the wine, women and song were not just legal but obligatory. But I wasn't jealous, far from it. He had not only extended my period of freedom, but had as good as given me a licence for loose living, which I should assiduously make use of. I might, perhaps, have a party.

I was enormously chuffed with this idea, and whisked through the bills and circulars without a care in the world. I then opened the letter forwarded by Era. It was from one Torquil Bannister of Mercia TV. He explained that he was instigating a new programme on the arts entitled, craftily, 'Imitating Life'. He puffed it to the full, with much talk of bold and unorthodox new approaches, of critical perceptions and popular lenses, but in spite of being sceptical about the programme itself I was still hugely gratified to be invited to appear. They wanted me (Torquil Bannister wrote) to be spokesperson for popular fiction, and they were hoping to find someone from 'the other side', as he rather menacingly phrased it, to promulgate debate. But it was all intended to be 'relaxed and entertaining' rather than 'confrontational', he assured me. And they would, of course, pay me a performance fee, plus expenses.

I needed no persuading. Telly – the hypers' holy grail! I opened the french window and went into the garden. Everywhere there was evidence of Declan's ministrations with mower, strimmer and hoe. The lawn – it actually looked like a lawn – might almost have been hoovered, it was so smooth and clipped and litter-free.

I got a deckchair out of the summerhouse and sat down, facing the sun, basking in the heat and my general sense of well-being. Fluffy leapt over the fence, bushy-tailed from whatever nefarious doings he'd been engaged in in my absence, and sprang on to my lap, purring energetically like a furry vibrator.

'Cooee, stranger!'

I turned my head and there was Brenda Tunnel, coming round the side of the house with Gareth, Clara, Jason and Michelle.

'Hallo, Brenda.'

'I saw your car in the front,' she explained, coming over to where I sat and studying me with an expectant smile as if I might have had myself elaborately tattooed while at the Buchfest. 'So I gave you a little breathing space and then brought them back to you!'

'Hallo, kids,' I said, getting up and embracing them. Their pleasure in my return was qualified, I could tell, by slight resentment; they kissed me dutifully but were aloof.

'Come on, Jase,' said Gareth, 'fancy a frame?'

'I don't think Harriet wants the whole house overrun the moment she's got back!' cried Brenda gaily.

'That's okay,' I said. 'Might as well get straight back to normal.'

237

'Do you want to see my Badness stickers, Michelle?' asked Clara. 'They're really suave.'

Within minutes the snooker table was set up, and the two girls had appeared in the window of Clara's room and pulled the blind down.

'Sit down for a minute,' I said to Brenda, fetching another deckchair. 'Would you like a drink?'

'Oh, no thanks, I won't. Have you had a smashing time?'

'Yes, very enjoyable – very busy, of couse,' I said, poor put-upon thing that I was. 'But I really can't thank you enough for having the kids. Were they all right?'

'I didn't know I had them, honestly,' said Brenda. She went on to tell me of how much they'd eaten, what they'd said, and how much of a tonic they'd been generally. As she talked and I watched and listened I concluded that they must have been a tonic of sorts, for Brenda was certainly in cracking form, billowing in a becoming ethnic print, and with some new reddish colour on her hair. I warmed to her. She was a good sport.

'I'm thinking of having a party, Brenda,' I said. 'Would you and Trevor come?'

'You bet, what fun!' was her reply.

I ventured on to more sensitive territory. 'How are things . . . I mean between you and Trevor, these days?'

'Oh!' she beamed, and wriggled her shoulders inside the ethnic tent, 'oh, *ever* so much better, thanks.'

That was it, of course. I realised in that moment what it was that was different about Brenda. It wasn't just the dress, or the hair; her boiler was stoked and lit. She was incandescent. All twelve and a half stone of nutty slack had the almost luminous glow of the well-laid woman. And perhaps it had been the presence of my children at Trevenda which had done it, by creating the necessary curb to marital conflict.

'I'm so pleased,' I said. 'That is good news.'

When the Tunnels had gone, and the children and I had eaten cheese on toast, I announced my intention of driving into Barford to collect Spot from 55 Tennis Court Road. Gareth claimed to have pressing engagements, but Clara agreed to come along for the ride. She rather admired Bernice, who doubtless struck her as a sort of Naughtiest Girl in the School writ large.

In the car on the way I pressed her about the Tunnels. 'Was it really all right? No disasters?'

'Not if you don't count her cooking.'

'It's okay, isn't it? What was the matter with it?'

Clara shrugged. 'It isn't like yours.'

This constituted a pretty fulsome compliment. 'Never mind, darling,' I said indulgently, 'you're home now. And,' I added, 'I'm thinking of having a party.'

'What, without Dad?' asked Clara, the voice of conventional morality.

'Why ever not? It will be a very good opportunity for me to ask all sorts of people Dad doesn't care for, that I owe hospitality to.'

'Such as?'

'Well . . . people from my publishers for a start, to repay all the lunches and things I've had off them. I thought of making it a lunchtime party.'

Clara considered this, her face a mask of mistrust. 'Do they have children?'

'Who?'

'Publishers.' She seemed to be asking about generic capability rather than specific fact. I realised I hadn't a clue about even the marital, let alone the parental status of the Erans. To me, they were life's eternal freewheelers, creatures of wine bar and restaurant, of boardroom and conference centre, of taxi, telex and media-launch. It was hard to imagine these darting, highly coloured gadflys staggering up to empty potties in the small hours, or bawling at pre-pubes to tidy their rooms. As for spouses, if spouses there were, I could not flesh them out into anything more than pin-people scurrying hither and thither, feeding the voracious egos of the Erans.

'I haven't a clue,' I said. 'But I shouldn't invite them anyway.'

'Good,' said Clara, 'so Gareth and me can invite friends?'

'I suppose so. A few.'

'What about music? Damon could do that for you.'

239

'No!' I practically clipped a traffic island in my perturbation. 'No, no, no!'

'Groo,' said Clara. 'Sounds really, really dull.'

'That sounds absolutely spifferoo!' cried Bernice, when I told
her. '*I* shall come, of course, and I might even persuade the
Venerable Bede to accompany me.'

'Good heavens.' I was suitably astonished.

'*Oh* yes.' Bernice tapped the side of her nose with her forefinger. 'Ways and means. The way to an academic's heart is
via his amour-propre. I shall tell him it's his chance to meet
some genuine schlock publishers.'

'But won't that put him off at once?'

'Absolutely not, he's all afire with the spirit of conversion.
You know that TV that was in the offing when you came up a
few weeks ago – well, it's definitely *on*.'

'Oh really, what is it?'

'Some horrid trendy arts thing that Merica TV are
putting out – '

'Not "Imitating Life"?'

'That's the one.'

'What date?'

'Can't remember – but it's the first one.'

I played my trump card. 'I'm on that one too.'

'Hell's teeth,' said Bernice in awe. 'Be gentle with him,
won't you?'

We were sitting on Bernice's patio, a sort of concrete jetty
around which foamed an impenetrable mass of unkempt
vegetation. Clara sat on the rusty swing-seat, drinking
something gaseous and fluorescent called Zzip!, and Spot lay
prostrate before us. He had put on weight under Bernice's
regime of goulash and inertia, and I reflected that both of us
could do with some jogging.

'You never said you were going on telly,' said Clara
accusingly.

'Well, I am.'

'What, with Mr Potter?'

'More like against, I should think.'

'How embarrassing,' said my daughter. 'You can't even

argue properly in real life, what on earth will you be like in front of a camera? It'll be a massacre.'

'For goodness sake, Clara,' said Bernice loftily, 'it's only a discussion about books.' I loved my friend, but with that one sentence she demonstrated her total ignorance of the world of publishing, both popular and otherwise.

The vegetation in front of us shuddered and rustled and finally disgorged Barty. He looked quite presentable, wearing a Barford University sweatshirt, and with his teeth in, but had spoiled the effect by wearing open sandals over stained nylon socks.

'Hallo, Barty,' said Clara. Oddly, she was not disgusted by Barty. Or at least, her disgust was mixed with respect for someone in whom disgustingness had found its apotheosis, and in adulthood too.

'Hallo, darling,' said Barty. 'Hallo, Harriet love. Fancy a game of darts, darling?'

'Okay,' agreed Clara. I watched doubtfully as Barty shuffled off with his arm round my daughter. Bernice at once turned to me with an expression of lascivious expectation.

'Well? How was it?'

I glanced round furtively. 'Where's Arundel?'

'At the library. What happened?' I told her, in graphic detail and not forgetting the matron episode. 'Stroll on, as hairy as that, eh?'

'Absolutely.'

'You do see life, Harriet,' said Bernice happily. 'And how do you feel about all this, now that the show's on the road? Guilty? Ashamed? Soiled?'

I pondered my reply for a full three seconds. 'No. Bucked.'

'Wa-hay!' Bernice lifted her clasped hands in the air. 'That's my girl!' She pulled out the front of her T-shirt and glanced down. 'I'm getting freckles. So what now?'

'I don't know. I was thinking I might write to George, and – '

'And what? Don't for God's sake do anything hasty.'

'I know, but I can't possibly carry on with this once he gets back.'

241

'Probably not. But it will have done both of you the power of good. Let the Greek keep charging your battery for as long as possible, and then pass the benefits on to George.'

I considered this option. It had a lot going for it, most of all commonsense and expediency. But there was one crucial flaw.

'I don't think I can give him up.'

Bernice gave me a look of affectionate contempt. 'You took him on, you can give him up. George has a perfectly serviceable tool as well, you know.'

'I know, I know . . . but I am hooked on Kostaki.'

'Then George will prevent you getting withdrawal symptoms. Literally.'

'I'm not sure.'

'Look, missis,' said Bernice, wagging an admonitory finger at me. 'Make your mind up. If you think Kildare's worth a divorce, that's your funeral.'

'That sounds a bit drastic – '

'Well, it's what you were implying, isn't it?'

'I don't know that I was – '

' – implying anything, oh no, of course not.' Bernice sighed despairingly.

I felt I had failed her. 'What should I do?' I asked humbly.

'Eat your Greek and have him too, of course! All the benefits of marriage plus bonuses.'

'I know,' I said, brightening, 'I'll wait till after my party, that gives me another couple of weeks, and maybe I'll have him out of my system by then.'

'Mañana, mañana,' sighed Bernice. 'Maybe.'

'I thought,' I said, changing the subject, 'that I'd invite absolutely everyone to my party. You know, a real mixed bag. It's time I brought all the threads of my life together – '

'– and made one ruddy great granny knot which you won't be able to untangle,' said Bernice, gloomily. But prophetically.

We talked for a little longer and then I got up to go. Bernice accompanied me to the games room – a damp and crumbling annexe where Barty had his darts board, and a dilapidated ping-pong table which rose in a kind of sharp ridge along the centre join. He and Clara were as happy as Larry, apparently, which all goes to show that you never can tell.

'Harriet,' said Barty, shuffling over and wagging a fistful of Crafty Cockney Super Flights in my face. 'Clara tells me you're having a party!'

Clara was lucky that we were in company, and separated from each other by the ping-pong table.

'That's right,' I said, through clenched teeth. 'Just a few friends, you know, nothing – '

'She's invited me along, bless her.'

I gave Clara the old optical gimlet, but she was terrifically busy examining the scoreboard. I could feel warm shudders of suppressed laughter from Bernice.

'Has she?' I said. 'Fair enough.'

'I shall look forward to that,' Barty assured me. 'Haven't been to a do in ages. Formal, is it?'

'Yes,' I snapped. 'Absolutely.'

To my dismay, Barty evinced delight at this information. 'Watch out girls,' he cackled, pirouetting round us like something from the dance of the living dead. 'I'll be there in my zoot suit!'

'Come on, Clara,' I said. 'Time to go.'

We collected Spot and went out to the car. Bernice was seismic with giggles.

'Now don't be too hard on her,' she said, putting her arm round Clara, 'you did say you were goint to invite everyone.'

Out of deference to my friend, and Barty, who had appeared in the doorway wearing a plastic Snoopy apron, I maintained an icy silence. Just as we pulled away from the kerb, a familiar green Jag drew up in front of us and Clara, keen to forestall my wrath, said: 'Oh look, there's Mr Channing!'

'So it is,' I said. 'Don't change the subject.'

Nonetheless I did notice as we drove off that Mike Channing was visiting 55 Tennis Court Road. And was admitted without demur.

I waited till Monday to visit Constantine, though over the weekend I saw him twice – once at a fork supper given by Barry and Lydia Langley, where he was introduced as 'our latest

243

doctor' and I as 'our local celebrity' and we were both rendered speechless by the ferocity of the chilli con carne; and then again at the Open House wine bar in Regis where I took Gareth and Clara on Sunday in order to get out of cooking lunch, and where he was present as the guest of Dr and Mrs Donleavy. I felt obliged to stop at their table and pass the time of day, but escaped as quickly as possible. It was awkward in the extreme to meet, socially, two men who both had intimate knowledge of my private parts, especially as Dr Donleavy was wedded to his work and probably saw all his female patients as no more than a cluster of tubes and channels on legs, and might at any moment be unable to contain his curiosity on the subject.

On Monday, at about midday, I put on my running gear and set off for Parva at a cracking pace, without the dog. I covered the distance in record time, and as I turned into the Prickhard I almost mowed down Kostaki who was painting the gate, dressed in denim shorts and flip-flops.

'Hallo,' I gasped, 'may I come in?'

In reply he rested the brush across the top of the paint can and escorted me into the house. In Anna's absence it was, as she had implied it would be, pin-neat. A scent of beeswax hung in the air, and the effect of screwing on the gleaming parquet flooring was that we moved along, humping and stretching like a bipartite caterpillar, so that I finished up with my head in the drawing room. The marmalade cat patrolled round me with his tail in the air like a flag, treating me to a snail's eye view of his neat, seamed anus.

Kostaki, disengaging, glanced over his shoulder.

'Didn't they used to get the servants to do the quickstep with dusters on their feet? This would have been just as effective and twice as enjoyable.'

I was, at last, used to his little ways. Fuck first and talk after. It was all very well for him, since his powers of recovery were phenomenally rapid. But if I had anything worth saying I had to make sure it wasn't poked clean out of my head before I got round to saying it.

'I've decided to have a party,' I said, sitting up. 'Can you come?'

'What date?'

244

'You tell me which Saturday's best for you, and I'll make it then. I haven't sent any invitations yet.'

He got up, fastened his shorts, and went to consult the diary by the telephone.

'Saturday fortnight?'

'Fine. It'll be lunchtime, because I want to ask the people from Era Books.'

'Including Screwball Major?'

I considered this question. 'Yes, I think so. I mean, I'll invite him, but I don't suppose for a moment he'll come.' I scrambled to my feet and went over to him. 'Kostaki . . . '

'Yes?' He put his arms round me and began licking my neck. 'You're all nice and salty.'

'It's called sweat. Look, don't you think it's time we – '

'Talked about Us?'

'Then you agree?'

'I think it's an appalling idea. Once you start talking about something it turns into a dead bird in a glass case. A conversation piece. Leave it alone and it flies around like it ought to.'

'But I really think we should – '

'Ever since I was a child,' he went on conversationally, pushing his fingers into my hair and his tongue into my ear, 'I have loathed and detested the word should. It smacks of cabbage and homework and cold showers. I so much prefer can and will and might . . . '

It was hopeless. My attempts to rationalise and regularise were being met with nothing but criticism from Bernice and levity from Kostaki. I had about as much chance of making him take the matter seriously as I had of preventing him, now, from manoeuvring me across the hall and up the stairs.

For the first time in weeks, as I submitted swooningly to Kostaki's impassioned manipulations, I thought, wistfully, of George.

Chapter Fifteen

Like any other red-blooded writer, I was prepared to endure virtually any indignity at the hands of the media in order that my (usually misguided) pronouncements might be enshrined in print, or carried over the airwaves in between pop records, or, best of all, be actually seen, articulated by myself, on the TV screens of those hapless viewers who had omitted to switch over to 'Minder'.

Therefore, in spite of misgivings about the premise of 'Imitating Life', and stark terror at the thought of public debate with Arundel, I set out one humid Tuesday in late June for Antwich, and Mercia TV.

My party was on the Saturday, only four days off, but I was confident I had things in hand. It seemed to me that if I was to enjoy myself, without George's invaluable organisational presence, I had best get the Little Men out in force. So I had splashed out on Attwood & Co., Caterers of Basset Regis (who, with a nice appreciation of cause and effect, advertised for Parties-Weddings-Functions-Children), whom Linda Channing had described as obliging and presentable. I had also commandeered Damon for the day as general dogsbody, and had grudgingly agreed, as part of our verbal contract, that he might provide background music for the occasion.

'Don't worry,' he said soothingly. 'I got plenty of your sort of thing.' I knew this to be true, but it was not so much the content as the manner that concerned me.

'If there's the slightest hint of a hitch,' I warned, 'off!'

'Of course,' he agreed, discernibly pained by my mistrust.

Declan was to take charge of car-parking arrangements, and the children had agreed to be responsible for any of their contemporaries who might turn up. This left me almost nothing to do but look decorative, act vivacious, and have fun.

I just hoped I should be able to manage the last. I had recently experienced my very first, tremulous stirrings of angst concerning my affair with Kostaki. Mine had been a fast-moving and highly intensive course in adultery, and the graph of my emotions had been correspondingly steep, reaching a dizzy zenith in Fartenwald and now slithering inexorably, inevitably, downwards.

The trouble was, I had got used to him. You get used to anything if you get enough of it, and I was getting a superfluity of Kostaki. It wasn't that I didn't still want to get laid by him. I had no say in that whatever, for he pushed the 'Go' button with masterly accuracy every darn time. But I did wish there was something else – a little more conversation, a few shared interests that were non-physiological, one or two frills and trimmings to our relationship. A little – dare I say it – romance. Besides which, it was exhausting. There were none of those drowsy, whispering, post-coital hours which I had envisaged as part of an illicit affair, no drives into the country for lunch at cosy anonymous hotels, no calls to say 'I love you'. We simply continued with our separate lives, and came together at intervals for voracious bouts of screwing during which he displayed no concern whatsoever for our respective reputations. No place was too public for him, no situation too risky, no audience too large. We walked a continual knife-edge of scandalous risk, upon which he thrived, but which was beginning to saw through my nerves. Only the previous Sunday I had conducted a lengthy coversation with Eric

247

Chittenden at a cocktail party with Kostaki's hand in the back of my trousers, and he had twice jumped me when I was out jogging, leaving the Ghikasmobile parked at the side of the road, as conspicuous in the empty Barfordshire countryside as a Harriet Blair novel in a headmistress's study.

There was no doubt that I couldn't carry on indefinitely. It was only steam heat that held us together, and I was running out of steam. The party, therefore, had taken on a different aspect in the light of all this. It was now beginning to look less like a celebration of liberated lust and feminine independence, and more like a graceful swan song. Bernice's advice did not now seem so outlandish. I *should* welcome George home, when he came, with open arms and nicely warmed bed . . . I should treat him to all that I had learned from Kostaki . . . we would resume our well-ordered, tolerant and sensible existence . . . and who knows but that I might not be able to continue seeing my lover from time to time, in order to keep my fires stoked and riddled?

Of course, my heroine Maria was subject to the same emotional fluctuations as myself. Before the Buchfest the problem had been to keep her in check so as not to disaffect my army of loyal readers. Now she was back on course (and in women's dress) and confronted by the pressing need to make a choice between the two men in her life. Kersey House had been relieved, as the saying goes, by the Royalist troops, and there had been much ostentatious gallantry on every hand, culminating in the rescuing of young Jamie from the jaws of death by Richard Hawkhurst. Biting both the bullet and her full underlip, Maria must needs go to where Richard (slightly and becomingly wounded) lay, and proffer her thanks.

'Sir,' she faltered, 'may I speak with you?'

Even from her position by the door Maria could see how his blue eyes glittered in his white face, and she felt the old thrill that was part fear and part excitement, as he beckoned her to draw closer. But his voice was softer than she remembered as he bade Martha withdraw, and a smile played about his bloodless lips.

'What would you, cousin?' he enquired. 'Now it is your turn to look down on me. Is that sweet, little Maria Trevelyan? Does it please you?'

'It does not, sir,' she replied stoutly. 'Indeed it grieves me to see you brought low. Are you in much pain?'

'It is nothing, a scratch merely.' He was curt, and she liked him for it. 'But I tire readily. Tell me what it is you have to say.'

She felt her cheeks burning with the childish blushes he must surely despise, and her voice, when it came, was scarcely more than a whisper. 'I wished to thank you for saving the life of Jamie Farrell.'

'Do you so . . . ' She knew those piercing blue eyes rested on her face, and she dared not raise her own to meet them. 'And what is young Farrell to you?'

'He has been a good friend to me . . ' She looked up, and spoke with passion now. 'A friend when I thought I had no other in the world!'

'No more!' Richard half-raised himself from the pillow, but fell back with an oath and repeated, more quietly: 'No more. I read it in your face, what it is that you feel for him, and I wish to hear no more of it. He fought well today, he did not deserve to die. But nor does he deserve those tender and impassioned feelings which shine in your eyes and cry out in your voice – '

For a moment he closed his eyes and tightened his lips in pain, and Maria reached out to touch his hand where it lay upon the bed. But he shook her off angrily.

'Go, cousin! I tire. Go – and send Martha to me.'

'I will do so.' With soft tread and troubled heart she left the chamber. She had seen her proud cousin brought low, but it had brought her scant satisfaction. For she had also seen, in that tortured white face, those blazing blue eyes, suffering not only of the body – but of the heart . . .

The satisfaction *I* took from all this was far from scant. I was back on familiar territory, in the very heartlands of the literary genre which I had made my own. Also, I had planned an ending of unrelieved gloom which would ensure that all the protagonists, and especially Maria, would emerge with honour, and without a dry eye in the house as far as my readers were concerned.

But that would have to wait till after 'Imitating Life'. My main concern as I sat in the buffet car en route to Antwich was that I should put up a good show before the cameras, and not disgrace myself in the confrontation with Arundel Potter, spokesman for Literary Standards. Bernice had phoned me concerning Arundel's preparedness to give me a lift, but I had declined, for two reasons. Firstly, I suspected she was traducing her husband, who had never had an altruistic impulse in his life and, if he had, would have rung me himself; secondly, I knew that whatever I might gain in terms of comfort and convenience by accepting the offer would simultaneously be snatched away by the psychological war of attrition which Arundel would certainly wage on my morale. If I was to be pitched against him before the cameras, the very least I could do was to arrive in good confrontational order, my arguments mustered, my self-regard stable, my enthusiasm untarnished.

Constantine, bucked as usual at the prospect of a new setting for his activities, had arranged to meet me in a pub in Antwich called the Flag and Ferret, and to drive me home thereafter. So I put on the black dress he had admired at the gymkhana, daubed Instan on my legs and red varnish on my toenails, and set off.

Mercia TV occupied a building like a breezeblock mausoleum on the northern outskirts of Antwich, as inconveniently placed as possible for those arriving by public transport. The taxi driver who took me from the station to the studios pointed out these disadvantages to me at some length and in a hectoring and accusatory tone. By the time we arrived I was disposed to overtip, and to apologise for the inconvenience I had caused him by being a guest of Mercia TV, both of which he accepted as his right and due.

'What you on?' he asked, as I turned to go.

' "Imitating Life",' I replied.

'Never 'eard of it.'

'It's a new arts programme.'

'Oh yeah? We need that like we need a hole in the head,' was his encouraging rejoinder.

I entered the foyer. The decor was poor man's Scandinavian, with a lot of pine-look laminate, and khaki carpet tiles. The walls bore the massed mugshots of Mercia TV's presenters, plus signed photos of their more eminent guests – one or two wholesome pop singers, a Chinese cookery expert, and a footballer with a perm. Behind the receptionist's desk was a slatted board, headed: 'Today Mercia TV welcomes – ' and nothing else. Beneath it was a tray full of plastic letters from which, one dared to hope, the words 'Arundel Potter and Harriet Blair' might have been formed. 'Una Paloma Blanca' wafted over the sound system. The receptionist was reading *Cosmo.*

'Good morning,' I said, in my best up-front, unabashed, self-publicising manner. 'I'm Harriet Blair, here to record "Imitating Life".' I produced my letter. 'Torquil Bannister contacted me.'

'Oh yes,' said the receptionist. 'Miss Drinkwater from Era Books is here already, she's in the hospitality room. I'll just call someone to take you through.'

'Miss Drinkwater?' I gaped foolishly. Marilyn? Erans in attendance were an unforeseen complication.

The receptionist consulted a large book. 'Yes, Marilyn Drinkwater, publicity director, Era Books. Yes? No?' She gave me a quizzical patronising smile. She had an orange crew-cut and a spotted bow tie.

'Yes,' I muttered. 'Marilyn, of course.'

'Take a seat, please.'

I sat down on a black vinyl banquette, reminiscent of the one in the waiting room of the Basset Parva surgery. On a large, shin-high table before me were an assortment of magazines and periodicals. The elaborate fans in which these publications had been arranged suggested that they were seldom if ever read by the guests whom they were supposed to divert. Irritated by the fans, I picked up a copy of something called *On the Move* and read, with mystification, of a grand-mother from Stoke Poges who had circumnavigated the earth on a specially modified tricycle to raise money for a community centre.

The receptionist dinked a few buttons with her purple-lacquered nail and waited, smiling at me sightlessly as she listened for an answer. 'Oh, Pia. Mrs Blair is here for Torquil. Could you come along and fetch her? Her publicity lady is in the green room with the others. Thanks, love.'

She leaned towards me, focusing this time. 'Pia will be down in a mo.'

'Jolly good.'

I stared once more at the grandmother. There were innumerable photos of her travels. Here she was in New Guinea, sturdy and indomitable among grinning headhunters . . . here in a souk, beads dangling from her handlebars . . . here, apparently, in the Yukon, in a plaid jacket and ear-flaps . . .

'Harriet Blair?'

A whiff of expensive scent assailed my nostrils and I looked up to see a slender, doe-eyed beauty with a cloud of dark hair, dressed all in white.

'I'm Pia,' she told me. 'Will you come with me?'

'Thank you.' I rose from the banquette. My bare legs, on being parted from the vinyl, made a noise like elastoplast being stripped from a rhinoceros. Pia floated ahead of me like a wraith, or dryad, her hair seeming to float around her head, her white espadrilles to glide an inch or so above the floor.

It was miles to the green room. Like some mythological adventurer being lured on by a will-o'-the-wisp I followed Pia through swing doors, up flights of stairs, into lifts and out again, across promising-looking outer-office areas, only to pass once more into the barren hinterland of corridors and echoing stone steps.

'It's such a silly building,' she cast over her shoulder. 'There's a new bit and an old bit but they didn't seem to join them up properly!'

'Too silly,' I agreed.

At last we reached a door which Pia opened, to reveal a group of people drinking, smoking, and apparently enjoying themselves. I at once spotted Arundel and Marilyn, and there were two others. One was a young woman whom I took to be Arundel's nanny from his academic publishers, the Barford Press. The other was a tall caddish man in a bounder's uniform of tight yellow shirt, electric-blue lightweight trews, and brothel-creepers. This was Torquil Bannister.

'Ah, the long-awaited Mrs Blair,' he said. 'The lovely Pia has brought you to us. Pia, let me look at you. Harriet, let me shake you by the hand.'

I clasped the nicotine-stained cod fillet which he extended to me, and then he asked whom I knew.

'Well, I know Marilyn, of course,' I said. I didn't like to admit acquaintanceship with Arundel in case they threw us both out.

'You got here all right then,' said Marilyn. 'How's the family?'

'Fine,' I said, 'as far as I know.'

Marilyn shrieked with laughter. 'Honestly, you are a scream.'

The others looked blank, not having been initiated into the secrets of the Era/Blair byplay. Arundel lifted one eyebrow.

'A drink,' suggested Torquil. 'White wine? Pia, vino, there's a love.'

Arundel's nanny stepped forward, bringing her charge with her. She was a plump, plain, breathless girl, a first-class Eng.Hons. if ever I saw one.

'How do you do,' she gasped, 'I'm Flavia Brayne.'

'How do you do.'

'And this is Arundel Potter, your fellow guest, but I believe you two may have come across each other. I know how parochial university towns can be.'

'Good day, Mrs Blair,' said Arundel, with admirable formality. 'What a small world.'

'So you two *know* each other?' cried Torquil.

'Scarcely at all ' 'Not really ' we both said together.

'Not that it matters,' said Torquil hastily. 'But it can be inhibiting to have to criticise the work of a friend.'

'Mrs Blair?' Pia handed me a small glass of wine, the colour and temperature of recent urine. 'And there are some snacks on the side if you're hungry.' I observed parsley-bedecked quiches on a side table.

'Thank you.'

'I'm surprised you didn't run here, Harriet,' quipped Marilyn, assiduously buffing up my imagie. 'It's only fifty miles.'

Amid polite laughter, Torquil said: 'Oh, a runner, are you?'

'Not exactly. Just a domestic jogger,' I replied, with the

becoming modesty so beloved of the Erans. Marilyn glanced round with pride. Flavia and Arundel began to chat, earnestly and quietly, and Pia started to cut a quiche into wedges.

Marilyn came to my side. I felt initiative drain from me as the Force of the Erans emanated from her and held me in its insidious power.

'Harriet,' she said, in a confidential tone, 'has Torquil explained what he has in mind?'

'Not in detail,' I said, turning politely to Torquil. As he began to invoke widened perceptions and extended parameters I conjectured, unkindly, that what he had in mind most of the time was sniffing ladies' bicycle seats. Torquil Bannister would not see fifty again. His face, ruddy with frequent ingestion of green room chateau pissoir, was adorned with a thick moustache, handy no doubt for filtering oxygen from Mercia TV's overused air, as a whale sifts plankton from the sea. His eyes, above a nose the shape of an inverted light bulb, were wet and blue like a couple of guppies swimming in skimmed milk. He was one of those men who made me inordinately glad that I had experienced Kostaki before I got too old to care.

' . . . so you see,' he concluded, 'we're really just after an entertaining show which deals with some of the questions the ordinary viewer would ask about art if he or she had the chance.'

'Always supposing,' I said, 'that the ordinary viewer has any in the first place.'

'Any what, Harriet?'

'Questions.'

Torquil slapped me on the back. 'I like your style, Harriet. I like it very much. I think – ' he leaned round and addressed Marilyn – 'we shall have a very nice show in the bag a few hours from now.'

Marilyn squeezed my arm affectionately, pleased that I had scored a hit with Torquil, though uncertain about my means of scoring it.

Pia came over, having failed to interest anyone in quiche. 'Torquil's marvellous, isn't he?' she breathed, in all seriousness.

'I should think so,' I replied cautiously.

'He's just so amazing with *people*,' she said. 'He can just *pull* the best out of them.' She made a gesture reminiscent of drawing a fowl. 'And of course he is *the* creative man at MTV at the moment. The sad thing is,' she sighed, weightily, 'we shall almost certainly lose him after "Imitating Life". It's just *so* innovative.'

'Still,' I said, joining in with gusto, now I understood that platitudes were the currency in which we dealt, 'people have to move on, and up, and of course it does make way for new young talent.'

'That,' said Pia with feeling, 'is so true, Harriet. Oh look, we're going down.'

Pia's last remark to me in the green room seemed, in retrospect, to have been prophetic. And like the helmsman of the *Titanic* I experienced a shudder of the gravest foreboding as, with Torquil before and Pia behind, we made our way down flights of reverberating speckled stairs to the studio.

'Now then, Arundel and Harriet,' said Torquil, 'Pia will take you to make-up.'

Once more we followed where the lovely Pia led, and this time wound up beneath the contemptuous gaze of Zandra, who pronounced Arundel to be colourless and myself florid.

'I'll deal with you first,' she said, tipping my head back. 'We usually have this trouble with our female guests, they seem to think they have to put the make-up on with a trowel just because they're going on telly. You have a naturally high colour, don't you, so I'm going to quiet things down a bit, and dry off these greasy panels.'

I squirmed inwardly, not least because Arundel, sitting next to me with a pink plastic bib round his neck, was listening with fascinated attention to this tirade.

'The men,' added Zandra, dusting, dabbing and tweaking, 'are generally a whole lot easier.'

'I'm bound to say,' said Arundel smugly, 'that I agree.'

'Right,' said Zandra, unimpressed. 'Your turn now.'

I did not wait for Arundel, but left him to Zandra's tender mercies, and went out into the passage where Marilyn was waiting to escort me to the studio.

255

'Just be your own super self, Harriet,' she advised as she ushered me along.

'I'll try.'

'Plenty of emphasis on the sales of your books both here and abroad, all the letters you get from readers, the satisfaction you get from bringing enjoyment to literally millions of people – '

'Don't worry,' I said. 'I won't let you down.'

The set of 'Imitating Life' comprised a group of cylindrical plinths, like assorted tinned goods. On top, as it were, of the baked beans, was a simulacrum of a film camera, on the tuna fish a pile of books, on the dog food theatrical masks, and so on. I deduced, from the presence of three anorexic tubular chairs and a rubber plant, that we were to be sited just off centre on the drinking chocolate.

'So, Harriet,' said Torquil, rubbing his hands with glee at the prospect of good sport, 'what do you think of our set?'

'Very striking,' I said.

Arundel arrived and we stood, he gingered up and I toned down, on either side of Torquil as he ran over the outline once more for our benefit. He then introduced the show's presenter who turned out to be a woman, Siobhan Flynn, tall, striking and American-designer-clad.

'Right,' said Torquil, 'I'll go on up and leave you to Siobhan. We'll kick off in about fifteen minutes.'

We settled ourselves gingerly on the drinking chocolate while people in headphones, cameramen and assorted Oxbridge camp-followers bustled about being Part of Things.

Siobhan Flynn turned out to know a lot more about me than I did.

'The great thing about your books, it seems to me, Harriet,' she said, 'and indeed about all good popular fiction, is its quality of honesty and innocence, and by that I don't mean naivety. To work, a mass-market novel must be written with integrity, would you agree?'

'I suppose so,' I said dimly. 'Although – '

'And of course a genuine respect and affection for one's readers, something which comes over very strongly in your work. You never short-change your public and I respect that.'

'Thanks,' I said.

'Now Mr Potter – ' she turned to Arundel. I wondered why he merited a Mr but I was just matey old Harriet. 'Mr Potter, broadly speaking I know your views, but may I ask, have you actually read any mass-market fiction?'

'Only,' said Arundel frostily, 'in the interests of research for this programme.'

'Fine. So you can, as they say, give examples to support any arguments you may have?'

Arundel whitened beneath his blusher. 'Of course.'

'I do hope,' said Siobhan, addressing both of us, 'that we can have a really entertaining and mature discussion here, and perhaps try to establish some sort of universal standard that could be applied to all types of fiction, high and middlebrow, literary and popular . . . let's dispel a few myths here today . . . '

She continued, but I did not listen. It was perfectly plain that she was a four-star pain in the arse. As I sat there I caught Arundel's eye and read there, astonishingly, exactly the same thought. We were destined to be, for perhaps the only time in our relationship, united in our profound and instinctive dislike of a third party. It was going to be all right.

A couple of hours later, the first show in MTV's new series 'Imitating Life' was in the can, and Arundel and I had successfully sabotaged the whole shooting match with an unprecedented display of mutual arse-licking which had left Siobhan Flynn twitching with frustration and everyone else redefining parameters like billyo.

'Amazing,' said Torquil over the tea and bikkies, at which Siobhan was not present, 'really. Amazing. You two really made nonsense of so much received thinking out there.'

'Glad you like it,' I mumbled. Arundel and I were now like a couple of embarrassed lovers after an ill-advised one-night stand, quite unable to address each other, or even to meet each other's eyes.

'You were both just terrific,' said Marilyn, spraying us with digestive crumbs. 'Arundel, put it there. I think you've done more good for books generally this afternoon than all the hyping and sniping has done in years.'

Arundel clasped her hand briefly, with an expression of his most falcon-like hauteur. 'I'm glad you think so.'

'Oh, I *do*,' said Marilyn ardently, 'I really do.'

Arundel and I left soon after that, scuttling away from the scene of our shameful betrayal of principles like a couple of rats leaving a sinking ship. Flavia Brayne suggested we all go the Coach House Hotel for a drink, but I made noises about catching the train and left Marilyn to maintain an Era presence at the gathering.

I caught a cab to the Flag and Ferret, and as I got out the taxi driver, a rather jollier character than the one who had taken me to MTV, remarked: 'What you going to this dump for, love? You don't look like a spit and sawdust girl to me. I could show you some real nice boozers in this town.'

'I'm meeting someone here,' I said. 'It's on our way home.'

'I should forget him, love,' advised the cabbie with a wink. 'Any bloke who brings a lady to the Ferret deserves to be stood up.'

'Why?' I asked. 'What's the matter with it?'

'It's a right hole,' he told me, 'that's all. Cheers, love.'

He was absolutely right. One glance at the public bar of the Flag and Ferret made me think quite wistfully of the Coach House Hotel. And the lounge bar, with its bleak and seedy pretensions to respectability, was if anything even worse. Except that there, alone at the bar (it was only just gone six) was Kostaki, wearing the elegant suit in which I had first seen him, looking every inch the disarming young country doctor and reminding me forcibly that my recent madness had not been without justification. His looks were enhanced by the extreme drabness of his surroundings. Our fling might be on the downward curve, but I was sure as hell going to enjoy the slide down.

'Hallo,' he said, in his dégagé way, 'what'll it be?'

'I'll have a drink first,' I replied, to show I'd learnt a thing or two under his tutelage, but he didn't smile. 'Everything all right?'

He shrugged. 'So-so.'

'Oh, *that* so.' I tried again. But there was still no change.

He settled his shoulders in an irritable gesture. 'Gin?' He addressed the Ferret's barmaid: 'Gin and tonic. And another of these.' It was Scotch. I eyed him charily.

'Do you want to hear how it went?' I asked tentatively, pouring tonic and taking a recuperative swig.

'Go on then.'

'It was fine! The interviewer was such a pseud that we effected a spontaneous outflanking movement. Me and Arundel, imagine, it was great!'

'I haven't met him.'

'No, well, he's a . . . look, what *is* the matter?'

'Afternoon surgery was packed. Abso-bloody-lutely teeming. Some people needed more time, but of course it was the one day I had to rush them all through.'

'I see.' I took another swig, a consciousness-deadening one this time, to keep the sour whiff of incipient acrimony at bay. 'I'm sorry.'

There was the suspicion of more shoulder-settling. It was aggravating, like Clara's shrug. I stared glumly straight ahead, and thought that this was the bottom line where adultery was concerned: a grotty anonymous pub in a provincial suburb, chosen expressly for its lack of popularity with the rest of the human race; the two soi-disant lovers – it seemed a misnomer at present – sitting silent and reproachful over stiff drinks; guilt, resentment and irritation hovering over their heads like three vultures anticipating a meal.

'Right then,' said Kostaki, pushing his glass away from him with both hands, and getting up. 'If you've finished, we might as well go.'

As I drained my gin and picked up my bag I realised, with something amazingly like satisfaction, that he sounded just like George.

The Ghikasmobile was parked in an alley behind the Flag and Ferret, where ramparts of leaking black refuse bags attested to the unappetising nature of the pub's bar snacks. We climbed in, still in silence; though with succour, so to speak, hard at hand, I could not be entirely gloomy.

Kostaki reversed out of the alley at speed, dislodging a few of the refuse bags as he did so, ground the gears, stalled, leaped forward and snarled ill-temperedly out of Antwich. We proceeded as far along the Barford arterial road as was discreet, before turning through an open gateway into a field and screwing.

Though the Fiat was small, its suspension was excellent, and the degree of discomfort, allied to our vague sense of mutual discontent, resulted in a more than usually explosive coupling.

Unfortunately the earlier humidity had given way to a thundery shower during my sojourn at MTV, and the effect of our violent activity was to drive the Fiat's tyres deep into the mud. We re-surfaced to find ourselves more or less rooted to the spot, with the gate now closed behind us and the car surrounded by a herd of silent and attentive cows, just back from milking. The herdsperson, rustic switch in one hand, personal stereo round his neck, brought up the rear, displaying considerably less interest than his charges in the spectacle of two adults struggling to uncouple and adjust their dress in the front of an 'S' registration Fiat. But I was all too familiar with the blank stare and syncopated walk of those wired for sound, and was consequently not surprised at this apparent sang-froid.

Constantine, pretending to ignore our bovine audience, switched on the engine and pumped the accelerator. The wheels whirred ineffectually in the mud, spraying the impassive cows with their own mire.

'You need a bit less throttle . . . ' I suggested.

'Possibly,' he replied. He was displaying once again his doctorly attitude towards the combustion engine, one of bravura detachment. He seemed to believe that if he activated the right parts often enough and with sufficient determination, the car would eventually move. It was, after all, the method he employed with regard to sex, and with signal success. Unfortunately I was not in the mood for sitting by while he totally loused up what was left of a long and trying day.

'It's stuck,' I said, 'for goodness sake.'

'I'm aware of that.'

'All you're doing is getting us further in.'

He closed his eyes. 'Please, Harriet. Allow me, will you?'

There was that echo of George again. The only difference, in fact, was that whereas George would certainly have been right, Kostaki was wrong. I looked sharply away, but the side window was by now coated with liquid mud and worse. Smarting with righteous indignation I stared straight ahead while the Fiat buzzed and sizzled beneath us.

The cows had regrouped at a safe distance, and now stood looking on in a well-ordered semi-circle, ears at the horizontal, jaws rotating, like a slightly animated school photograph. The herdsman stood at one end, in the position of headmaster. I thought as I watched him that I detected the beginnings of cogent thought, and I was right, for he suddenly removed his headphones, switched off the stereo, and came over to us. He was a squat, muscular youth, with a T-shirt advising us to 'Relax'. A forlorn hope under the circumstances.

Constantine continued to ignore everything but the Fiat's dashboard, but the herdsman was a match for him. He simply leaned across the bonnet and tapped on the windscreen with his stick. With the engine still running, Constantine rolled the window down and stuck his head out irritably.

'Yes? What is it?'

'Need a hand, squire?'

I smiled appreciatively. 'How very kind.'

'We'll get there in the end,' said Kostaki, ignoring me.

The herdsman transferred his attention to me. 'If you was to come over in the driving seat, him and me could bounce you out.'

'What a good idea.' I laid an as-it-were wifely hand on Kostaki's rigid forearm. 'Did you hear that, dear?'

Kostaki switched the engine off at last. 'No.'

The herdsman was nothing if not thick-skinned. 'If you hop out, squire, and the lady takes the wheel, we could bounce her out. Give her a good shove.'

This time he emphasised his point by opening the driver's door. Kostaki, the poor dear – taut, pale and silent – climbed out, and slammed it behind him. I negotiated the gear lever, realising as I did so that something was missing: my pants. Somehow in the heat of the moment my St Michael cotton polyester apricot hip-huggers had been overlooked. I

261

took a cursory glance round, but there was no sign of them. Not to worry, I was now in the driver's seat in every sense, and even if I did have to get out, the skirt of my sundress was of a respectable length. I switched on the engine and they began bouncing and shoving. Kostaki's beautiful suit soon looked as though someone had chucked a tureen of brown Windsor all over it; it really was too bad.

It didn't work. After about three minutes the two men stood back, mopping their brows, and I was smitten with remorse and got out.

'Hopeless,' I remarked. 'And just look at you.'

'This really is an infernal bloody nuisance,' said Kostaki warmly. The exercise had done him good. It was nice to hear him sounding like a human being again. 'What the hell are we going to do?'

'Got any sacking?' enquired our adviser.

'I don't carry it around in June,' replied Kostaki.

'It's a crying shame I haven't got me donkey jacket,' said the herdsman. He surveyed us both speculatively, and I knew what he was thinking. I had on nothing I could consign to the slough of despond without risking arrest, and neither did he. We both looked at Kostaki, whose jacket had taken on a curried appearance.

He went even paler. 'Now, steady *on* - ' he began. But a collective moo from the cows interrupted him, and the potential transaction was nipped in the bud by the arrival of a car on the other side of the gate.

'Oh dear, oh dear,' remarked a thin, contemptuous voice from the driver's window. Too late I recognised the maroon Morris 1000 of Arundel Potter.

'Looks like the cavalry,' remarked the herdsman.

It looked more like nemesis to me. Bearing in mind that the best form of defence is attack I marched over to the gate and confronted Arundel, and his passenger, Marilyn Drinkwater, as they disembussed.

'We seem to be in a bit of a mess,' I said brightly and clearly, conscious of Arundel's gimlet eye upon me. 'I met Constantine and he kindly offered to give me a lift, but now look what's happened - honestly, would you credit it?'

'Not really,' said Arundel. 'What in heaven's name are you doing parked in a herd of cows?'

For once, my modest talent for invention came to my assistance in a real and practical way.

'Must you ask?' I chided him gaily, glancing at Marilyn to enlist her woman-to-woman sympathies. 'After all that plonk and strong tea?'

It was perfect. Marilyn emitted a hoot of delighted laughter. 'Oh, Harriet, you do get into some scrapes, how killing!' Once again I had shown myself to be a good sport with a nice sense of humour, even where the exigencies of the bladder were concerned.

'We're stuck in the mud,' I explained, before Kostaki could deny it in the face of all the evidence. 'I don't suppose you've got any sacking?'

Arundel bowed his head in a lofty affirmative, but quelled my gasp of delighted relief with: 'What a pity I don't have the ashes to go with it.'

'What?' I stared at him blankly.

'Arundel feels,' said Marilyn, 'that he said one or two things on MTV that he would prefer to forget. *I* thought it was all absolutely splendid.'

'Oh.' I glanced from one to the other of them. There was something here, some murky undercurrent, some hidden vein that I could not fathom, and now was emphatically not the moment to try. 'Well,' I said with ghastly chirpiness. 'Shall we get the show on the road?'

As Arundel opened the rear doors of the Morris I caught his eye fleetingly, and if looks could kill I should have been rendered carrion forthwith. I should have known, of course, that our brief and treacherous bout of intellectual heavy petting would end in tears. For half an hour's cheap thrills at MTV's expense Arundel had forfeited his lofty superiority over me. And hell hath no fury like an academic caught with his standards down.

Constantine advanced, hand outstretched, his sleeve steeped in a rich rustic soup of ordure. The look *he* gave me was none too kind, either.

Gamely, Marilyn shook his hand. 'Nice to meet you,

doctor,' she said, and something in her tone suggested that she had heard of him before, perhaps in the context of the Buchfest. Arundel approached, sacks over his arm, and I hastily effected further introductions.

'This is very good of you,' snapped Kostaki, through a face that seemed to be entirely clenched.

'Not at all,' replied Arundel.

The herdsperson stepped forward. 'Evening, name's Clarke.' There was no way of knowing if he meant Clarke as in Kent, or as in Lord.

'How do you do,' said Arundel.

'And this is Daisy, Dolly, Maisie, Molly, Fairy, Folly . . . ' Clarke made an expansive gesture, clearly expecting some sort of laugh. The four of us and the cows stared at each other with consummate stolidity.

'Right,' said Arundel.

Marilyn and I stood by the Morris and watched as Kostaki, Arundel and Clarke spread sacks.

'What a lucky thing we happened by,' said Marilyn, 'and I spotted you.'

'Yes, wasn't it,' I agreed.

'Your friend is such a fascinating man,' she rhapsodised. 'Such a fine mind. There's real intellectual rigour there, something one doesn't come across very often . . . '

She burbled on, and I got to wondering how she came to be travelling back in the Pottermobile in the first place.

'What have you done with Flavia Brayne?' I interrupted, rather rudely.

'Goodness,' said Marilyn, 'you make it sound as though we performed unspeakable rites on her still-warm cadaver.' She laughed shrilly. 'She said she'd quite like to visit her married sister in Antwich, and Arundel offered me a lift into Barford. I can get Suburban Electrics there, it's quite a saving.'

'I see.' I surveyed Marilyn. For a congenitally pasty woman she was sporting quite a flush. Suburban Electrics, my eye.

'Oh look!' she cried, 'they're going to have a go!'

Reluctantly I transferred my attention to Operation

Shitstorm. There was now a piece of sack tucked beneath each
tyre, which gave the Ghikasmobile the appearance of having
webbed feet. Kostaki was behind the wheel, and Clarke and
Arundel stood one on each side, at a safe distance. Beyond the
car Daisy, Dolly and the rest of the girls still stood in a neat
semi-circle. The resulting tableau resembled a scene from some
abstruse and impenetrable Greek tragedy.

'Okay, squire,' said Clarke. 'Chocks away.'

Kostaki started the engine and pressed the accelerator.
There was an unpleasantly familiar sizzling sound and the four
bits of sacking became chewed string. Clarke, to my consternation, flapped his arms to attract Kostaki's attention, and
then made a 'V' sign.

'I say,' said Marilyn.

'Second!' yelled Clarke. 'Get in second.'

'Oh I see,' she said, appeased.

'Hold it, squire!' Clarke and Arundel rearranged the
sacking, Kostaki got into second, and we held our breaths.

We watched and mentally urged our champion on. I
found myself bearing down as if giving birth . . . 'There you
are, sir, want to have a hold? It's a lovely bouncing two-litre
Sierra Estate . . . '

'Hoorah! Well done!' cried Marilyn, clapping her hands.

The tableau was broken. The Ghikasmobile shot out of
the slough, scattering the cows in all directions. Kostaki steered
it in a wide arc and drew up facing the field gate. Morris and
Fiat eyeballed each other through the bars.

Clarke collected up the sodden sacks and offered them to
Arundel.

'Quite honestly,' said Arundel, nostrils crimped, 'I don't
think I'll bother.'

'Fair enough,' replied our genial assistant. 'I'll split.'

'Very well,' said Arundel, looking mystified.

'Thanks again for all your help,' I said. 'We really are
grateful.'

But Clarke was already tuned back into his personal
muse, and was on his way, with a glazed eye and a funny walk,
his bevy of bovine beauties sashaying before him.

Kostaki opened the gate. Arundel was examining

something in the morasse from which we'd just extracted the Fiat.

'Again, many thanks,' I said to Marilyn. 'See you soon, I have no doubt.'

'Oh, no *doubt*,' she agreed. 'And very well done on this afternoon's performance. I shall tell them all that you were super, as usual – I don't know how you do it. Goodbye, doctor.'

'Cheerio and thanks,' said Kostaki, not offering a hand-shake this time.

' 'Bye, Arundel, and thank you.'

We climbed into the Fiat and Kostaki started up once more. But of course the Morris blocked our exit so we were obliged to sit there, puttering impatiently, while Arundel walked back with maddening slowness, and with something in his hand.

To my surprise he came to my window and knocked on it lightly with the knuckle of his forefinger. 'Open up.'

I rolled the window down further. 'Yes?'

Arundel favoured me with his most reptilian smirk, and lifted into view a soiled and sodden scrap of material, held fastidiously between finger and thumb. Only the label was relatively clean and it bore, unmistakably, the signature of the patron saint of the high street.

'My dear Harriet,' said Arundel. 'The call of nature must have been urgent indeed for you to overlook these.'

There followed that which in my novels I should have described as a pregnant pause; a pause broken only by the distant lowing of the cows, and now, unmistakably, the crowing of a cock.

'Really, Arundel,' I said roguishly, 'been at the washing lines again? Take me home, doctor.'

Chapter Sixteen

'You mean to say he never even mentioned it?' I squeaked incredulously over the phone to Bernice the next day.

'Not a dickie bird,' replied my friend. 'So you see he can't have set that much store by the incident.'

I had other ideas about the cause of Arundel's reticence, but this was not the moment to expound them.

' . . . the arrogance of guilt,' Bernice was saying. 'You think every damn thing begins and ends with you.'

'Not at all,' I said plaintively. 'It was jolly embarrassing! Think how you'd feel if someone appeared at your window brandishing a pair of your pants.'

Bernice sighed. 'Brandishing's nothing. It's a helluva lot better than putting them on himself, or using them for a face mask. Besides, you said, you denied them thrice.'

'I was bluffing. And he knew it.'

'Oh, for God's sake . . . !' said Bernice. 'You're just angsting away for the sake of it. Let's talk about the party. I was thinking that you're going to need an ice-breaker. Something to get them all pulling together.' She paused. 'Or perhaps not. Something to get them *mixing*.'

'Well, what?' I asked sulkily.

'Ask people to come as their occupations.'

'Sorry?'

'For instance, Arundel would come in a gown and mortar-board, Kildare in a surgical mask . . . that sort of thing. It works quite well. I mean, you're on speaking terms with a bona fide vicar, aren't you?'

'Yes,' I said doubtfully.

'There you are then. Vicars are great. And you can be the archetypal romantic novelist, a vision in pink marabou.'

'But what,' I said feebly, 'about the people with boring occupations?'

'One or two boring people don't do any harm,' replied Bernice airily.

I considered the matter. 'Well, maybe. I suppose if I spread the idea around, there's time . . . '

'Of course there's time. It's not full-blown fancy dress, just an underlining of identities.'

Put like this, the scheme seemed fairly innocuous. Something occurred to me. 'What about you, Bernice?' I asked. 'What will you come as?'

'Don't worry, I've been thinking about that,' she assured me. 'I've never done a hand's turn in my life, so I shall come as what I'd *like* to be.'

'What's that?' I asked.

'A tart with a heart,' she replied.

I disseminated this idea by means of telling a few selected communicators – Vanessa, Brenda, Dilly, and my children. I had had an almost hundred per cent acceptance to the party, and reckoned that if only a few people complied with the directive it would be enough to make things go. I had not heard from the GM, which after the events of Fartenwald was no surprise, but at least he would infer from my invitation that the hatchet was buried.

I rang Kostaki myself. 'I see,' he said. 'Fine, yes, I'll do my best.'

No, things weren't what they were. We had parted on reasonable terms after the Antwich episode, having of course returned to the Prickhard first, there to ensure that the sun did not set on our wrath. But just the same I knew that the George-like tone which I had noticed first at the Flag and Ferret, and again in the cowfield, had been the knell of passing lay.

But perhaps it was no bad thing. The circumstantial evidence was piling up against us ominously. There had been the night of the dinner party, with the unexpected arrival of Akela and her troops; the sudden discovery of Lance Lowe at the football tournament; our eventful threehander with the GM at the Dynamik; and, most recently, The Case of the Apricot Hip-huggers.

Perhaps infected with the sense of a chapter in my own life closing, I became obsessed by an insane desire to finish the first draft of *TRT* before the party. In a mood of ruthless professionalism I sat down at the tripewriter and prepared to sunder Maria, Jamie and Richard amid the well-orchestrated ping of heartstrings.

Richard was about to peg out. The wound, apparently so slight, had become infected, but because pity was anathema to him he had kept the imminence of his demise from Maria. He had also (not wanting to appear a sissy) concealed his passion for her. All this granite-jawed selflessness had resulted in Maria being confirmed in her original opinion that her cousin was a tight-arsed, toffee-nosed so-and-so without an ounce of feeling, and she had sought solace in the muscular charms of Jamie. But alas, the Parliamentarians had returned, and this time there was no withstanding them. Richard, with his dying breath, told Maria to flee while she still had the chance. Too late she realised what might have been. Jamie, not to be out-done in the chivalry stakes, declared that he would not abandon the master who had saved his life, but would fight to the death at his side. Honour dictated that the only course left open to our heroine was to don once more the guise of a lad and take charge of the evacuation from the burning manor house . . .

. . . *she turned and looked back once more at Kersey, so proud and fine, now a helpless prey to the hungry flames of civil war. Once – how long ago? – she had come here as a poor and humble relative. She left, now, as the last hope of the proud Hawkhursts. She had arrived as a stubborn and ignorant girl. She left as a woman. But she took no pleasure in her alteration. For behind her she left the man who had declared his love for her too late, and who, she prayed, had been taken into death's blessed embrace before the ravening flames devoured him . . . And there, too, was that other man, he whose dark and thrilling intensity had first stirred passion in her, but who now, surely, faced death too.*

She felt a touch upon her arm and glanced round to see old Martha looking up at her with a look of such wise and penetrating sympathy that for the first time in this day's long ordeal Maria felt the hot tears sting her eyes.

'Oh, Martha,' she whispered, and covered the old servant's hand with her own. 'Oh, Martha, what am I to do?'

'I know, missy, I know,' soothed Martha, now using the affectionate diminutive of an equal. 'But the future is your trust now, and 'tis a sacred one. 'Tis a heavy burden for a maid, but you were ever a strong one.'

'But I shall always remember . . . ' Maria broke off, unable to continue for the weight of sorrow bearing down upon her.

'Ah, the remembrance tree,' sighed Martha. 'Pity it is that remembrance is a dead tree, and a grinding heavy weight for young shoulders to carry.'

Suddenly, at this, Maria lifted her head, and set her face towards the west, turning her back on the funeral pyre that was Kersey House. Her voice, when she spoke, rang out once more with hope.

'Then, Martha, I shall not carry it! I shall lay down the remembrance tree and march forward into life.' Together, and proudly, they went on.

I switched off the tripewriter. Life has few moments to offer as sweet as that of finishing a book. Of course, I knew I hadn't seen the last of it. For a start, I had to do a re-write, and sort out one or two of my more dubious suppositions about seventeenth-century England. Then Vanessa would lay hold of it, and set about the serious business of making her professional mark ('there's no question Harriet is a spontaneous natural story-teller, but she does need a firm editorial hand'); after Vanessa it would pass into the province of Dennis the copy-editor, anxious to elevate his essentially mundane role to the status of key operation ('I mean punctuation is the good manners of writing, right?'); and finally *TRT* would reach the printers, Cobbold & Sons of Southampton, who were also not

above putting their oar in ('Battle of Havelocke 1680 surely?').
They were all usually perfectly correct and the book would
eventually come clunking back, essentially the same, but
outwardly hideously disfigured, like something out of "The
Monkey's Paw'.

Still, any Erans who goaded me, covertly or otherwise,
while drinking my booze on Saturday, would get more than
they bargained for.

Next day, Friday, I summoned my domestic lieutenants
for an 'O' group. The newly confident Damon pre-empted any
query by saying at once:

'I got you some good sounds together for tomorrow.'

'Why, thank you Damon.'

'Mother of God,' spluttered Declan. 'In broad daylight?'

I turned to him benignly. 'It's only a little music,
Declan,' I said, 'not group sex.'

Declan's face assumed an expression of thunderous self-
righteousness, as though my very denial had confirmed his
vilest prejudices. Damon continued as if there had been no
interruption.

'Yeah, some nice sixties stuff, bit of James Last, Ray
Conniffy type of thing . . . '

'It doesn't have to be too staid,' I reminded him sternly.

'Gotcher.' said Damon.

'And if you could give the downstairs a real spring clean
this afternoon . . . ' I suggested.

'Will do, natch,' Damon promised. 'I'll give those toilets
of yours a birthday.'

He went his ways and I turned my attention to Declan,
who was still sweating disapproval through every pore.

'Now, Declan,' I said briskly, 'let's get the garden looking
tip-top.'

'I been working like a nigger, so I have.'

'Of course you have, it's only a few finishing touches that
are needed – '

I observed a rebellious glint in Declan's eye. Finishing
touches were not in his line. He preferred broad strokes of the
machete.

'I'll settle for them wasps,' he declared, taking up a

271

bargaining position. There was a wasps' nest at the end of the garden, which caused little trouble to anyone.

'I'm not sure whether – '

'If you're filling the place with people you need to be shot of them wasps,' he growled threateningly.

'Perhaps you're right. And you're quite happy to organise the parking?'

'I don't mind.' I knew, actually, that he was ecstatic at the prospect of a couple of hours as authorised bully of the middle classes.

'And of course you'll join the party afterwards,' I said ingratiatingly, 'and what about Mrs O'Connell . . . ?'

'She's not a one for socialising,' snapped Declan.

And Declan was? I was still tussling with this apparent anomaly as he stamped off to his shed behind the greenhouse, there to mastermind the demise of the wasps. It was nice to see him happy, but I had the gravest misgivings about the insecticide to come. The song 'Great Balls of Fire' might have been written for Declan, whose preferred method of dealing with wasps was to thrust a parcel of smouldering straw down the entrance of the nest. But the last time he had engaged in ritual slaughter of this kind, his victims had wised up. A phalanx of super-wasps, seeing Declan approach with a pitchforkful of burning straw, had zoomed from their subterranean fortress and attacked him. Declan had retaliated by whirling the fork with its smoking load about his head, like a demented hammer thrower, and calling down a murrain on the whole insect tribe and wasps in particular. Fragments of burning vegetation had flown in all directions, and drifted wantonly into the neighbouring field full of standing corn. Only the most urgent and intensive use of the hose by Damon and myself had prevented a catastrophe of the first magnitude. I had since left a large can of proprietary wasp-destroyer in Declan's shed, but without much real hope of success.

Saturday, as they say in books, dawned fine and hazy, with the promise of a perfect midsummer's day to follow. The flat fields of Barfordshire seemed to purr with bees and grasshoppers as the sun broke through and in these most ideal of conditions my garden seemed to acquire what I always hoped for but rarely seemed to achieve, an appearance of artful artlessness.

The crack troops reported early, starting with Declan, hugely pleased with himself after dismissing the wasps with only minimal incineration of the farmer's hedge. He was dressed to slay, in a deafening plaid jacket and important-looking brogues that might have been hewn from the living bog oak.

'Declan,' I said, 'you look terrific.'

His response to this was to treat my threadbare jeans and Toms T shirt to his most strafing appraisal and ask: 'Will you be changing?'

'But of course! Today, Declan, I'm going to look like a proper romantic novelist.'

'Lord bless and save us.' He darkened with horror. Declan was genuinely squeamish about my job. But as he went off up the garden to take charge of the parking lot, nothing could disguise the fact that he was in outstandingly good form.

Damon arrived next. Like Declan he made no concessions to the temperature in matters of dress, and was apparelled à la Sky Masterson in a black suit and shirt with a white tie and two-tone shoes. In the darkness of my barn where he had elected to set up shop, he was like a living negative. He had brought huge amounts of equipment, in a battered van.

'Do you need any help?' I asked.

'Clara's coming,' he replied. 'It's cool.'

Right on cue, my daughter appeared, dressed in the awful shapeless clothes which make the slim and young look even slimmer and younger. She had squirted some pink hair dye on the front of her fringe.

'You're going to give Damon a hand, are you, darling . . . ?' I asked.

'That's right,' said Clara defiantly. But my nascent suspicions were smothered at birth by the arrival of Spot. He was usually whitish with black bits. This morning he appeared to have been tie-dyed with cochineal.

'My God,' I said.

'No, it's Spot,' exclaimed Clara. 'I sprayed him with my Hair-Glo. You know all the best lady novelists have bright pink hair and Pekes to match, so I did Spot for you. It'll get you a few laughs, anyway,' she said, with a chilling note of scepticism.

'Thank you.' I looked down at Spot. The black bits had turned purple. He wagged his tail and panted, revealing a gruesome fuchsia tongue.

'Is it poisonous?' I asked.

'Of course not. And it comes out.'

'Oh . . . good . . . '

Damon and Clara disappeared into the barn, and Gareth hove in view, dressed in his football gear – 'It's what I do, Ma, okay?' – and went away again almost at once to fetch Brett Troye whom he had enlisted as fellow greeter.

Next to arrive were Attwood & Co., Caterers of Basset Regis. Linda Channing's description of them as obliging and presentable had been, I considered, an extremely liberal interpretation of the facts. As with many such organisations – a selection of others being removal companies, carpet layers and furniture delivery men – the team comprised three: a smart alec, a geriatric and a mental defective.

The smart alec was the eponymous Attwood, who paraded about my patio with his thumbs in his waistcoat, telling me that the heat was against me, and my petits bateaux de fromage would certainly wilt, but then I as the customer appreciated that and would accept full liability for the exigencies of the weather.

All this time it became clear that while he was in charge of the bullshit the other two did the work. They quietly set about organising the buffet in the kitchen. The elderly one had a nasty cough, and the not-so-bright lad had a tendency to bring things into the house, stand stock still for a minute or two, and then take them straight out again. But the operation seemed to be progressing, so I went up to change. There was no point, as the saying goes, in having a dog and barking yourself.

I emerged twenty minutes later in the next best thing to the cloud of pink marabou suggested by Bernice. I wore the purple silk from Boutique Meridiana, with some pink cotton trousers underneath, Indian style. I had gone mad in the jewellery department, with beads, bangles and dangly earrings, and I had with me Spot on a length of purple dressing-gown cord.

The dreadful Attwood redeemed himself a little by greeting me with a glass of the Spanish champagne I was paying a competitive price for.

'May I say the hostess looks très glam?' he asked. I gave him a queenly smile and strolled out into the garden, glass aloft, Spot trotting after like something that should have been pickled.

I had just sat down, graciously relaxed, in one of the deckchairs which were scattered invitingly about, when Gareth's head appeared round the corner of the house.

'Hey, Ma!' he called, his voice rising to compete with the Beach Boys invoking 'California Girls', 'There's a stinking great Roller out here!'

How typical of the GM not only to turn up unannounced, but early, and with his tall and mournful chauffeur, Anstey, staggering beneath the weight of a huge basket of flowers. As the two of them processed down the garden towards me I was conscious of people peeping and prying from every available vantage point.

'Mrs Blair!' grated the GM, surveying me. 'Get you!'

He himself was wearing a tight double-breasted cream suit, with a blue and brown striped shirt and a tie whose only justification can have been that it was the emblem of some distinguished club. Above this ensemble the GM's face gleamed ruddily, but not, I suspected, from heat alone.

'Oh . . . for me?' I cooed appreciatively as Anstey lurched forward with the flowers. Spot bared pink fangs; he looked as though he'd been using plaque disclosure tablets. 'It's all right,' I explained, 'he's part of my costume.'

The GM laughed throatily. 'Anstey, why not take the flowers into the house for Mrs Blair?' he suggested. 'And then park the motor.'

Anstey staggered off, glads bobbing, and I hung on tight to the purple dressing-gown cord.

'Could your wife not come?' I asked pointedly.

'Shame, no,' said the GM, 'she's opening a family fun

275

day. But I thought why not? . . . Mrs Blair, no hard feelings I trust?'

'I'm sorry?' I said with a vague, distracted smile. 'I'm not with you.'

'I like your style,' said the GM, with perceptible relief. 'Well, I must say I call this very pleasant! Ve-ery pleasant.'

He accepted a glass of champagne from the dumb waiter and collapsed on to one of my folding chairs with a sharp crump of canvas under stress. I took a deep draught of my own drink. Things had not got off to a very promising start. Spot panted pinkly at my feet, gazing up at my face as though awaiting instructions. In the parking area I could see Anstey at the helm of the metallic grey Rolls, backing and filling manfully under Declan's gloating supervision.

The air vibrated with awkward cross-currents. And of Kostaki there was still no sign.

That was at twelve-fifteen. By one-thirty the novelty of the GM's presence had long since been swallowed up in the roaring, squawking, eclectic tide of other guests. The music thumped on, now no more than a descant for the drunken hubbub below. Everyone had survived the attentions of Attwood & Co., so far. The drink flowed on. No cars had been scratched. Kostaki had still not arrived.

I was as tight as a tick. Nervous anticipatory drinking had given way to the steady fuel consumption of the condemned woman. Why had I asked all these people? Did I really know them all? And if so, did I want to know them any better? Neither my husband nor my lover was present, yet the air in my garden positively pullulated with sex. The very tadpoles in the pond looked, to my jaundiced eye, like a pack of jet-black super-sperm, gathering for a massed ovarian raid. As I stood on the patio sipping my tepid bubbly Attwood materialised at my side, patronising and confidential in his white coat, like a doctor with the result of tests.

'Mrs Blair, would you like dessert served now?'

'Um . . .'

'And would you like the cheese to be offered at the same time as an alternative, or when everyone's had dessert?'

'Er . . .'

'May I suggest the former? We can always hold some cheese back to offer afterwards, and in this heat . . .'

'Quite.'

'Whatever you say, Mrs Blair.'

It was all going perfectly well without me. I retired into the kitchen, passing as I did so the Attwood menials on their way out to gather up dirty dishes, while Attwood himself began uncovering tureens of strawberries and towering alps of meringue and whipped cream with a flourish. All of a sudden something cut through the miasma of alcohol and gloom: the phone was ringing.

I put my glass down and fled across the hall to the sitting room, then changed my mind and bounded up to the bedroom, two at a time. As I reached the top of the stairs I bumped head-long into Mike Channing, dressed in *Financial Times* pink. I thrust him aside and burst through the bedroom door. As I did so, the phone stopped ringing.

'Bugger!'

'Wash your mouth out, I answered it for you,' said Bernice, who was standing by the bed with the receiver in her hand. She wore a white crochet dress, a shell necklace and a scattering of dark red love bites.

'Thanks,' I said, and snatched the instrument from her. She left the room with the large person's legendary light-footedness and closed the door behind her.

'Hallo?' I barked.

'It's me.'

'Oh, hallo. Talk about yesterday's mashed potatoes.'

'I'm late.'

'I know.'

'Sorry, not a thing I could do, one of my old ladies had a heart tremor.'

'Oh dear.' Remembering the Fartenwald crack about pre-conception care, I took that one with a pinch of salt.

'I'm on my way now. Party going with a swing?'

'I think so.'

'See you soon, then.'

' 'Bye.'

I put the receiver down and stared out of the window. My wine-soaked mind lurched forward a pace or two. What the hell had Bernice been doing in my bedroom?

In spite of everything, I had my pride. I did not wish to be found alone and palely loitering by Kostaki when he arrived. No, I would be out there in the thick of it, sharing jokes, exchanging confidences, showing that I was not the sort of woman who needed a man in order to feel complete.

Accordingly I appropriated another glass of champagne and went out to mix with the gay company.

The heat hit me like a smack in the face. I had left Spot tied up in the shade beneath the kitchen window, but when I went to retrieve him he was no longer there. The end of the purple cord trailed limply in his water bowl. I could only hope that whatever he was up to, it was not actionable. Although the law of probability would be on his side. 'I swerved sharply, Your Honour, to avoid hitting this large pink and purple dog . . . '

Moving among my guests was rather like a ride in a brightly lit ghost train. Bizarre and disconcerting images rose up before me at every turn, emitting weird sounds. Here was Stan Nutkin, in stetson and spurs, munching a vol au vent and apparently exercising some hitherto unsuspected animal magnetism over Baba Moorcroft, in an apron ('I'm only a housewife') . . . here was Stan's wife Nita, in suedette bolero and gauchos, confiding to Trevor Tunnel that a 'finger buffet was absolutely ideal but texture is so important, oh hallo, Harriet!' . . . Eric Chittenden, a vicar from the waist up, was Lee Trevino from the waist down, in yellow and black hounds-tooth trews . . . 'The trouble is,' complained Lydia Langley, 'that since March I've had builders in my back passage,' . . . Mike Channing was telling Tristan about books. 'You would call that a serious book, in my business we would say that it was not user-friendly, see the difference?'

. . . both Tristan and Vanessa had arrived wearing dustbin lids ('hardcover editors') but had long since discarded them. Vanessa now sported red shorts and a white sun-top and was engaged in telling Gareth, with much vivacious wriggling, that since she was dressed in his club colours she should be on his team. She had made a bad error of judgement with regard to his age – Gareth was hypnotised by so much bare, adult, female flesh, but only I knew how unlikely he was to respond to her hectic advances when close at hand hovered safer company, in the form of Sabina Langley. Poor Vanessa. On the rockery were Arundel, Marilyn and Barty (the latter formally attired, as promised) all sitting on Arundel's academic gown. Barty waved his glass at me – 'I'm having a smashing time, darling, just keeping a watchful eye on the lad here, you can't be too careful!' – and Arundel crimped his lips in his most poisonous smile. Marilyn was completely Brahms and looked as if she might do something disgusting at any moment. I moved on.

Up by the greenhouse I stumbled on Tanya Lowe, wandering about anxiously with a length of chain in her hand.

'Hallo, Tanya,' I said, 'how's your glass?'

'I've lost my Sukey,' she answered, plainly distressed. 'Is your garden enclosed?'

'More or less.'

Tanya shook her head dismally. 'I only brought her because she seemed under the weather.'

I wondered how she could tell. 'Don't worry,' I said. Glynis Makepeace shot past us in full uniform, muttering something. 'Don't worry, she's not exactly a pup, is she?' The GM jogged by, breathing heavily. 'I mean, she won't go far.'

Eric appeared, and I passed Tanya on to him. I walked on, past Declan's shed, and between the dwarf apple trees to the parking lot. Anstey was perched on the bumper of the GM's Roller, reading the *Sun* and smoking a panatella. At my approach he rose wearily to his feet.

'Don't disturb yourself,' I said. 'Have you had plenty to eat and drink?'

'I have to watch my stomach, madam,' replied Anstey. 'Ulcers. I brought a nosebag.'

I went between the massed ranks of cars to the blackthorn hedge which divided my garden from the neighbouring field and stood in the blackened gap created by Declan's wasp activities to admire the view. The greenish-bronze corn trembled in the heat. The air was full of a hypnotic pulse of twittering birds and chirping crickets . . .

But as I stood there, taking stock, I became conscious of another sound, regular and insistent, and near at hand. It was as though someone were banging the hedge with a carpet-beater, and emitting a faint grunt with the effort of each blow.

I braced one foot against the bank and peered through the gap. Still I could see nothing, though the noise seemed to be getting louder and more rapid, reaching a crescendo. Braving thorns and spiky twigs I leaned even further forward, craning to right and left, and now I saw something. Unprepared as I was, I at first took it to be the fat, hairless muzzle of some quaint animal – a coypu, perhaps, or breed of fancy pig, with crenellated ears waggling back and forth. But this impression lasted for only a second, until I realised that what I was looking at was the back end of a copulating couple. The pig's muzzle was a set of buttocks, and what I had taken for ears were the feet of whoever was underneath.

Fascinated, I climbed right on to the bank to see who it was. When I did, I could only wonder why I had not guessed before. For there were Brenda Tunnel and Declan, going at it with a vigour that would not have disgraced the pistons of the Flying Scotsman in its heyday.

'Cecil . . . oh, Cecil!' gasped Brenda, grabbing handfuls of the O'Connell wire wool and pulling. 'Don't stop now! Cecil, you're wonderful . . . !' I retreated from the hedge and left them to their big finale. For the first time since my party had begun, a big silly grin spread over my face. Cecil, eh . . . ?

As I reached the apple trees Gareth appeared, with Sabina in tow. 'Having fun, kids?' I enquired affably. I was only glad he had escaped Vanessa's attentions.

'That funny waiter told me to tell you someone else has arrived,' replied Gareth.

'Oh really, thank you!' I cried, and hastened back, via the ghost train to the front of the house. In the angle of the chimney breast I discovered the GM, tie loosened and vowels coarsening by the second, grappling with Akela.

'Everybody all right?' I said.

280

'Great party, love . . . ' mumbled the GM soupily, keeping a detaining hand on Akela's lanyard, 'terrific grub . . . gorgeous girls . . . marvellous . . . '

'There's something going on by the gate,' remarked Akela. She must have been enjoying herself, she was trying to get rid of me.

What was going on was the Ghikasmobile, parked at a sharp angle with the front left-hand wheel on the pavement. Kostaki himself was standing in the road, holding the passenger door open.

I lurched, beaming, to the gate. 'Hallo!' I cried. 'At last!'

'Don't speak too soon,' said Kostaki, whose face, I noticed, was the ghastly shade of hummus grey. 'I've got something for you.' There was a stifled commotion in the passenger seat and then someone got out.

It was George. He had a large surgical dressing over his right eye.

'Harriet,' he said, with feeling. 'Thank God. What the blazes is going on here?'

'I'm having a party,' I said, opening the gate and admitting the two of them. George and I exchanged kisses. 'Hallo, darling. What have you done to yourself?'

'I can see that,' he said. 'What for?'

'I don't know. For fun,' I said hollowly. I only wished I could be sure about that. George wore an immaculate pale grey suit with a white shirt (only slightly bloodstained) and a blue silk tie. Kostaki had on a white coat with a thermometer in the pocket and a pair of bermudas.

'I'm very afraid,' said Kostaki urbanely, taking charge as he had done in Fartenwald, in circumstances at least as bizarre as these, 'that I backed out of my drive in rather a hurry and just clipped your husband's hire car – '

'It's a ruddy write-off,' said George.

' – absolutely my fault and quite unforgivable,' went on Kostaki smoothly. 'No serious damage, but when I found out who George was I thought the least I could do was run him over here. We left the other car at the Rickyard.'

'Thanks awfully,' I said. I kissed George again, and

realised I was inordinately pleased to see him. 'Look, Constantine, do go and find a drink and something to eat, there are heaps of people you know . . . '

'Right you are.' Kostaki beat a retreat, coat flapping.

I linked my arm through George's and led him up the path. 'Darling, I'm so sorry about all this. I wasn't expecting you.'

'I know. But Harriet, I just had to see you. I had to.'

I was really touched. 'Did you?'

'Yes.'

'And now you're here.'

'Yes.' He glanced about jumpily. 'Look, could we go inside – somewhere quiet? I need to be alone with you. I've only got thirty-six hours.'

'Of *course*.'

Infected by his impatience I ushered him round to the french window and into the house, like a member of the Resistance with an English airman. Even so I heard a cry of 'Is that *George* . . . ?' ring out above the babel, and knew that our precious moments of privacy would be numbered.

I took him into the bedroom and we sat down on the edge of the bed. He passed his hand over his eyes. He really was in a state, poor love. All the same, I noticed what I'd been in danger of forgetting – that he was at least as tall as Kostaki, and had brown eyes, and was nicely tanned from the Arabian sun. With one big, built-in advantage. I was married to him.

I leaned over and began loosening his tie. It was nice not to be jumped, for once. I was going to enjoy this.

But he flinched as though I'd held a flick knife to his throat.

'What are you dressed like that for?'

I looked down at myself. 'Oh, this . . . we're all dressed as our jobs.'

'When did you become a fairground palmist, then?'

I laughed heartily, George not at all.

'Look, Harriet . . . '

'Yes?' I smiled lovingly at him. 'It *is* nice to see you.'

'Is it? Yes.'

'Yes. It is.'

'The thing is . . . ' He laced his fingers together and squeezed them as if trying to wring water from his knuckles. 'I've been having an affair.'

'You have?' An affair? George? *George* had been having an affair? I felt hysteria rising in me like the semi-digested Spanish gigglewater which sloshed dangerously in my stomach.

'Who with?' I asked. I didn't give a flying fart who with, I was just trying to re-group my stricken forces.

'No one,' replied George.

'I see.'

'I mean, no one you would know. An older woman.'

This struck me, in my debilitated state, as hilariously funny. George was middle-aged, for God's sake! Who had he been poking, an octogenarian?

'How much older?'

'Well, a bit. But she doesn't seem it,' he added hurriedly, defending his taste in women.

'Someone else's wife?' I asked hopefully. That at least would be a tick against my name in the Great Book of Life.

'Certainly not,' said George, rather more like his old self. 'A widow.'

'But a merry one, obviously,' I remarked bitterly.

George blushed fierily. 'I won't hear a word against her,' he said. 'None of it was Anna's fault, I was completely infatuated – '

'Who?'

'I was. Completely.'

'No, but who with? Anna?'

'Yes. I think it's over now, though. But it shook me, I can tell you.'

I wondered if I told him everything, now, whether we might strike some kind of bargain. Or, alternatively, commit hara-kiri.

'What did Anna make of it all?' I asked, with genuine interest.

'Oh, it was nothing much to her,' said George, with uncharacteristic modesty. 'She's a woman of the world, marine archaeologist, a man in every port sort of thing . . . ' he sighed. 'It was just a fling. But I'm so terribly, terribly sorry. I came here to tell you that. The guilt's been destroying me. Can you forgive me?'

I had an idea I'd written the lines for this encounter in one of my earlier books.

'We've been through a lot,' I said, quite untruthfully. 'Why throw it all away at this stage? Things may not be the same, but perhaps that doesn't matter. We have a good marriage, and that counts for something, doesn't it?'

'Harriet,' said George solemnly. 'I don't deserve you.'

That much at least was true.

We went down into the garden and George got a hero's welcome. It was a funny thing, but he'd behaved at least as badly as me, and flown hundreds of miles in order to tell me so. So why did he look like a new man? I was quite sure if I'd gone all the way to Riyadh to apprise him of my doings I should still have been stretched face down on the carpet licking his handmade shoes and sobbing for forgiveness. All the same, he had arrived at the optimum moment. I would try to forgive him his little fling with Anna Ghikas, especially in view of what I was keeping back. And his protracted convalescence from guilt would ensure that he was unreceptive to rumours about me.

Yes, it had all worked out for the best. Then why did I feel so bloody? Some kind of cockney rock was pounding over the loudspeakers. Barty and Dilly were doing the twist. Akela and the GM were imbuing the palais glide with their own brand of sullen fire. Bernice and Mike were . . . well, Bernice and Mike were going it a bit, quite frankly. They were actually locked in one another's arms without even the shallowest pretence at dancing. Bernice's abundant flesh bulged through the interstices in her crochet dress, giving her a quilted appearance. The daintily scalloped hem was rising ever higher over her generous thighs.

'Mike?'

It was Linda, tall, neat and every inch the high-powered woman executive, in a Thatcher-blue suit and stilettos. Mike looked round at her with the slow, relaxed affability of the inordinately well-refreshed.

'Yes, dear?' Two words that have launched a thousand marital blaggings.

'I just wanted to tell you you're a conceited, pusillanimous, two-faced, double-dyed shit,' said Linda. And pushed the two of them into the pond.

I turned away. I was absolutely beyond surprise. The faces of Attwood & Co. were gathered at the kitchen window, with eyes like saucers. Just by the french window Spot was wolfing down petits bateaux de fromage from a willow-pattern serving dish. So at least he was back, and the police had not called. I summoned him, retrieved the cord and tied it to his collar.

'Come on, boy,' I said, 'let's go for a little walk.'

On the way I looked in on the barn, having it in mind to extend cordial thanks to Damon and Clara for their efficient and blameless contribution to the day's proceedings.

The two of them were sitting on the floor, holding hands.

'Hallo, Mummy,' said Clara. It was the first time in months she'd actually sounded like a child. 'What I really want to do is leave school and go on the road with Damon and the disco.'

Damon struggled to his feet, perhaps less out of deference to me than to relieve the all-too-obvious congestion in his black trousering.

'She's a great kid,' he opined loftily.

I think that was what really got to me. Great kid? My beautiful, intelligent, haughty, horse-mastering daughter – a *great kid*?

'Damon,' I said, advancing like some avenging phantom into the barn, 'Damon, you have abused your position in my employ. You're fired.'

'It's cool,' he replied without rancour. 'I was leaving anyway.'

I rounded on Clara. 'Clara!' I snapped – and then the wind went right out of my sails. How on earth could I come the heavy parent when the whole property was overrun with drunken adults whose thoughts alone, never mind whose deeds, would make anything contemplated by Damon and Clara look like a brownies' picnic?

'I'm going for a walk,' I finished tamely. And then added: 'Your father's back, why don't you go and say hallo to him?'

'Daddy, ace!' shouted Clara. Fleetingly, Damon and I were united in our sense of rejection. Then I swept out.

I went along to Stu's field, and stood in the shade by the gate, calling her by name. I didn't like her much, but there is something soothingly consistent and detached about animals, removed as they are from the vagaries of passion and of conscience.

To my surprise Stu hurtled towards me with her ears pressed back as if planning to jump into my arms like a horse in a cartoon. Almost immediately I saw why, for behind her galloped her field-companions, geldings both, nostrils like blast furnaces, poor old tools at the ready, the equine embodiment of the aphorism that it is better to travel hopefully . . . Stu was in season.

She galloped almost to the fence, then sensed that she was being cornered, snapped at me, wheeled about at her hapless suitors and pursued them with a piercing whinny of outrage to the far corner of the field. The entire incident had taken about thirty seconds. I sighed wearily. Was I actually the only creature in the entire parish of Basset Magna who was not getting, or planning soon to get, their end away?

'Oh, Harriet!'

No, there was at least one other. I brightened. It was Tanya Lowe, on her way home, with the redoubtable Sukey waddling on her chain.

'Lovely party,' she called. 'Made a really nice change.'

Knowing what I did of the goings-on chez Lowe, I did not doubt it.

'Glad you liked it, Tanya,' I said. 'And I see you found Sukey.'

'Yes, silly old thing,' said Tanya affectionately. 'It's up the kennel for her now, I reckon she's coming on heat. Cheerio, Harriet.'

' 'Bye, Tanya,' I said.

Spot and I watched her go. Spot sat still, eyes half-closed, tongue lolling, ears at half mast. I should have known that look. Sukey had a bright pink backside. We could expect a litter of little Spookys.

Back at the house the pond incident had resulted in a hasty regrouping of forces. Everyone was busily trying to demonstrate that whatever they personally had been up to, it had only been a manifestation of the party spirit and definitely not to be taken seriously.

It was too late for Mike and Bernice, though, who were standing on the lawn like a couple of mud wrestlers while Nita and Baba mopped them with paper napkins. Marilyn, for reasons of her own, was kneeling with her head over the pond. Linda was weeping in George's arms, and George was looking over her head at Arundel, listening attentively to whatever Arundel was saying. His look of rapt concentration led me to believe that whatever it was, it concerned him directly.

Something told me that the study was the only place to go. After all, *TRT* and its forebears might soon be my last and only toe-hold on the slippery slope of self-regard.

I opened the door to find Kostaki and Vanessa there before me, standing and gazing down at the tripewriter like a young married couple admiring their first-born.

'Hallo there,' said Kostaki. 'Just popped up to do some work?'

He couldn't fool me. I recognised the voice which, like the conjurer's free hand, distracts attention from the one being removed from a lady's underwear. But I was much too tired to play games.

'No,' I said.

'Oh, Harriet, my *love*,' gushed Vanessa, 'I was just looking for the upstairs loo and I stumbled on your den. And you've *finished*!'

'Only the first draft,' I said discouragingly.

'Never mind, just the same – what a lovely surprise!'

There was an awkard silence. But not for long. Kostaki took the thermometer from his pocket, studied it, and pronounced: 'A hundred and four. I badly need fluids. Excuse me, ladies.' Gone, and never called me lover . . .

'Isn't he a scream?' said Vanessa. I stared at her

cloddishly. She adjusted her expression to one of serious sensitivity. 'But Harriet, your last few paragraphs, they are *so* moving. I was just saying to Kostaki – '

'Vanessa,' I said.

'Yes?'

'Take this,' I said, removing the final page of *TRT* from the tripewriter, putting it with the rest, and handing her the whole lot. 'Take this moving story of pride and passion. Find the room you were looking for. And shove the whole turgid lot up your arse.'

To be fair, she went chalk white, before emitting a hyena-ish laugh and diving for the door just as George appeared there with a face like Mr Barrett of Wimpole Street.

'Oh Harriet – !' she screeched. 'You're marvellous. George, your wife is absolutely marvellous!'

'So they tell me,' said my husband.